THE GUILDFORD TOWN CIRCUS SHOW ★ ★ ★

SURREY HILLS STEAM Co

SKY RIDE WITH CRADDOCK & MULFORD

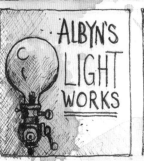

ALBYN'S LIGHT WORKS

WOKING WATCHMAKERS DUST PROOF CASE

STEERLINGS LOCKSMITHERY

THE BROOKS

CROWN

WHEELER AND Co.

GOLDEN & AGE

FABER has published children's books since 1929. T.S. Eliot's *Old Possum's Book of Practical Cats* and Ted Hughes' *The Iron Man* were amongst the first. Our catalogue at the time said that 'it is by reading such books that children learn the difference between the shoddy and the genuine'. We still believe in the power of reading to transform children's lives.

CHRIS MOULD's
WAR OF THE WORLDS

A GRAPHIC NOVEL

INSPIRED BY THE H. G. Wells CLASSIC

faber

The War of the Worlds first published in 1898
This adapted graphic novel edition first published in 2024
by Faber & Faber Limited
The Bindery, 51 Hatton Garden, London, EC1N 8HN
faber.co.uk

Design by Ness Wood

A CIP record for this book is available from the British Library

ISBN 978–0–571–37739–8

2 4 6 8 10 9 7 5 3 1

MIX
Paper | Supporting responsible forestry
FSC® C007785

Printed and bound in the UK
on FSC® certified paper in line
with our continuing commitment
to ethical business practices,
sustainability and the environment.
For further information
see faber.co.uk/environmental-policy

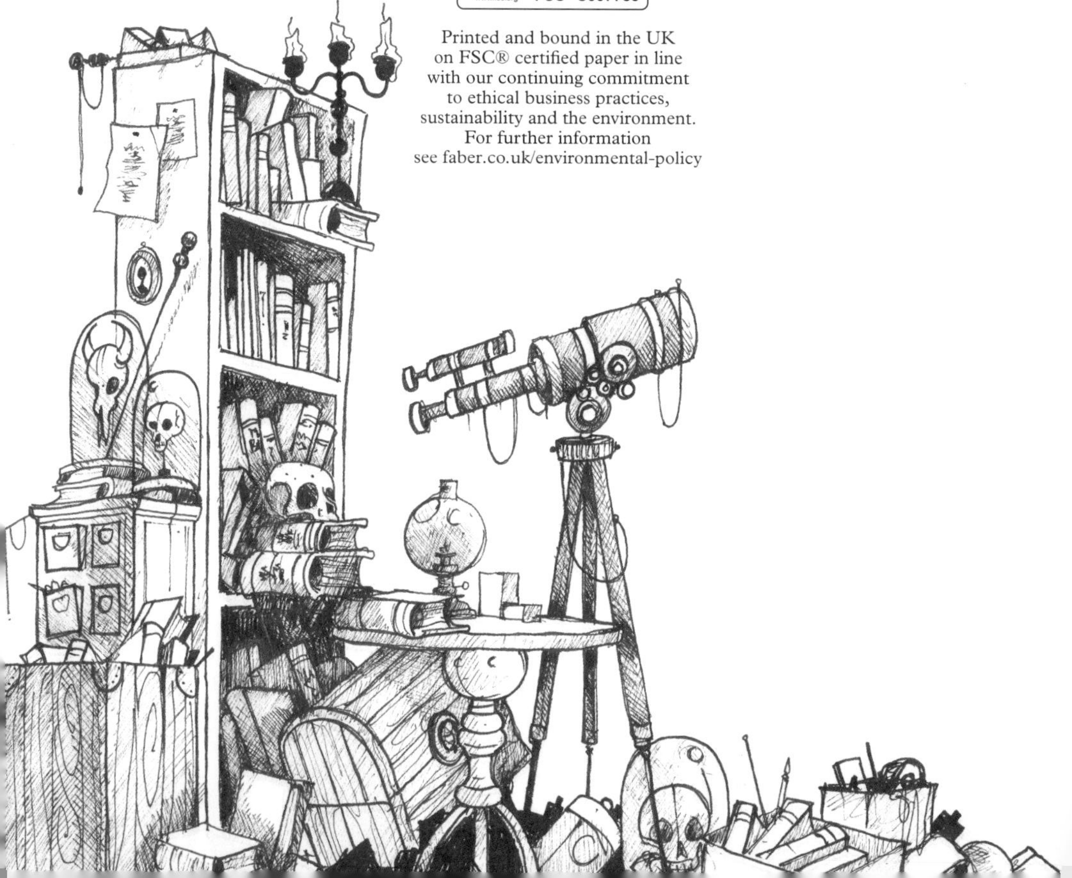

For Alfie, with love CM

CHRIS MOULD has illustrated the gamut, from picture books and young fiction to theatre posters and satirical cartoons. As well as writing his own fiction and illustrating Ted Hughes' *The Iron Man* to much critical success, he has teamed up with author Matt Haig for the bestselling *A Boy Called Christmas* series. He lives in Yorkshire with his wife, has two grown-up daughters, and when he's not drawing and writing, you'll find him . . . actually, he's never not drawing or writing.

H. G. WELLS (1866–1946) was an English novelist, journalist, sociologist and historian best known as the 'grandfather of science fiction' for the impact of his novels including *The Time Machine*, *The Island of Doctor Moreau* and *The War of the Worlds*. *The War of the Worlds* is known for being one of the first novels to depict a war between aliens and humans. Wells was at one time a science teacher and used his ability to explain scientific concepts simply in his work.

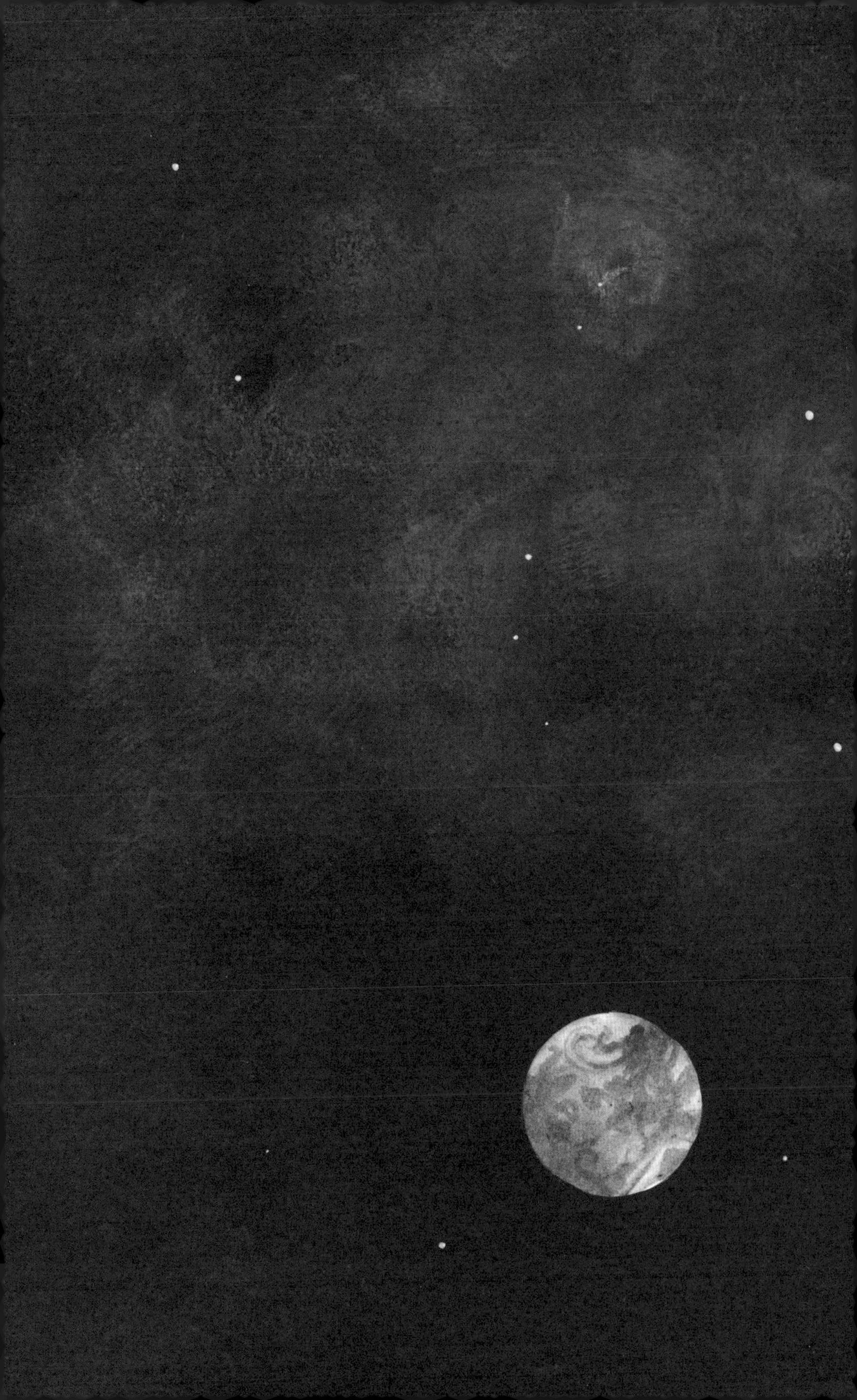

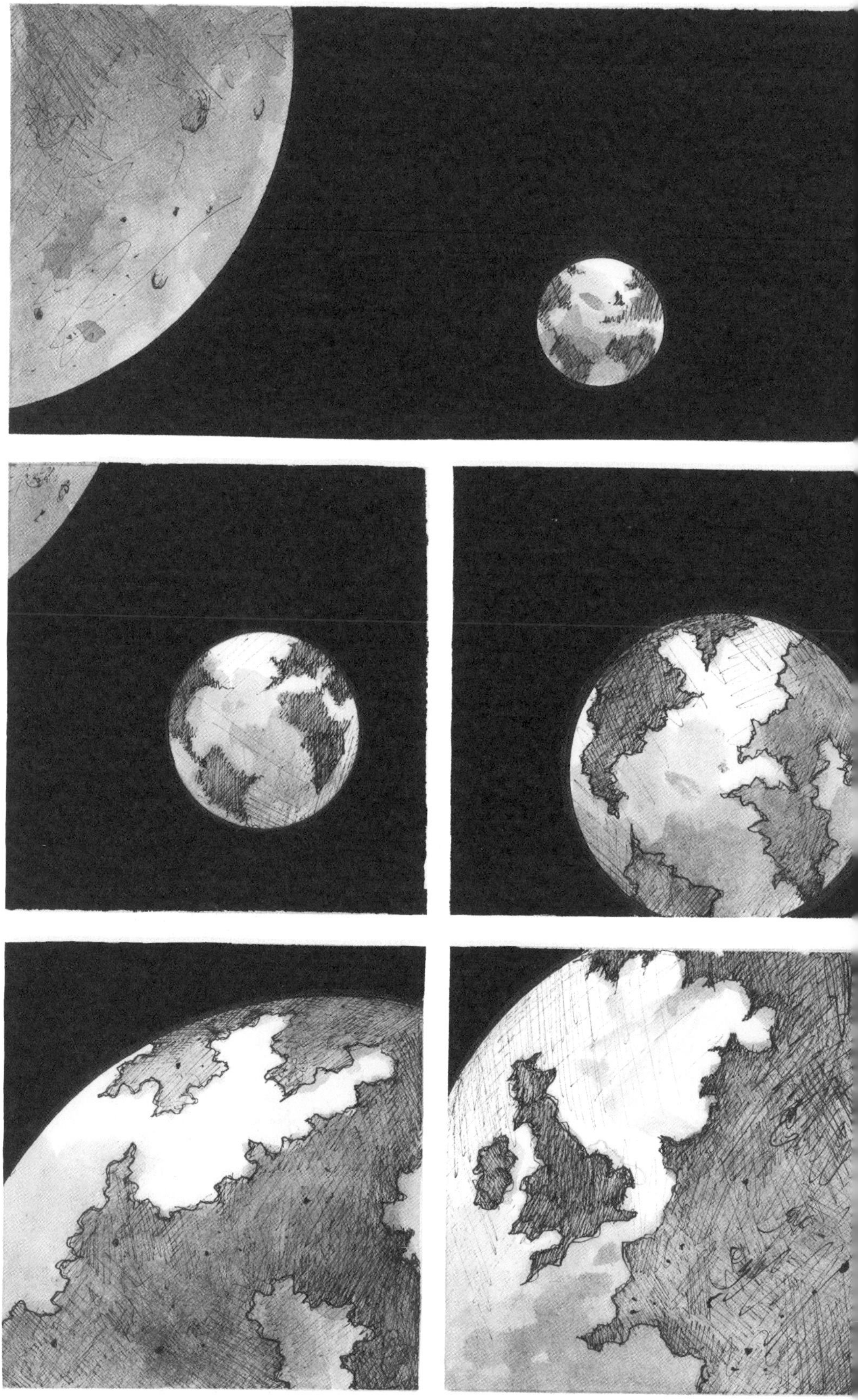

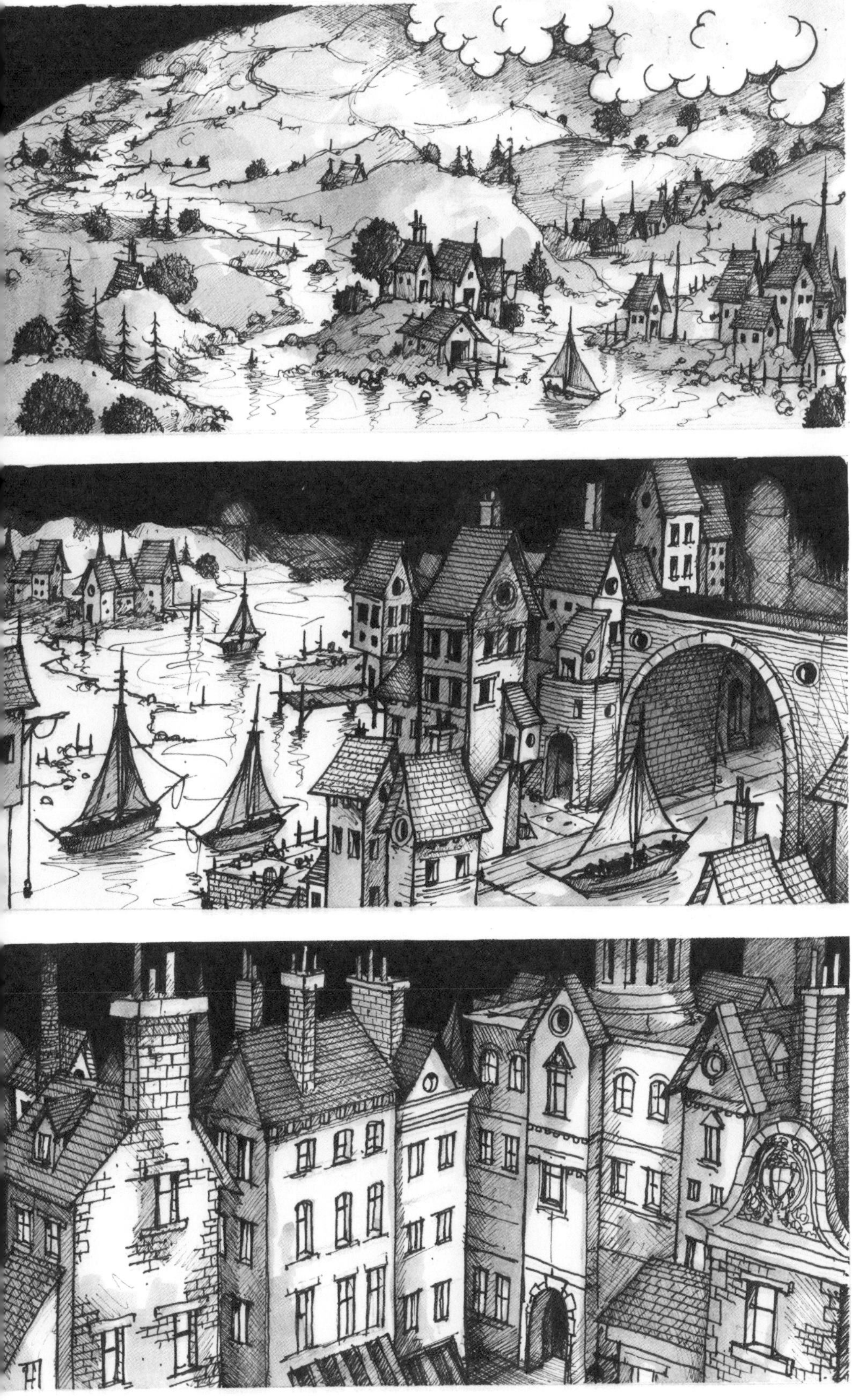

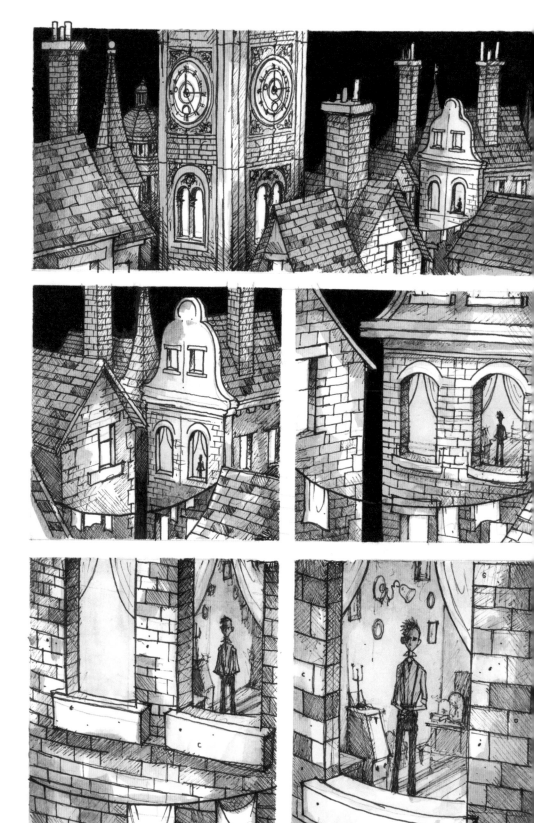

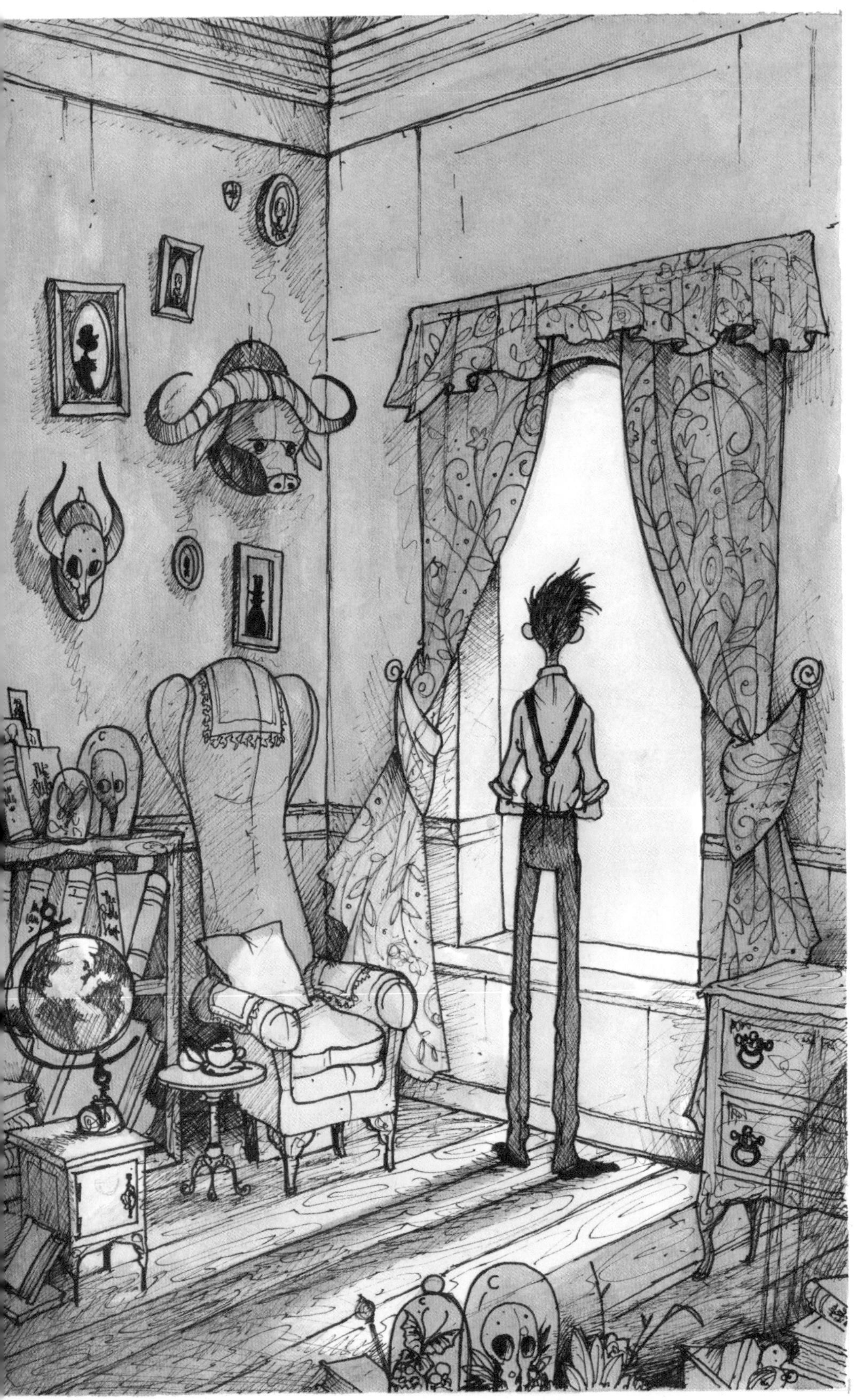

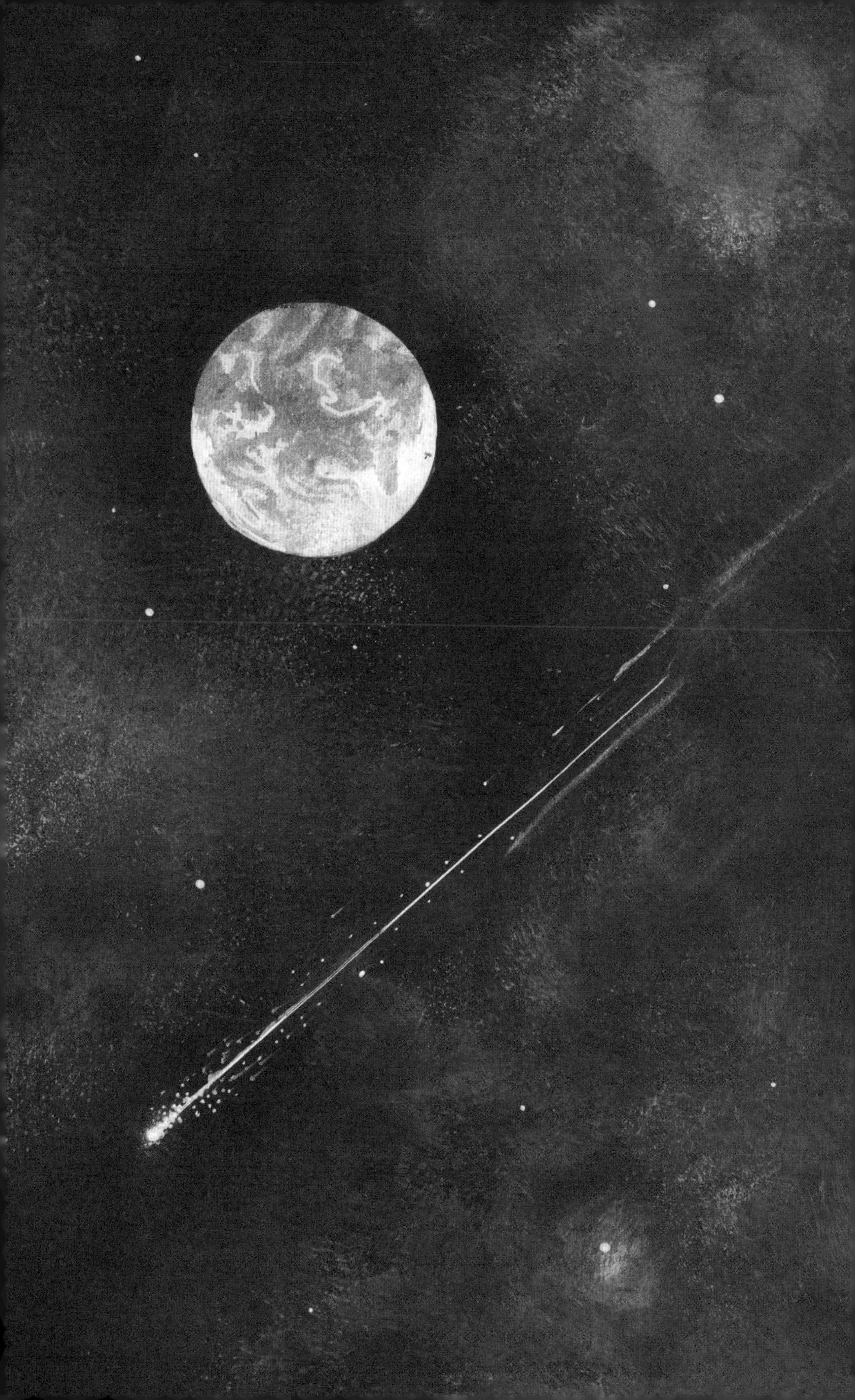

Chapter One

Where We Began

FOR AS LONG AS I STARE INTO THE BEYOND, the world seems to keep on turning, as if nothing ever happened. We are, all of us, still here. It feels safe for now. But when darkness comes, I look anxiously into the night until sleep overtakes me. It has needed so much time to return to what we once knew and we are always aware of the chance that they might come again.

My name is Leon. Let me tell you my story. I must take you back to the mid 1890s, just ahead of a long dry summer that would be sure to test our tolerance to the heat.

Until they came, I worked long hours as a clerk in the city hall. The days dragged themselves through the week. More often than not, my imagination would set me adrift. I had always made attempts to escape reality – in the books

I read, in the stories I imagined, and in the drawings I made. Surely we were not the only ones who existed within this vast galaxy that engulfed us? How could it be that ours was the only world from which life had emerged? There was so much around us that remained unexplored. And so it was often that I found solace in my own search for what may be. I drew endlessly and dug deep into my mind for what might exist somewhere else. Strange places and beings. Landscapes unknown to us.

I had met Anya at the laboratory at Ottershaw, where she worked, uncovering the secrets to disease and infection. I was fascinated by her studies under the microscope and the way she made sense of the things I knew I could never understand. And above her workspace was the observatory that held the answer to the worlds beyond ours.

In her free time Anya helped her good friends Orla and Ivan to look after the children at the orphanage. She would play with them and teach them, and they grew close.

We spent all our time together, except when work took her far north on long trips where she would give lectures on her findings. I missed her greatly, as did the children. Anya would always say that missing people was a good thing: 'It means that you are fortunate enough to have those who mean so much to you.'

When time allowed, I would join her and the children at the orphanage, and in good weather we'd parade to the park. We packed food and games, and I drew the birds with Esme, the youngest child. On one occasion we spotted a nightingale hiding in the thickets.

'He has a beautiful song, but when he sings at night, he warns of danger,' I told Esme.

'Is that true?' she asked.

'Perhaps it is,' I said. 'I don't know for sure.'

'Why don't you know?'

'I don't know everything.'

And we would watch him hop around until he spotted us and flew away.

Anya adored the children. Often, I would listen to their exchanges. How Esme would quiz her endlessly. 'Where are we going now?' 'Who will be there?' 'How long will we be?' Esme worried about most things and didn't like change in her routine. She would cling to me until the others made her play.

There was no greater sound than to hear their happy voices – and no better sight than to watch them enjoy the open air. I had never known happiness as a child, and Anya and I aimed to make life better for them in whatever way we could. In the years before it all happened, they were our whole life and we were theirs.

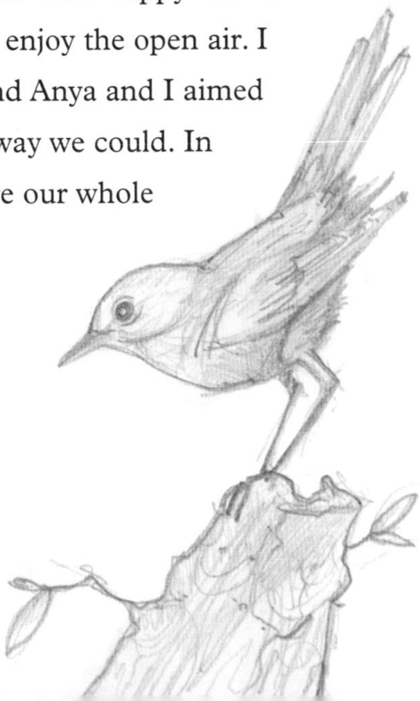

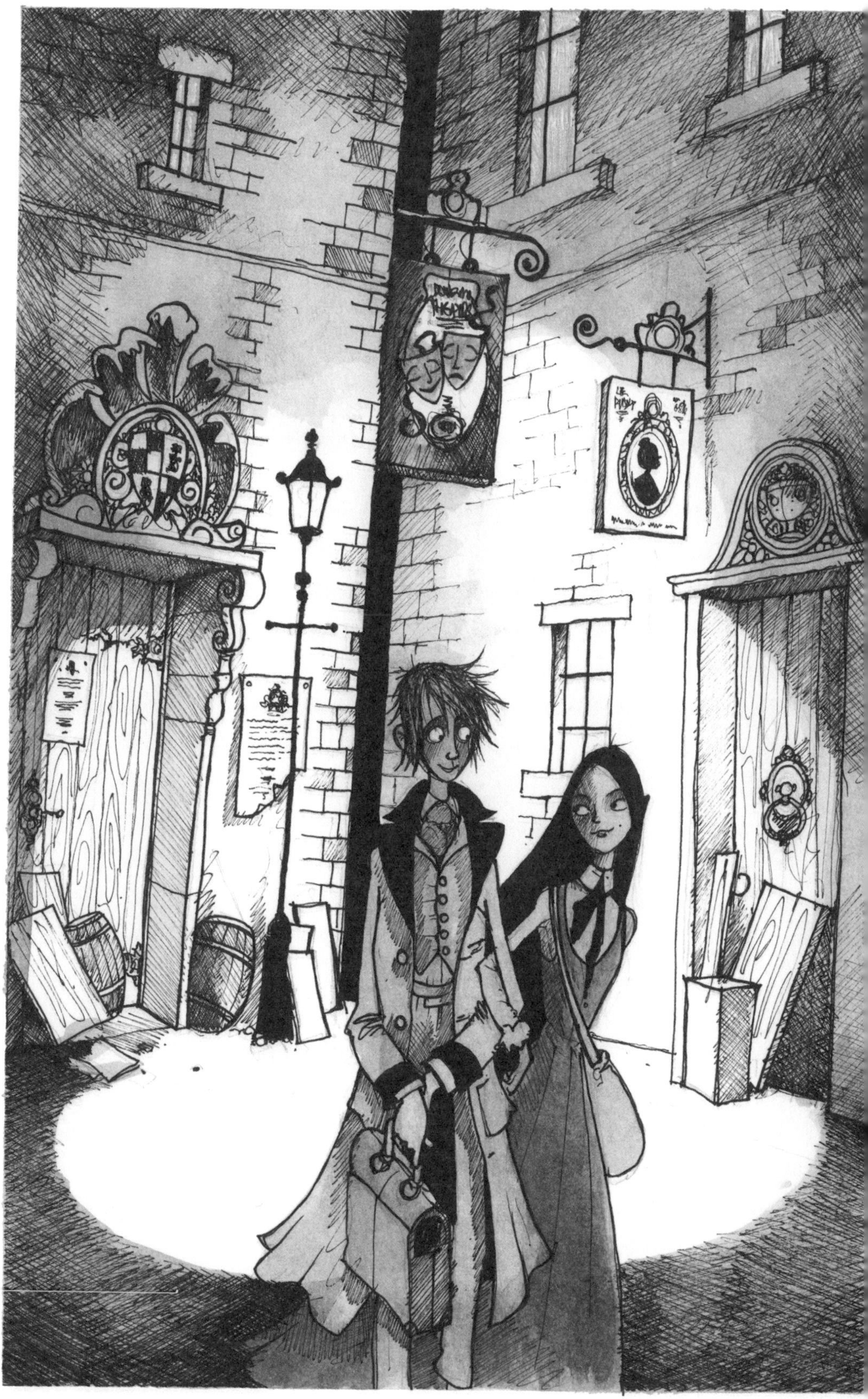

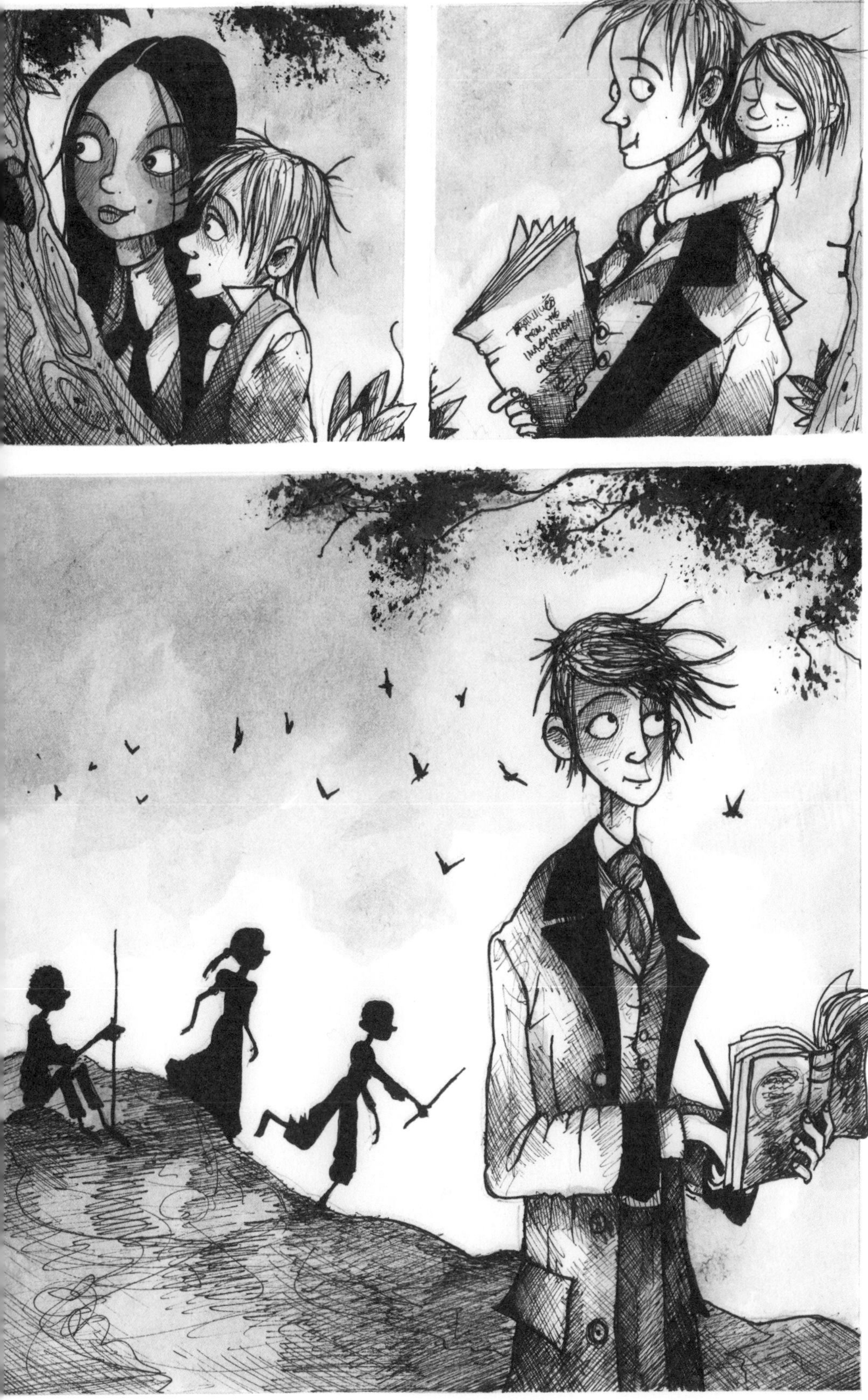

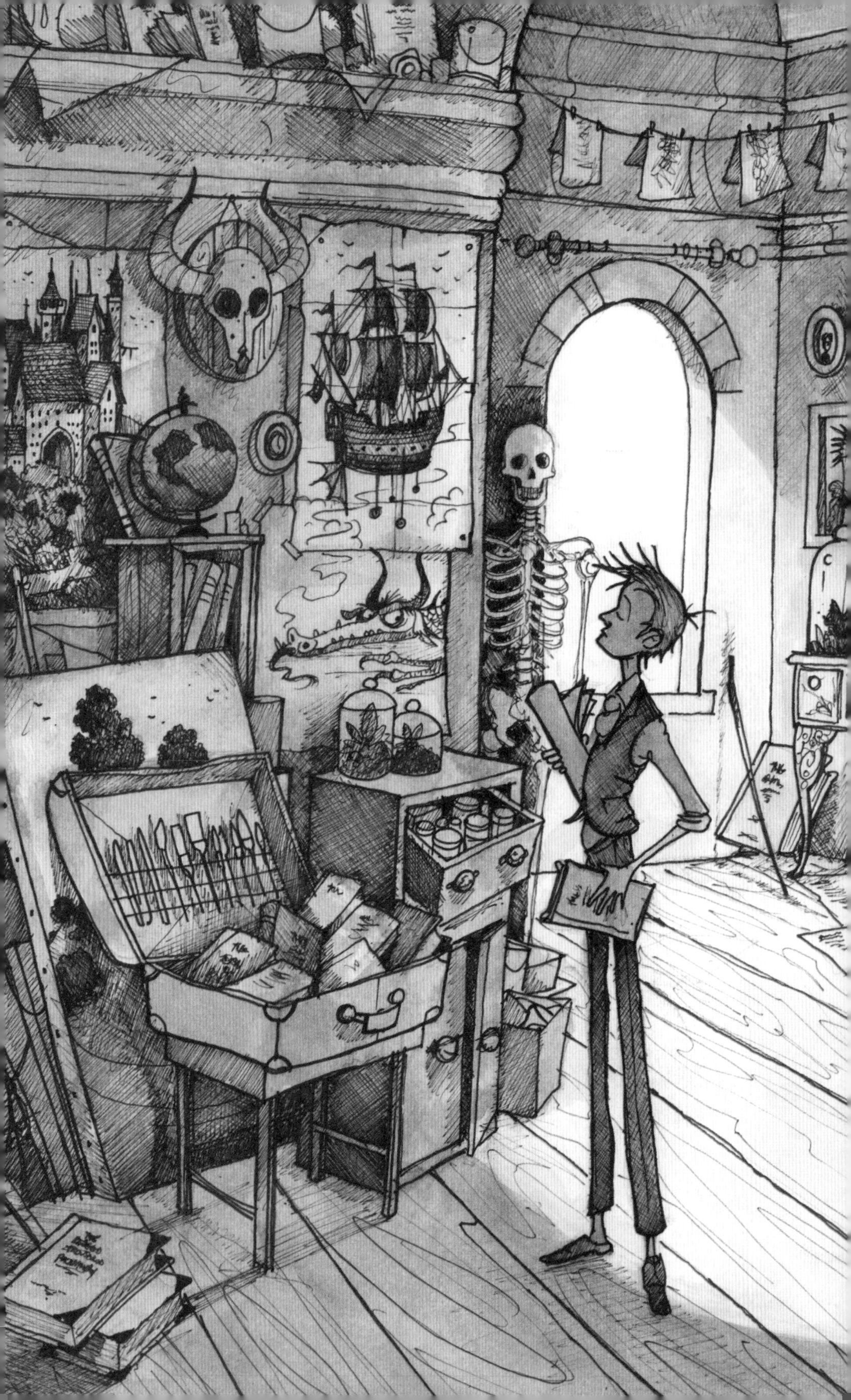

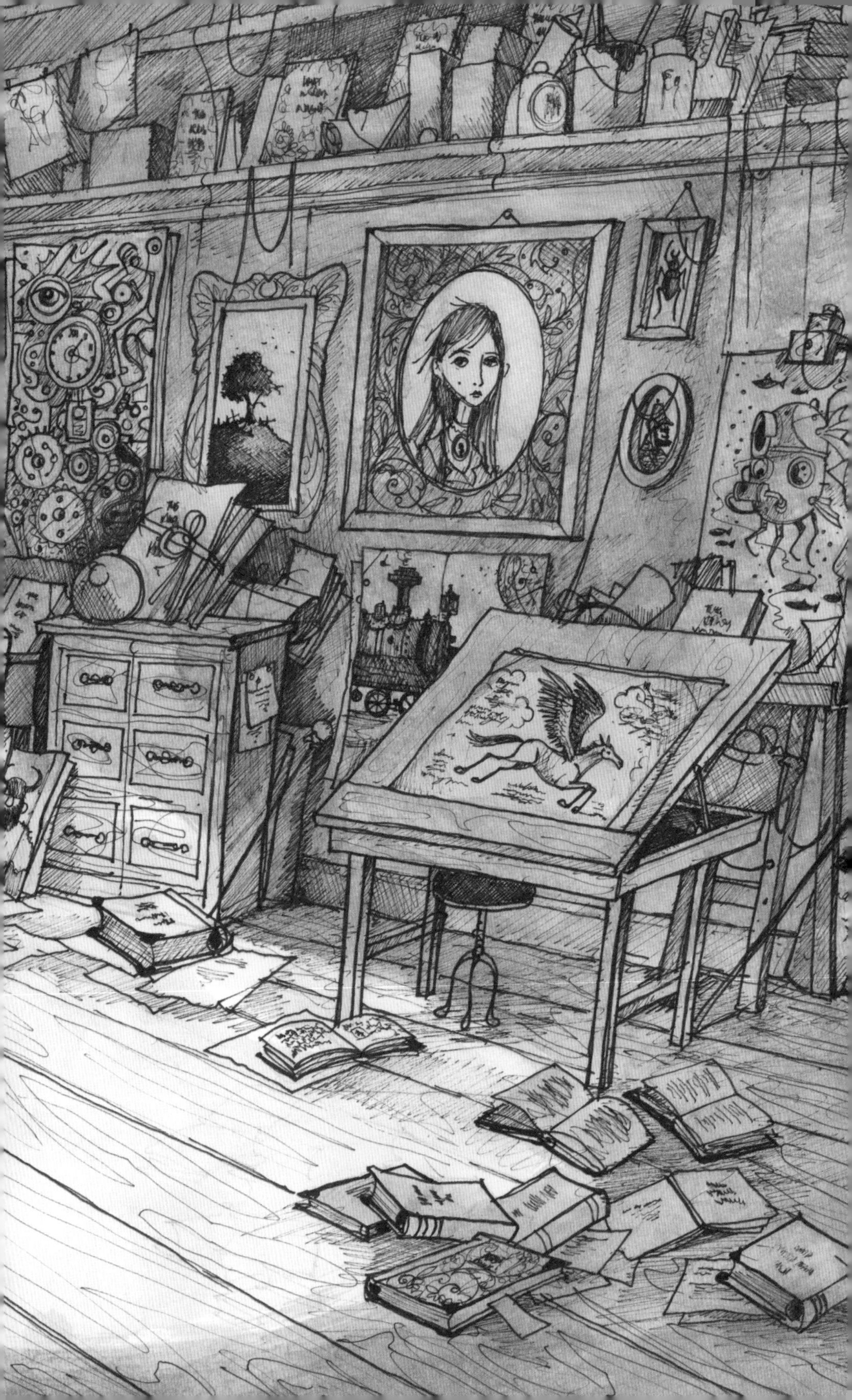

However, still I dreamed of other worlds and, whenever the opportunity arose, I spent hours with my head buried in elaborate maps and fantastical drawings. I obsessed over the curiosities housed in the museums and galleries of London, and I studied the works of great artists from the past. I was enthralled by the mysterious beasts and creatures that dwelled in paintings hundreds of years old.

Worlds beneath and above our own, filled with every detail imaginable. Alien landscapes marked with symbols and hidden meaning. All deemed to be works of fantasy.

Did those artists somehow know more than us? What had we yet to discover? Were they warning of things to come?

In the observatory at Ottershaw, I met an astronomer who showed me comets and shooting stars, and I saw the moon so closely that I felt as though I was standing on its very surface. Surely there was life right there, just as here?

I had yearned for so long to learn of the mysteries of other realms, of their strange lands and inhabitants.

Perhaps I had wished too hard.

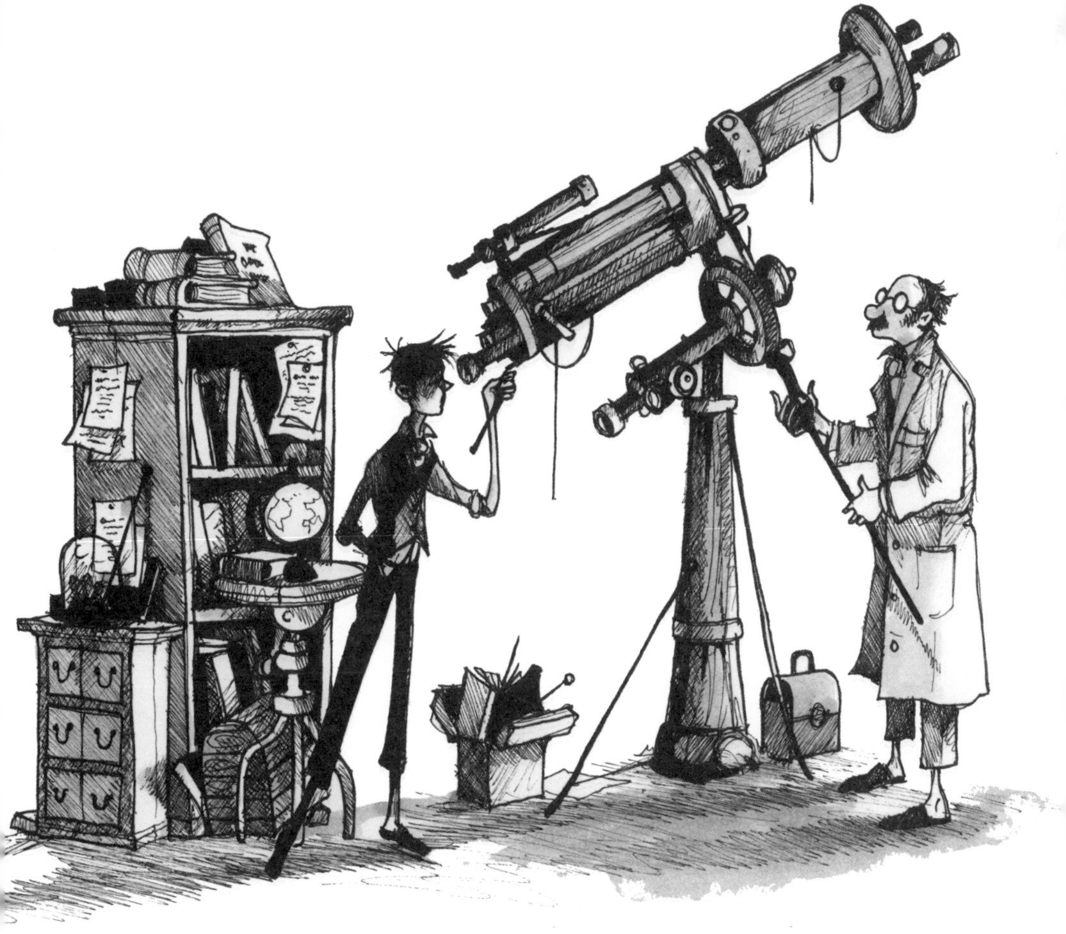

Chapter Two

The Eve Of War

NO ONE WOULD HAVE BELIEVED that during the last years of the nineteenth century this world was being watched keenly and closely by intelligent life from afar. That while people busied themselves to and fro with their various tasks, they were being scrutinised and studied. Perhaps as narrowly as a man with a microscope might examine the creatures that swarm and multiply in a drop of water.

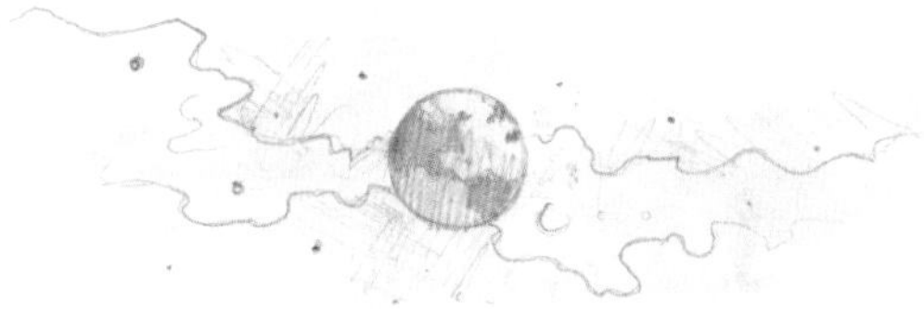

Across the deep gulf of space, this earth was being watched by envious eyes, and, slowly and surely, great plans were drawn against us.

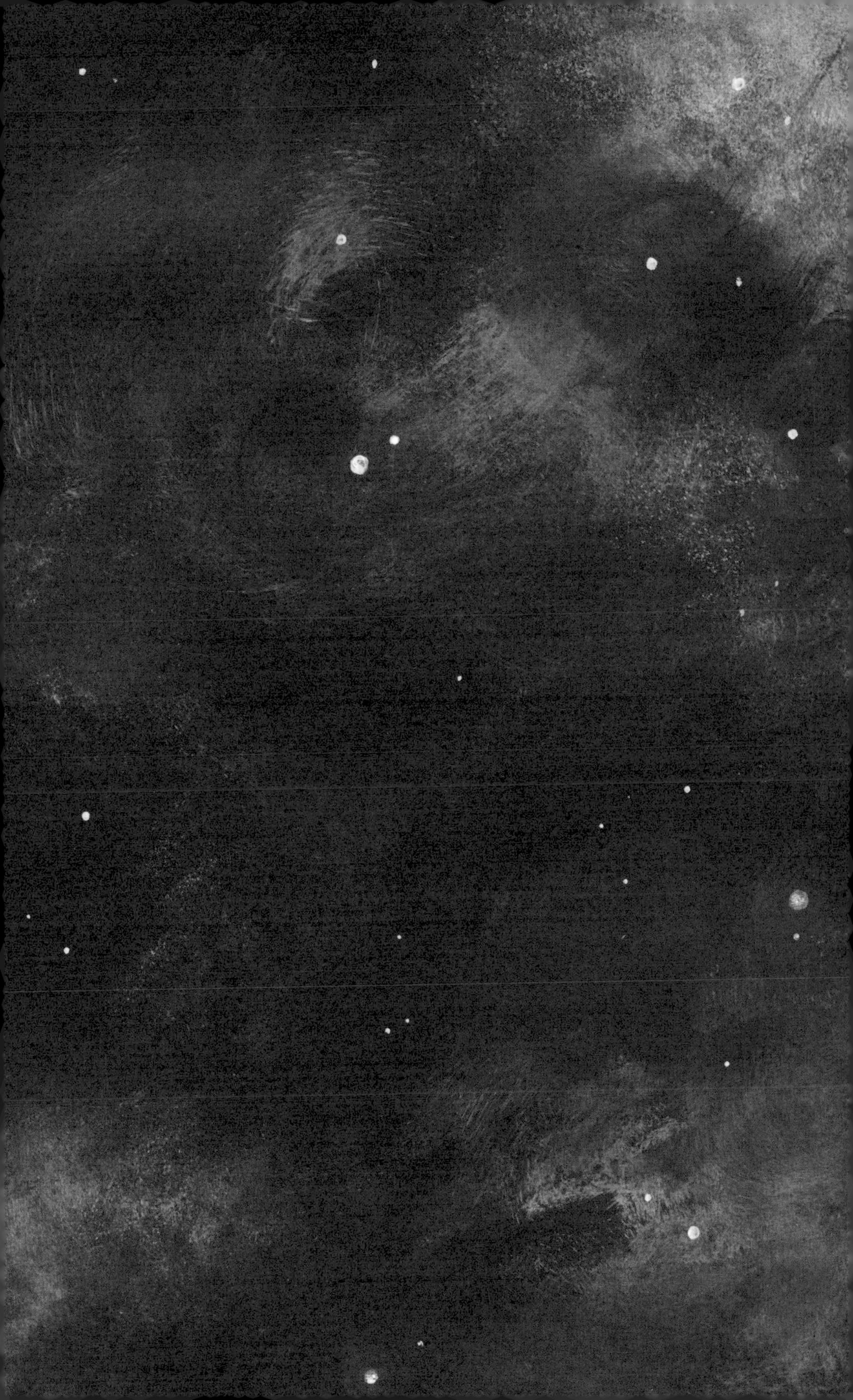

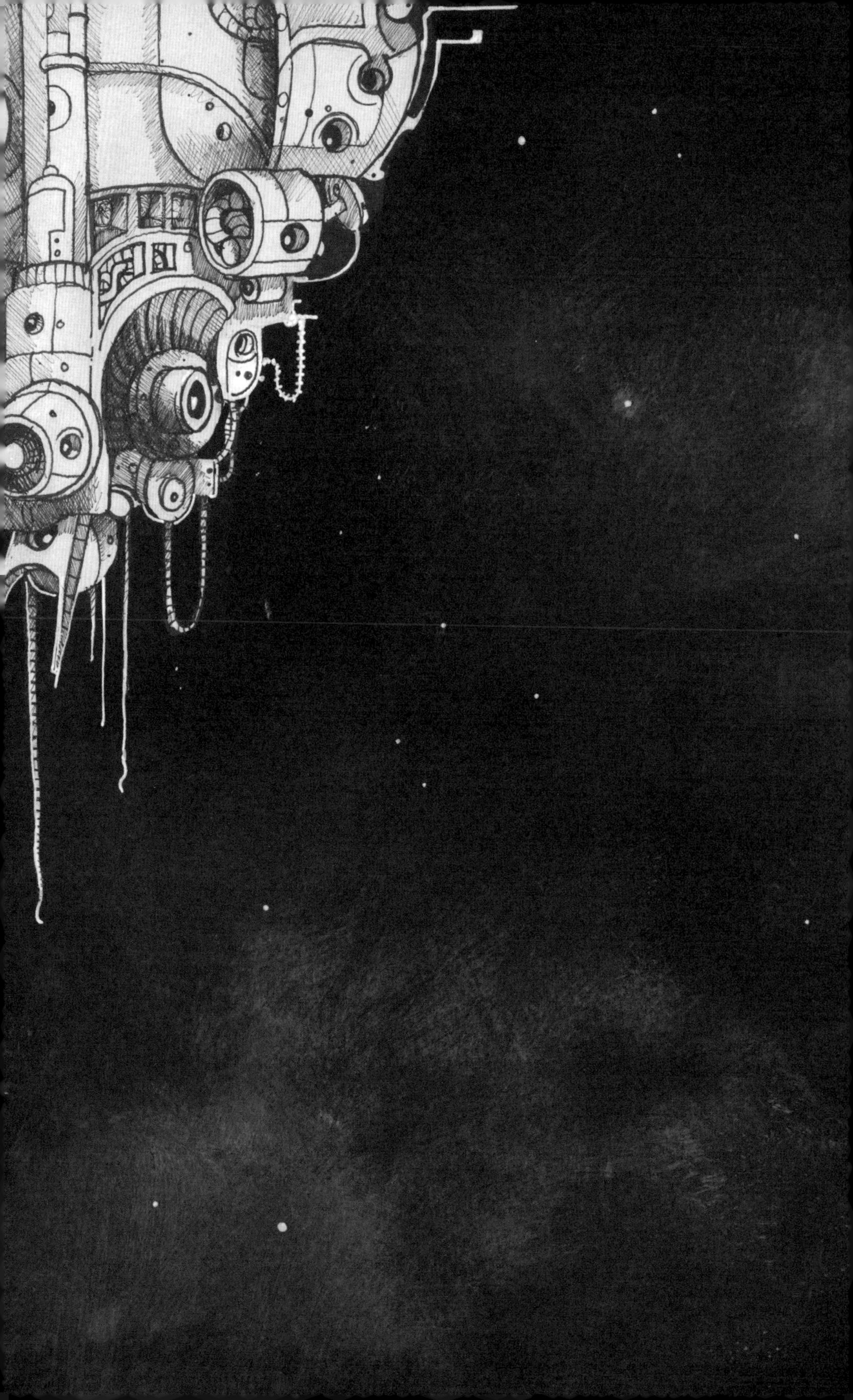

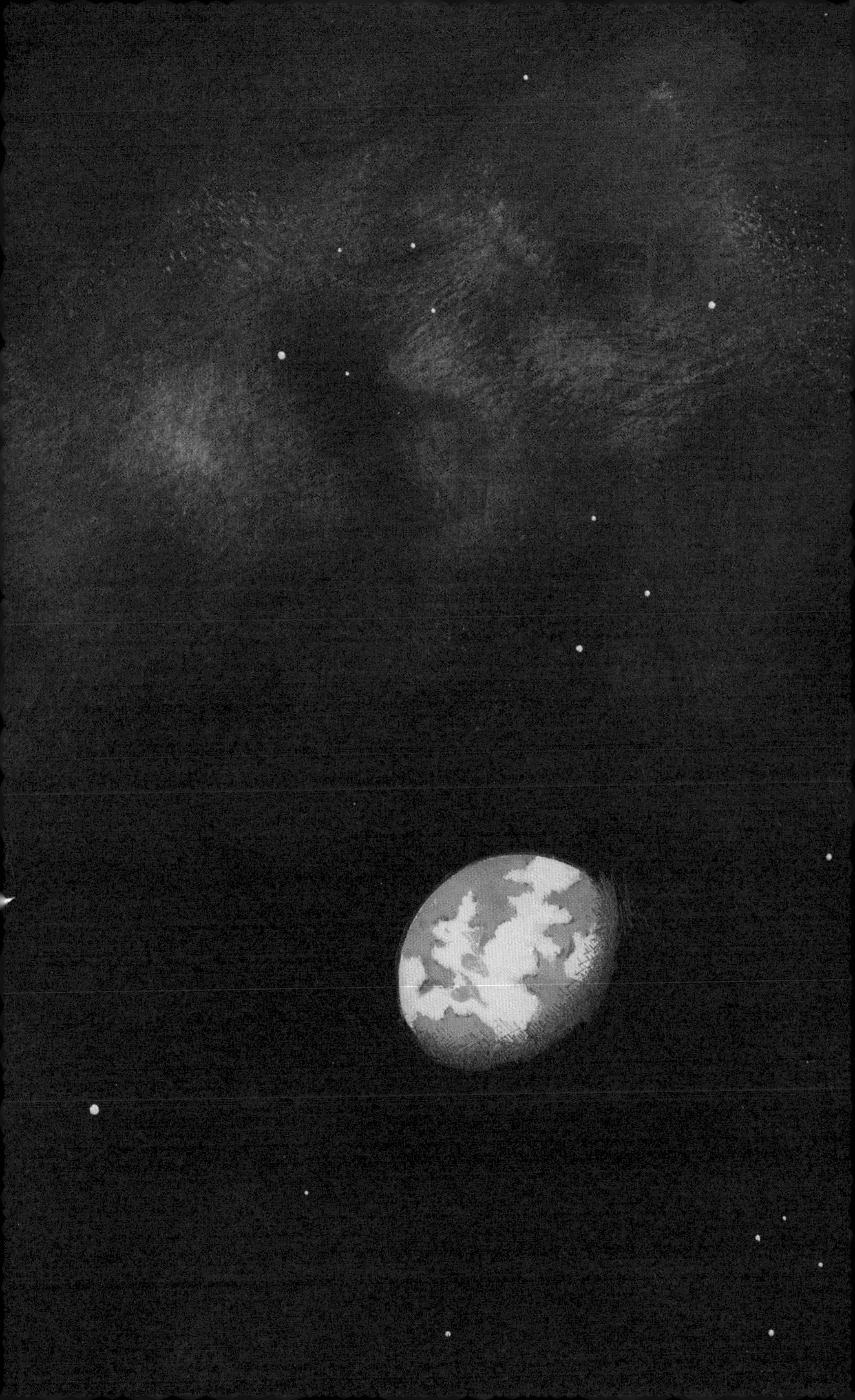

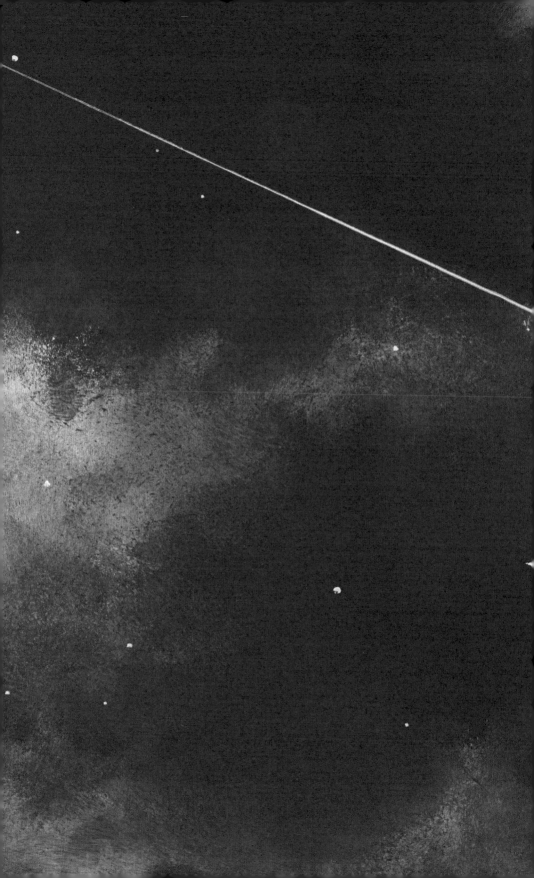

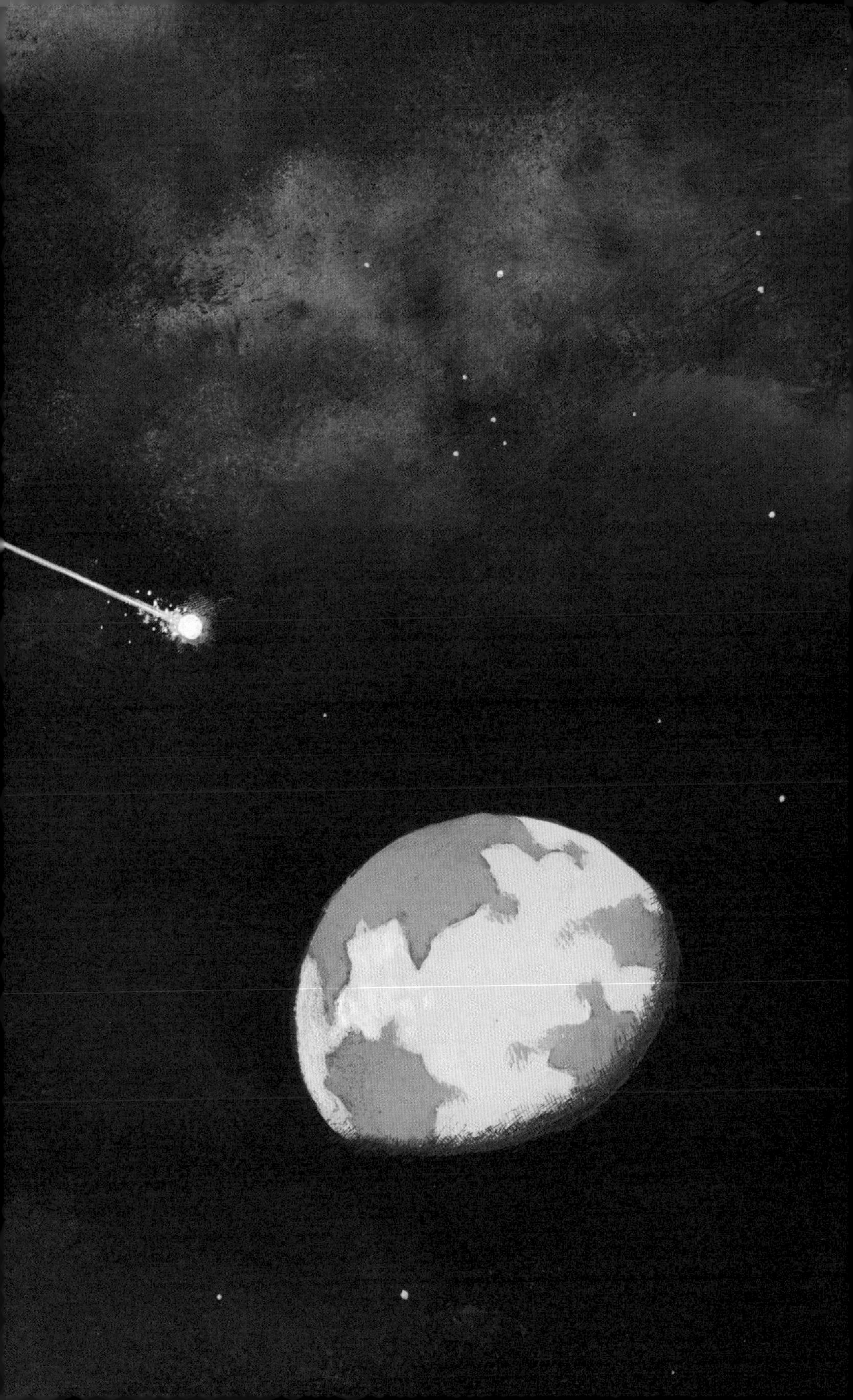

It was late in the summer of 1894. I remember it well. That first day of August had been blisteringly hot. A blazing light had been seen leaving the surface of Mars and, though it had gone largely unnoticed, I had been lucky enough to witness it for myself. Ogilvy, the astronomer at Ottershaw, had invited me to look upon it from the observatory. He was always generous in his welcome and made sure there was food and drink whenever I appeared.

'The stomach rules the mind,' he said.

We viewed the spectacle with much excitement. He surmised that it was more than likely a meteor shower and shunned my idea that we were being signalled by something from afar.

'The chances of anything manlike on Mars are a million to one.'

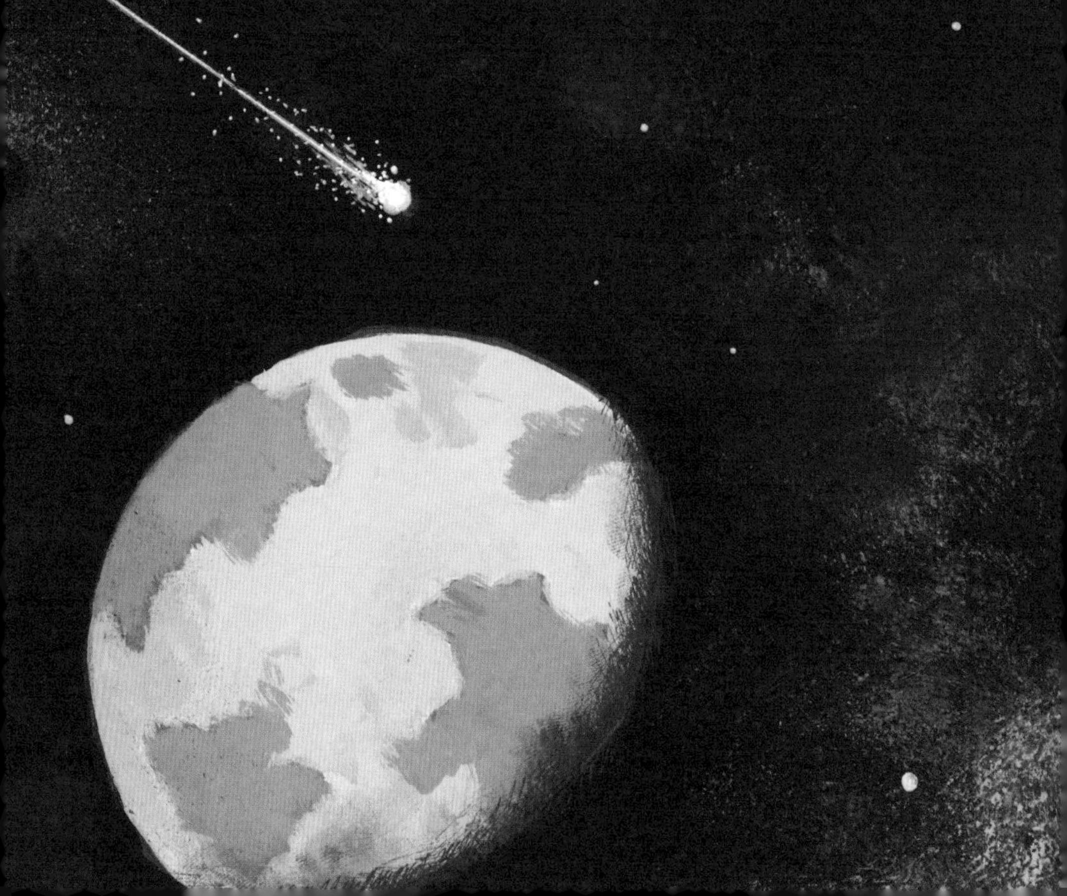

Chapter Three

The Visitors

WHAT APPEARED, AT FIRST, to be a falling star was seen in the early hours over the south of England: a jet of flaming gas burning its way through the atmosphere towards Earth as the world slept on a peaceful summer's night.

By dawn I had been asked to join Ogilvy to observe what had become of this spectacle.

'There is something I must ask of you,' he said as we left hastily across the drought-hardened fields.

'Of course,' I said. He had helped me in so many ways.

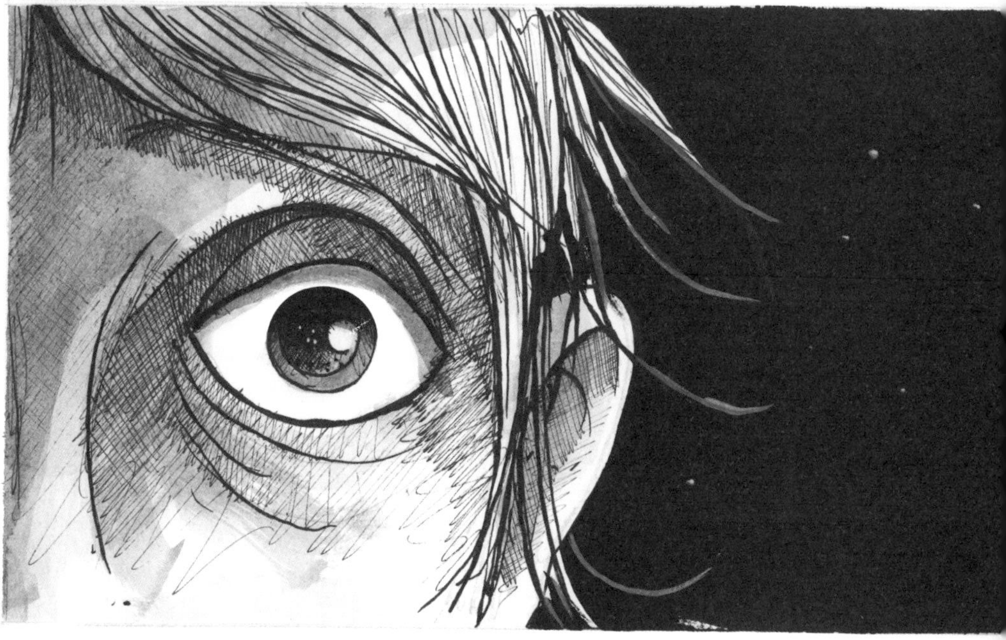

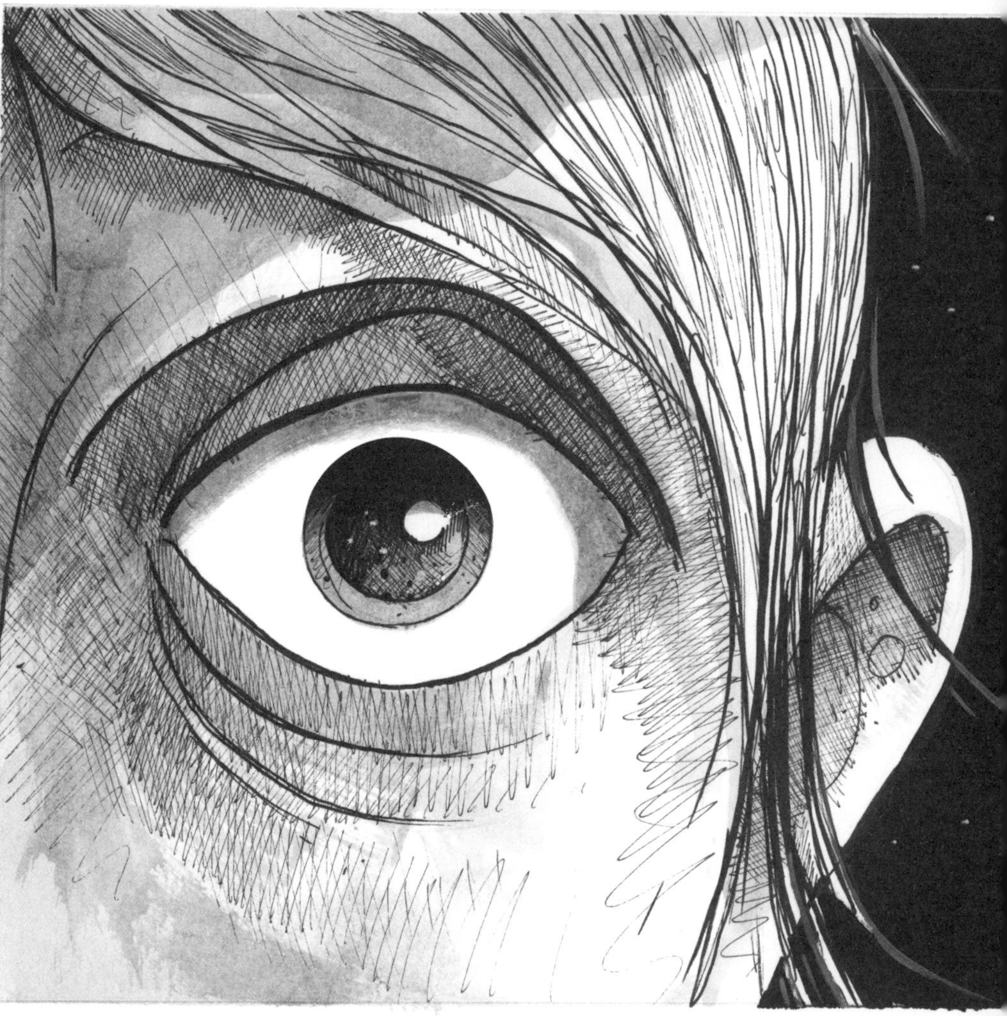

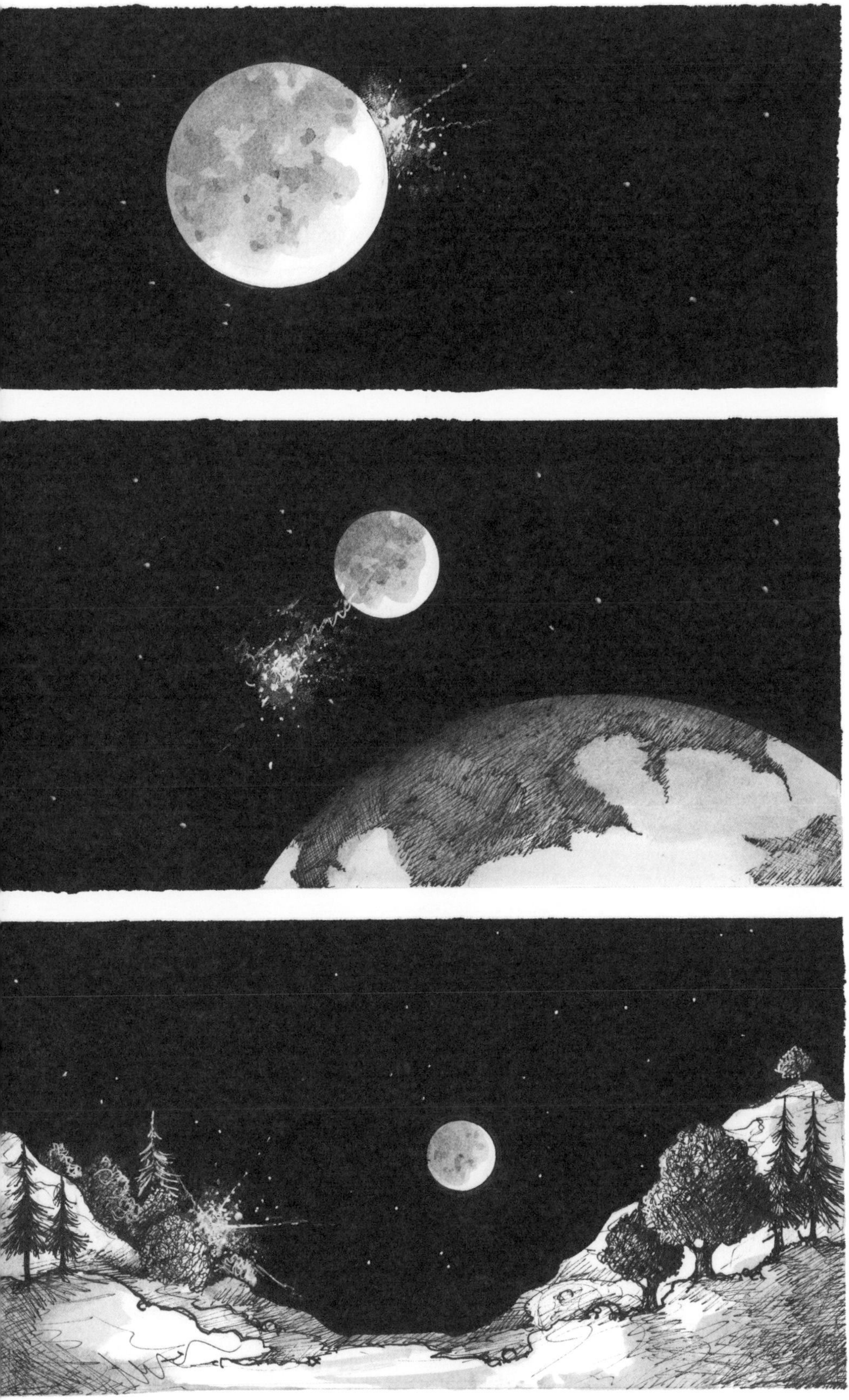

'You must make use of your drawing skills. Create a record of this momentous occasion. It's likely there will be no other visual diary of these events. Draw whenever and wherever you can. Make notes. Remember as much as possible. You never know what might prove to be important. Your information will be vital in the near future and in years to come.'

I was flattered and I agreed. In that moment I felt that, after all this time, my work suddenly had real purpose. There was never a day when I didn't carry my journal, my pens and brushes.

We found its remains upon the common at Horsell. The sun stared down at us. It was already hot, and while we began to inspect the situation, a growing crowd gathered in fascination. What seemed like a large capsule had embedded itself in the earth, forming a deepened pit. On close investigation, it appeared that its domed surface housed some kind of all-seeing eye. It viewed us intently, I was sure.

A chill came over me, as I stared at it, fixed upon the shape.

'Where on earth did this monstrosity appear from?' a man asked me.

'I can assure you, sir,' I replied, 'I watched it come from afar. This thing is not of our planet.'

'Nonsense,' he said, and laughed heartily, but his grin quickly turned to a grimace.

Those who have never seen Martian life can scarcely imagine the horror. Even at this first glimpse, I was overcome with fear and dread.

The Earth stood still as we watched, almost unable to move.

In that moment, from the depths of the pit, the capsule rose out of the earth on three long mechanical limbs: unfolding and extending steam and dust blasting from the steel shafts that made its legs. It turned as if to look through the glossy black lens. A huge eye observing the world around it. It followed its gaze, creaking and grinding in our direction. Steel cables hung at its back, trailing freely, seemingly half machine, half creature.

What was its purpose? What was this thing on metal struts striding into our path?

Everyone turned and made hastily for the trees. The thing lurked slowly after us, pounding the earth.

Something seemed to grip the air, pulling us up in our tracks, as if to seize us.

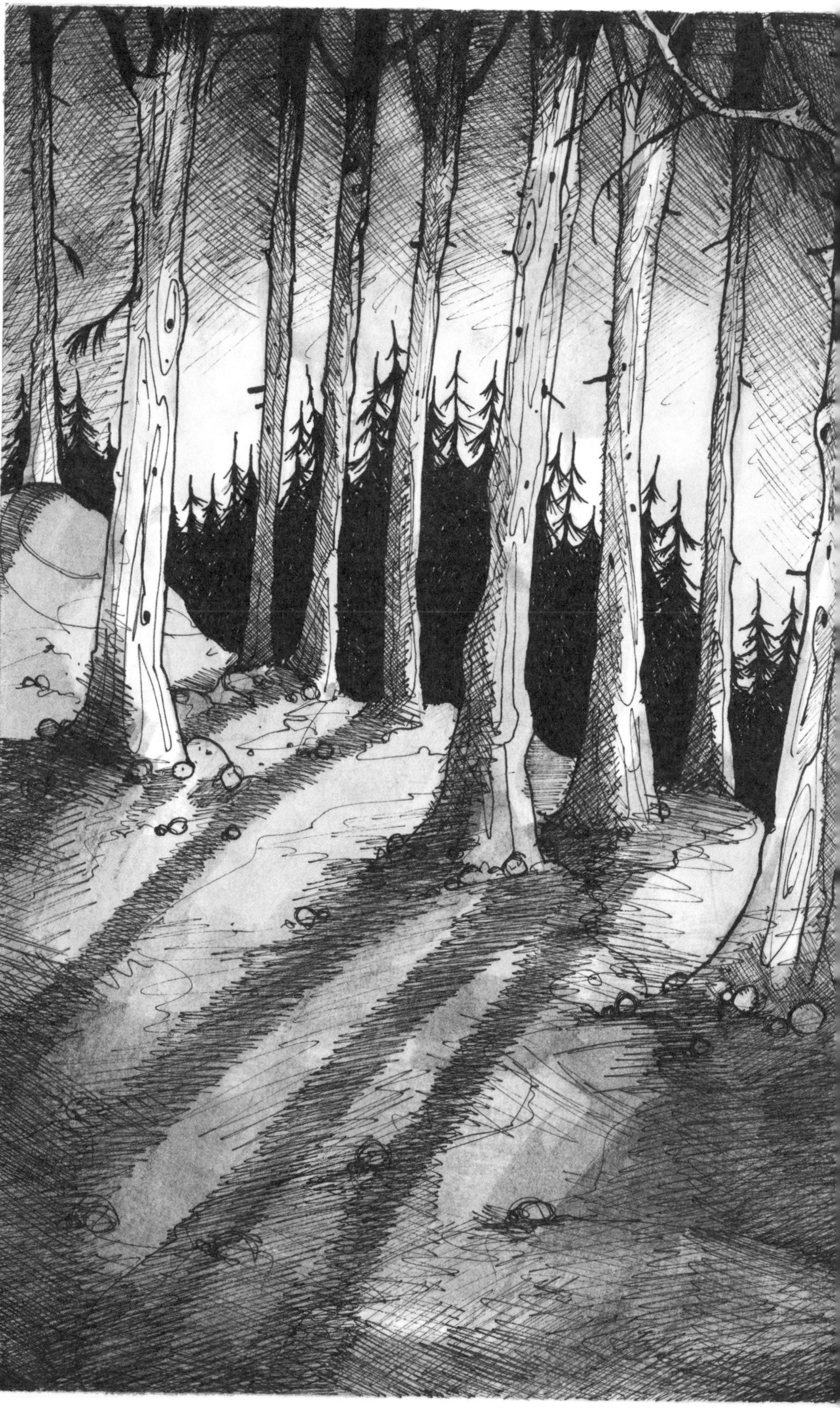

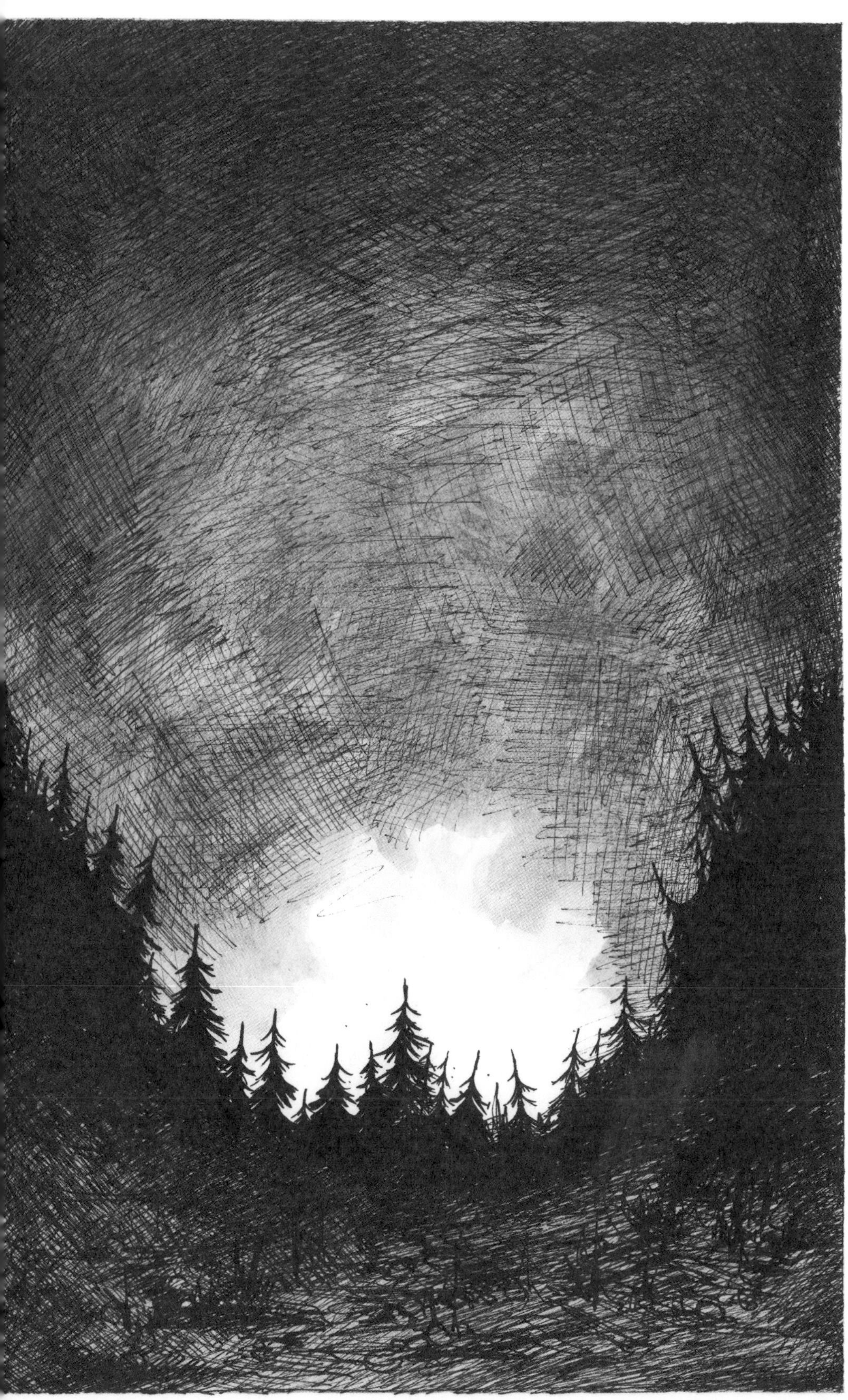

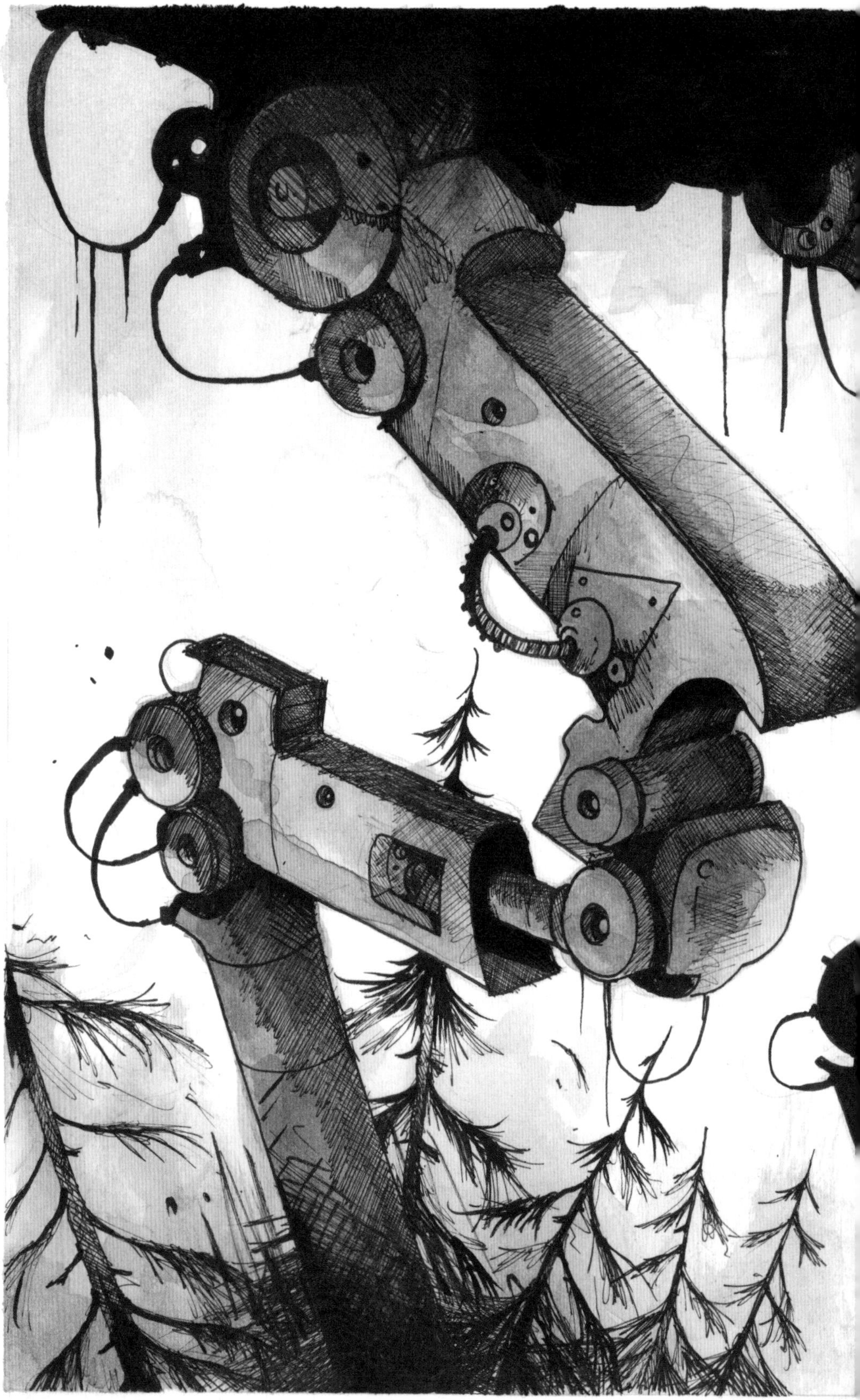

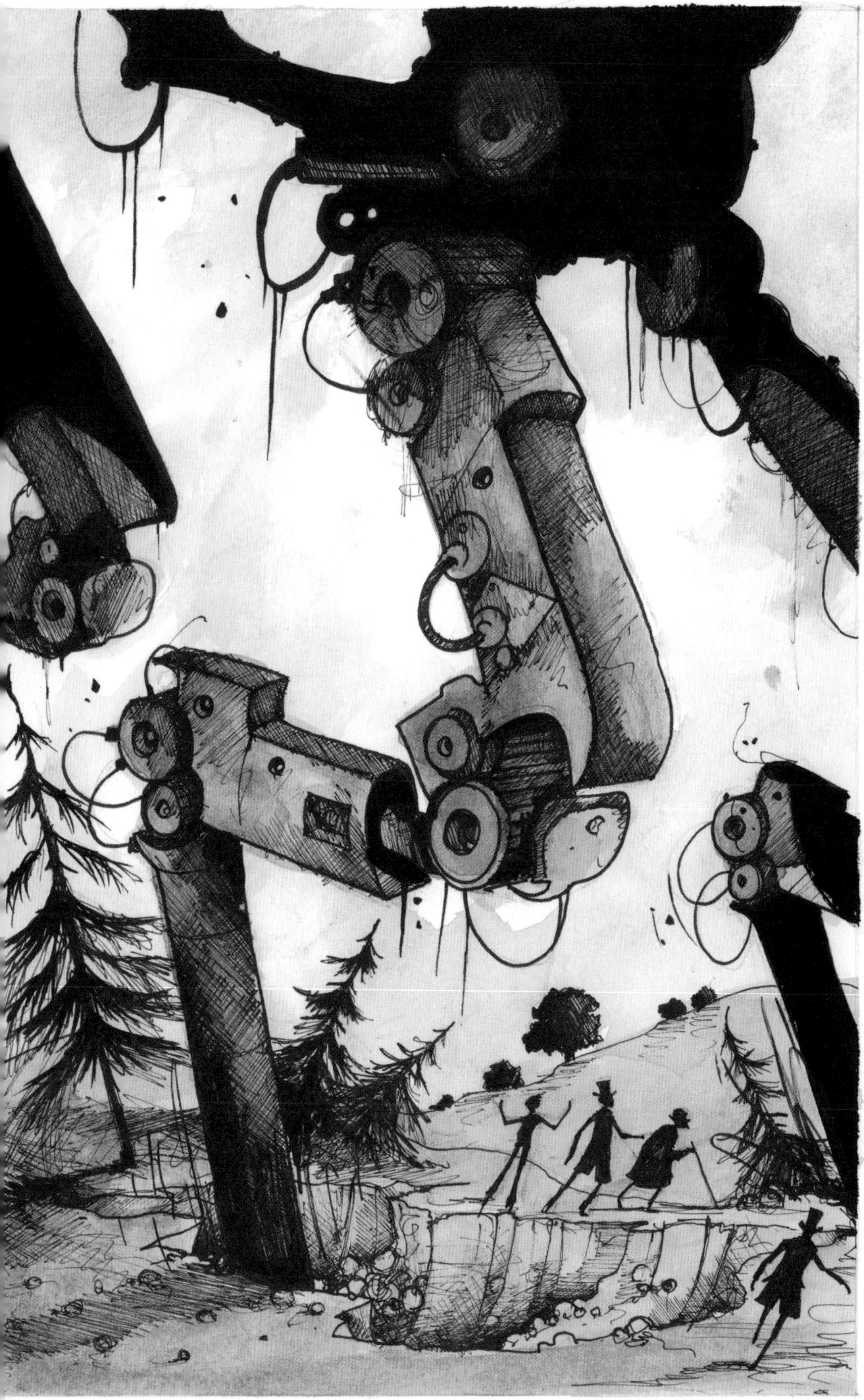

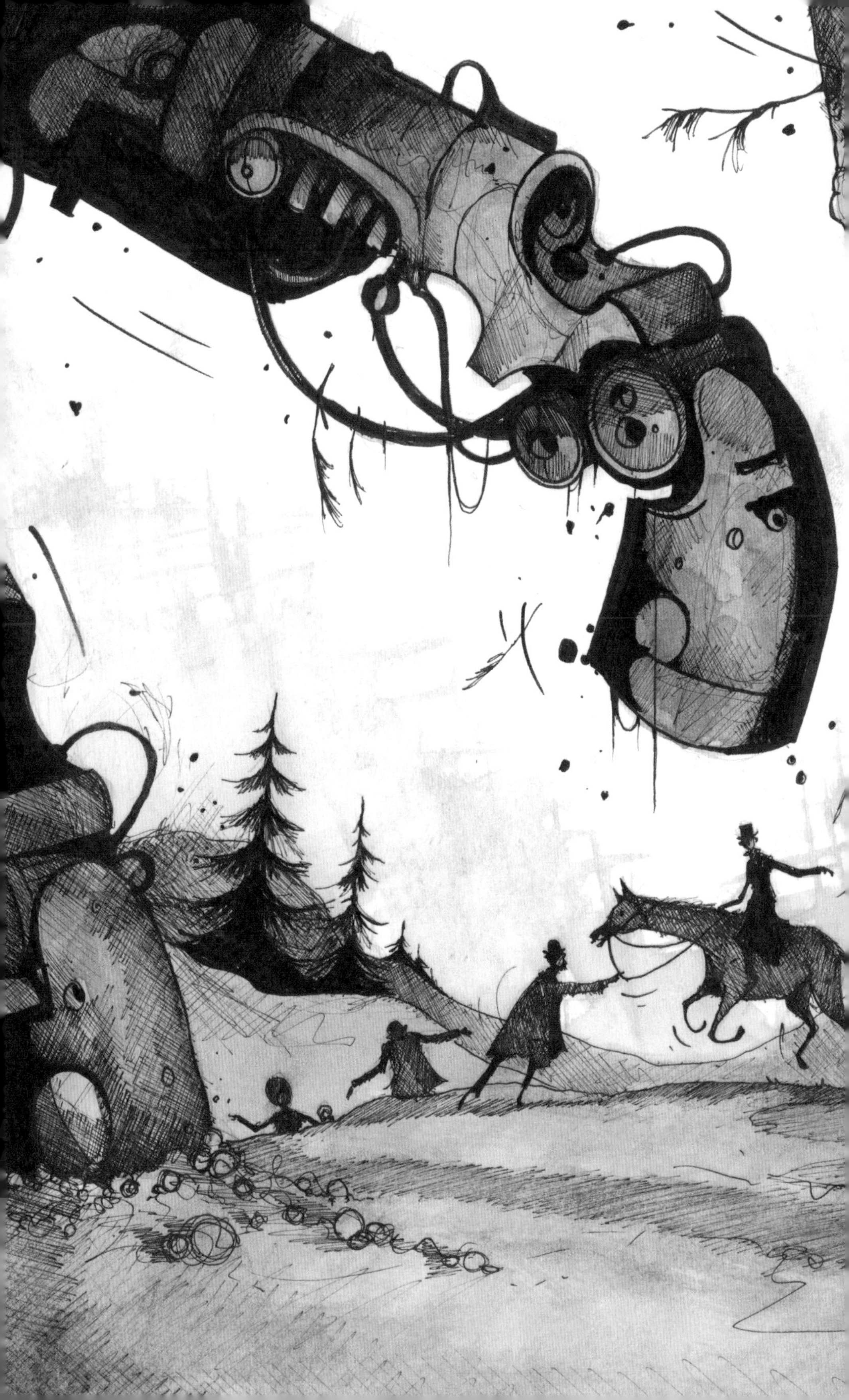

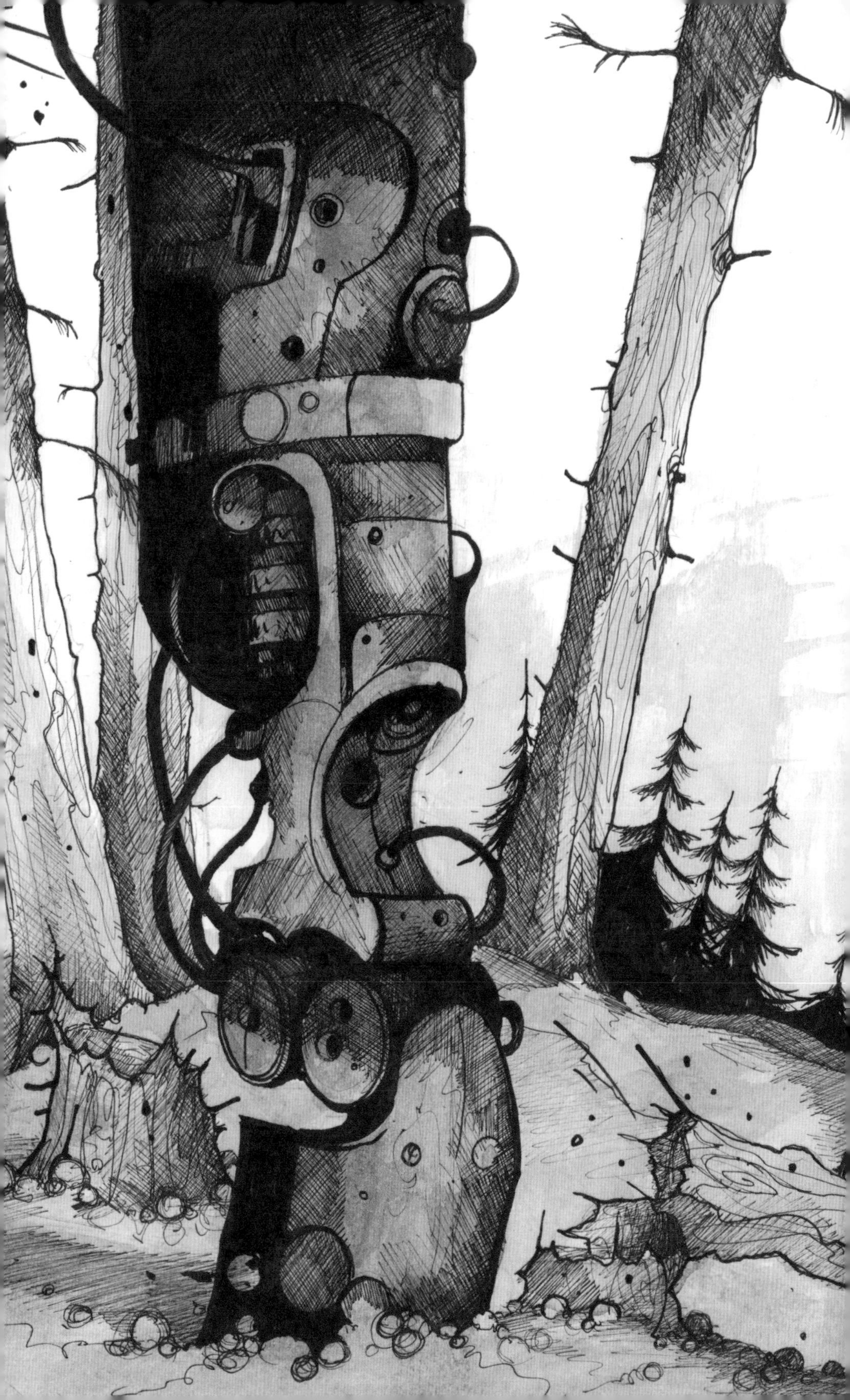

Pine trees burst into flames all around. This attack of sorts could only have come from the tripod that now towered over us, for there had been no flash nor fire nor pounding thump from a cannon.

An invisible grip appeared to freeze what surrounded us. In an instant, a wave of shock – unseen but immensely powerful – evaporated life at will, a blinding flash upon impact. Where the pines had been, the ground smoked and crackled.

In horror, Ogilvy and I began a stumbling run through the heather to make our escape, but in our bid to flee among the others, I lost sight of him. Fumes stung my eyes. I tried desperately to see up ahead, but I could only make sense of the few yards in front of me. The shadow of my companion, barely visible, was slumped to the ground on my horizon. Then, underfoot, there was a crunching sound beneath my boot. I stopped and felt around with my hands in the hardened earth. I found Ogilvy's spectacles broken, the glass falling between my fingers. And his hat, perished and burnt.

For now, I must put my pen aside. I can say no more.

Chapter Four

The Machines Arrive

I RETURNED HOME AT NIGHTFALL IN a terrible state, still shocked from the loss of my good friend and the events of that day. I felt desperate to explain all that I'd seen to Anya. She had always made such good sense of things. My appearance startled her. I took a drink, and while dinner remained neglected on the table, I told her my story.

'They will come here,' she said. 'And what about the children? They'll need moving to safety. This will all be too much for Orla and Ivan. In younger years they would have coped.'

It was in this moment that I felt that my fascination for other worlds had brought these creatures here to our doorstep and put us all in danger. There was no logic to my thought right there and then, least of all me blaming myself. But somehow the thought was there.

Anya's face was deathly white. I tried to reassure her as best I could. However, she was adamant that she should protect the children, and she formed a plan. She would leave the next day, at dusk. They would travel at night, she said. If the towns were being targeted, it made sense to head to the safety of the countryside. We had friends at Timber Hill: a farm, secluded and with space. She could get word to the lab from there.

If I'd known then what we would witness with our own eyes, I would never have let her go.

The next afternoon, we gathered the children. Taking food supplies from the orphanage, we loaded the cart as the sun dropped low. As expected, Orla and Ivan refused to leave their home, so we moved furniture and supplies into the basement and made sure they had all they needed below ground. On no account were they to venture upstairs until they heard further instruction.

It was still humid. We took the quiet track over the fields. (I rode my horse alongside Anya's cart.) The children sat silently, unknowing and clutching each other.

Ogilvy's words echoed in my mind. I had to capture whatever I could, using my skills. It would make all the difference. And so, in spite of the danger, I resolved to return home and make a record of whatever might happen next.

We stopped at the point of our parting; I stepped down from my horse and Anya from the cart. I felt the sudden need to compose myself. Something welled up inside me, and all my thoughts came to the surface at once. The awful realisation that I might never see them again. The idea that they might grow older without me, or me without them. And my guilt at having even had such thoughts. I swallowed the lump in my throat.

Anya and I held each other tightly and, before I could say it, she reminded me: 'We are lucky that we have each other to miss in the first place.'

'Where am I going this time?' asked Esme, tugging at my coat. I knew the move would unsettle her.

'To safety,' I told her.

'But I'm safe here with you,' she said.

'You'll see me soon.'

'Promise?' she said, the grip of her small hands slowly letting go as the cart began to roll forward again.

'I promise.'

'This will keep you safe.' Esme reached out and handed me a folded piece of paper.

I opened it up to reveal her drawing of the nightingale.

'If there's danger, he will sing at night,' she said. 'Just like you told me.'

I could not speak in that moment. The very act would have unleashed a whole wave of emotion from me. The urge to appear strong overtook. I forced a smile, tucking the folded paper into my breast pocket, and waved goodbye.

I knew their journey would be long and difficult.

I watched them until they were out of sight.

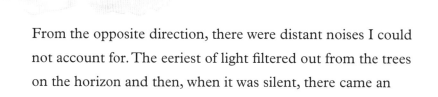

From the opposite direction, there were distant noises I could not account for. The eeriest of light filtered out from the trees on the horizon and then, when it was silent, there came an unsettling feeling that something dreadful was about to happen.

I made my return alone through the night and, as I did so, I saw a star fall above Woking, heading into the pine woods to the north-west. It was another capsule.

I sensed the horse was nervous as we made our way along the canal.

Something caught my eye in the distance, moving rapidly down the opposite slope of Maybury Hill. It was the machine: the monstrous tripod we had encountered on Horsell Common, higher than several houses, striding over the young pine trees and smashing them aside in its pursuit.

How many of them would come? What did they want? I had so many questions while watching that walking engine of glistening blackened metal with its ropes of steel hanging from it.

In another minute, a second tripod appeared. The two companions met and marched together across the landscape. In my panic to turn and escape, I pulled the horse too sharply. We stumbled and somehow I was thrown sideways into the water.

By some miracle, the horse did not bolt and I wasted no time in clambering back onto it. Without stopping to look again, I steered away and made my escape along the line of burning woods.

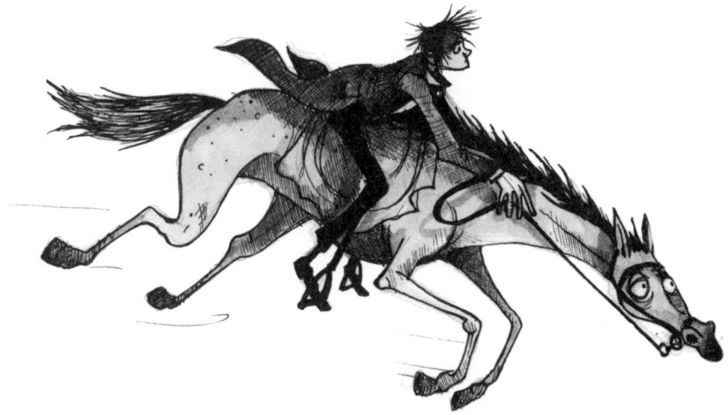

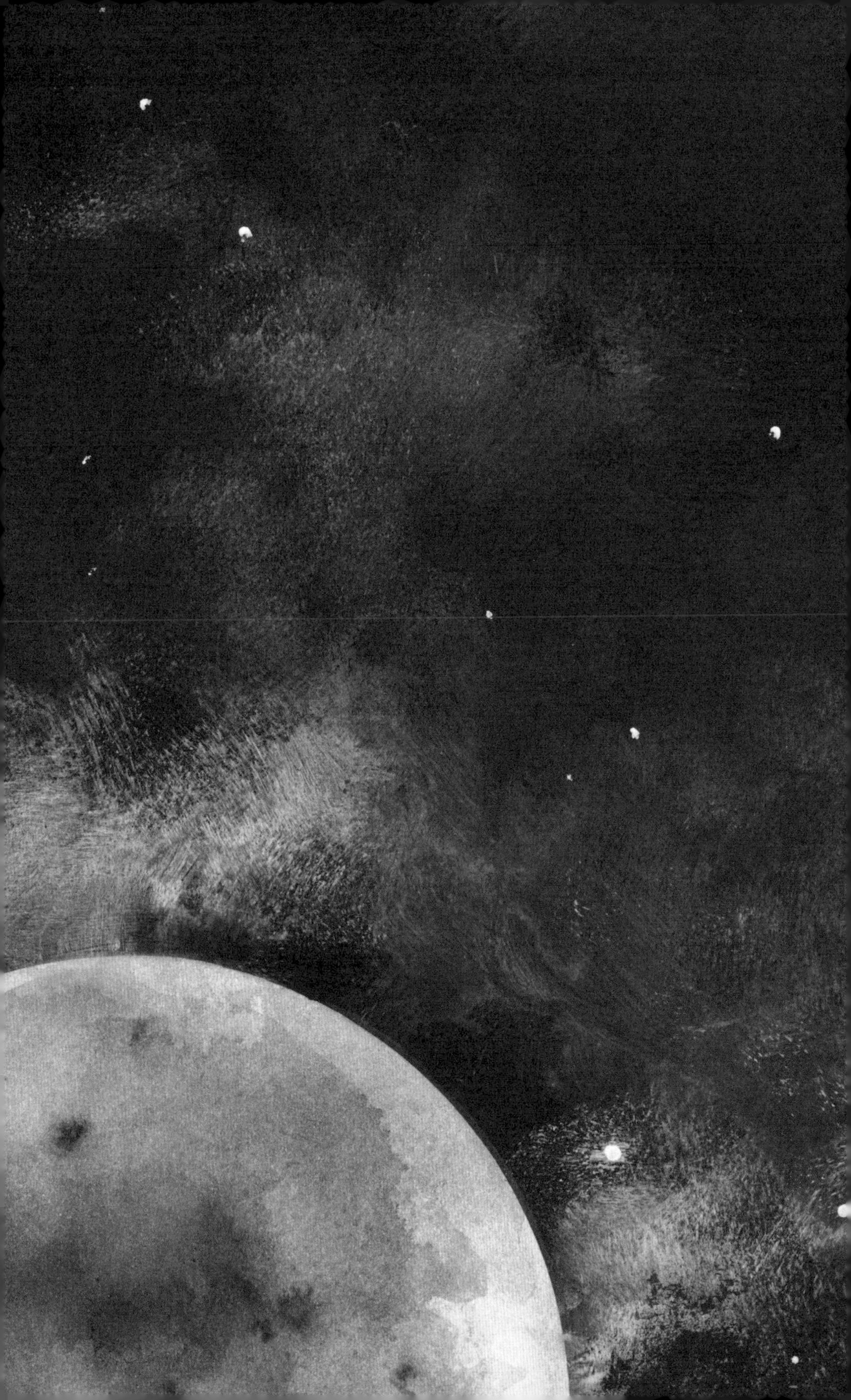

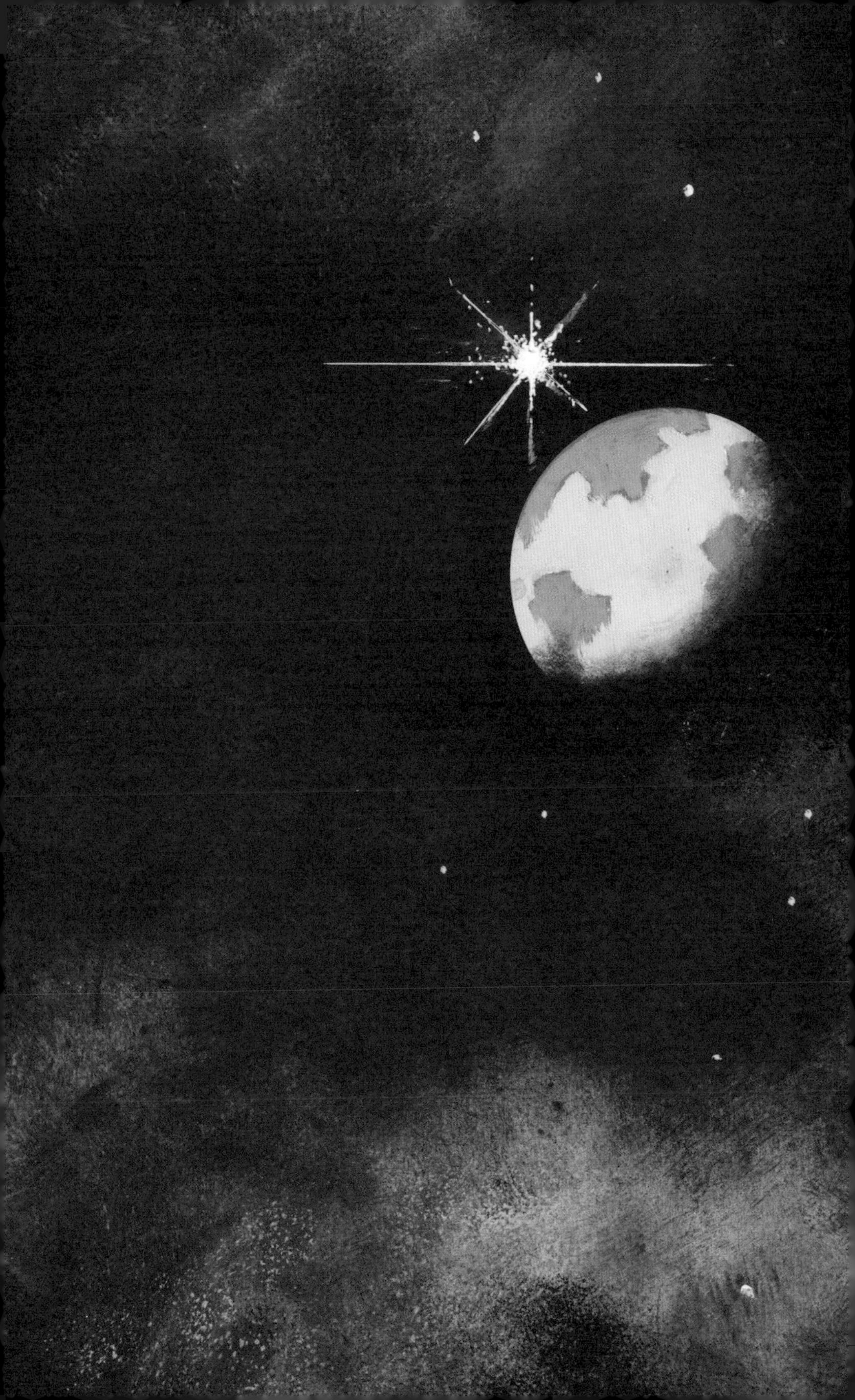

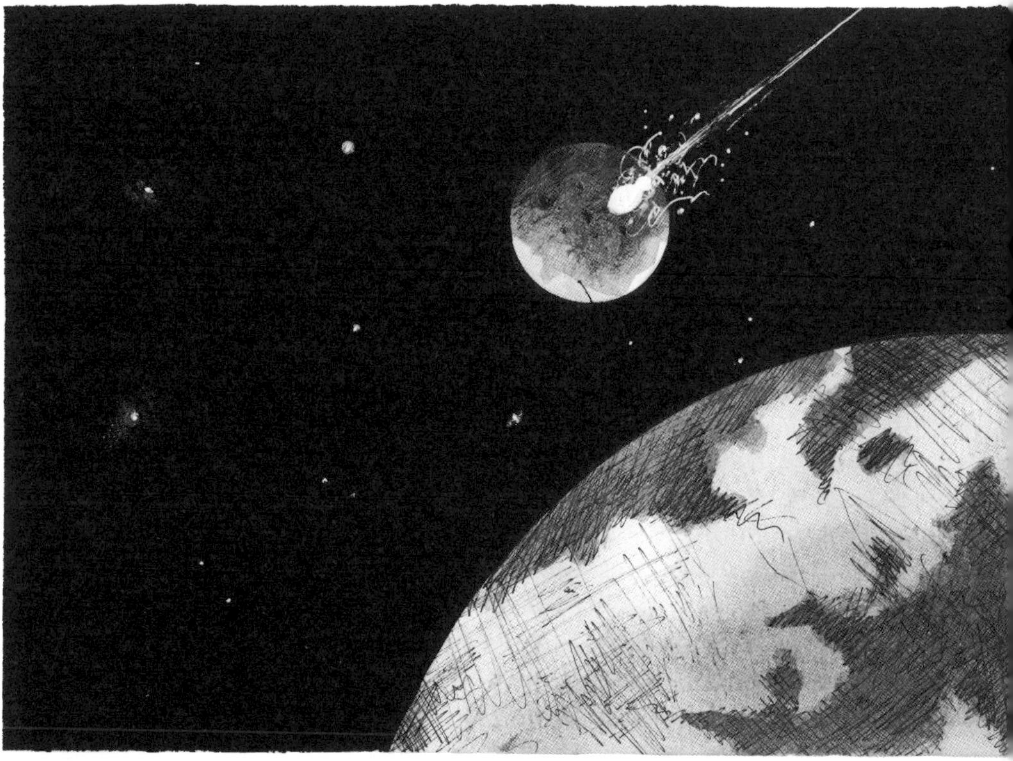

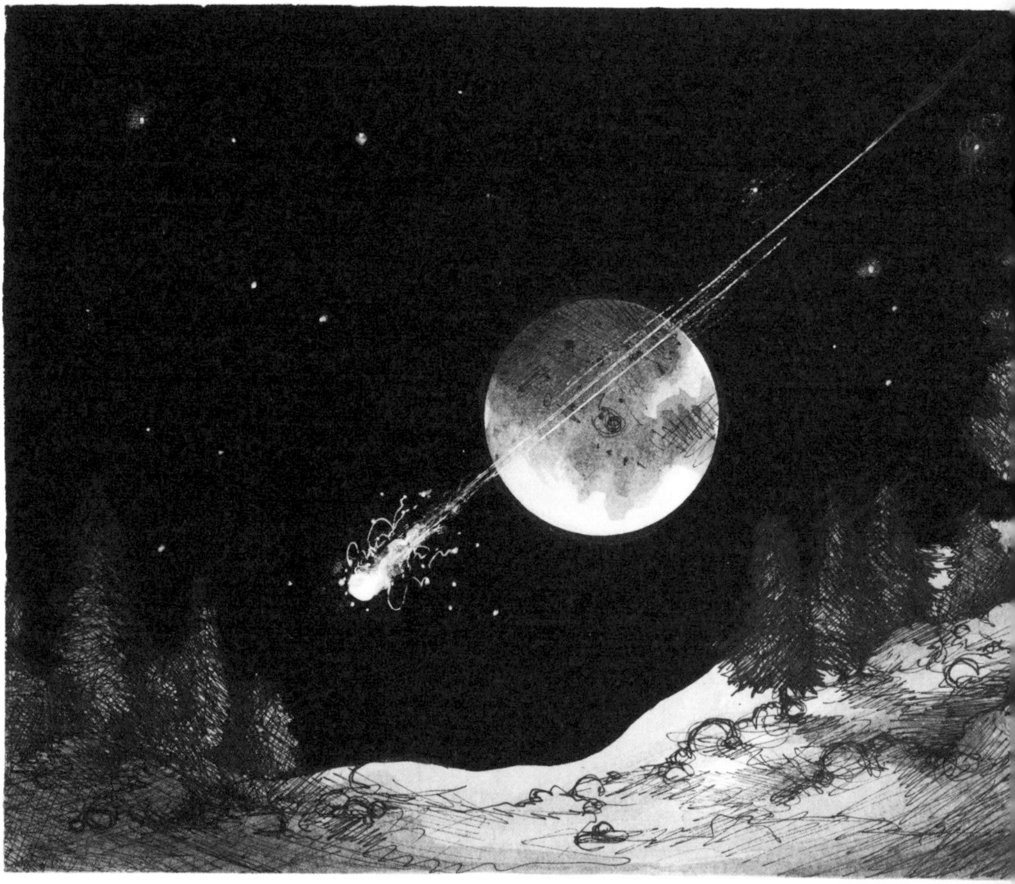

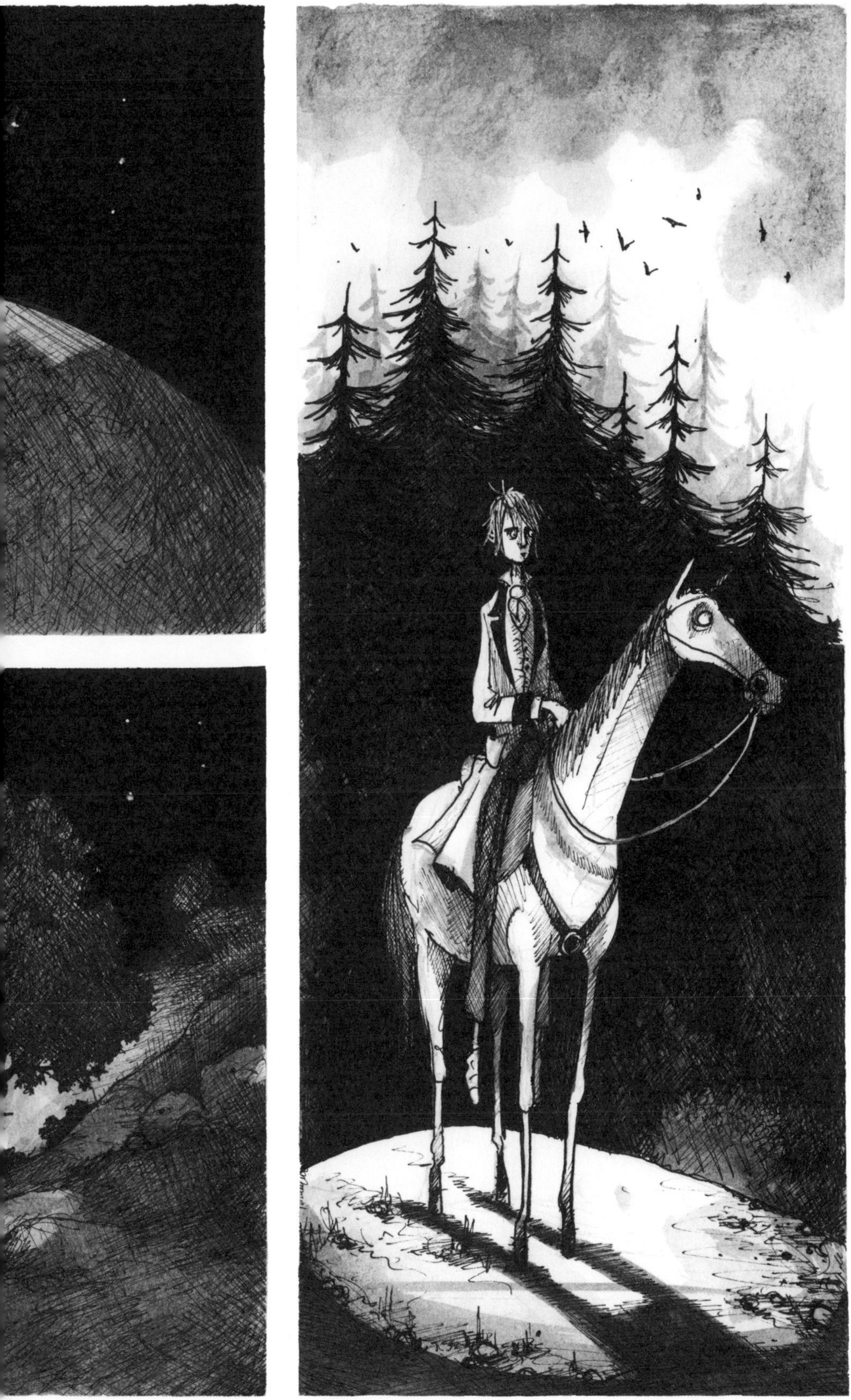

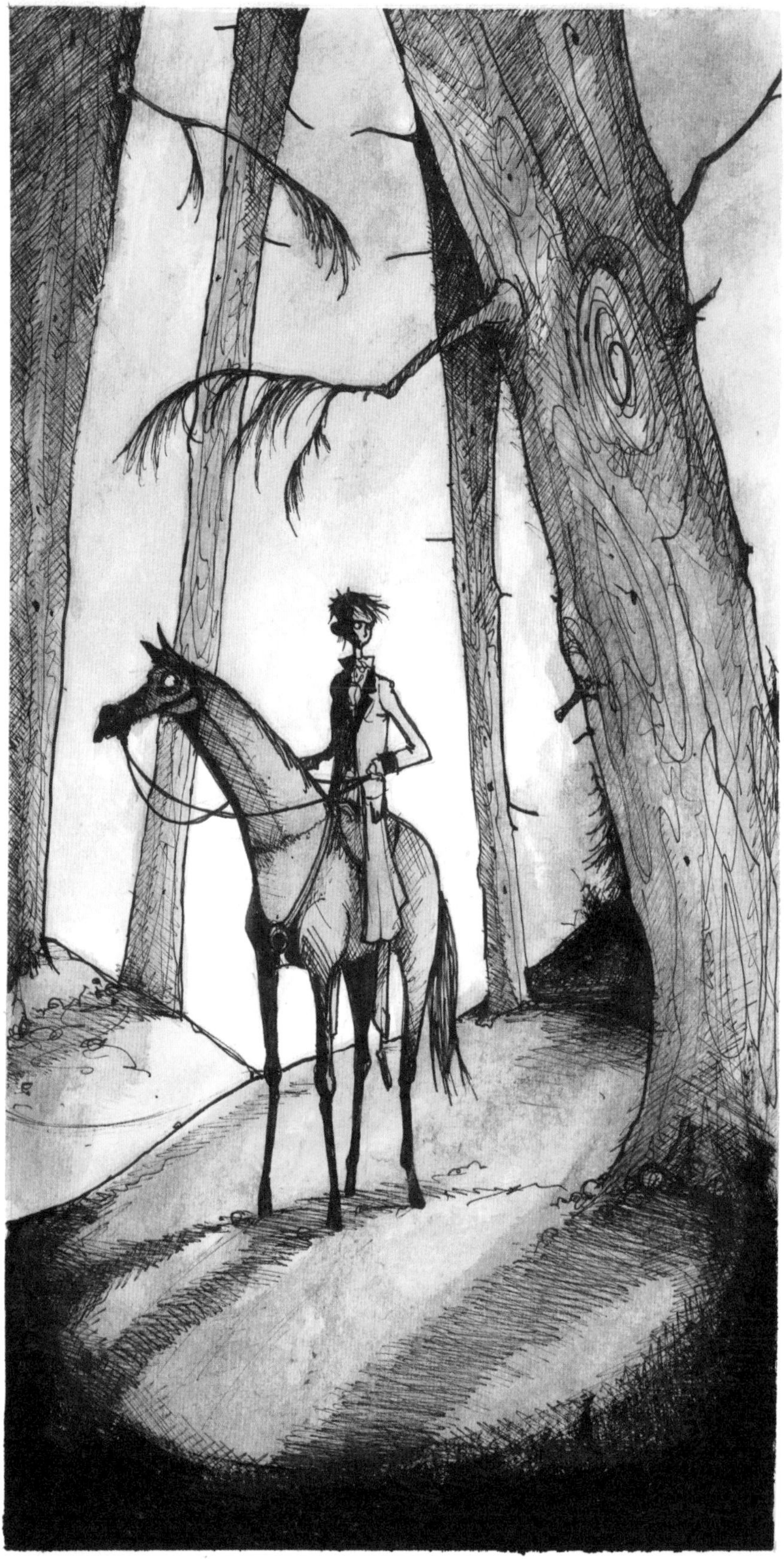
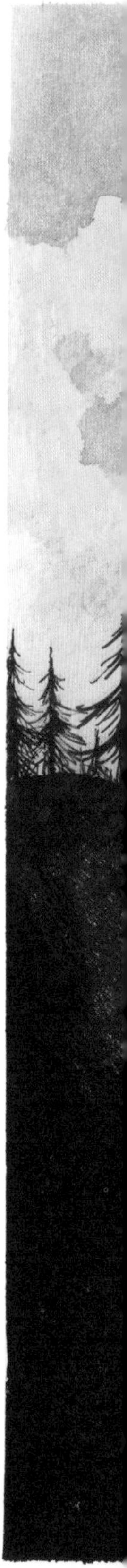

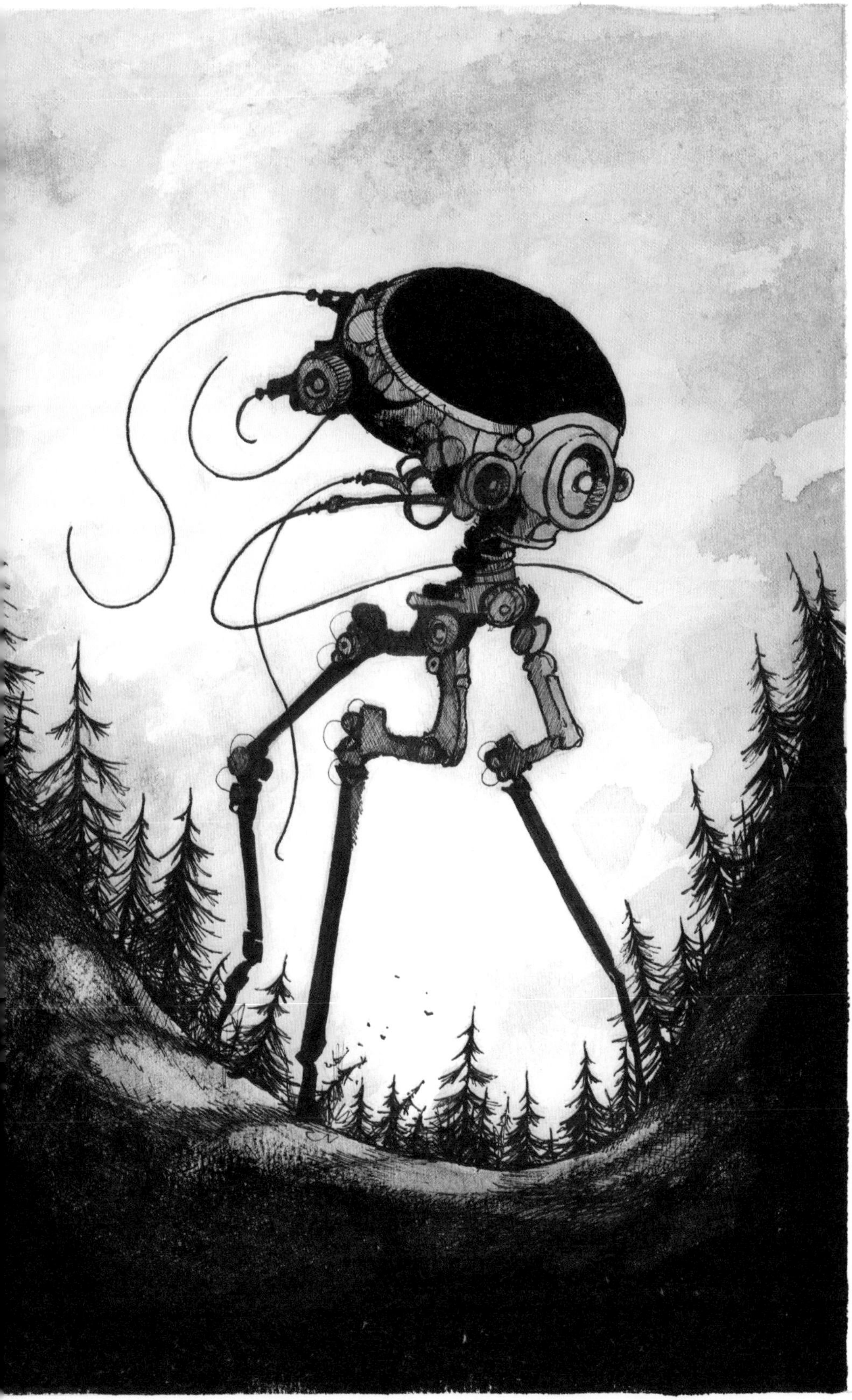

Chapter Five

Damage

I FOUND MY WAY HOME, where I sat trancelike in shock at the foot of the staircase. I shivered in a pool of water, attempting to collect my thoughts.

When I'd gathered my senses at last, I threw my clothes across the banisters and wrapped myself in a large sheet to dry off. Eventually I lay upon the bed, my hair still damp across the pillows. I drifted into deep sleep and was not aware of anything else until I awoke early the next morning.

What had become of Anya and the children? Had the machines headed their way? Had more capsules landed? What horrors awaited us all?

Unable to rest, and with my horse now lame, I dressed and left the house on foot to see what had become of our homeland. I could make out distant flames and trails of smoke rising from various points across the landscape. It seemed as if the whole world was on fire.

I had only ventured a short way before I discovered the catastrophic scene of a wrecked train. The engine, it seemed, had plunged through the bridge into the water and was still billowing smoke. Its passengers rescued by now, I hoped. The whole place was eerily silent.

Some way further along I met an exhausted artillery man on the common.

'I am Troy,' he said, and he held out a bloodied hand to shake mine.

'I am Leon. You must come back with me and take shelter. I live close by. It won't be safe for long, but I can prepare a good meal and we can see to your wounds.'

'You don't mind turning back? I would be most grateful,' he said.

'We must,' I replied.

When we reached home, I cooked and, before we ate, I cleaned and dressed his injuries while we talked.

'I fear for my family and their safety,' he told me. 'I am newly married. We have a child – he's only a few months old. Who knows what kind of a world we're bringing him into now?'

'We cannot blame ourselves,' I insisted, but as I spoke I somehow questioned it and wondered what we had done to deserve our predicament.

'Who did you leave behind?' he asked.

And so I told him about Anya and the children – and my task of recording what was happening. He flicked through my journal, fascinated by my work in the same way that I had been captivated by the paintings and drawings I had studied.

'What about photography?' he asked. 'Have you seen the results? The imagery is incredible. Surely that would be a more accurate record?'

I nodded. 'In some cases, yes. But it's not mobile enough. Or indeed quick enough. Achieving a view to make sense of it would be difficult and dangerous. And the added notes made in the moment will prove vital in later studies,' I continued. 'Or so I hope.'

'Your work is incredible. It is also *vital*,' he insisted. He paused, staring into thin air.

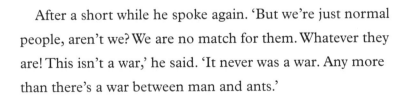

After a short while he spoke again. 'But we're just normal people, aren't we? We are no match for them. Whatever they are! This isn't a war,' he said. 'It never was a war. Any more than there's a war between man and ants.'

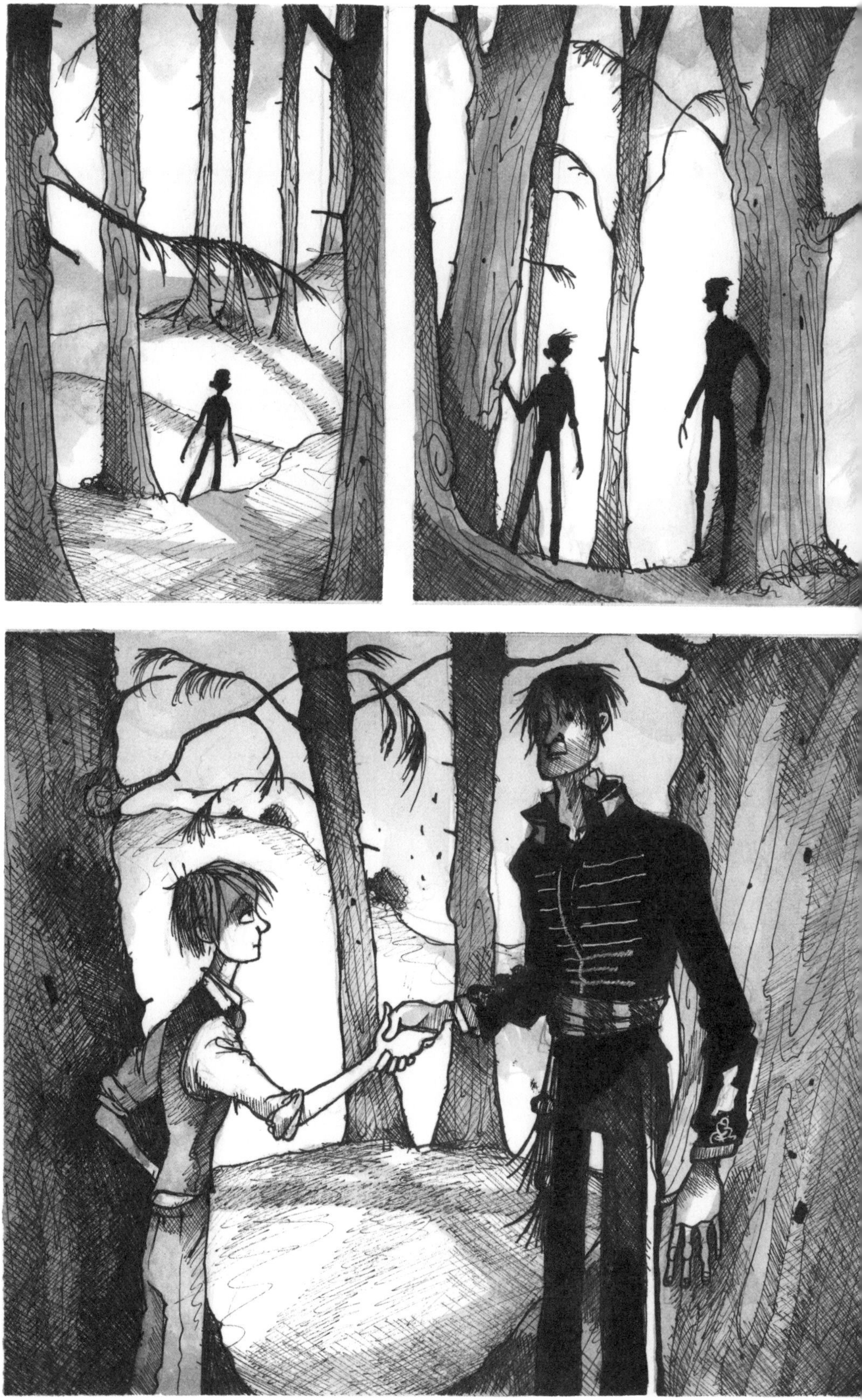

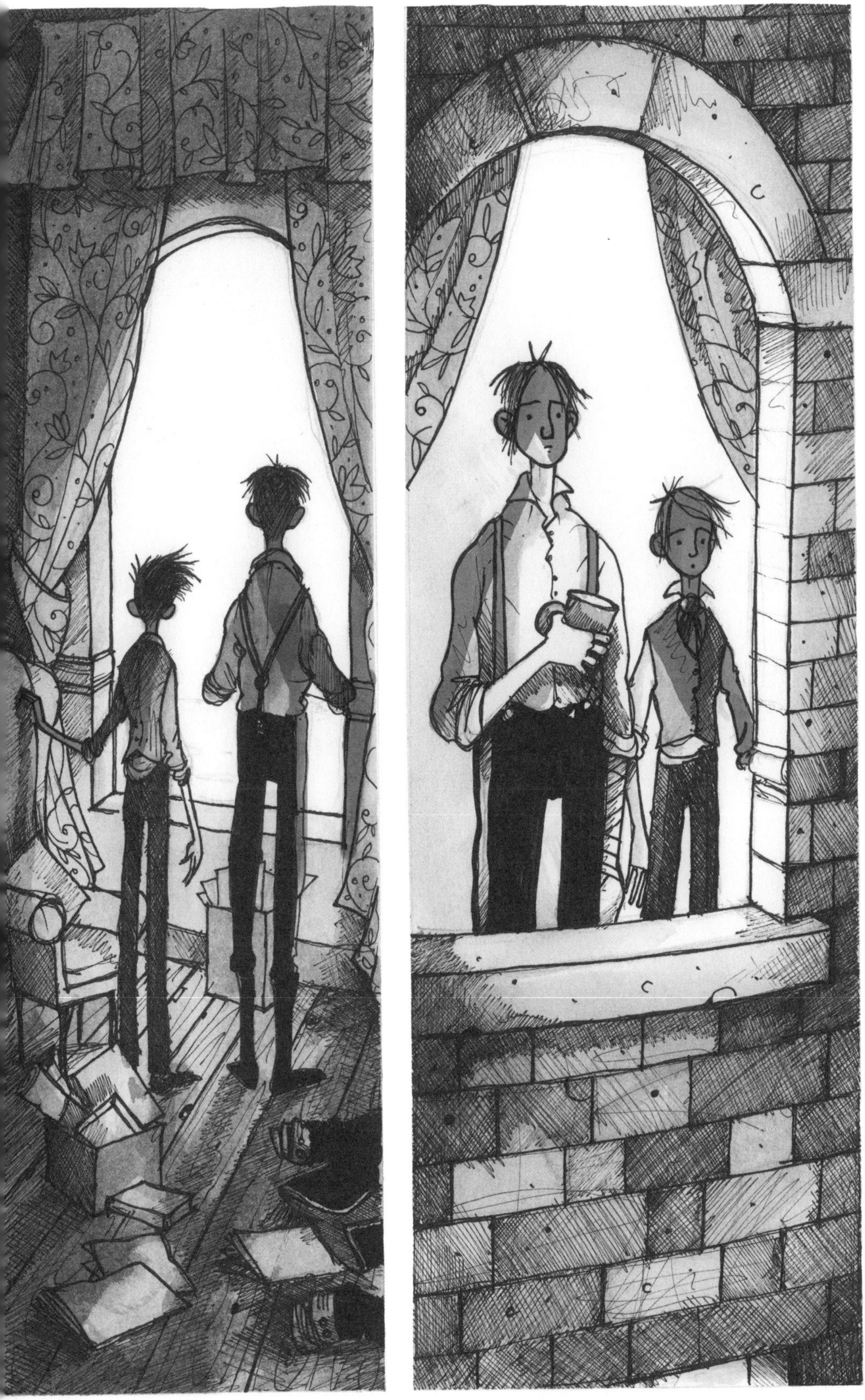

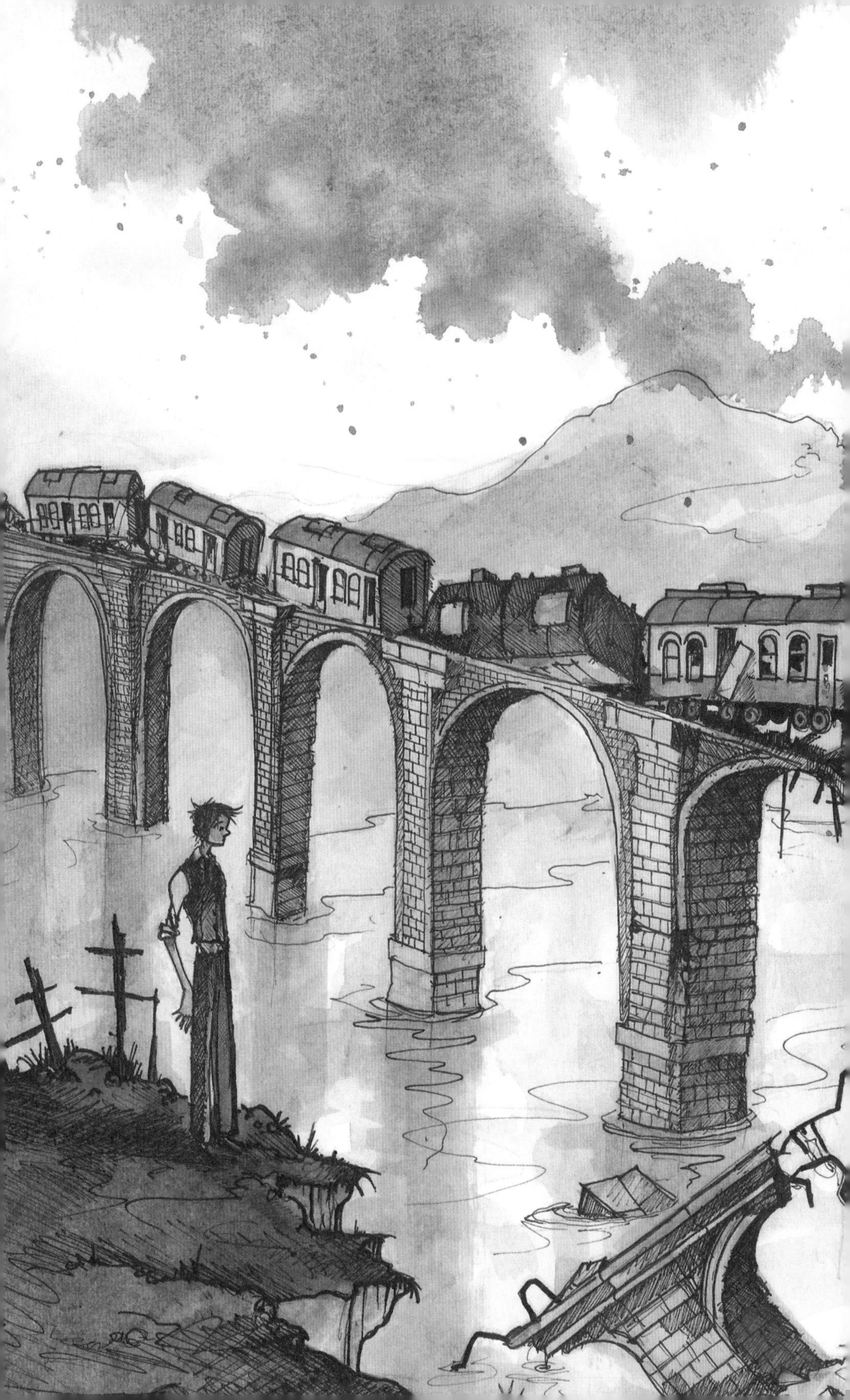

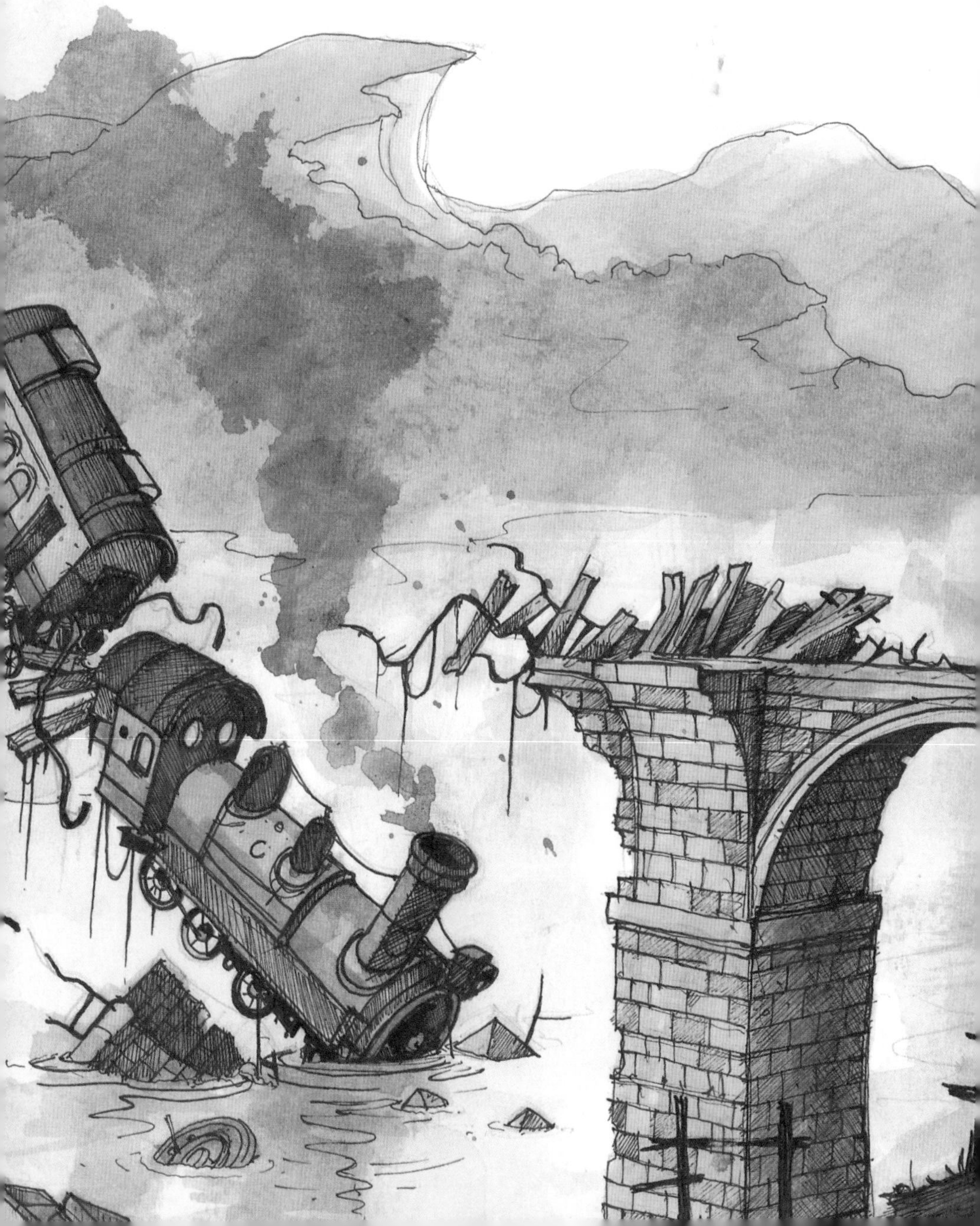

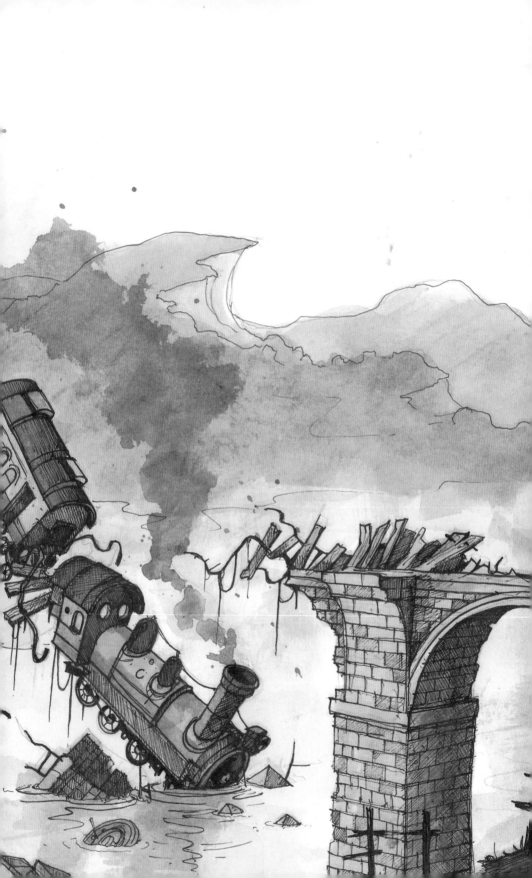

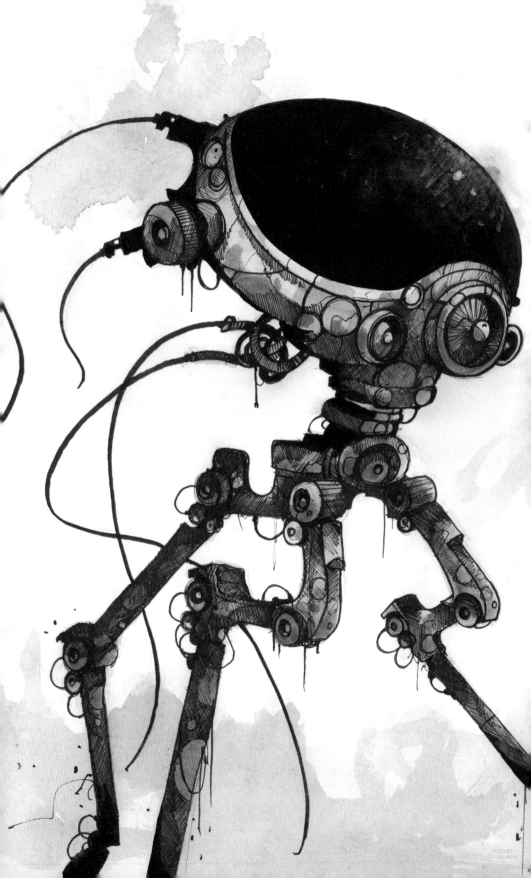

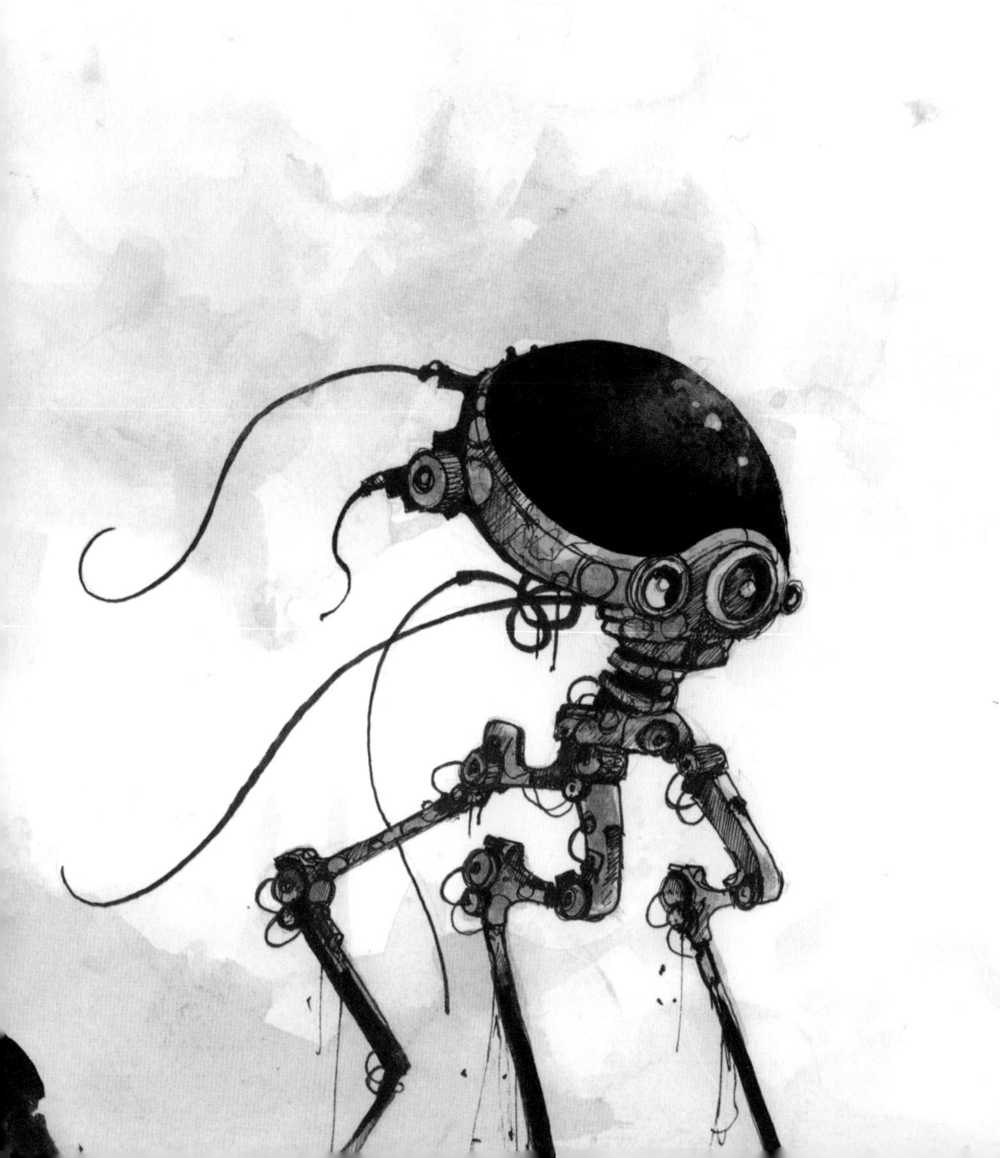

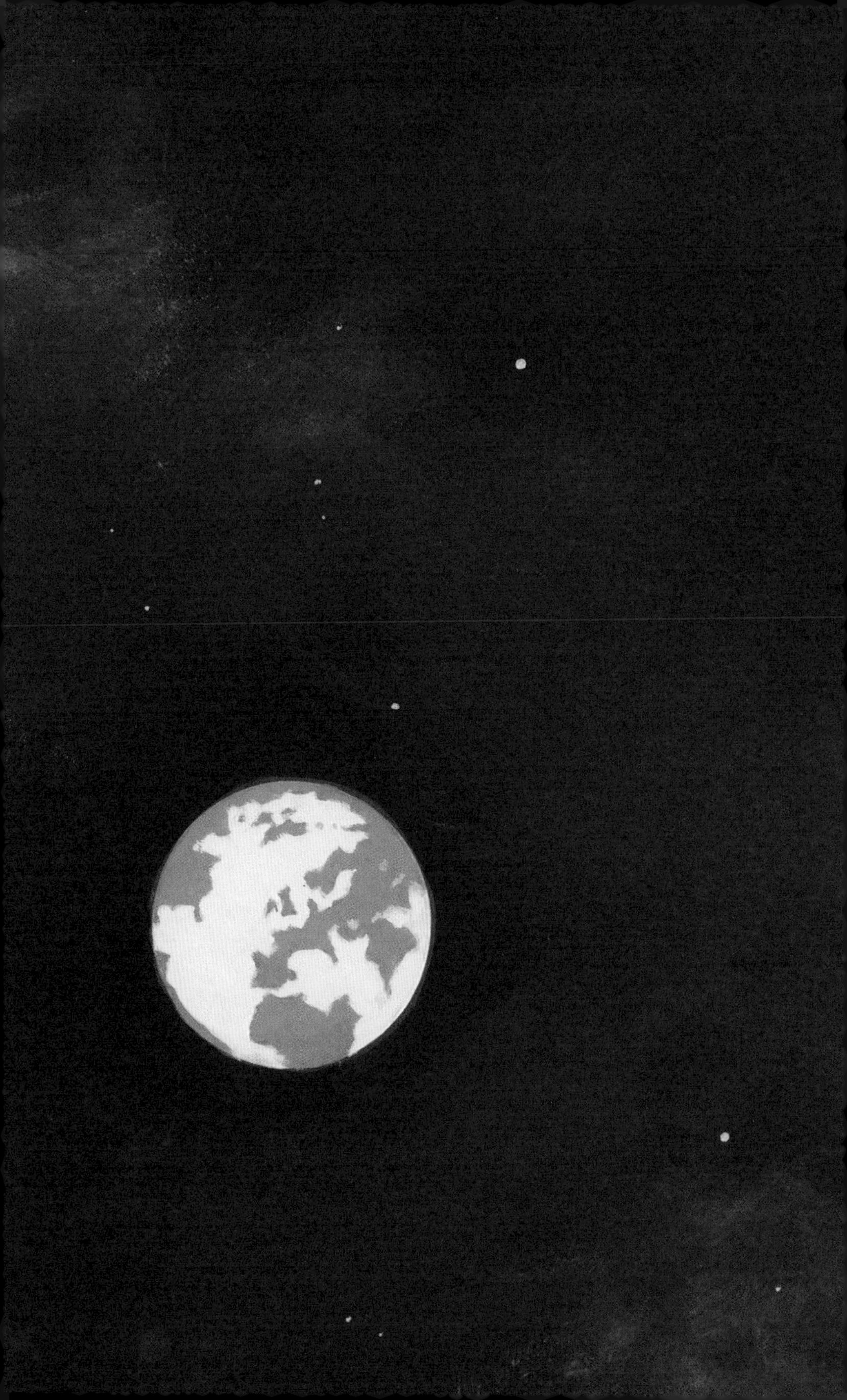

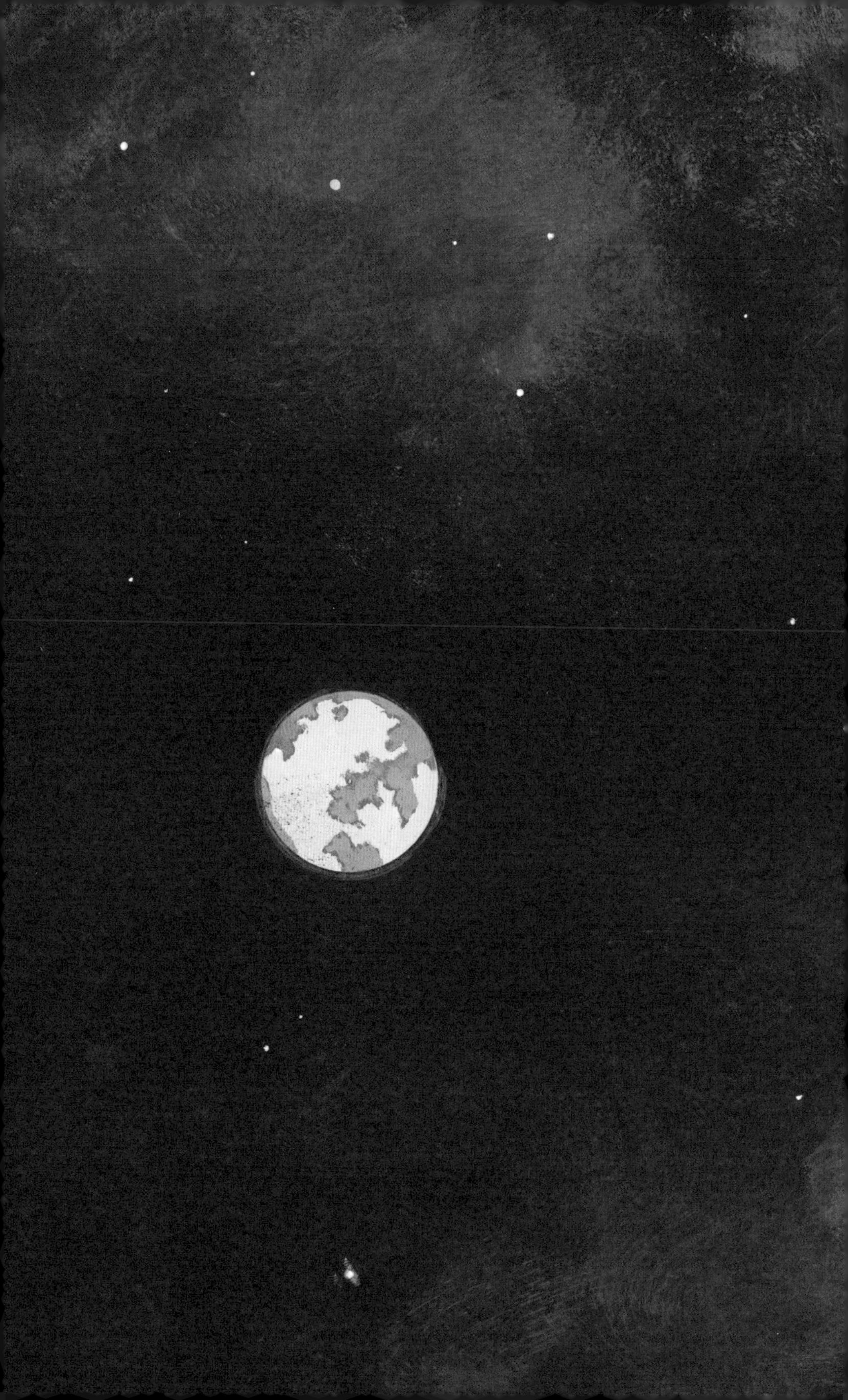

'But what do they want with our world?' I asked. Questions tumbled out of me. 'What drives them here? What do they seek to take from our ancient existence? How could we be of use to an advanced species who can travel across the galaxy as they can? Do both they *and* the machines live? Or are they one and the same thing?'

'Time will tell us,' was his only response.

'Time may run out altogether,' I said, and that brought an abrupt silence to our thoughts.

As the trails of smoke cleared and daylight broke, we could see further damage around us. In the distance, more tripods moved busily, toing and froing in their stride around the pits where the capsules had fallen. Their metal bodies glistened in the sun. And, here and there, trails of black smoke billowed around them.

Chapter Six

Gun Smoke and Combat

'I APPRECIATE THE WELCOME and convenience of your home, my friend. But this is no place for either of us,' insisted my companion. 'I'd suggest, if you don't mind, that we take what we can carry and head out from here. It will be safer away from the towns and villages,' he said, feeling revived after food and sleep.

I agreed and made no hesitation. We decided to leave together and then go our separate ways: he towards his battalion, while I would follow what activity I could find. We raided the cupboards and took what was sensible to transport.

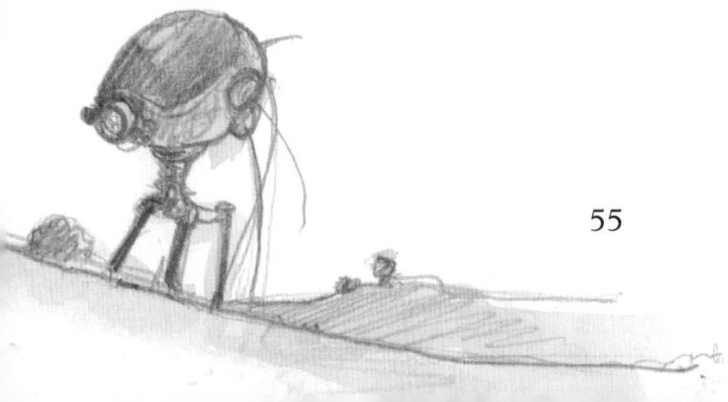

The summer grew hotter by the day and we knew that the heat would add to the struggle ahead. Indeed, we had already gone many weeks without rain. We took fresh water in flasks and drank what we could. Before setting off, we dabbed our faces and I ran wet fingers through my hair.

As we walked, we found discarded personal belongings along the way. Abandoned vehicles, spilled luggage that had been looted in opportune moments. Remnants of lives scattered across the landscape.

We took the well-trodden path to the orphanage before we broke into the woods at the foot of the hill. The twisted frame of a bicycle stood propped against the orphanage wall. Above us, plumes of smoke rose from the damaged rooftop. I stood motionless and fixed in a daze. I was unable to move myself away. My thoughts flashed back to the sounds of the children ringing in my ears. The timbers were exposed – splintered, burnt and torn apart. The slates smashed into dust.

'The Martians have walked this route. Ploughed through our town. We are nothing to them. Mere insects beneath their feet,' I muttered in despair. I needed to search the basement. I needed to know that Orla and Ivan were still safe down there.

'I'm sorry – we must hurry!' came the soldier's voice softly. 'We need to keep moving. We shouldn't stay still for too long.'

So reluctantly I turned away. For now I could only pray for Orla and Ivan's safety.

Throughout the morning, we came across droves of people with handcarts. And as we neared a rail station, we could see crowds bustling onto the platforms with luggage, desperate to escape. In addition, a flustered, overheated and noisy gathering had developed near Shepperton Lock where the ferries crossed, and it was clear that there were far more people than the boats could carry.

The commotion of the crowds was suddenly broken by the haunting howl that accompanied the arrival of the Martian machines. It was followed by the creaking groan of their steely joints.

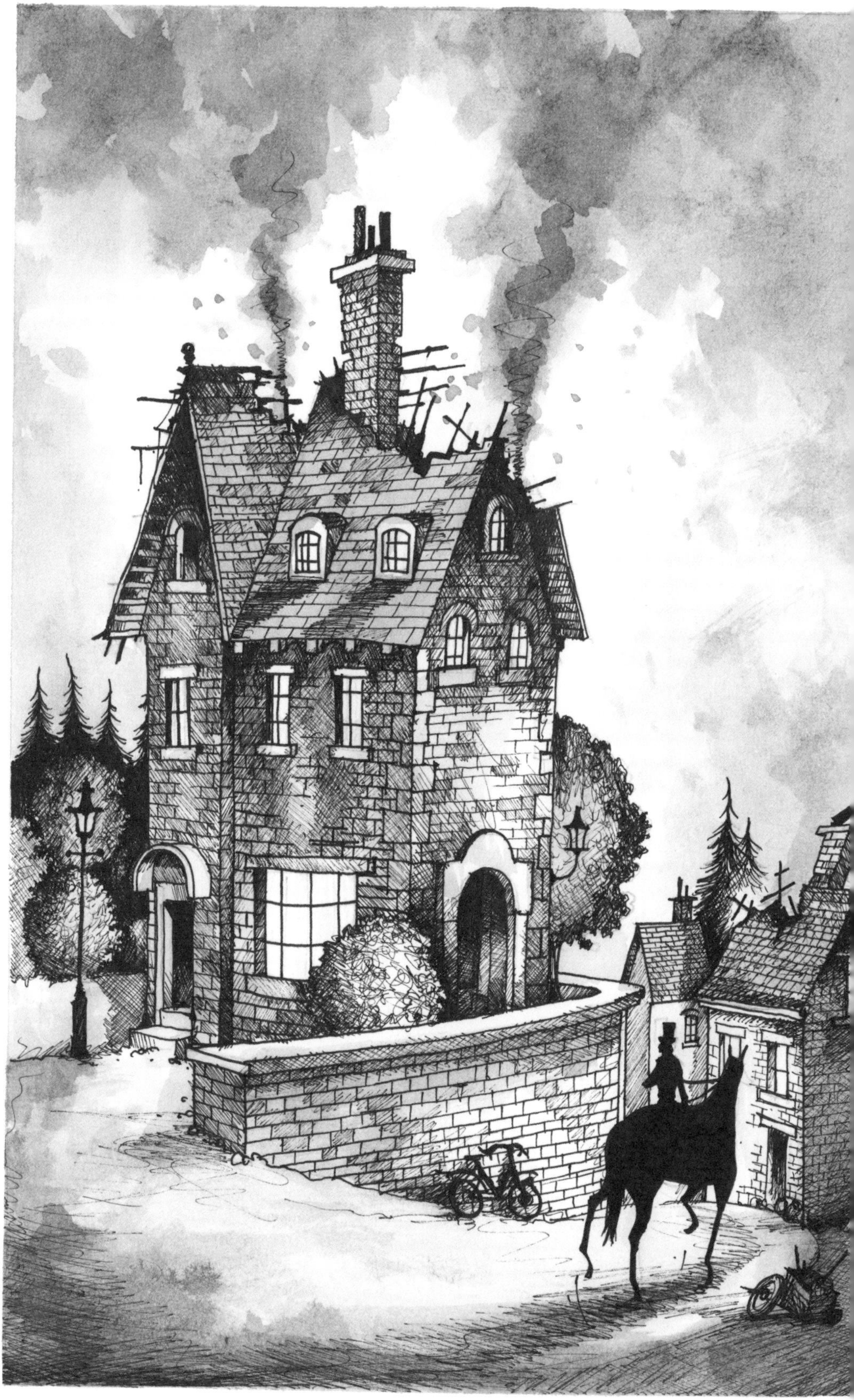

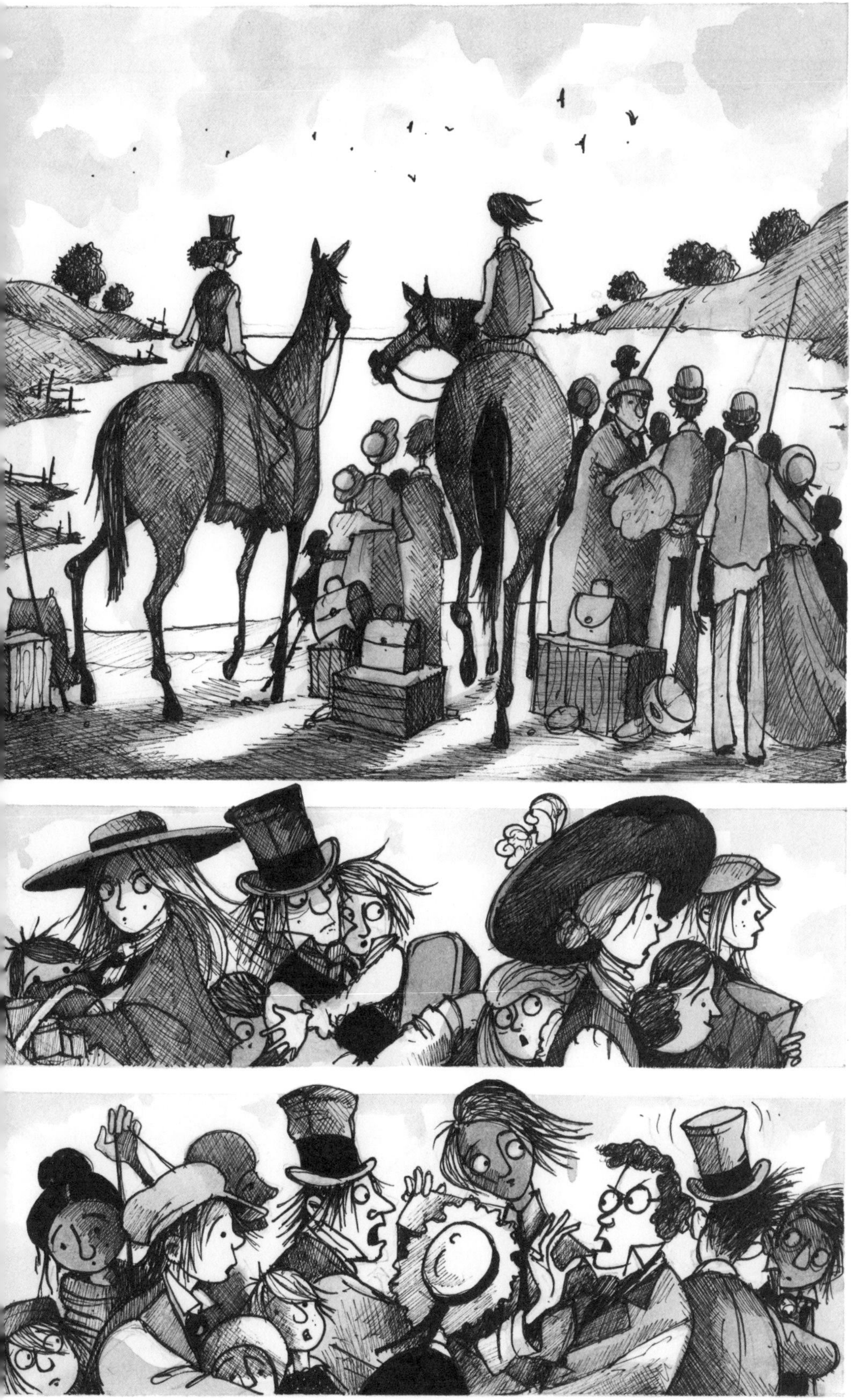

Within moments, their shapes appeared through the blazing hot shimmer of the afternoon, black smoke billowing around them. The pounding of their three-legged walk shook the earth beneath our feet.

Screams alerted the rest of the crowd, and the alarm caused desperate clambering and pushing. This was as close as anyone had seen them. The Martians towered over us, and the crowd surged in waves but without anywhere to go. It was unsure whether whether it was by intent or accident but several people had ended up in the canal's waist-height water, with hats bobbing, bags drifting and skirts flailing across the surface.

Others, including myself, followed – perhaps in the hope of avoiding being seen. Many of us plunged the depths and held ourselves under. The suffocating smoke rolled across the water's surface like an early mist and pushed the crowds downstream. Without warning a force seemed to grip us, as if we were seized tight without being touched.

Retaliating artillery fire burst into life from somewhere nearby. Almost instantly a shell exploded into the head of a nearby machine, bursting into flames

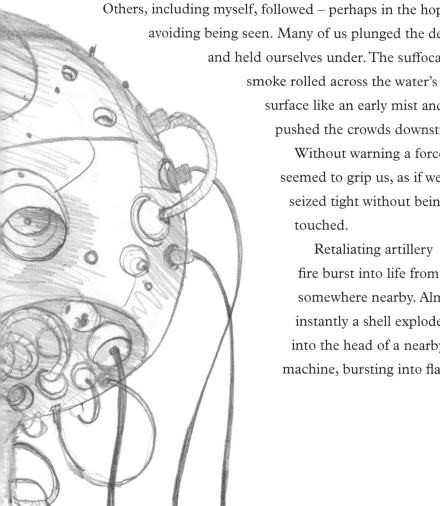

with a flash. The decapitated colossus reeled and crashed through the steeple of Shepperton Church before momentum drove its heaving bulk into the river where it lay, splayed and steaming.

Shrapnel showered across the water, pelting the surface. The screaming seemed to grow louder. I perched, chest-deep and unable to move, within the cover of an overhanging tree, holding my bag above the water, and waited for the chaos to settle.

In that moment I have a vivid memory of a huge foot of a machine coming down barely an arm's length from my half-submerged body as the four remaining tripods careered overhead. Up close I glimpsed the shiny metal surface. It fizzed and smoked. As it passed, the tightening force around us released its hold. A fragment of the strange metal floated by. Without thinking, I grabbed and held it. And then I placed it safely in my bag.

For the second time, amid the confusion of the attack, I had lost my companion. I shouted out, but my voice was quickly drowned in the havoc.

And then, very slowly, I realised that by some miracle I had again escaped.

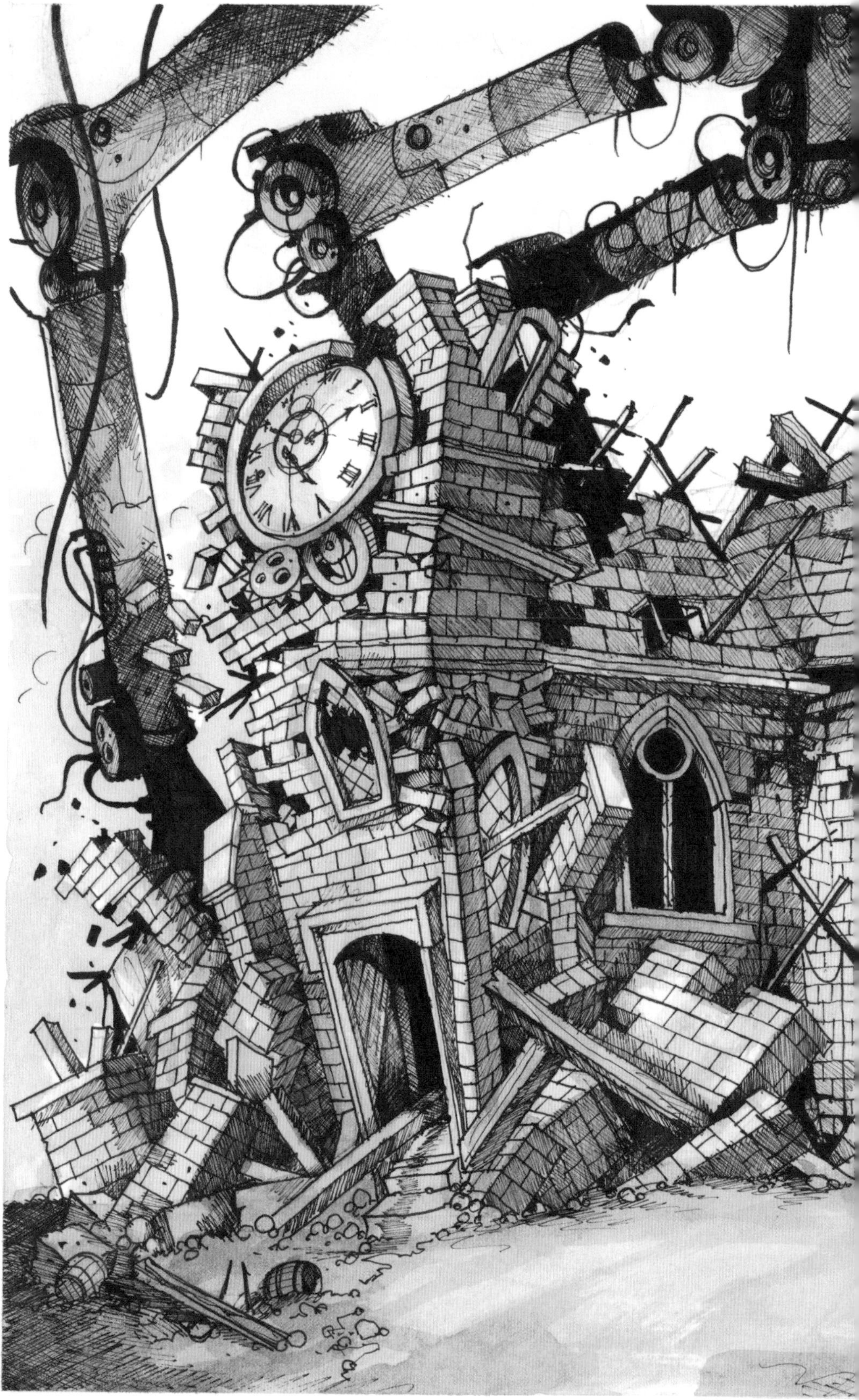

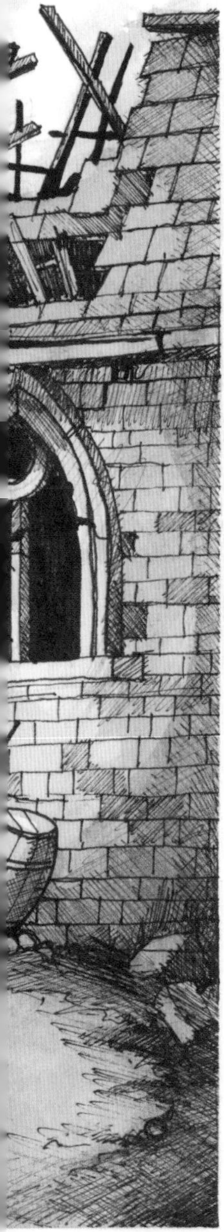

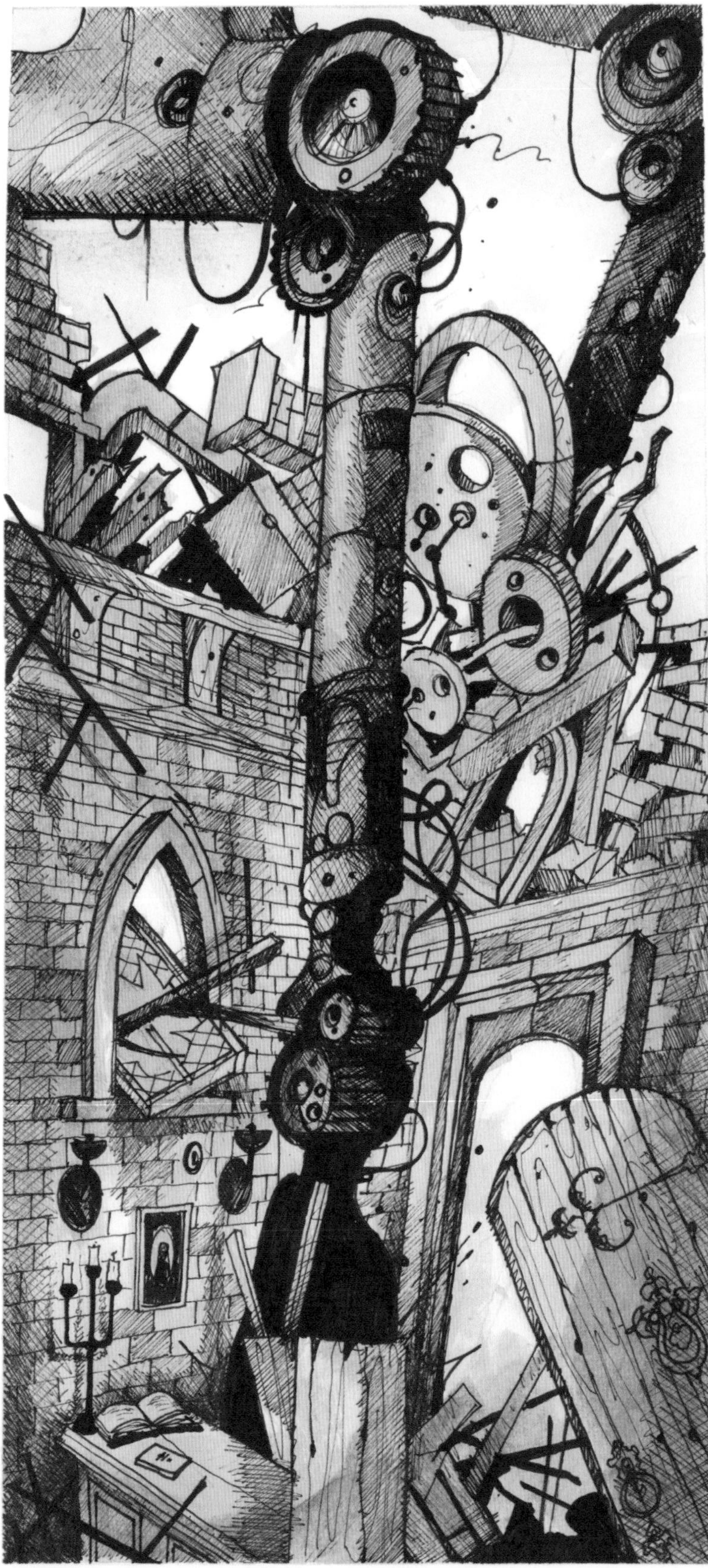

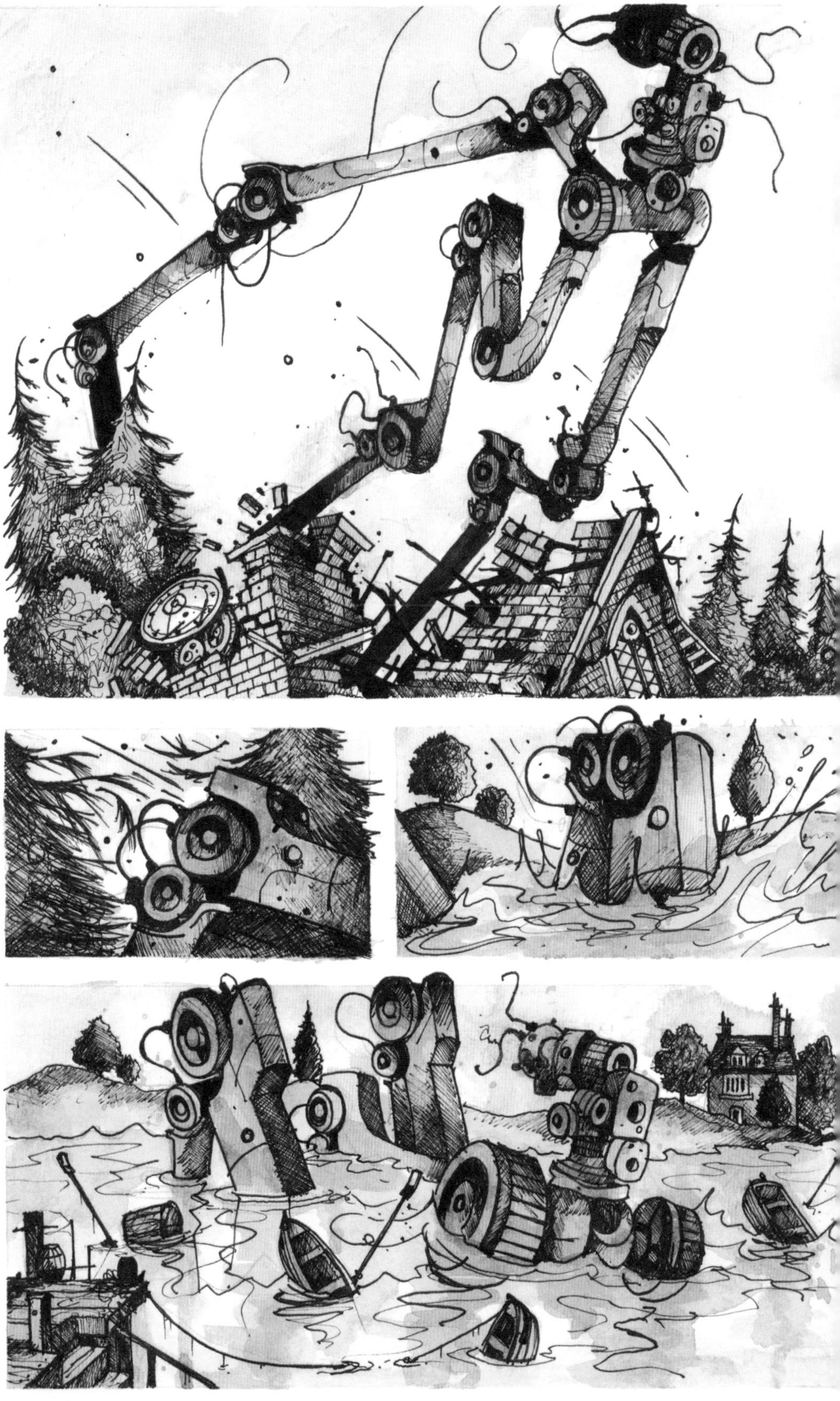

Chapter Seven

They Walk Through London

THROUGHOUT THE NEXT FEW DAYS, I observed capsule after capsule falling to earth, bringing reinforcements to the Martians. Where they could, the military responded with deafening firepower, pounding them with shells and bullets, but the aliens were not easily defeated. The artillery man had been right. This was not a war that the human race could win. The determination and the will to survive no doubt apparent. The reality of what we faced was something else.

I shrank from sight, retreating under the cover of trees, but the haunt of their howling sirens carried over the treetops. They emitted their black smoke that hung heavy in the air. I looked on in horror as, in the distance, people were choked and poisoned by the dense black fog that engulfed them.

Desperately I found a ruined empty building at Halliford, in the hope that I might escape the suffocation and that the Martians would not return to something they had already destroyed. I salvaged whatever I could of food and fresh water. My mind was filled with anxiety for Anya and the children. What had they seen of the destruction? And what had they suffered? I was tortured by terrible thoughts.

This building had only been recently evacuated. I searched and found a newspaper from the previous day and learned of the attack up in London. The headline leapt out at me. Refugees wandered the length of Oxford Street. Crowds of people wheeled handcarts along Marylebone Road. Fugitives streamed over Westminster Bridge. Desperate evacuees crammed the carriages and platforms of every railway station. Swarms of vehicles and horses battled for their position through the streets. Trails of the black smoke lay on the main route out to St Albans. People crowded the ferry terminals, and there was jostling and fighting as people were pushed back with boat hooks and fell into the water amid the stampede. This was the first I knew of attacks beyond our immediate surroundings. How far had they reached?

I put the newspaper back in its place and found a dust-covered radio perched above it, tucked behind books and crockery.

It was worth a try. At first I got nothing. Just a faint crackle and the occasional incoherent sentence. I persisted. And then suddenly: '*This is Mercury Radio broadcasting.*' Then nothing again. I twisted the dials impatiently. I moved the radio from one corner of the room to another until dance music could be heard. I lowered it carefully onto the table and turned the dials gently until the sounds became clearer. A melodic tune put me momentarily in a peaceful spot, sending my mind daydreaming back to Anya.

However, as I heard the following, I sat in shock, the hairs standing up on the back of my neck: '. . . *We interrupt this broadcast to bring you extended information regarding the devastating attacks across the globe . . .*' The signal drifted and white noise drowned out the voice. '*Continued attacks on the west of . . .*' More white noise. '. . . *and further inland, spreading across the continent . . .*' I persevered with the radio signal until I could surmise that attacks prevailed across Europe, then eastward into Persia, across to India and as far south-east as Ceylon.

Finally, right at the end, I caught a line about London, how the River Thames was littered with the remains of a broken city. The suffocating smoke was drifting out to sea.

I think I heard it correctly. That one of the tripods had stepped into the water. It had ground to a halt before stumbling and crashing, half destroying Westminster Bridge in its path. I could only surmise that it had been unable to keep aloft on its tall struts amid the strong current of the water. The strength of the Thames was forever unforgiving.

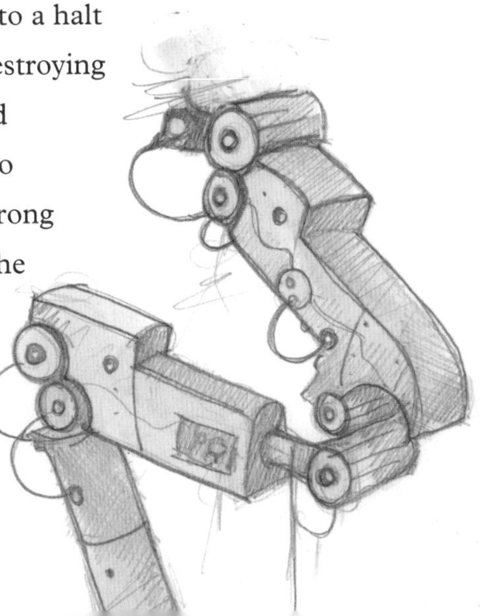

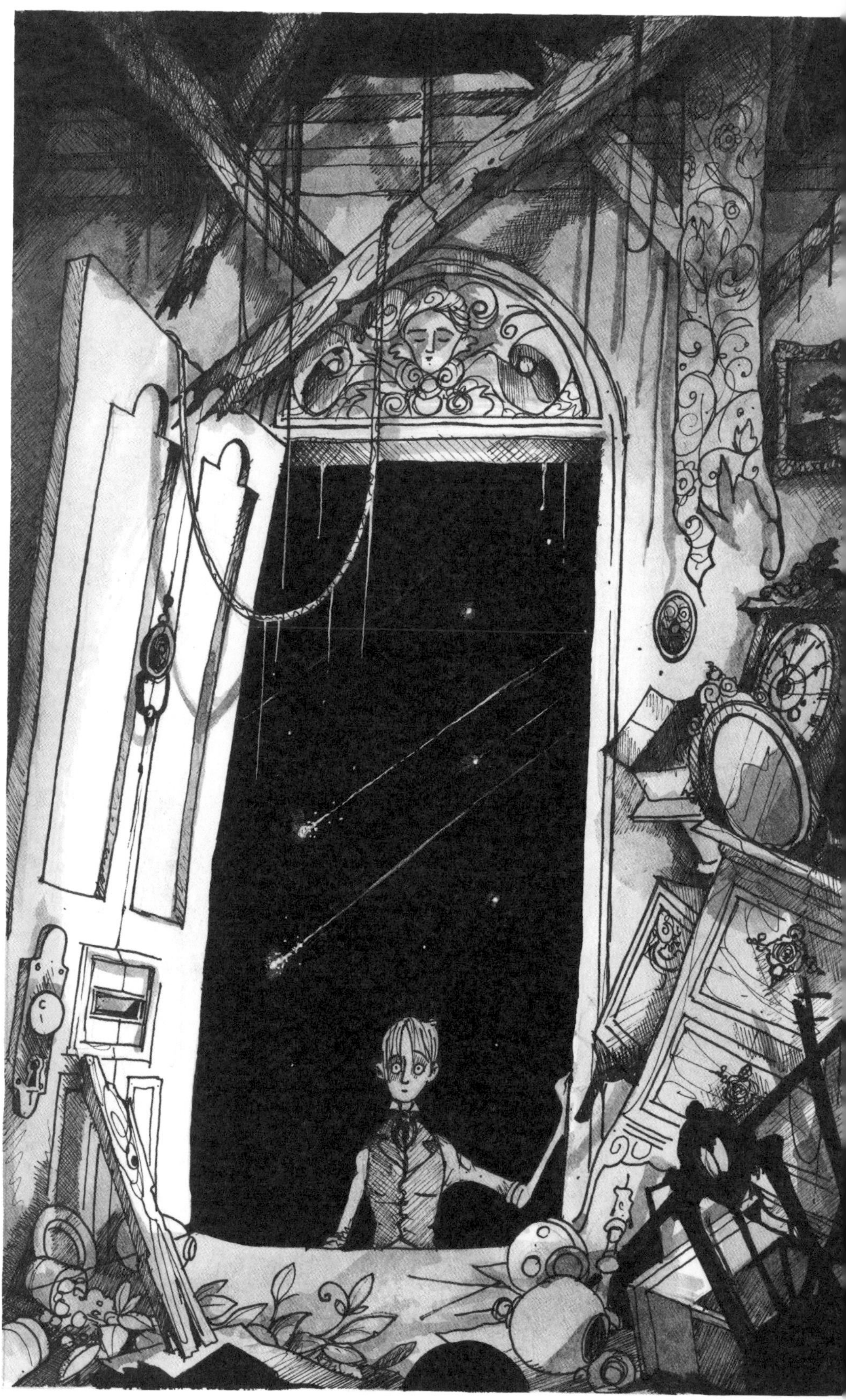

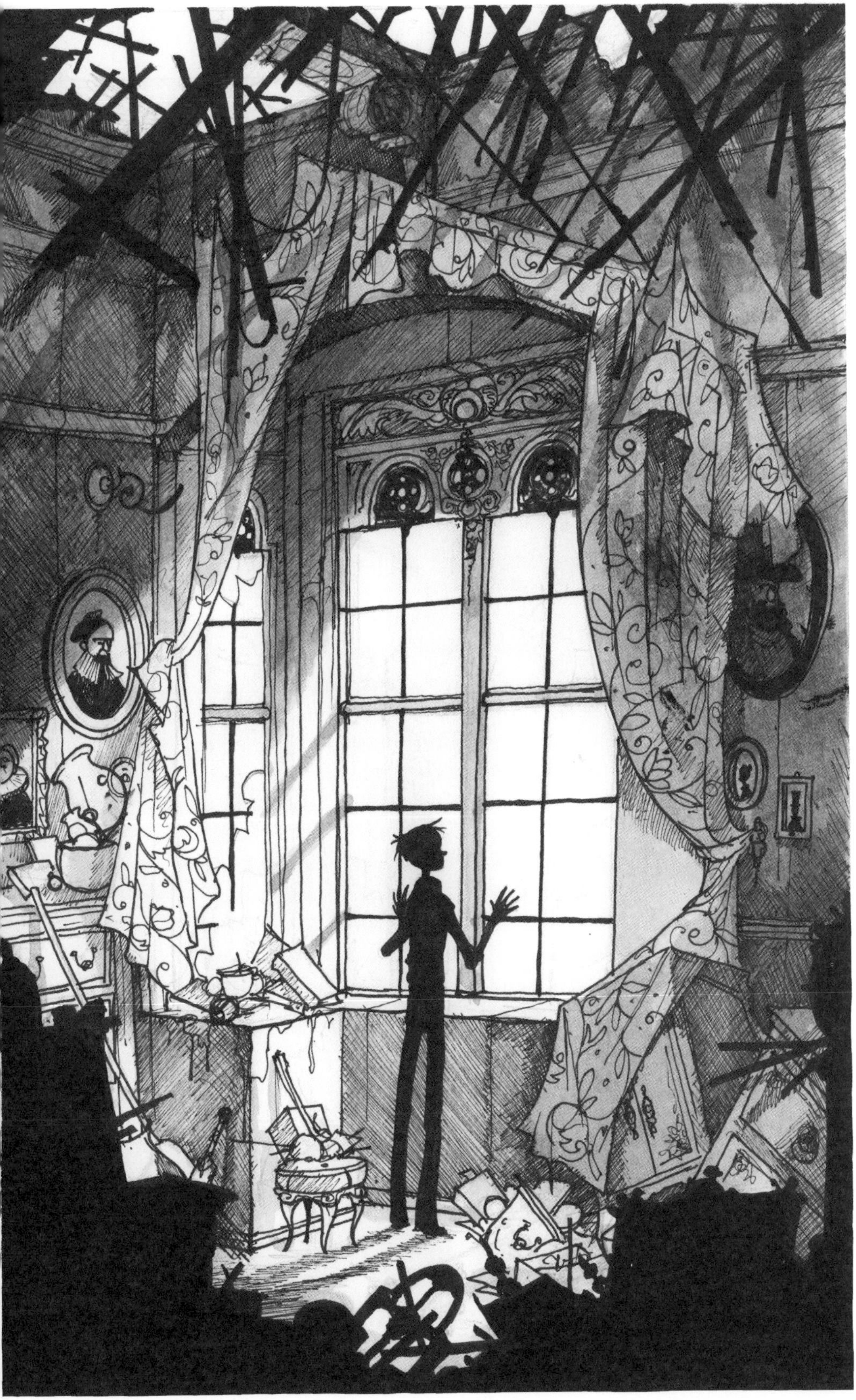

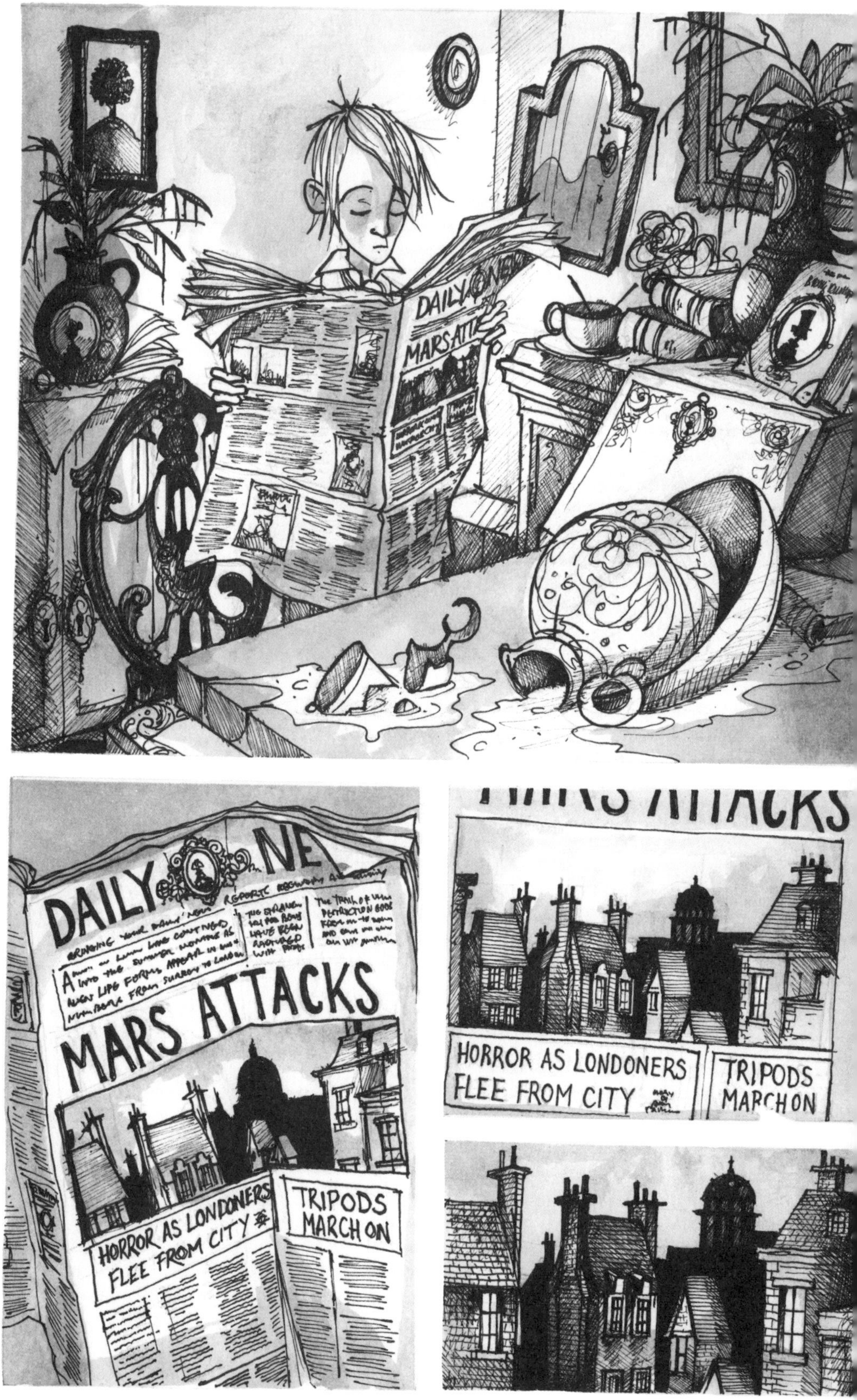
DAILY
MARS ATTACKS
HORROR AS LONDONERS FLEE FROM CITY
TRIPODS MARCH ON
HORROR AS LONDONERS FLEE FROM CITY
TRIPODS MARCH ON

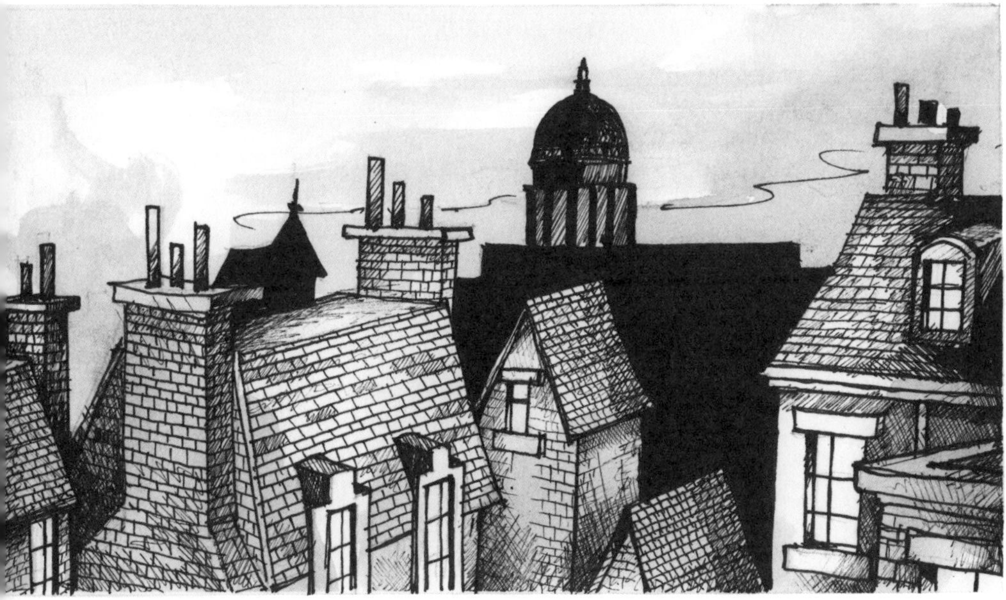

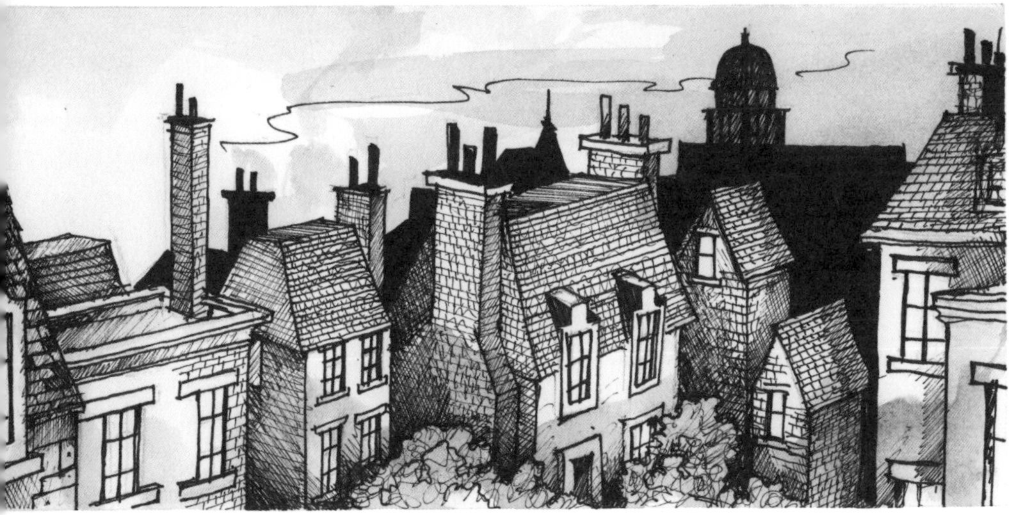

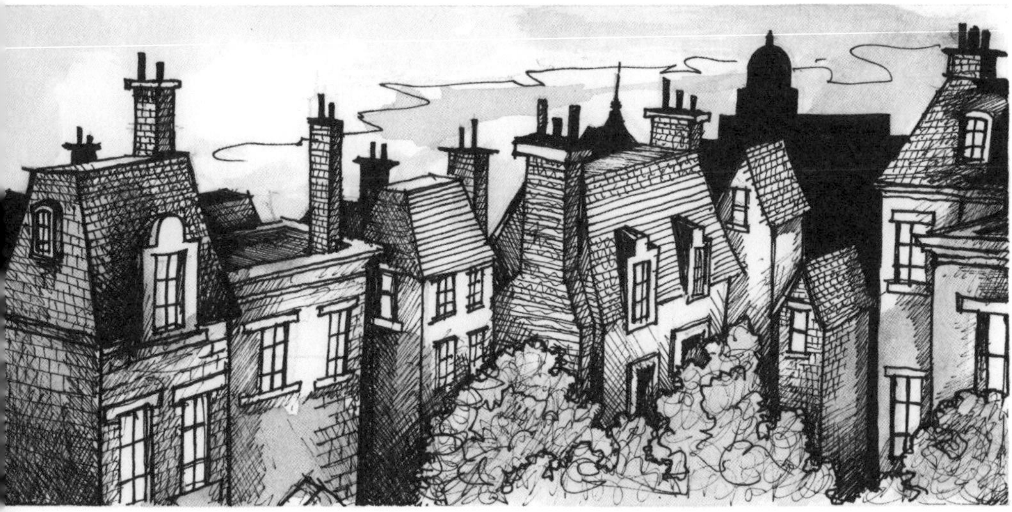

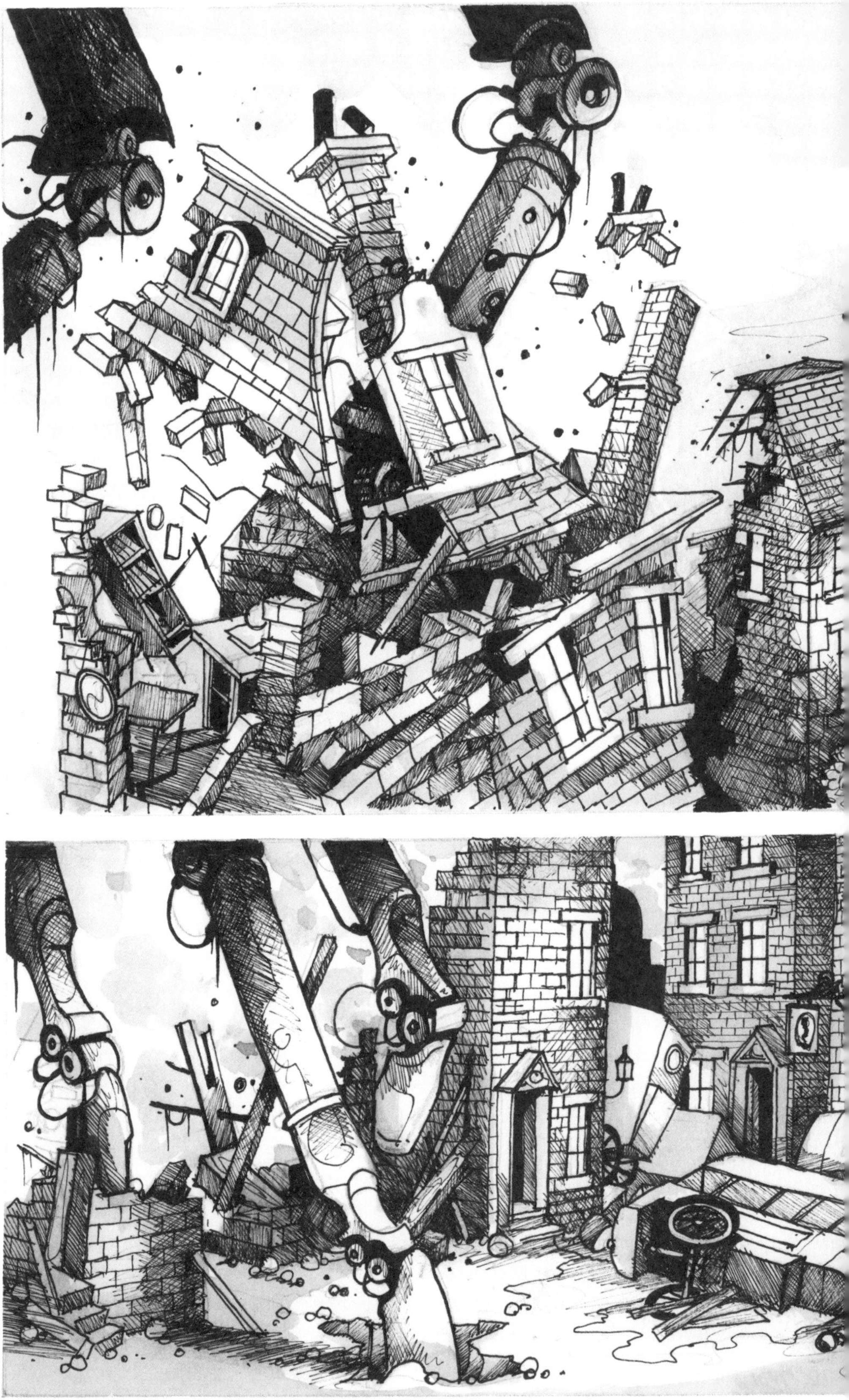

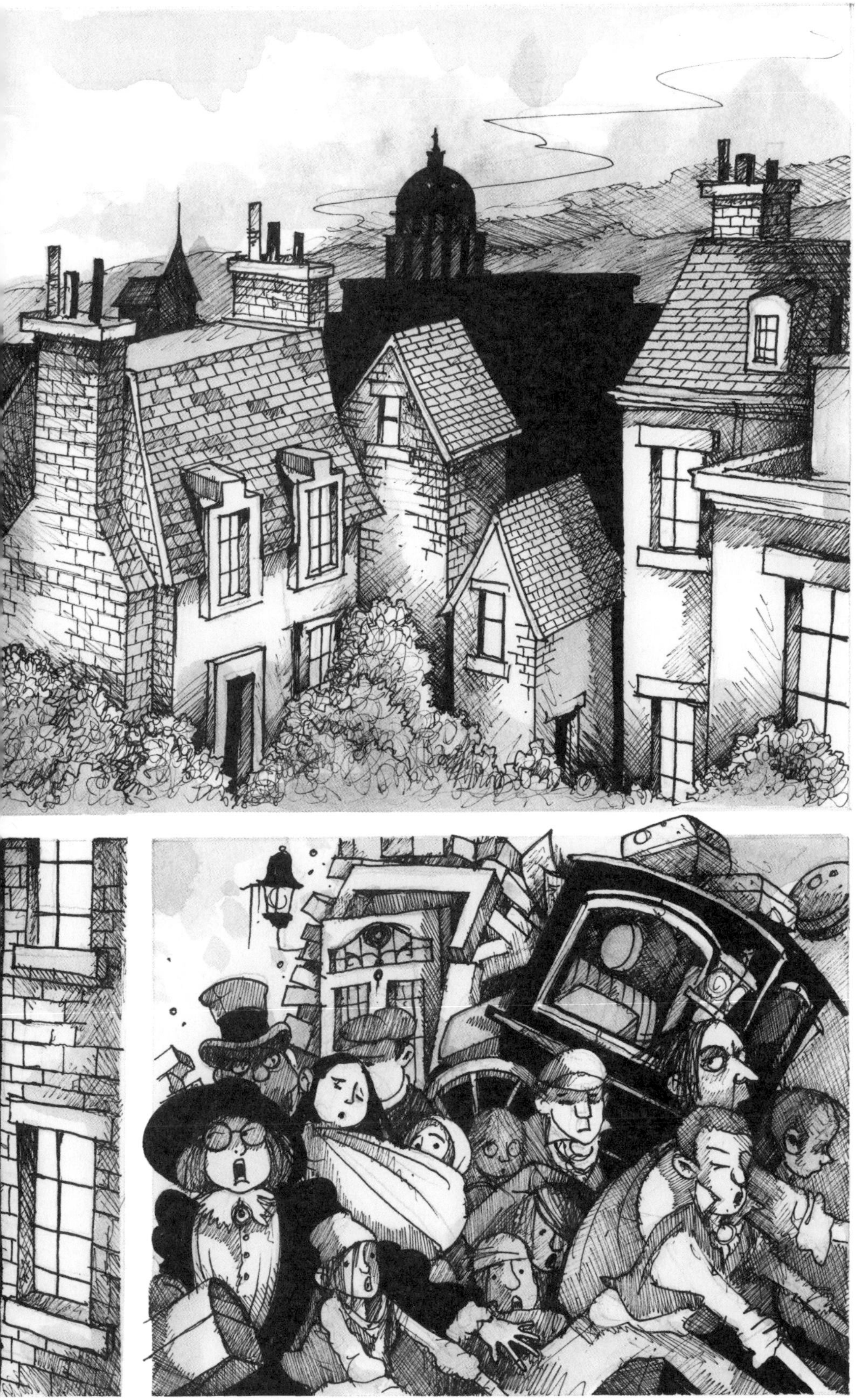

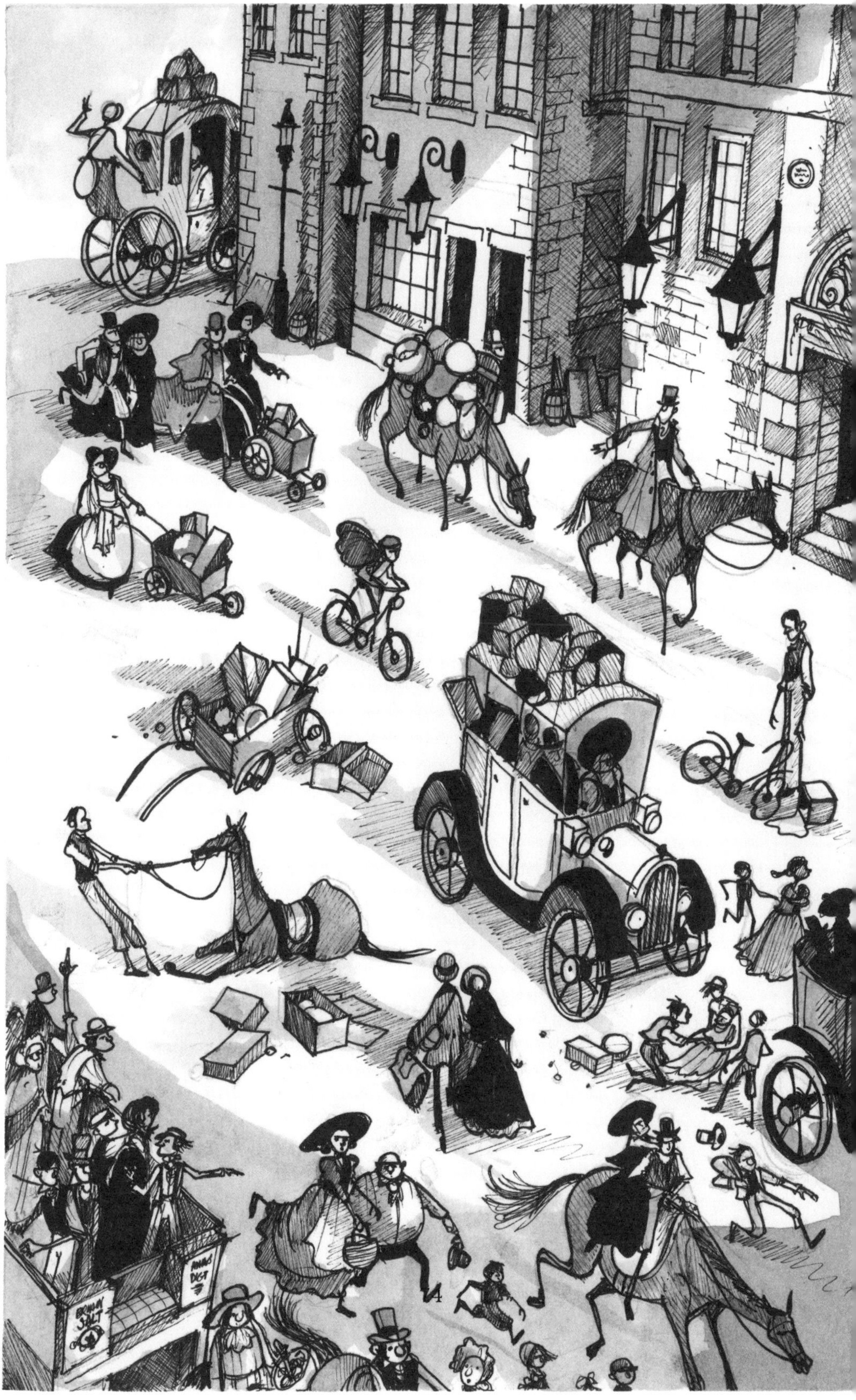

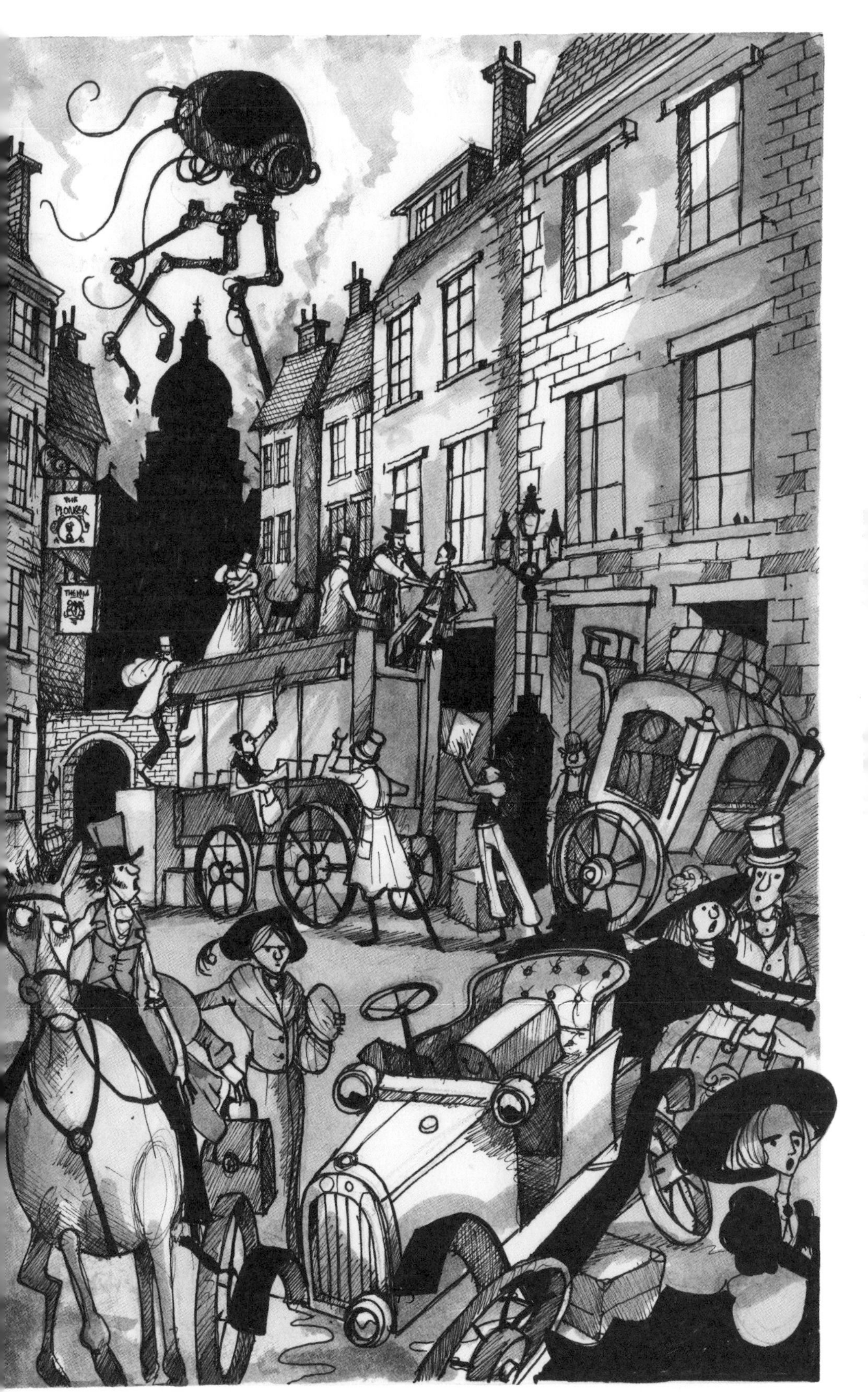

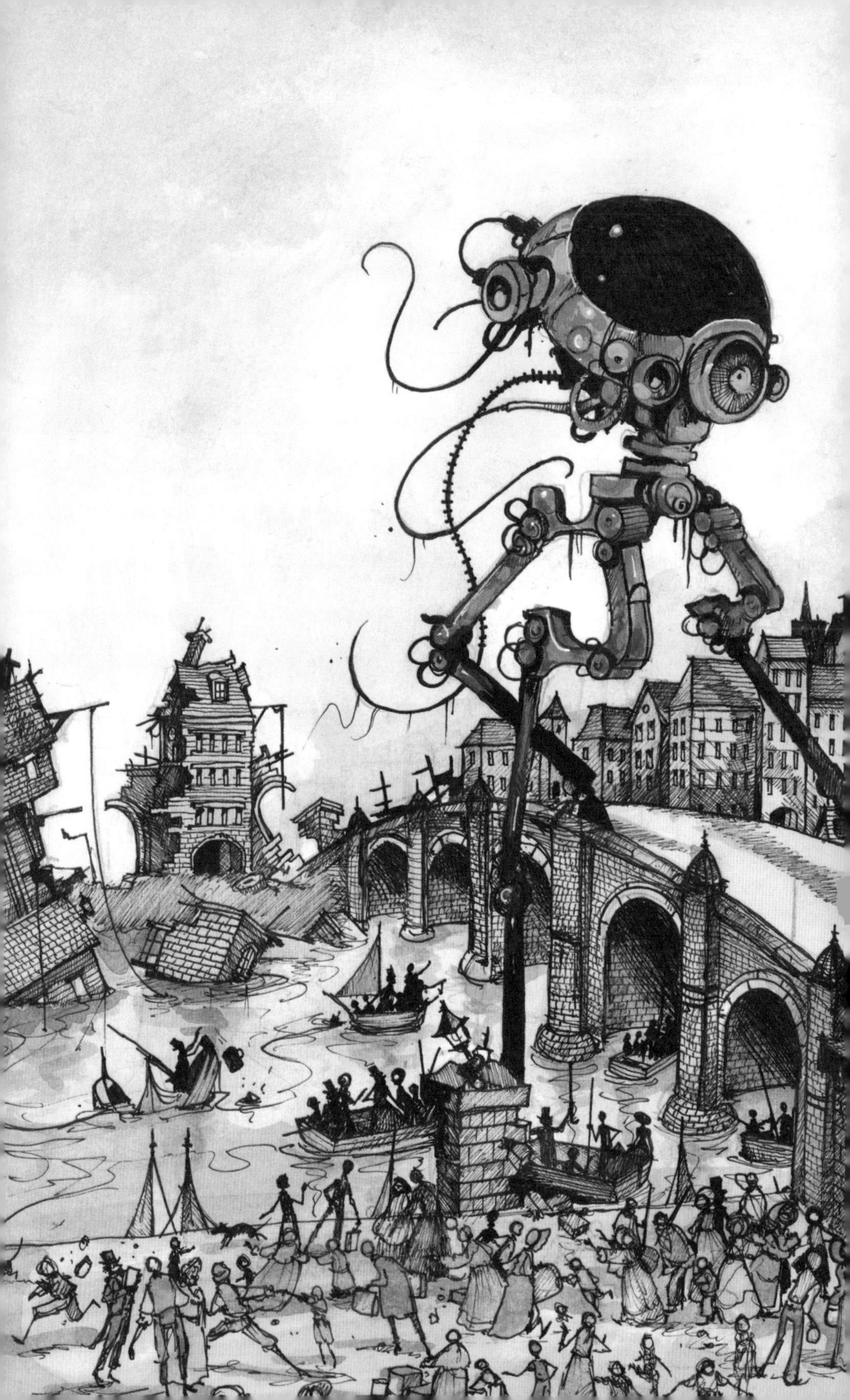

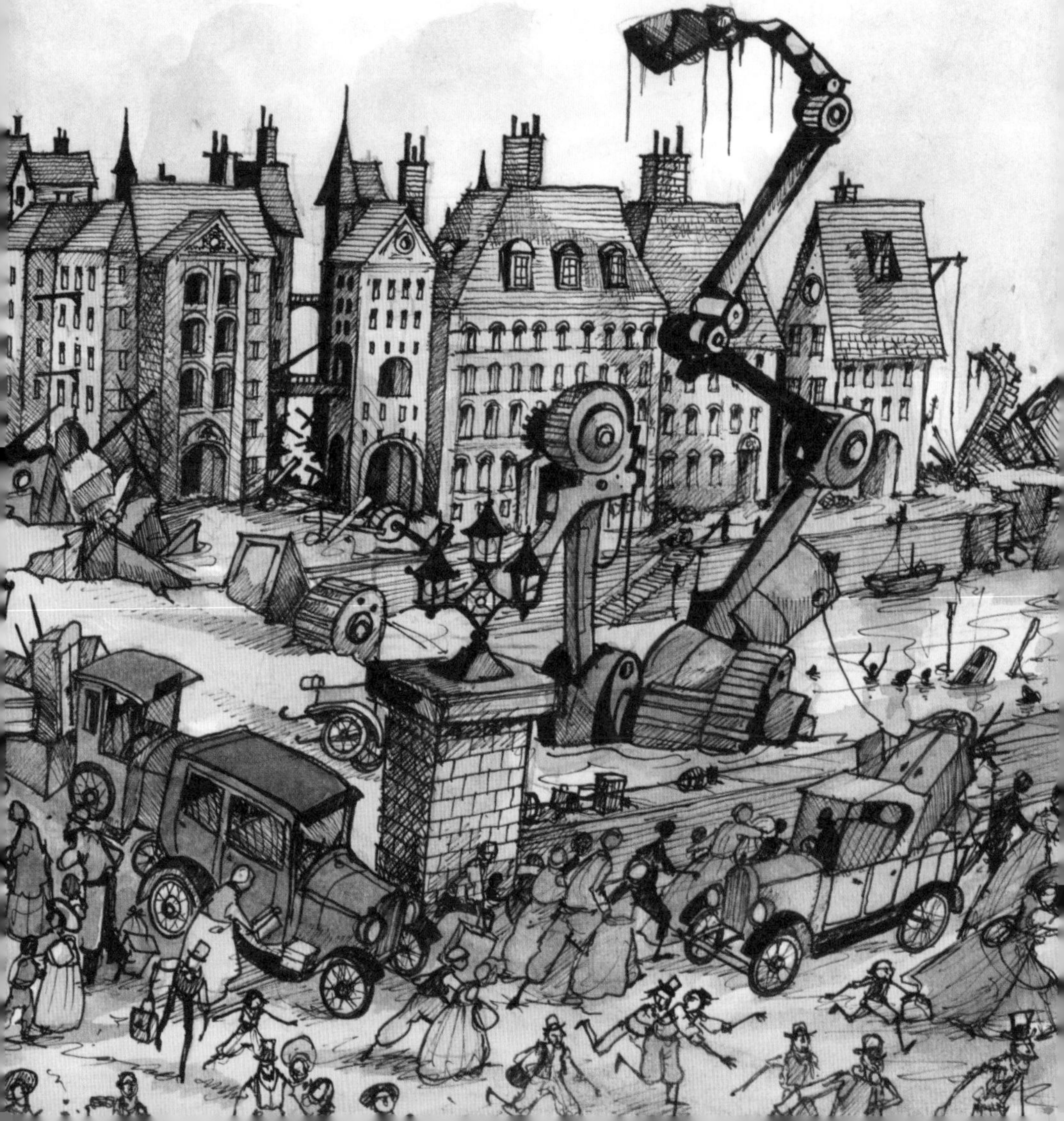

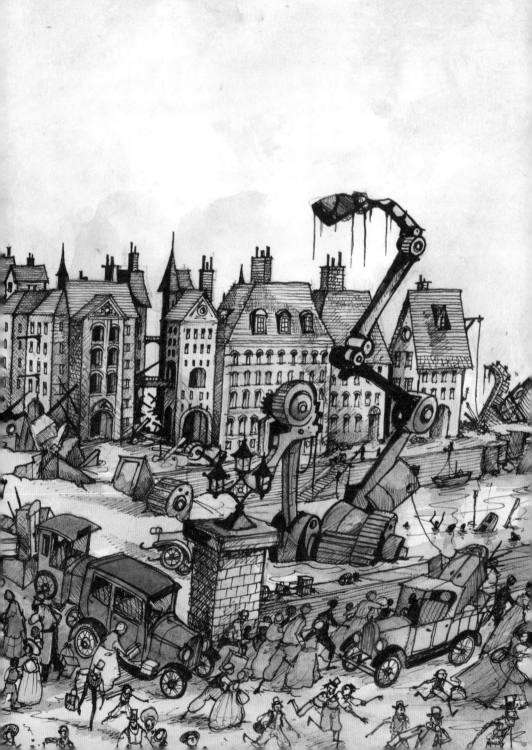

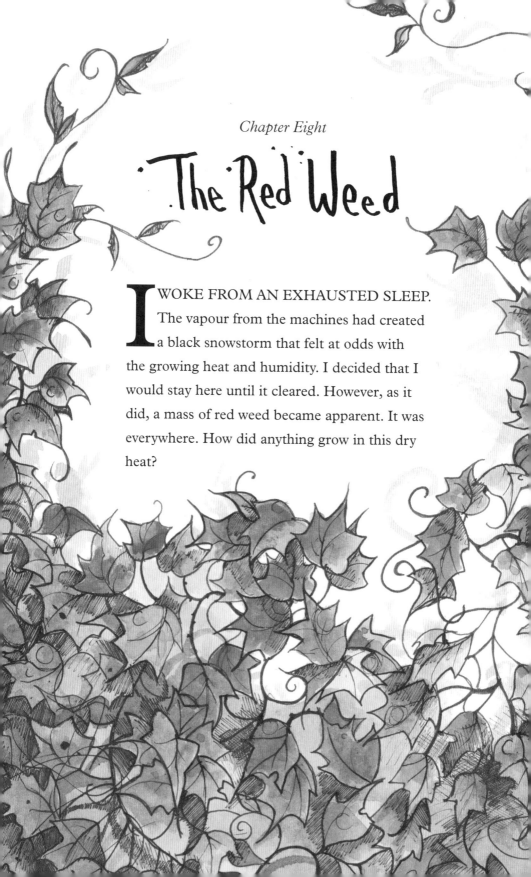

Chapter Eight

The Red Weed

I WOKE FROM AN EXHAUSTED SLEEP. The vapour from the machines had created a black snowstorm that felt at odds with the growing heat and humidity. I decided that I would stay here until it cleared. However, as it did, a mass of red weed became apparent. It was everywhere. How did anything grow in this dry heat?

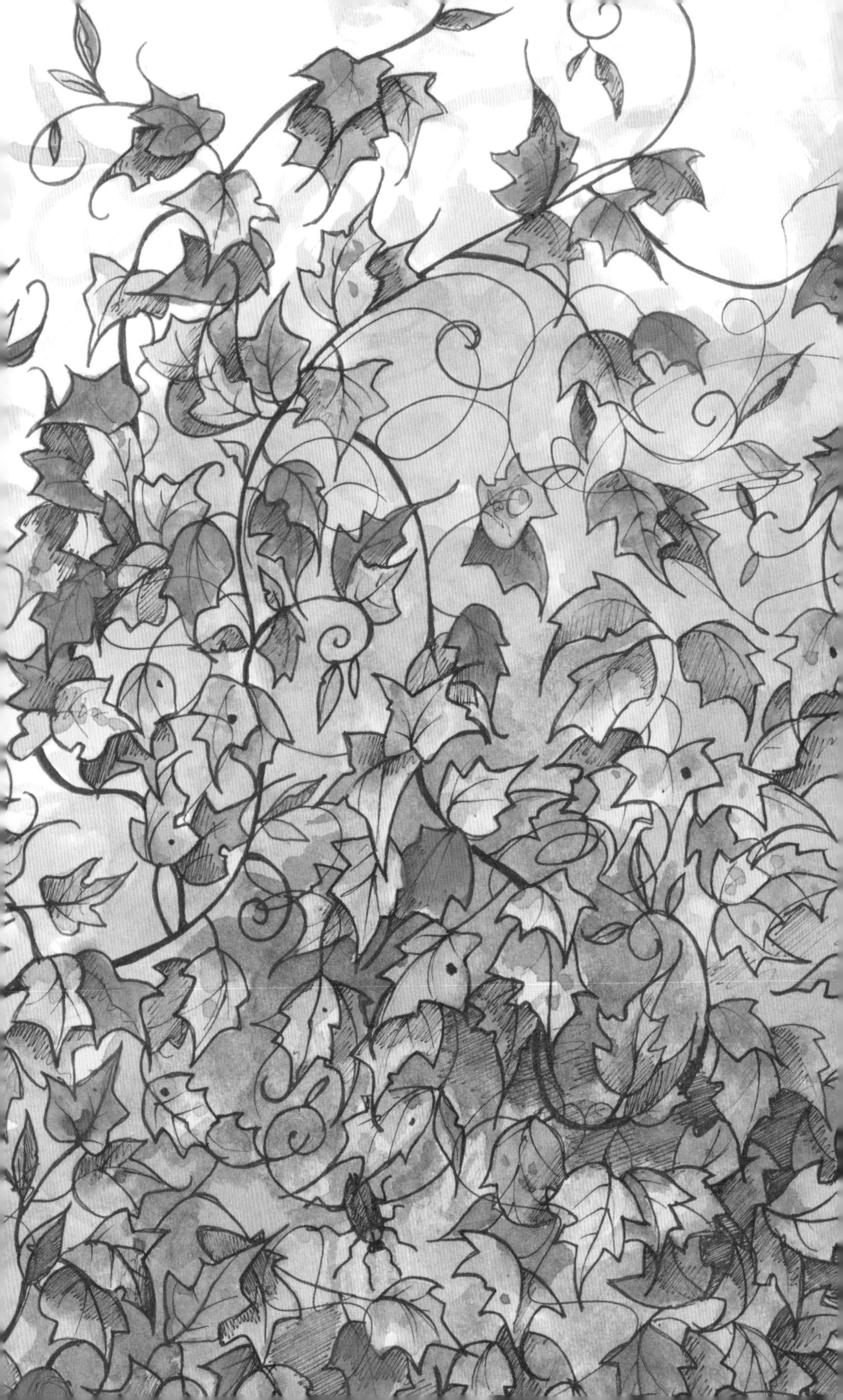

From my position I waited and watched through the broken windows. Still there were people escaping through Halliford. Dragging their whole lives in cases and bags. The strange sound that accompanied the machines came closer and then, in a breath, one appeared so close atop a nearby hill it took the fleeing crowds by surprise and I saw something I wished I had never seen, so dreadful that I almost can't write it down.

The invisible grip these things seemed to have, it stopped the people in their tracks. Then one of those blackened filthy steel cables reached out and took hold of someone. Capturing them somehow. Swallowing them up inside its mechanical frame. I looked on, aghast. And now I, too, was motionless and petrified. What did they want with us?

As I stood in shocked silence, a rumble of brickwork sounded from the rear of the building along with a metallic rattle. I listened. It came again. I made my way round to the back. And from there I saw that the building had collapsed into the ground and one of the machines now stood sentinel at the mouth of the pit. Once more I viewed the things up close, this towering stanchion of living, breathing steel. Half of it had a slick oily sheen and the other half was rusting and oxidised.

It was then that I realised that my hiding place was, by chance, the very site where one of the capsules had just landed. And, around it, its companions busied themselves like ants. I saw other machines: spider-like contraptions that appeared to dig and bury in the pit. There were great pistons and valves, jets of steam spitting violently. Spluttering and struggling as they worked their limbs to and fro. Horror-struck, I could not take my eyes off the sight before me. The red weed grew rapidly out from the deep hole. Perhaps these things brought the seed with them underfoot. Whatever it was, it grew at an alarming rate. A second machine appeared. They were now too close for comfort and, fearing that I might be seen and captured in that horrible way, I retreated anxiously to the basement.

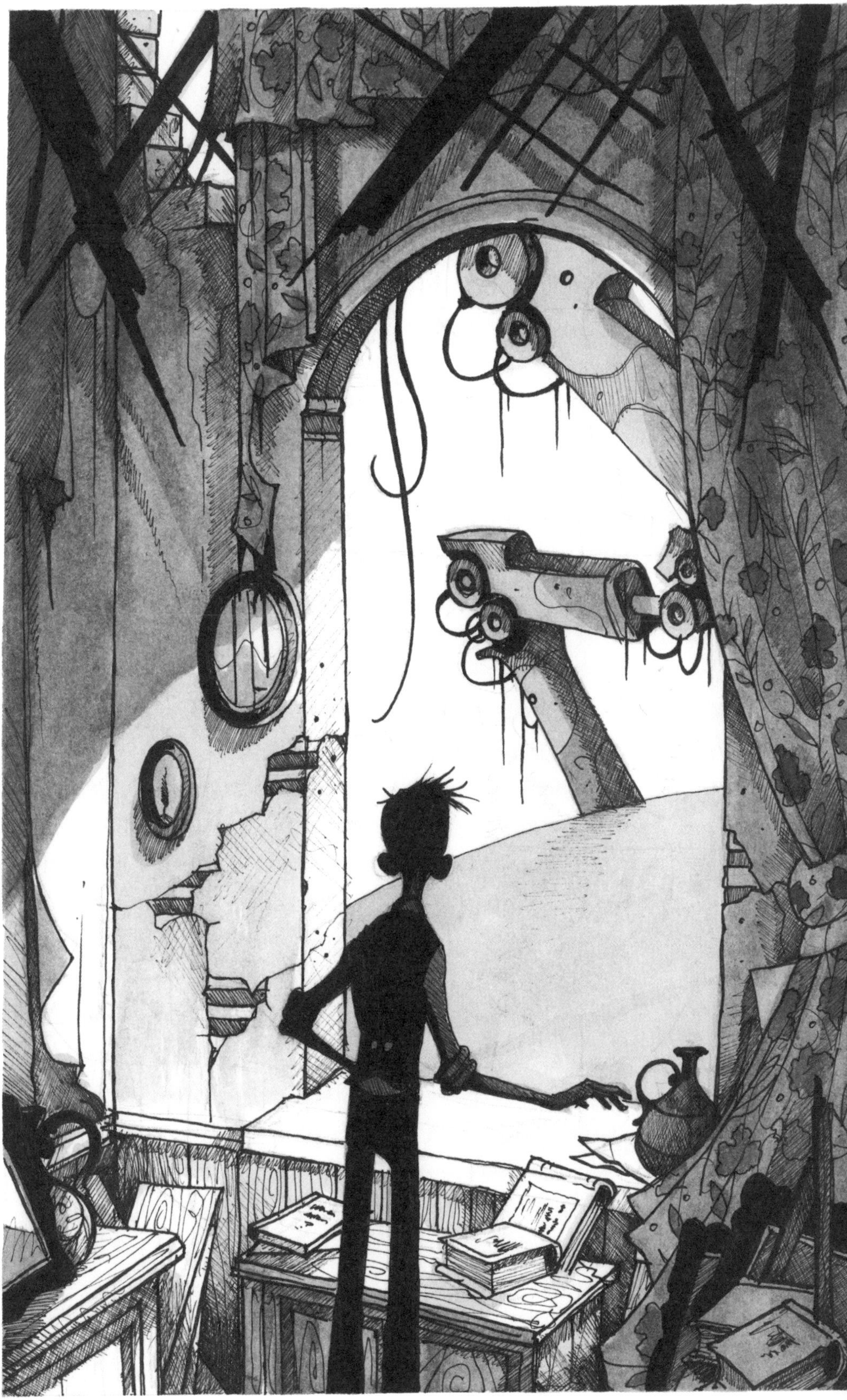

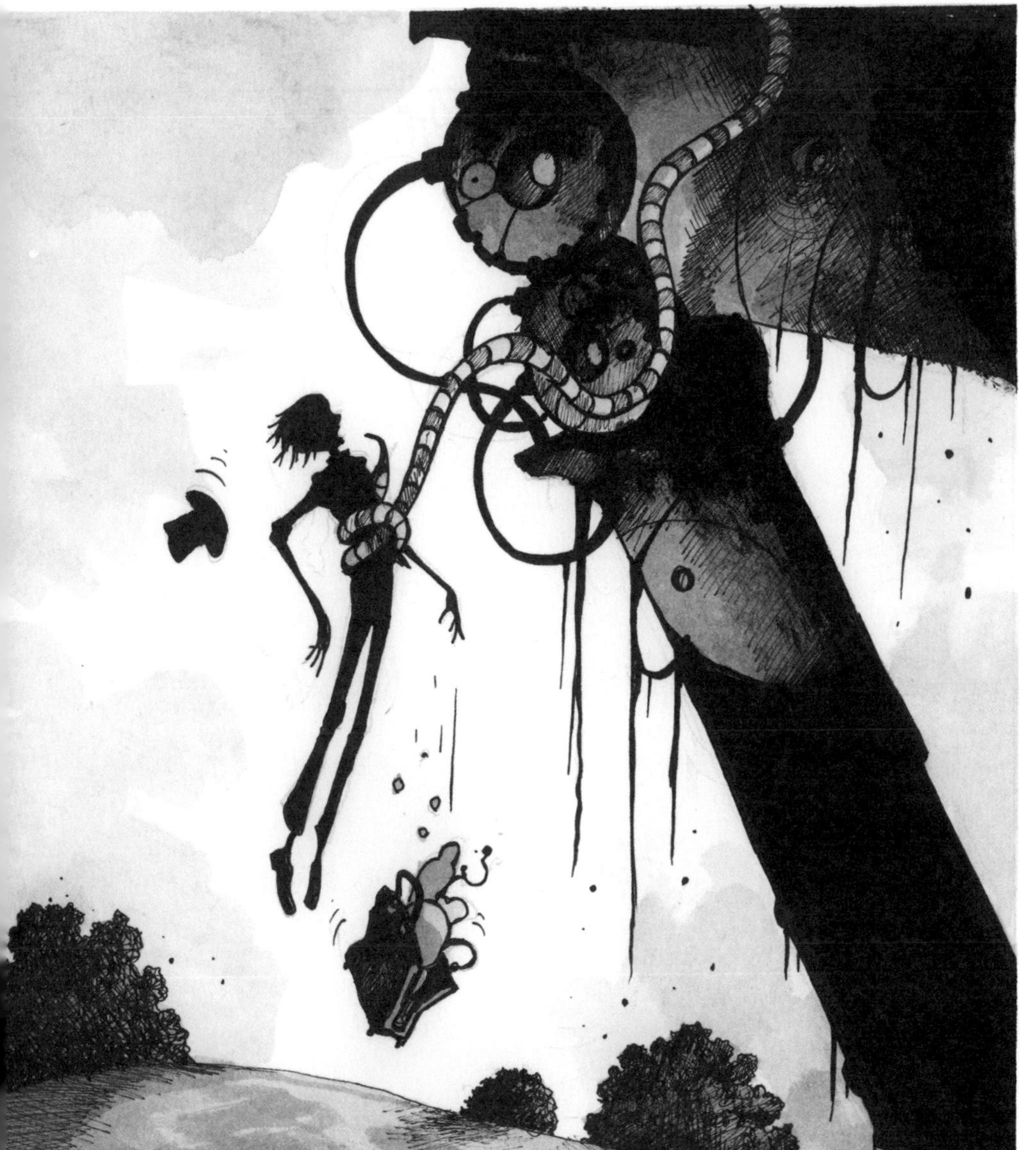

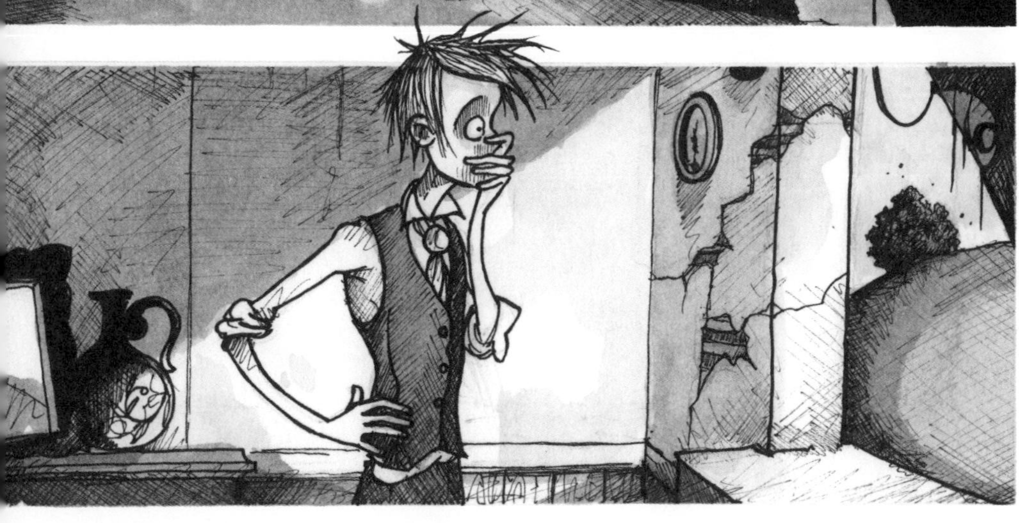

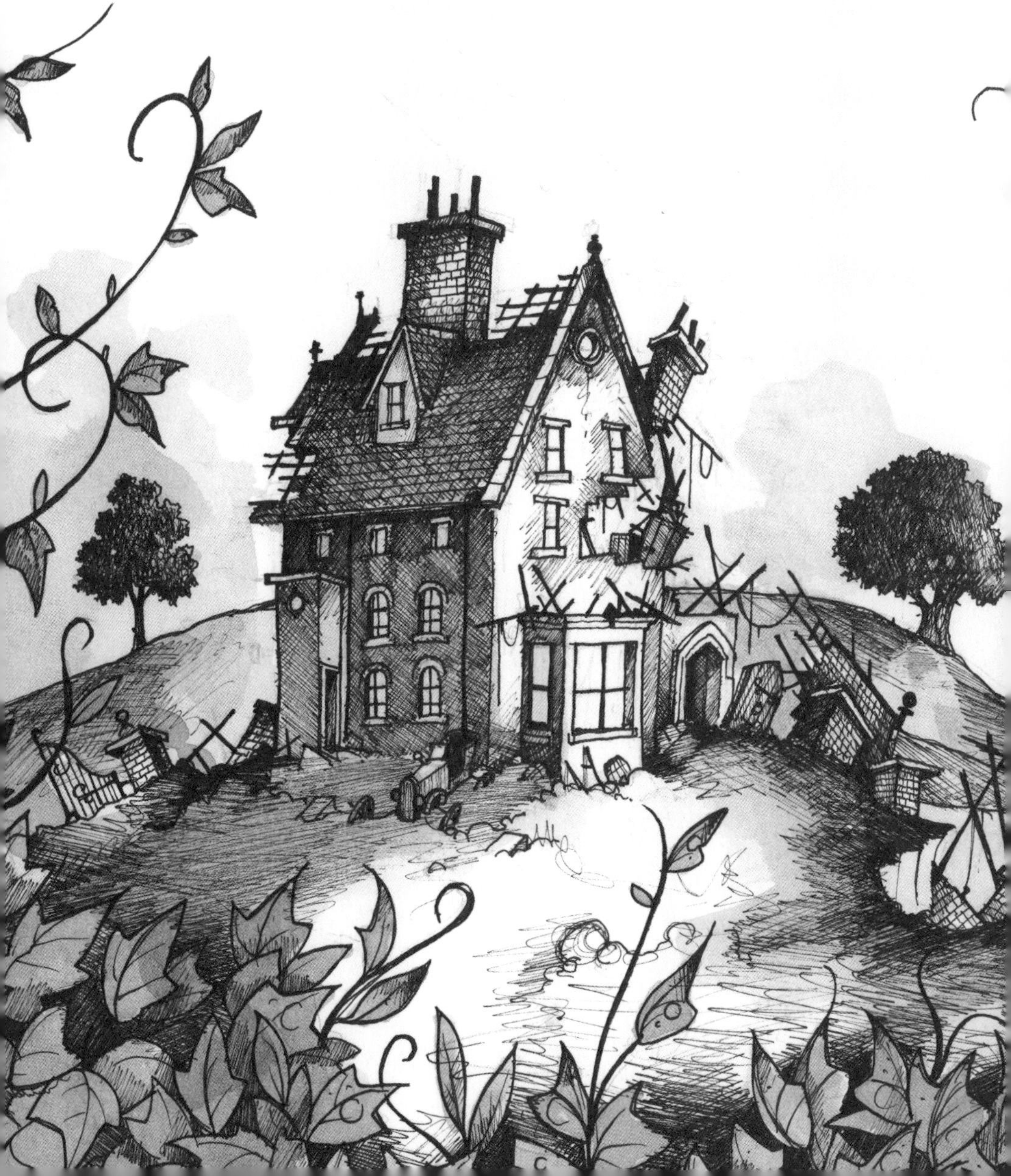

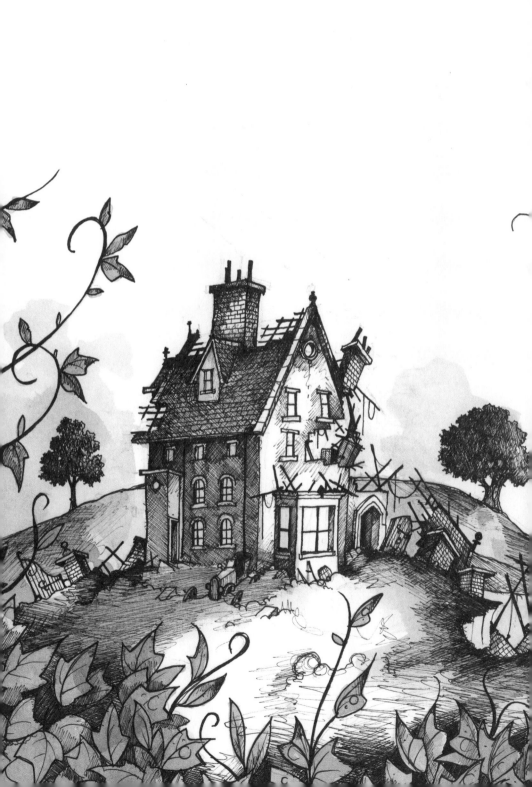

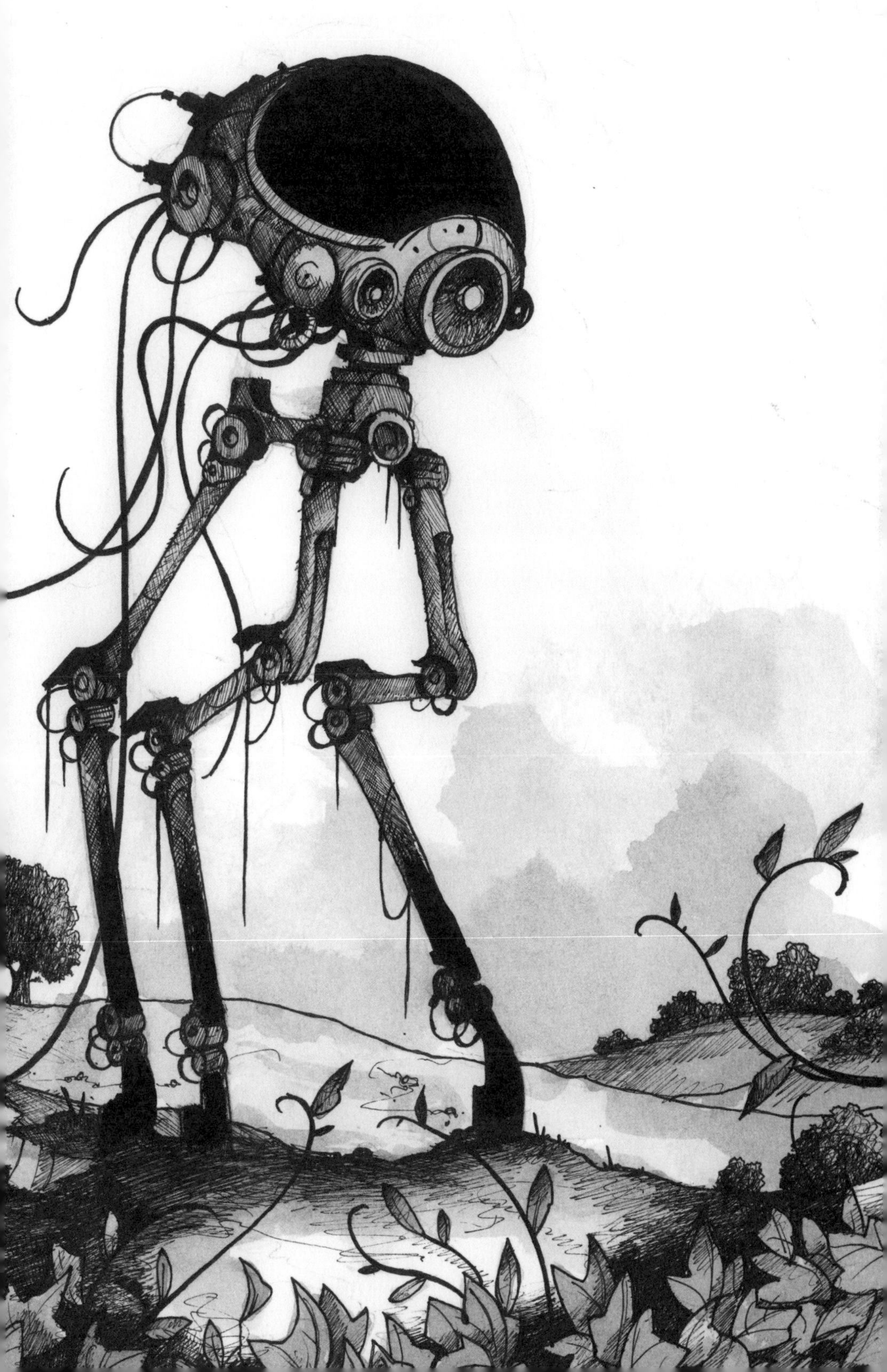

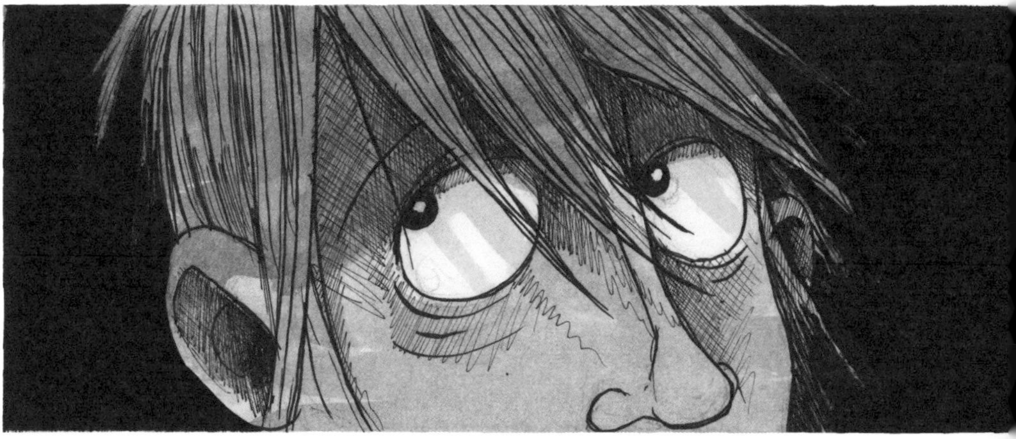

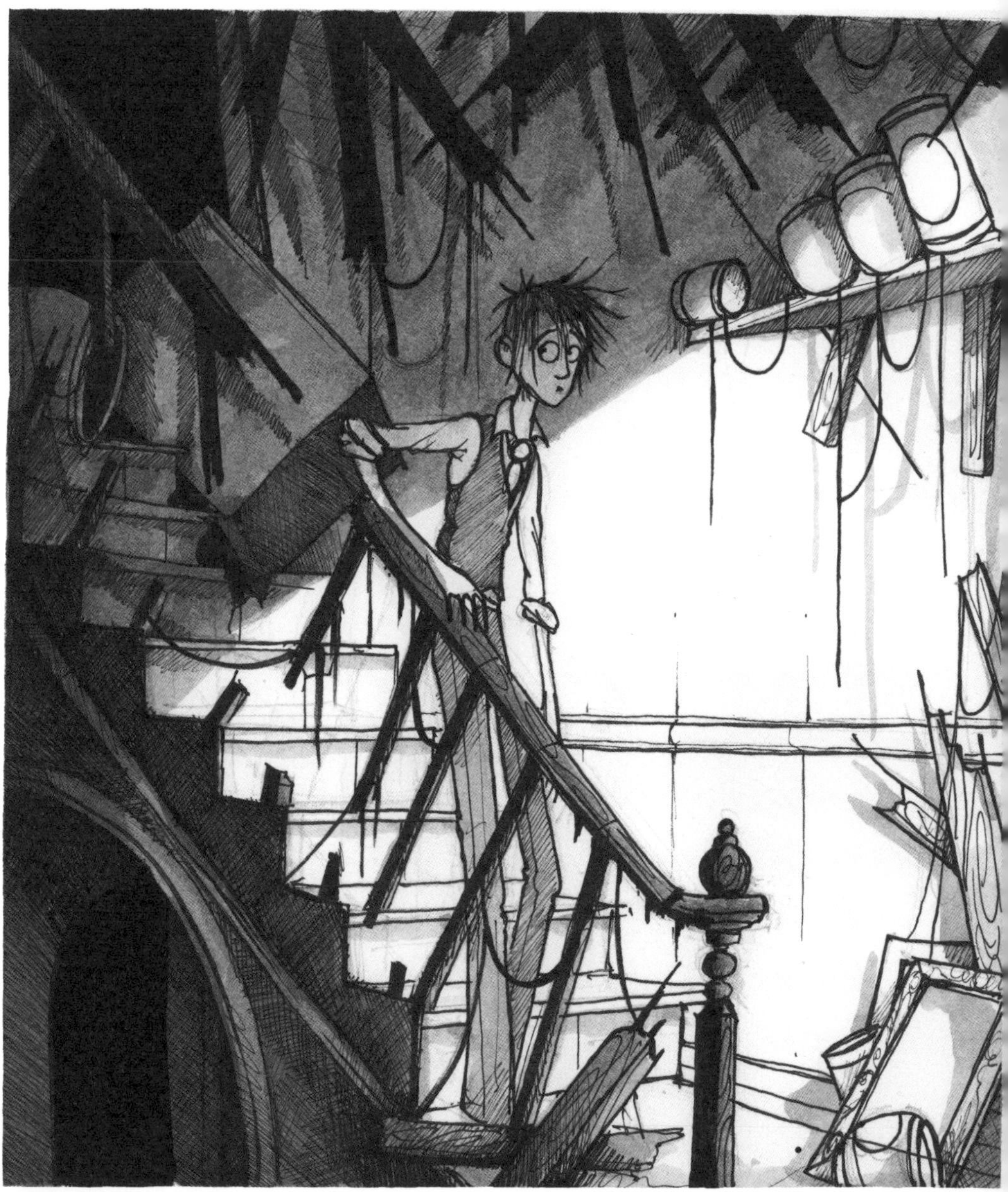

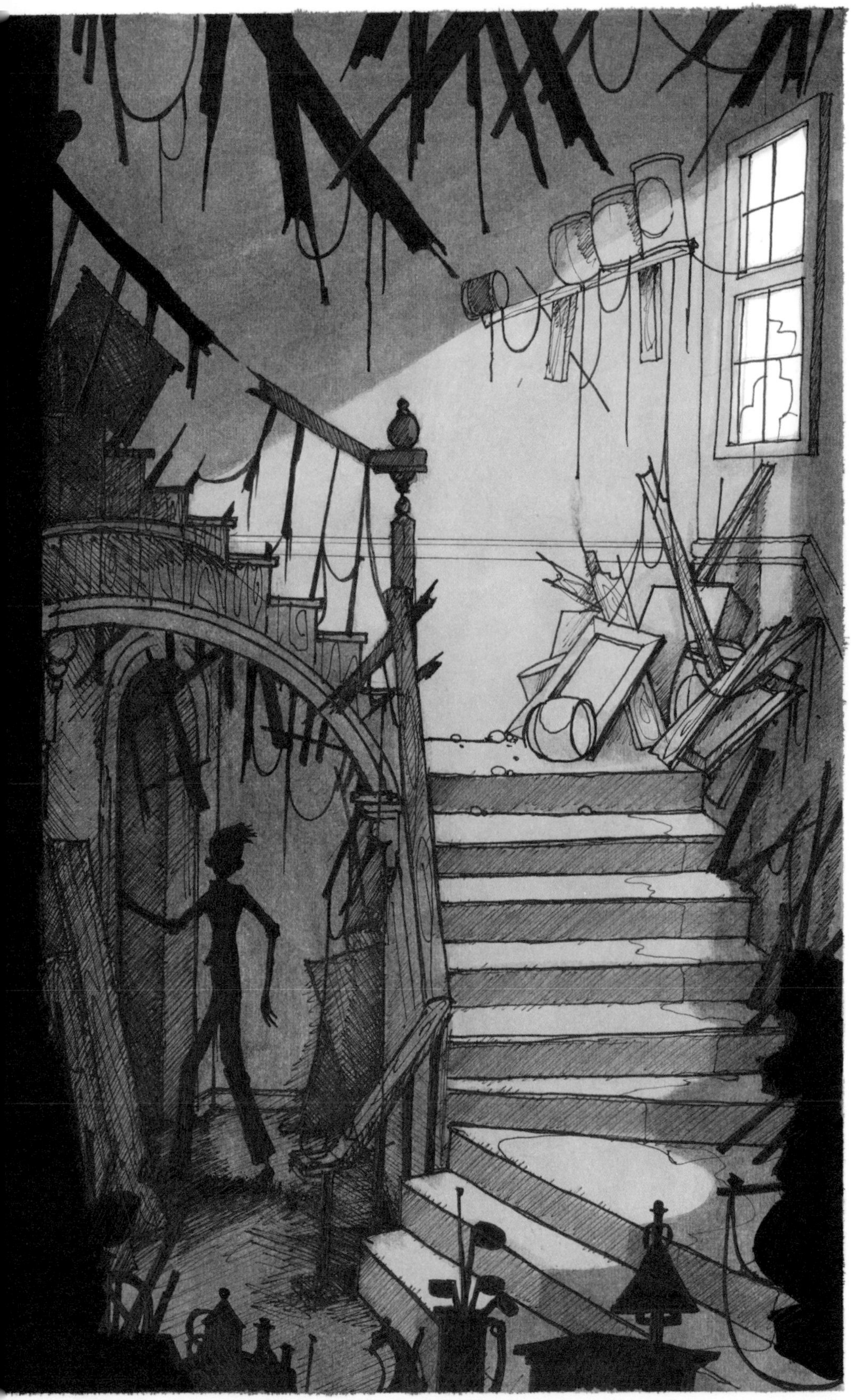

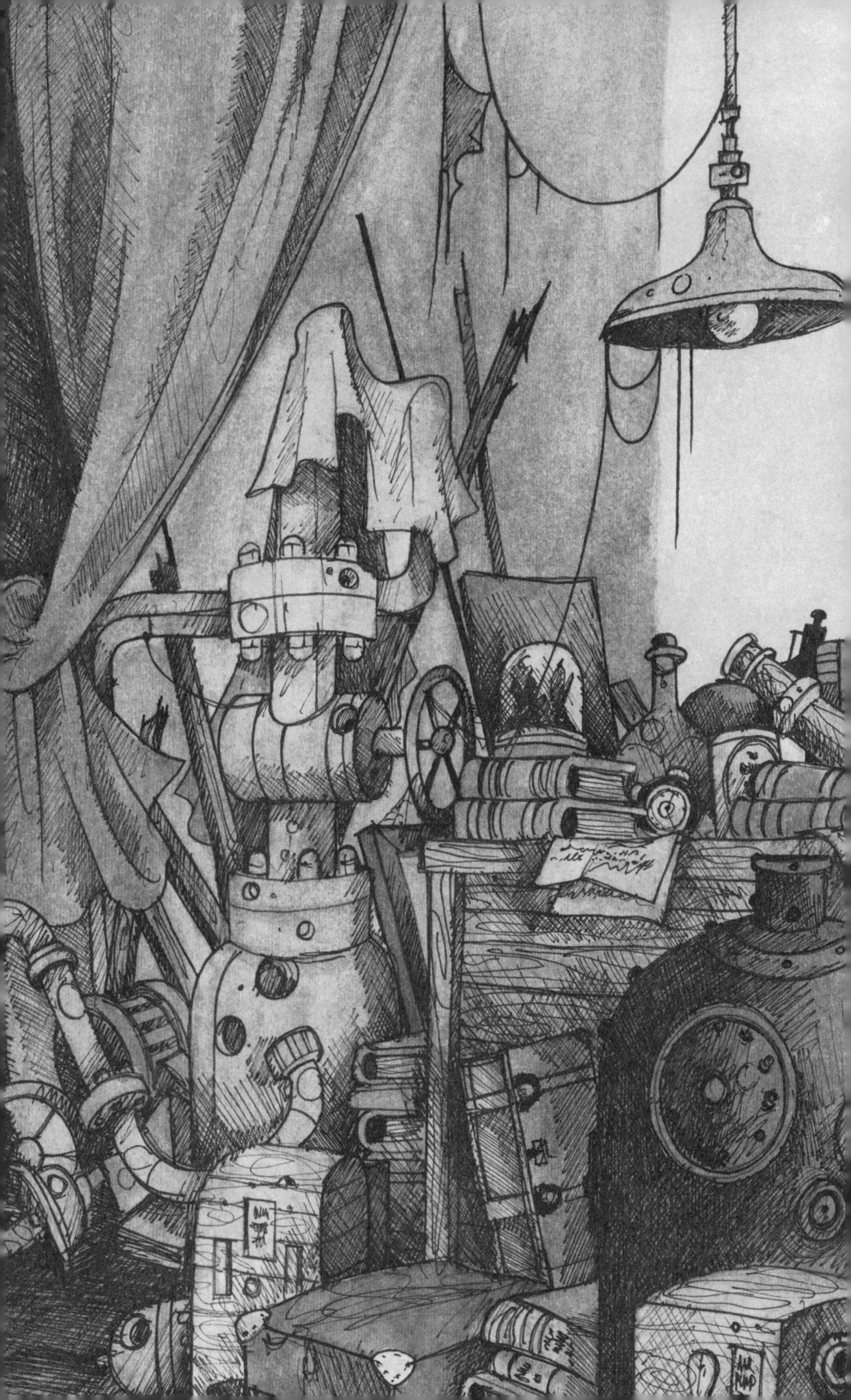

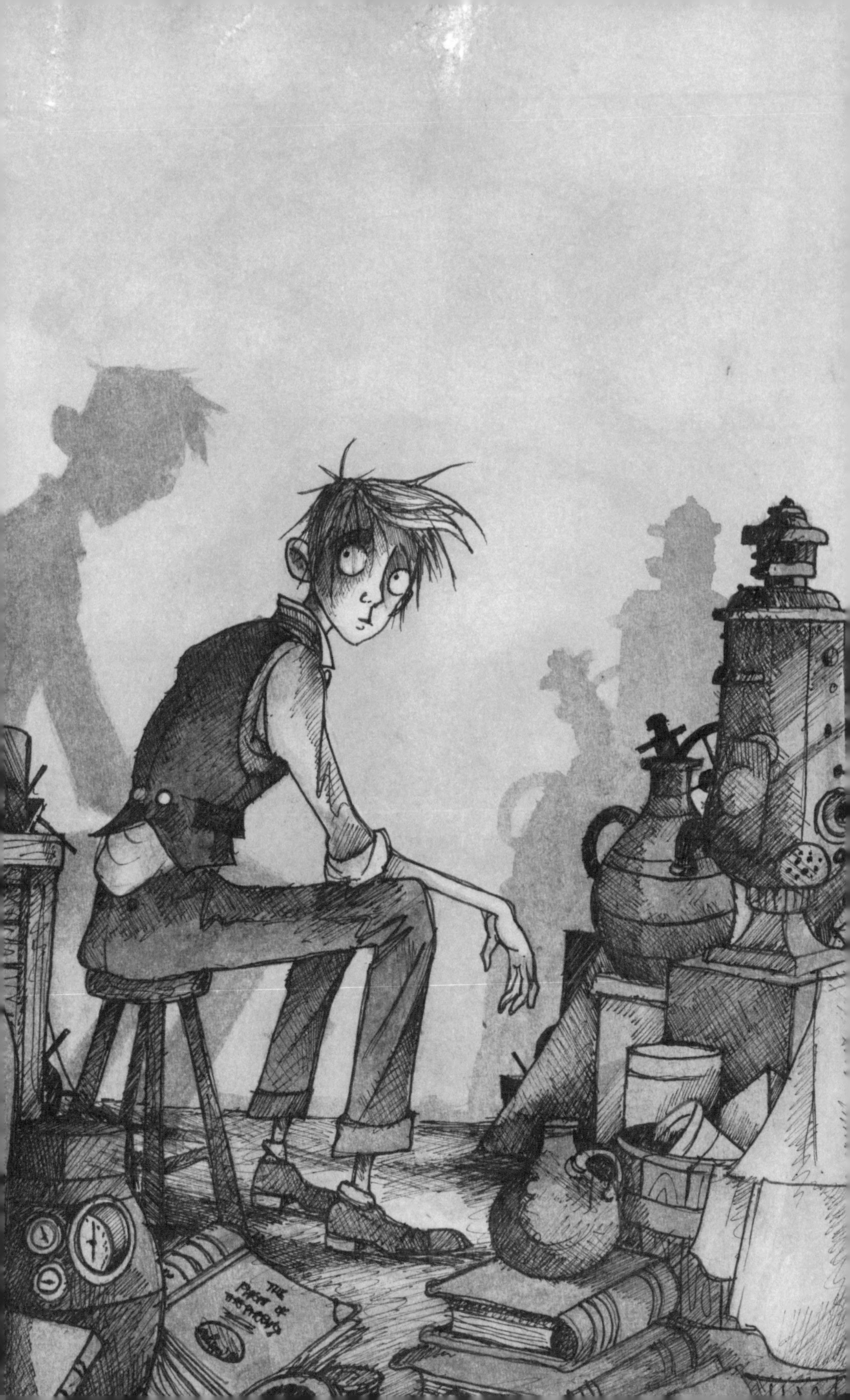

Chapter Nine

Close Encounter

I SAT IN TERROR IN THE DARK, unable to make real sense of the scenes I had witnessed. I would not move until I felt safe again. My only sign from the outside world was a pinprick of light that pierced a hole in a wooden shutter in the brickwork. I watched it fade and I knew that night had come again.

The next morning brought me new horrors. The chinking sound of gently tumbling bricks woke me from a broken night's sleep. I dared to open my eyes. I could see that the red weed had crept through the gaps in the masonry. Had it been there all along? Did it really grow that fast?

Slowly, a single elongated steel tentacle pushed through the crumbling wall, curling its way among the debris. I lay petrified and motionless, and imagined that the startled whites of my eyes lit the room and gave me away.

I made half an attempt to bury myself deeper into the rubble and the broken timbers, but every move I made seemed so ridiculously loud I gave up and stayed as still as I could. The metallic tentacle snaked its way over the fallen bricks and beams, feeling and searching.

At one point it touched the sole of my shoe, almost grabbing, and I nearly cried out. Had it found me at last? I began to tremble violently. What would it do? I could look no longer. I closed my eyes again and listened and waited. Sweat ran down my filthy hair, now stuck to my forehead and my face.

Then, as as it had appeared, it had gone – and I experienced such relief that I felt tears well up in my eyes. I was still so frightened that I lay there for the whole of that day, unable to move. It was at least cool where I rested.

While I hid alone in darkness, though, my brain whirred. My hand turned the corners of my journal in the dark, and I felt at the piece of metal in my bag. It seemed to jump when I touched it and there was a sensation against my skin. The cogs of my imagination cranked into life. My mind wandered to the red weed and the Martians and how it came to be that they were here. But, more than that, how they would survive. What was this crimson growth that came with them? Burying our treasured emerald landscape with its red mass.

I thought and thought. I drifted in and out of sleep and I heard Ogilvy in my dream.

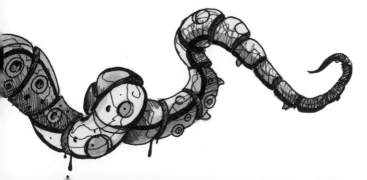

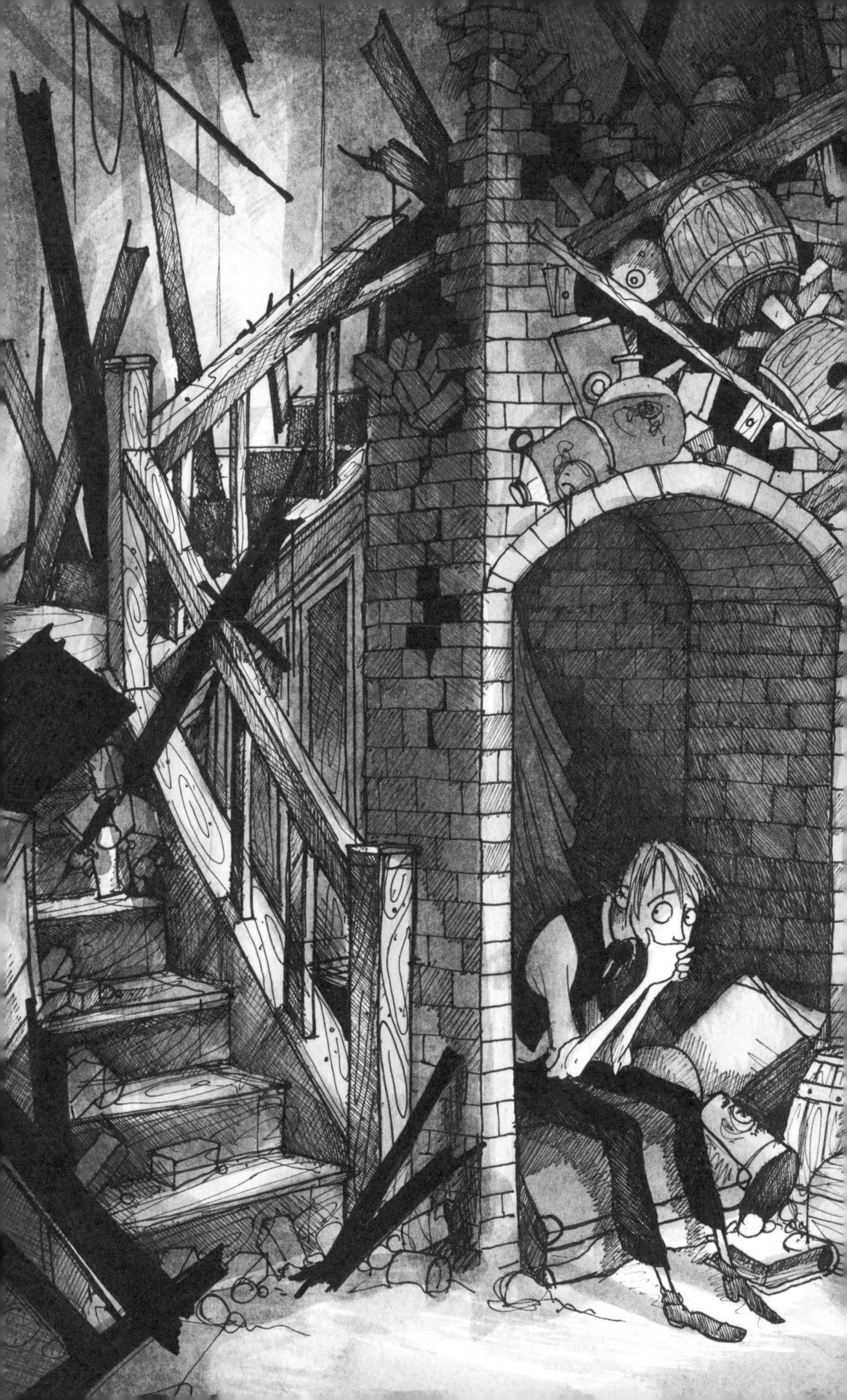

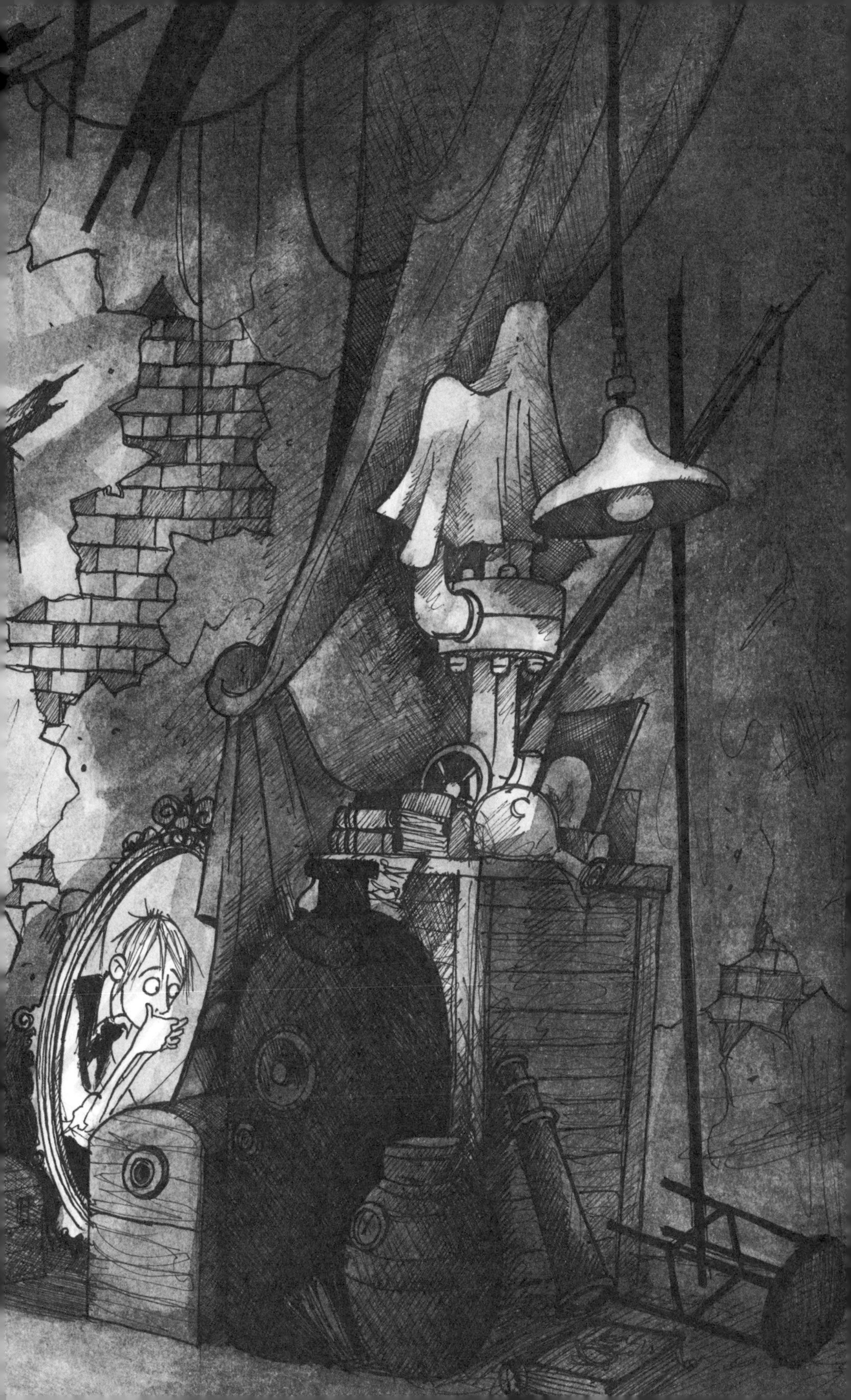

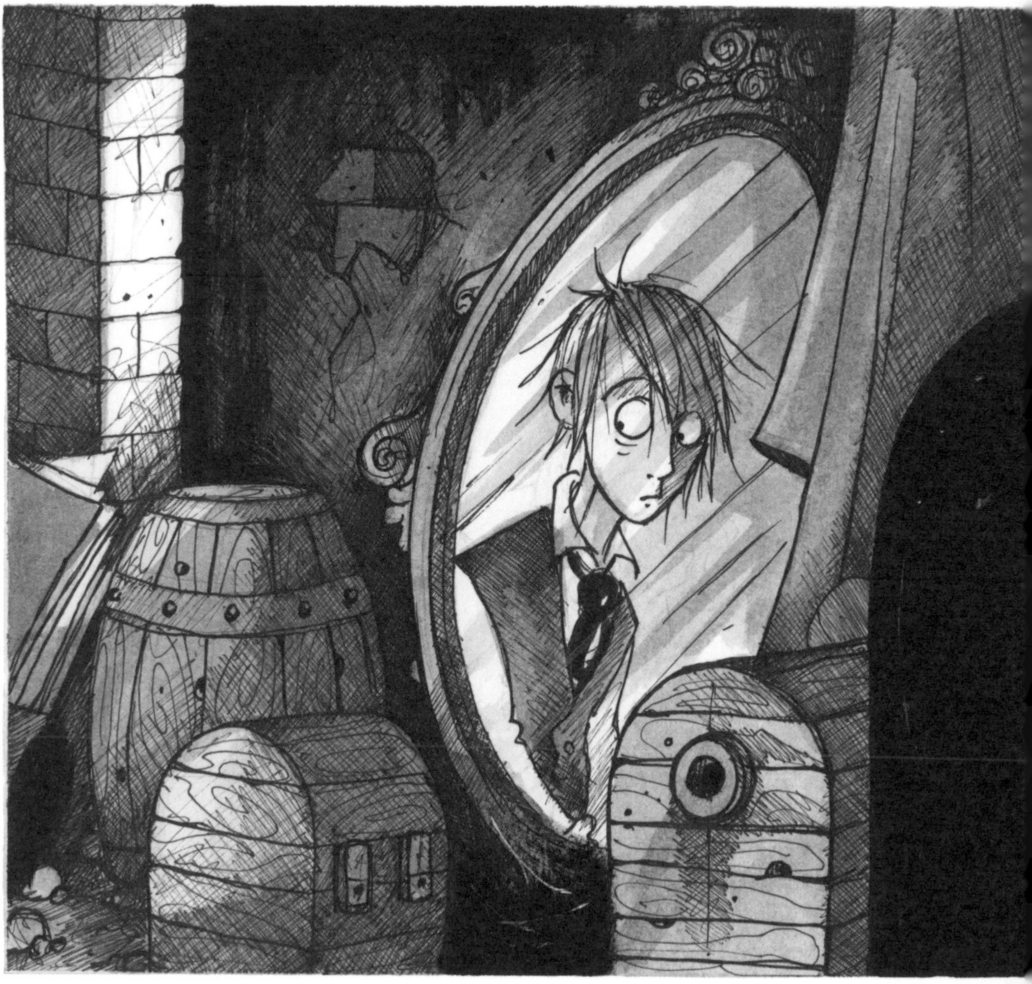

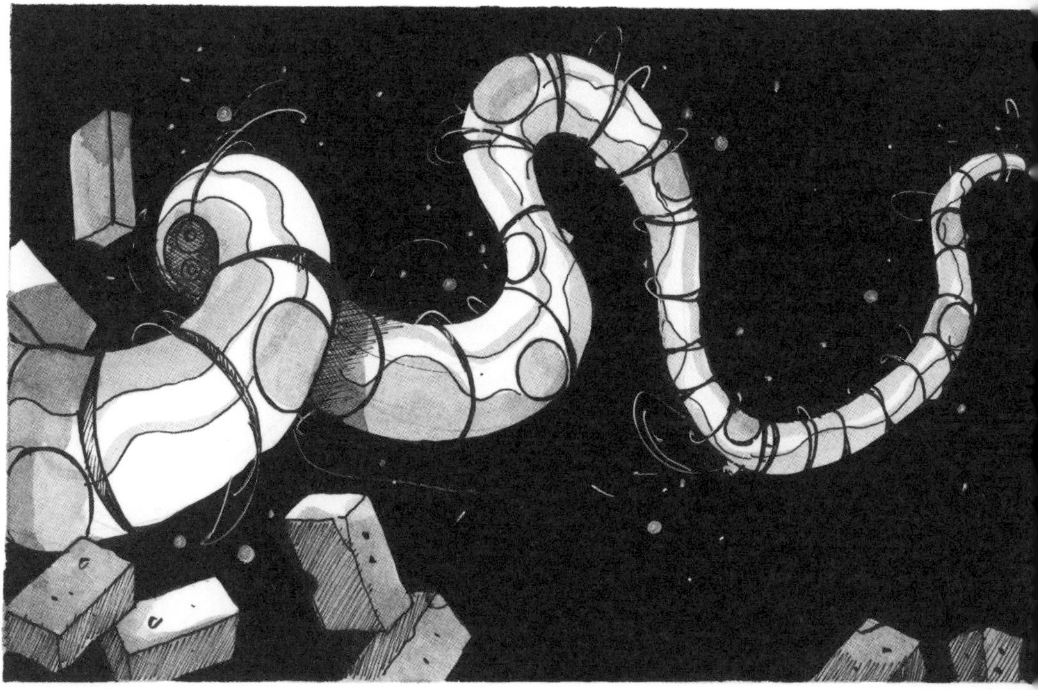

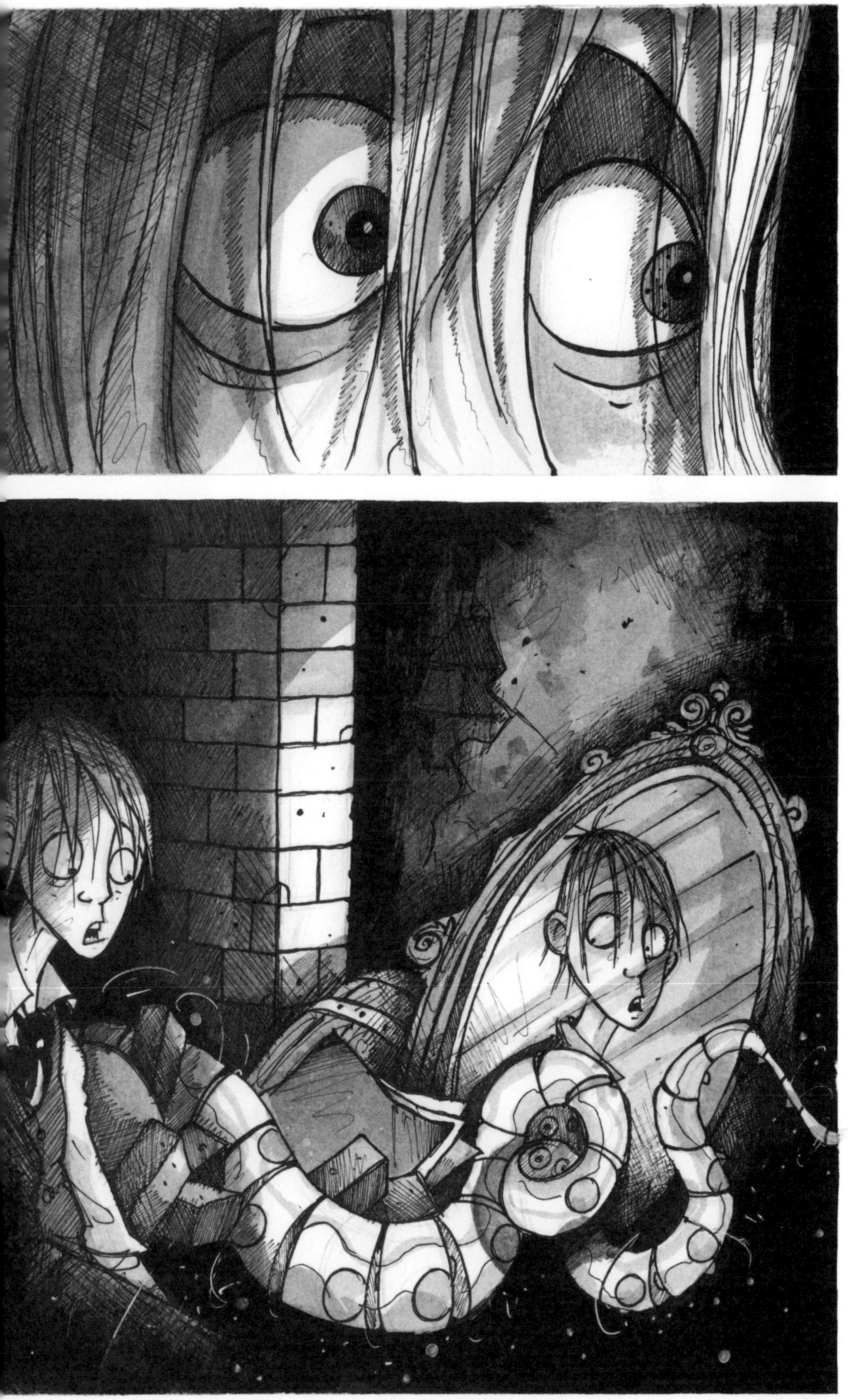

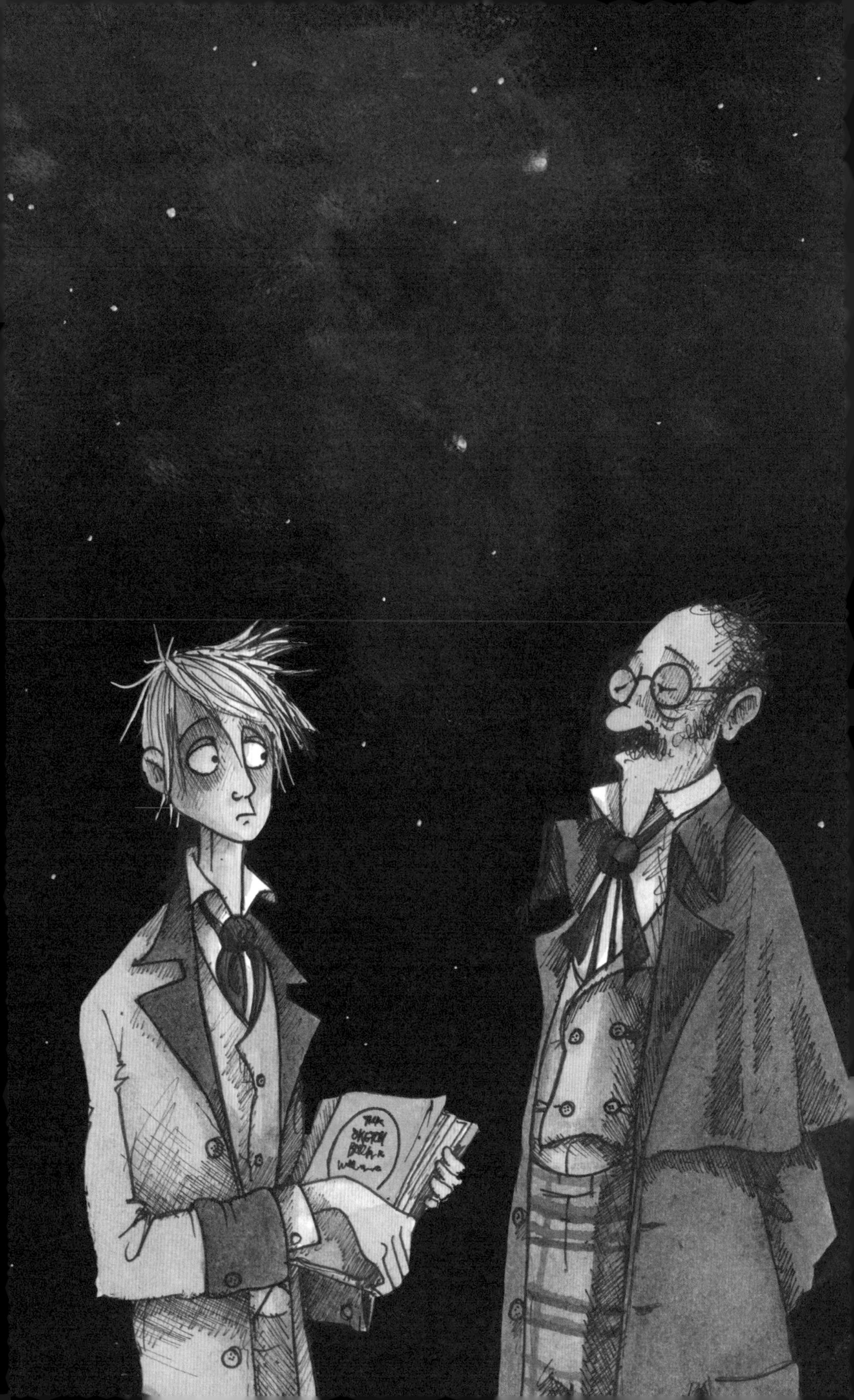

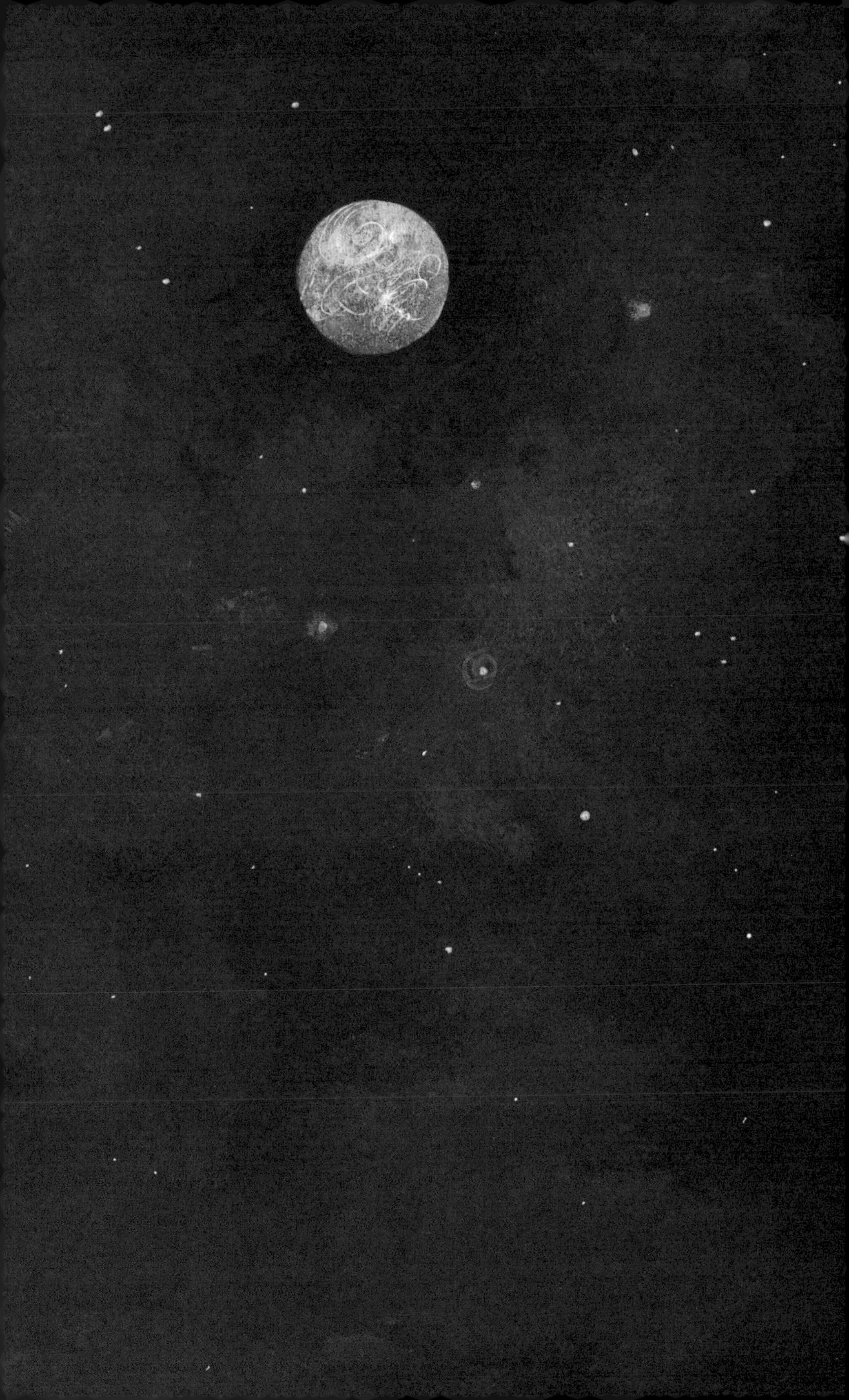

‘*Where did this thing do its worst?*’ he asked me. ‘*It’s where the sun bakes the ground hard. Where there is nothing but scorched land.*’

And his voice came so clear I felt as though he was right there. ‘*It’s where the green is strangled by the heat of the long hot summer.*’

In a fevered madness, I told myself that if I ever emerged from this moment alive I would help to solve this mystery and be rid of our unwanted visitors.

It was not until the following day that I was brave enough to venture back to the main floor of the building. By this time I was starving hungry and badly in need of water.

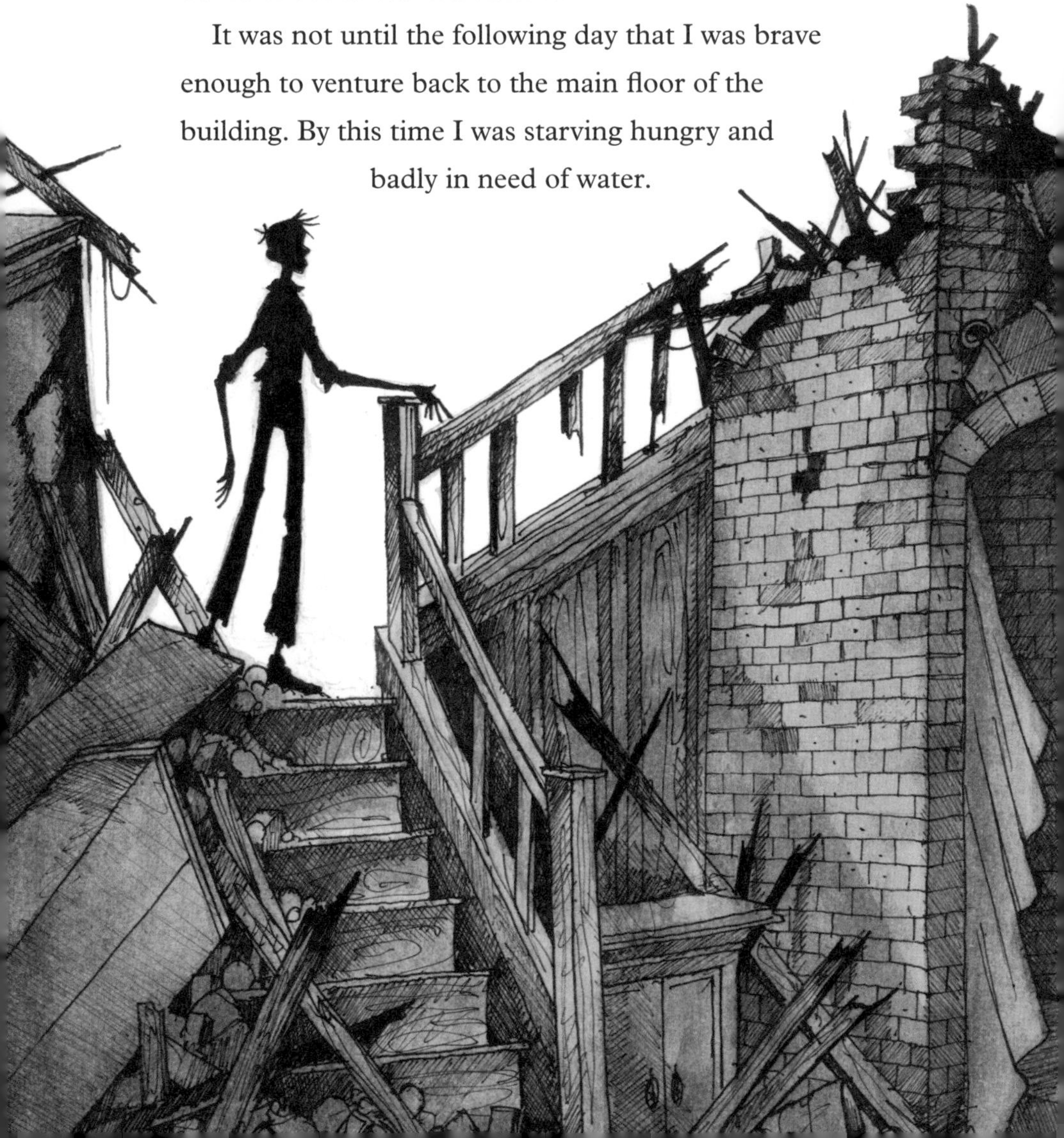

Chapter Ten

War Looms

AT GROUND LEVEL I NOTICED that the red weed had continued to grow, penetrating the walls and obscuring my view outside. I didn't dare to touch it or pull it away so that I might see. The sound of wings flapping attracted my attention. A bird perched in a broken circular window at the gable end of the building. I had not seen or heard such a thing for days.

I remembered Esme. She loved the birds so much. I longed to see her face and hear the children's voices and feel the excitement of a busy house. Thoughts of the burning orphanage flashed in front of my eyes. I was brought back to reality when the bird flapped and turned and flew out.

I peered through a crack in the wall to find that the vapour had cleared and the machines had moved along. I worked out that if I could escape through the lower and larger gable window, I could head back west over the fields.

Here was my chance, in a brief moment, to make my escape. My heart beat fast. I had to do it while I could see the way ahead. I climbed out of the window, carefully avoiding the broken glass, and raced out to the fields. My legs trembled as I ran. The heat smothered me as I emerged. It made the running harder. I kept on, my heart thumping. I ran and ran and it felt like a long way before I stopped to catch my breath. I dared not look back.

It would take me two hours to make my way carefully to Ottershaw, where I would head to the lab beneath the observatory. I knew nothing of the circumstances there. I hoped desperately that the building still stood. And, more than that, I hoped that there might be experts there who could help me. Who might make sense of my observations. I felt at my journal and at the sliver of metal in my bag that buzzed and fizzed at a touch.

As I approached, I could see that the observatory building had survived. I burst through the door, overheated and overexcited, on my knees.

When I looked up, Anya was standing before me. At first I could not believe it was her. I rubbed my eyes in disbelief. I moved closer and cupped her face in my hands. We stood in silence, held tight, our gazes fixed on each other.

'How are you here?' I asked.

'I've been here most days,' she told me. 'There is a safe route from the farmhouse at Timber Hill. I was asked urgently for help. We're doing what we can to make sense of this war of worlds.'

'And the children?'

'Don't worry – they are safe on the farm. They miss you. We are all of us safe. But you shouldn't go to them.'

She was right. Yet I was so desperate to see them and knowing how near they were was hard. However, we knew that it would unsettle them and agreed against it. The decision pulled at my heart. I had no desire to tell her what had become of the orphanage, and that I feared for Orla and Ivan. For now I would hold on to that painful secret.

I looked around the room. Anya and her fellow scientists had been studying the red weed. There were dissected roots and branches on the worktops. Hand-drawn diagrams, frantically scribbled chemical formulae and solutions were pinned to the walls.

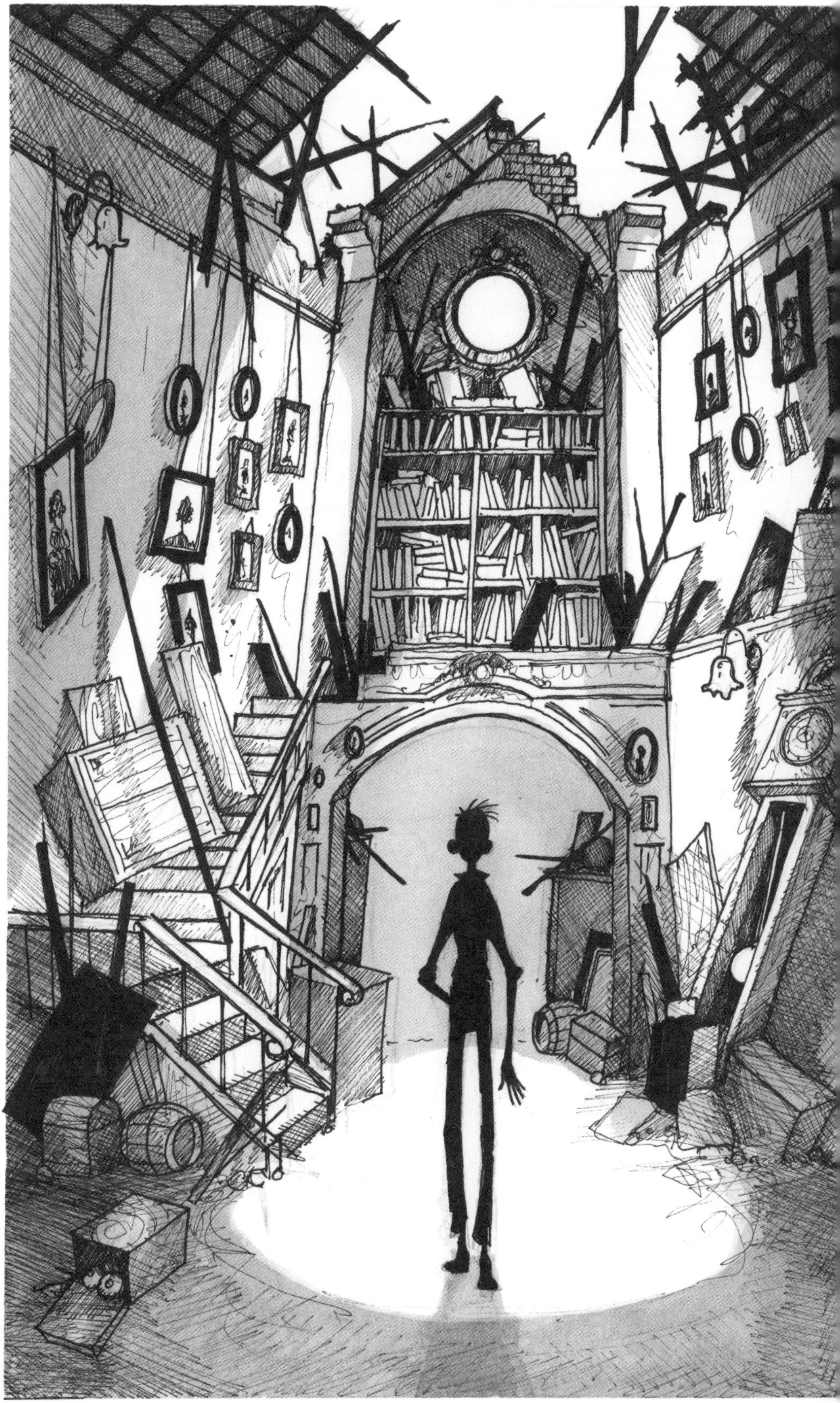

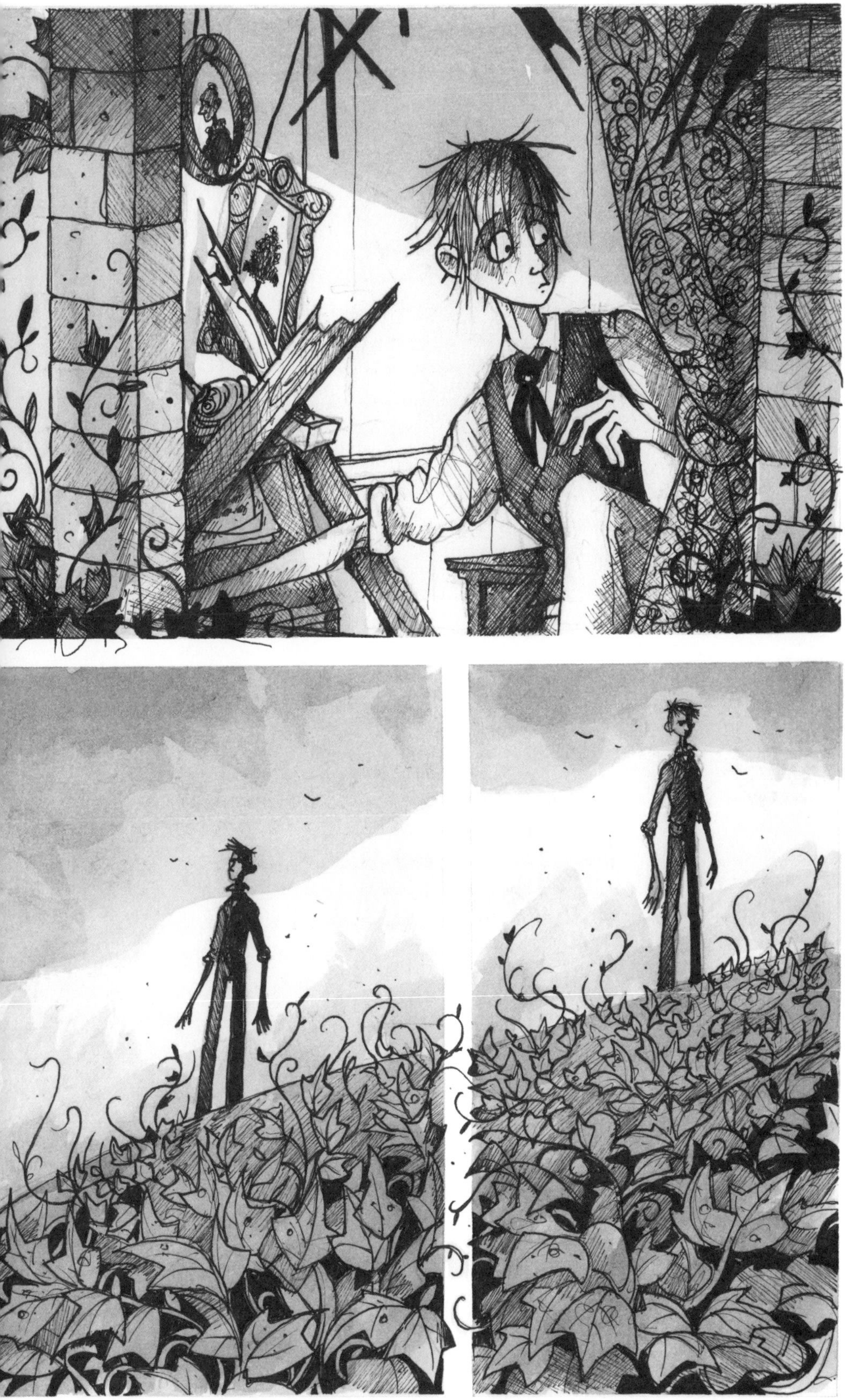

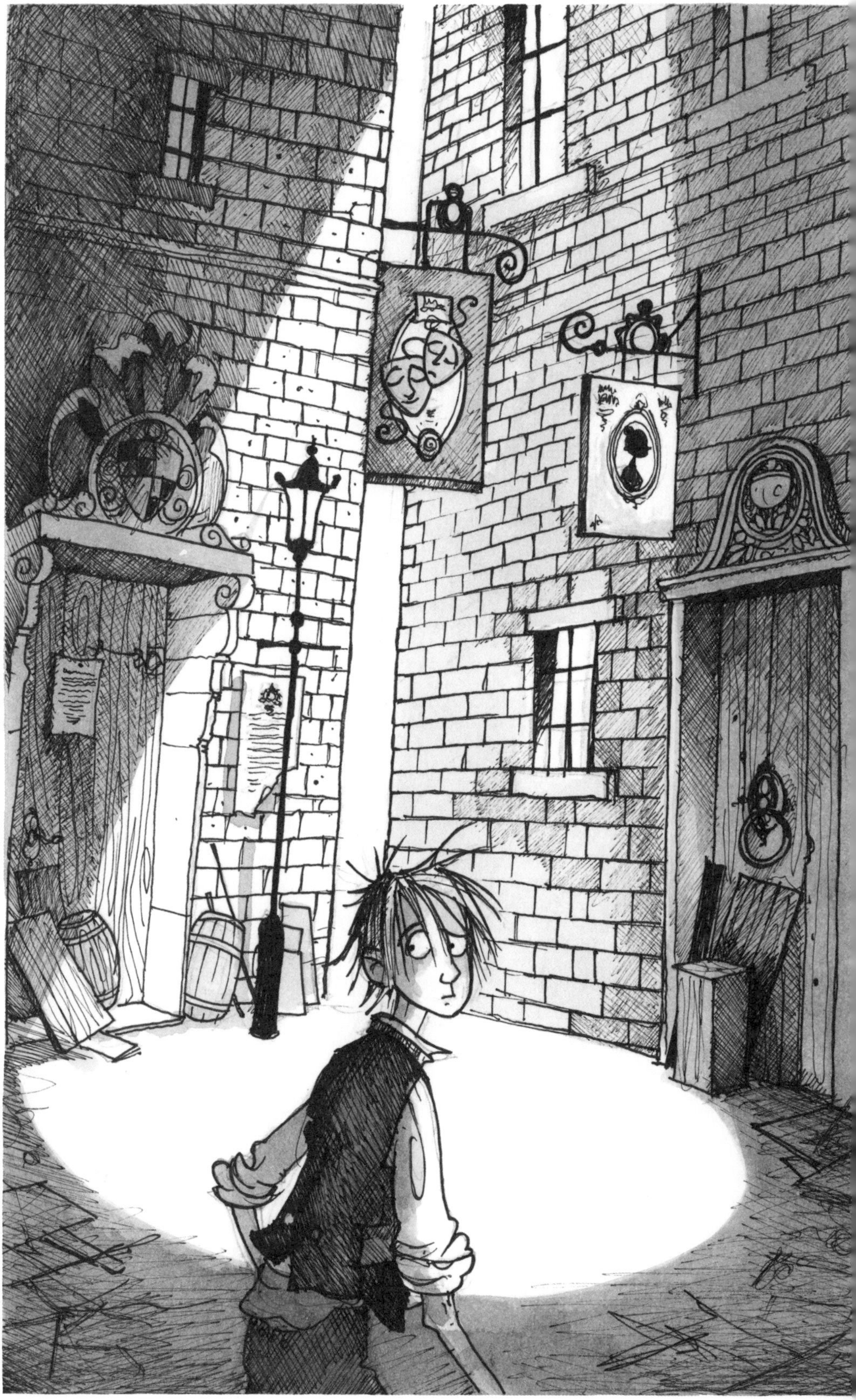

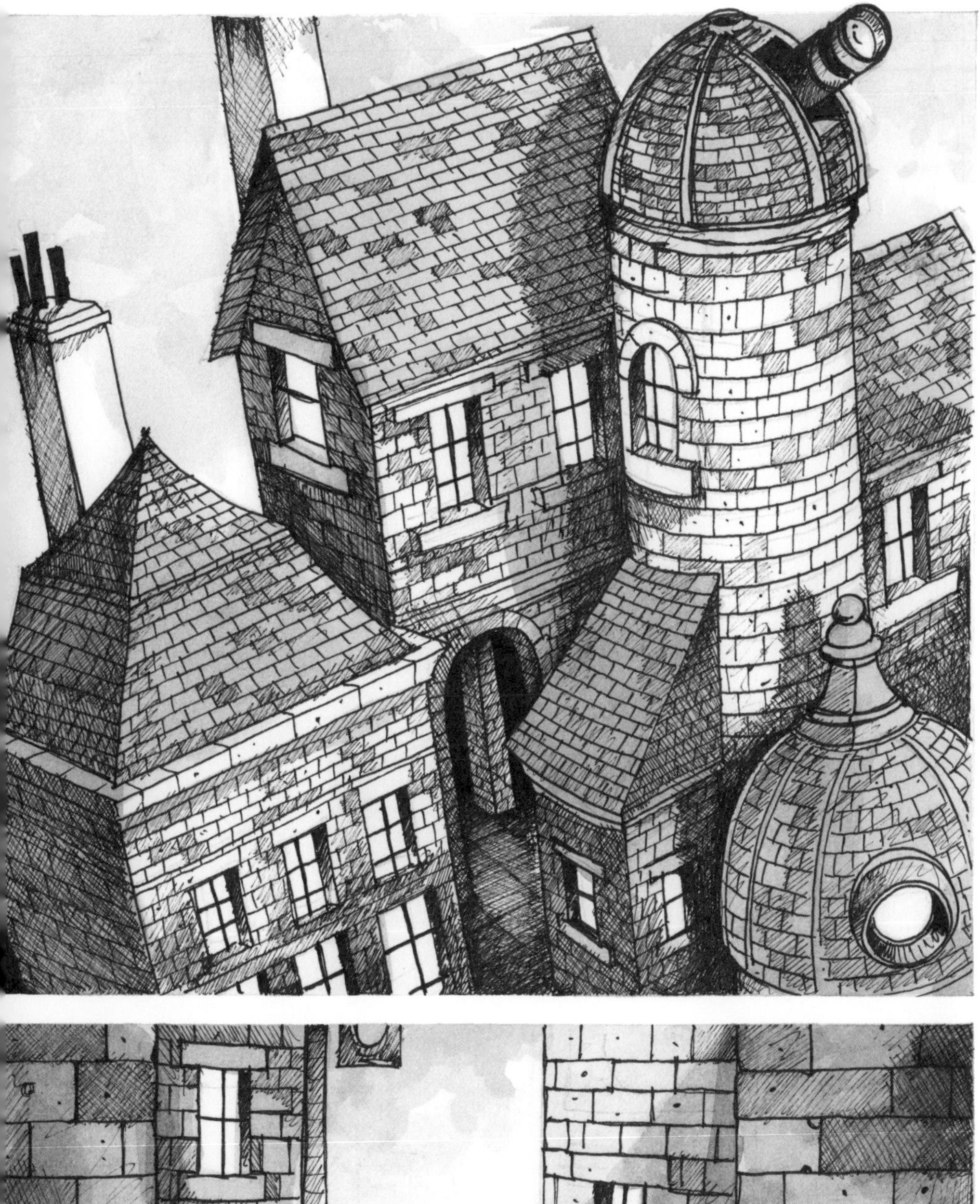

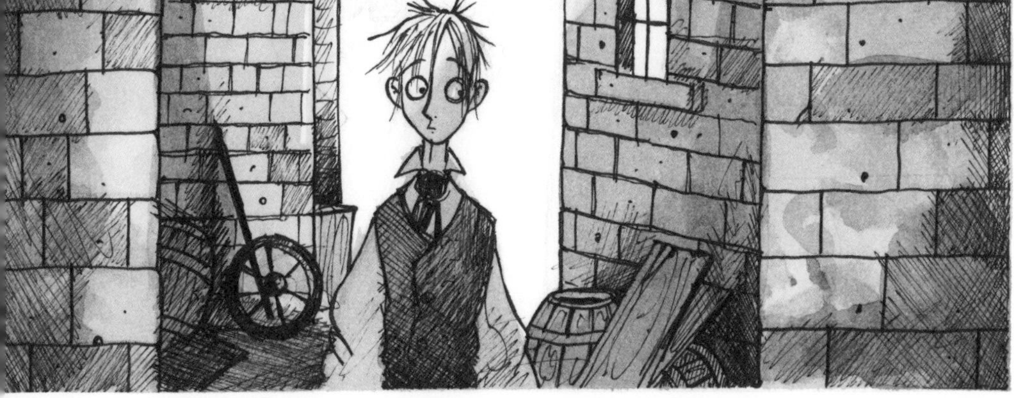

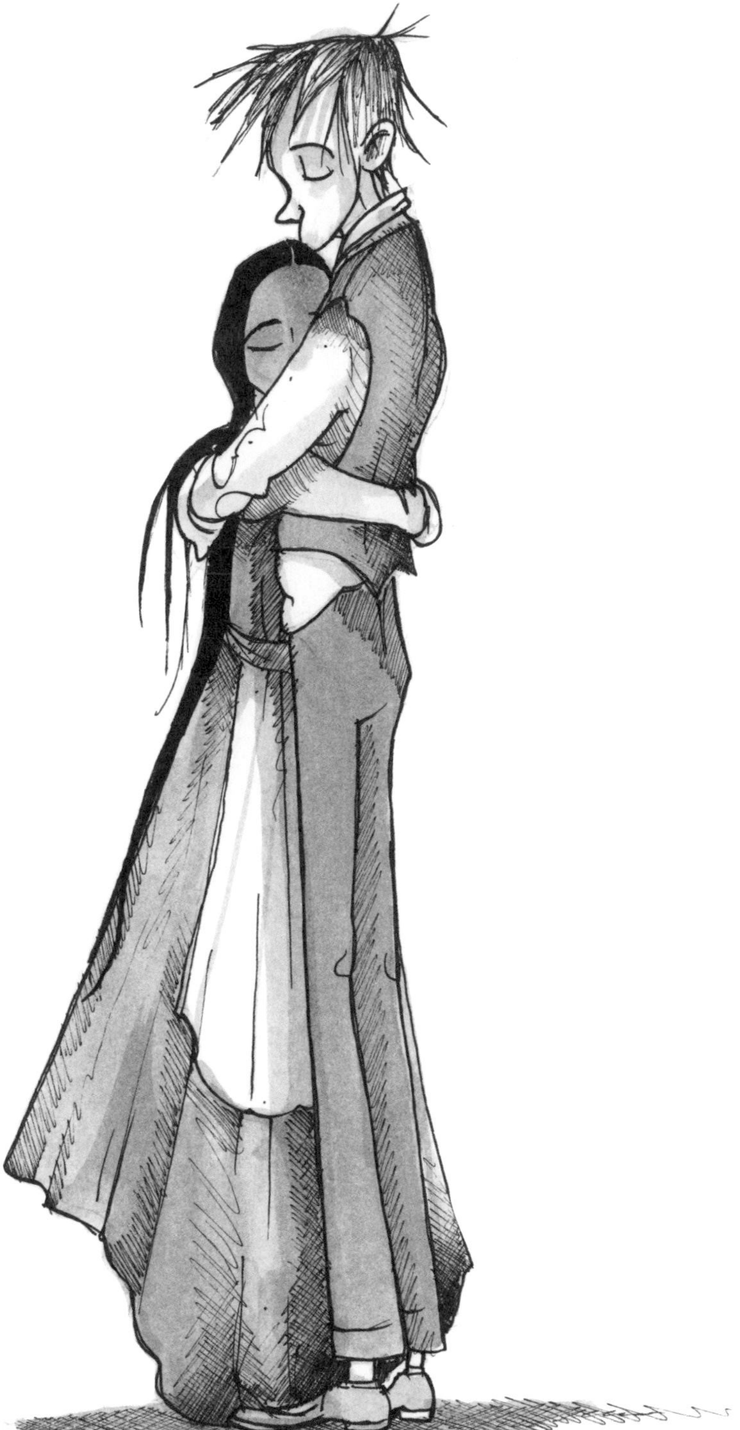

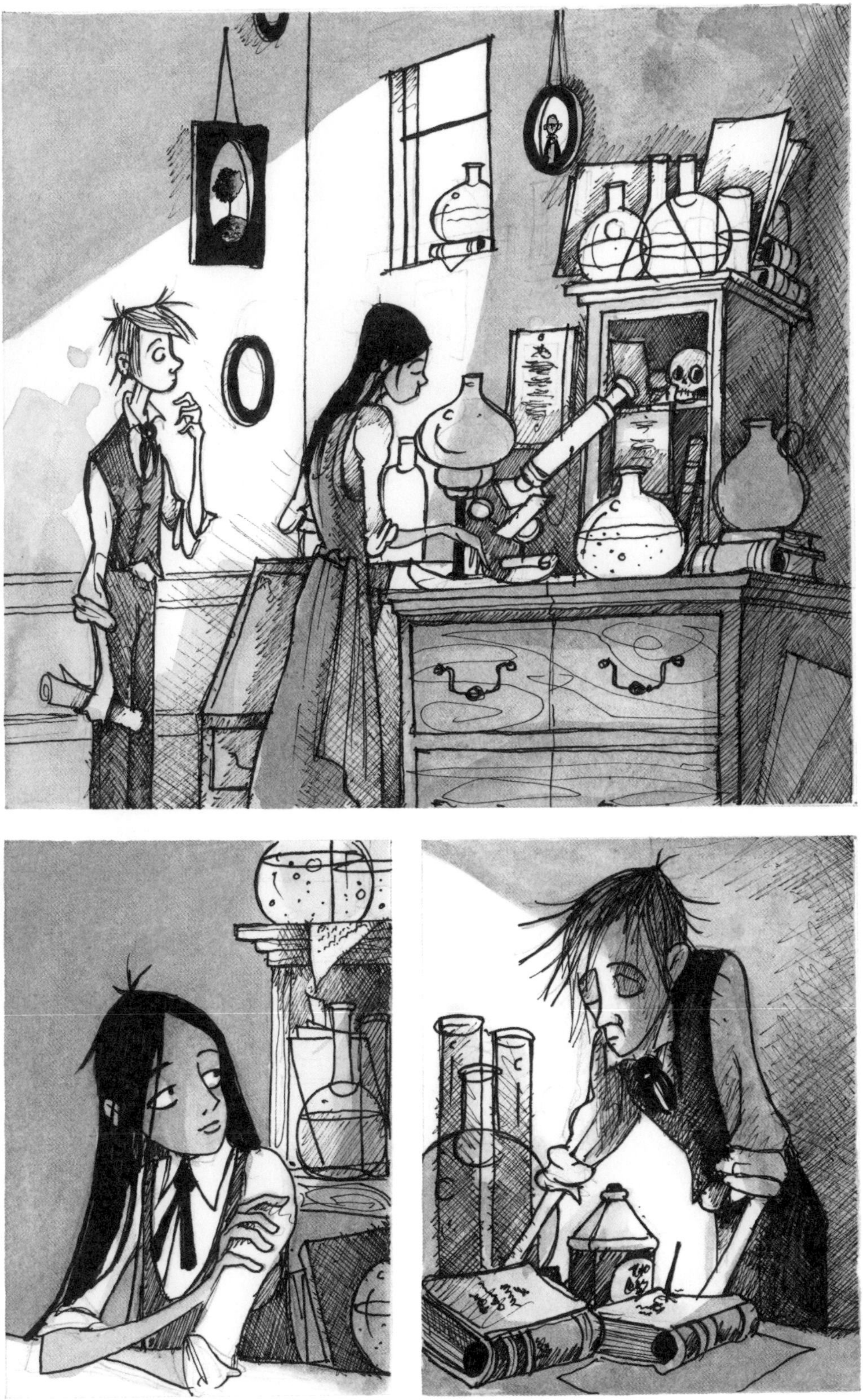

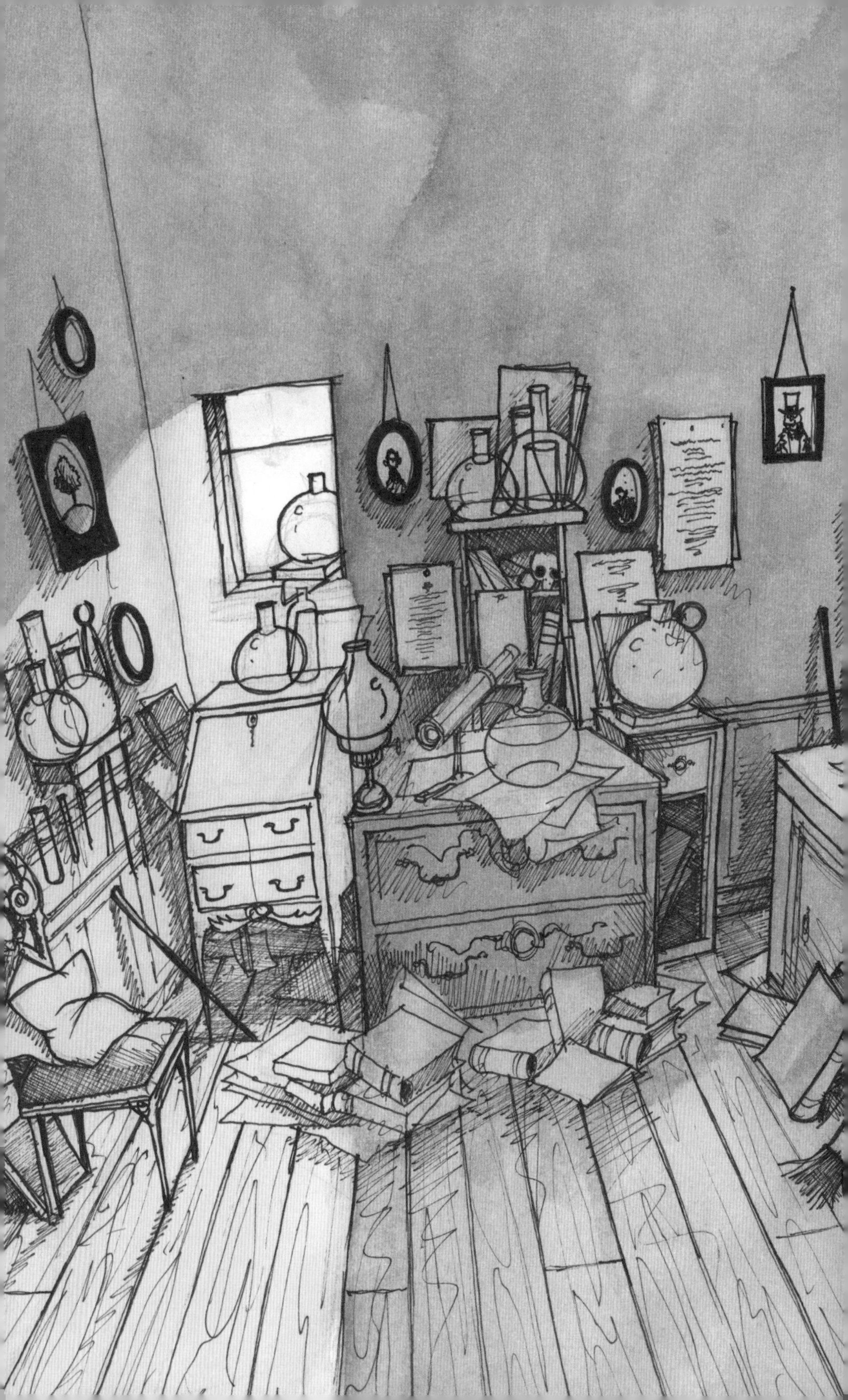

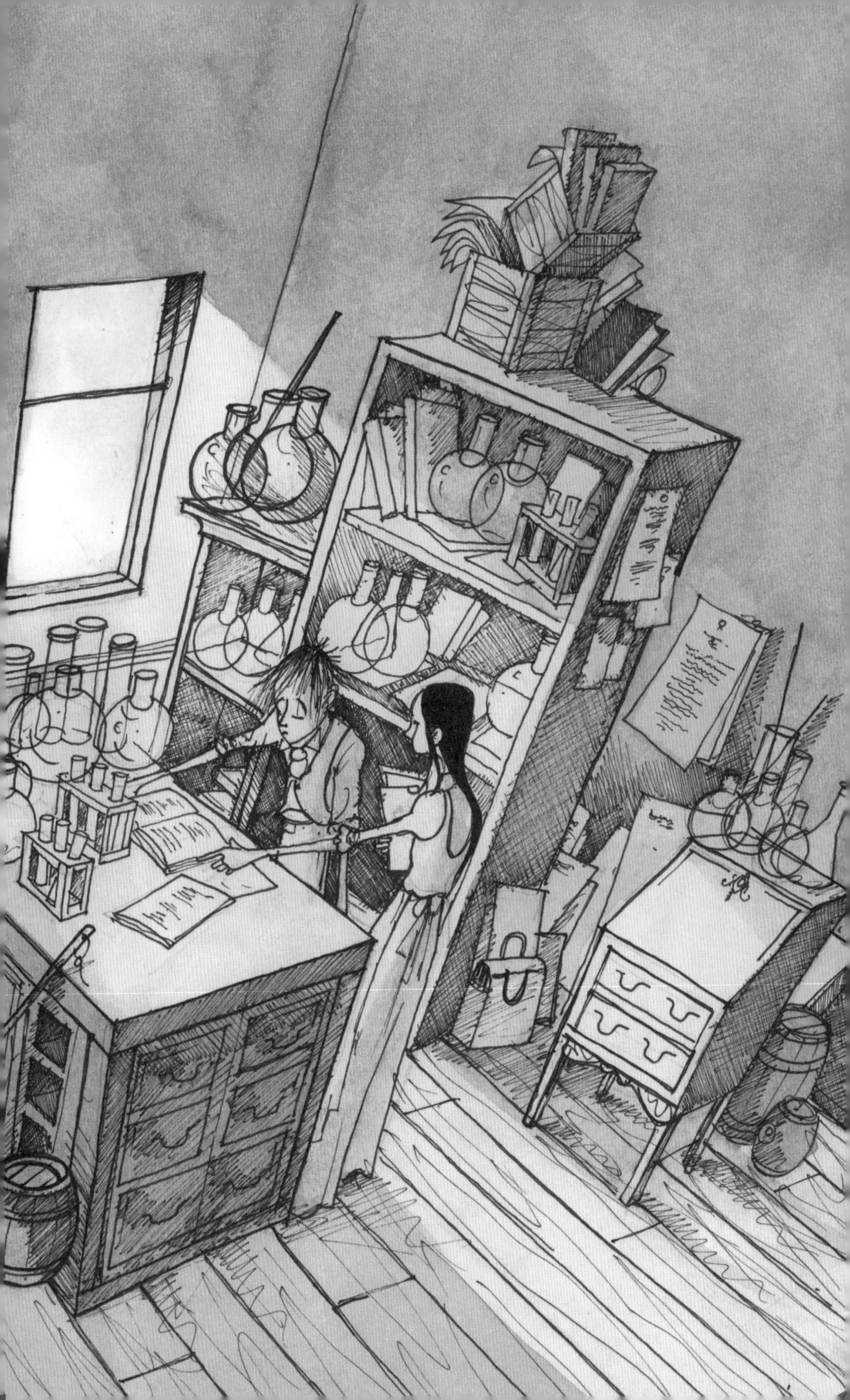

They had samples of all the stages of growth, and a scientist watched a fast-expanding cutting that looked as if it was spiralling upwards, even as we spoke.

Anya drew my attention back to her. 'What brought you here?'

'I have something to show you,' I replied. 'It might make a difference.'

I unpacked my journal on Anya's desk, and the scientists surrounded it in fascination. I showed them how I had studied the machines in my drawings. Their structure, their movement. The things I had seen up close. Where and how they walked across the landscape. The scientists made detailed photographs of my work, recording every page.

Then, using my journal, Anya marked the machines' activity on a map that was pinned to the wall. She pondered over it, confused.

'Their huge legs allow them to make ground quickly,' she said. 'But what's curious to me, unless they are wandering aimlessly, is that all their routes seem to be made twice as long as they need to be.'

It was then that I shared the best of my findings: the shrapnel from my bag.

'Where on earth did you get this?' Anya asked.

'There was contact with the artillery at Shepperton. One of them collapsed in pieces into the canal. Shrapnel fell around me. Those things are not just machines,' I told her.

'What do you mean?'

'It's as if, somehow, they live and breathe. This thing, this shrapnel – it hasn't stopped moving. It buzzes with life.'

Anya cleaned her spectacles with a cloth and placed the metal under a microscope.

'Fascinating,' she said as she examined it.

She observed the sample in many ways, under different lights, and using all kinds of optical measures. She cut into it, observed its centre, and tested its strength.

The team gathered their evidence excitedly. Work could continue much further here with my sample and studies.

I placed the journal back into my bag. 'I can return when I have more.'

'Leon, wait!' cried Anya. 'Those drawings.'

'Yes?'

'They're made . . . up close. You were near? It's not safe. We have enough to help us. Please, no more.'

I shook my head. 'I promised Ogilvy I would record everything I could. Otherwise we have nothing. I'll be careful.'

'But you mustn't,' she pleaded.

'Anya, I'm sorry. I really must. My work is just as important as yours.'

There was an awkwardness in our goodbye. A disagreement

that we did not have time to settle between us. We promised we
would both remain safe and that was all we could say.

Our meeting had been brief, but it had meant the world to
me that she and the children were safe. Knowing they were
there gave me a further boost and a hope that I had not had for
some time. A hope that life would return to us in the way that
we once knew.

Before I reached Horsell, I could see along the way that the
artillery had amassed a large army on the common. Row after
row of cannons. Crowds of men on horseback, and droves on
foot, armed to the teeth. They pitched tents and made fires and
ate and drank. As I observed all this, my earlier hope seemed
to drain away. Thoughts of what I'd witnessed crept into my
mind. Determination was our greatest weapon. It would not be
enough.

In the distance, the haunting howl of the tripod walkers
sounded over the Surrey hills. Closer and closer came their call.
I knew I should take shelter somewhere near, and quickly.

Chapter Eleven

When Worlds Collide

THE SKY DELIVERED A LOW RUMBLE that felt like a warning from afar. Blistering heat stifled the air. I waited anxiously from my position, nesting in a thicket of sharp thorns and harsh dried-out shrubbery. Unable to tear myself away from the dangers – half scared to move and half wanting to see what would unfold so that I could add to my journal.

And then all too soon they were upon us, crashing through the forest in their monstrous stride. With the machines still out of range for the artillery, there was an anxious moment of anticipation before firing could commence. The invisible grip took hold and slowed everyone down. Then suddenly, in the blink of an eye, men and horses were thrown into the air, obliterated by the Martians' power. Clods of earth launched upwards, then scattered down with a heavy force. Artillery fire burst into life.

Their pounding steel limbs ploughed into the dry earth as a wave of cannon fire powered towards them. The noise alone was shattering. The whole scene was barely visible through the clouds of smoke across the common. Penetrating these gargantuan beings was near impossible. Here and there, a single success sent a cheering roar across the fields: a tripod collapsing headlong into an ancient oak and setting fire to its canopy.

Nothing, though, could match the supernatural might of the alien attack and they ripped through the opposition. How could our artillery possibly stop machines that simply evaporated what was in front of them?

Overhead, the growl of thunder had been drowned out. The darkening clouds had been ignored amid the flames and gun smoke. But now it came. A great storm. A storm that had waited patiently through the summer while the earth dried out. A release of pressure from above would send a whole season of rainfall in a matter of hours.

At first, there were just a few scattered heavy splashes, but then a downpour followed with such ferocity that it was painful to stand beneath it. I found shelter deeper within the woods from where I watched. Flames and fumes engulfed the trees around me. There was nowhere to hide.

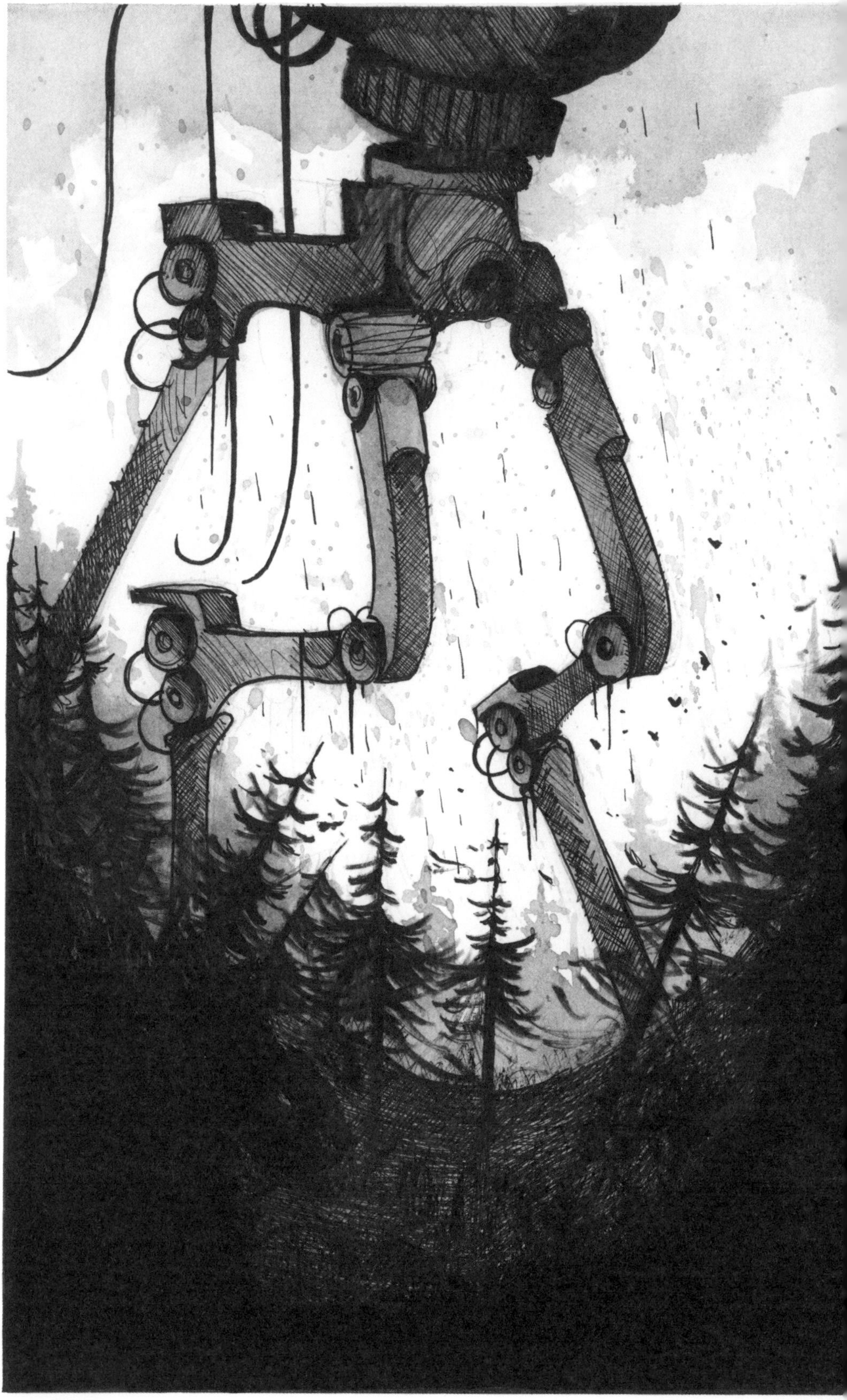

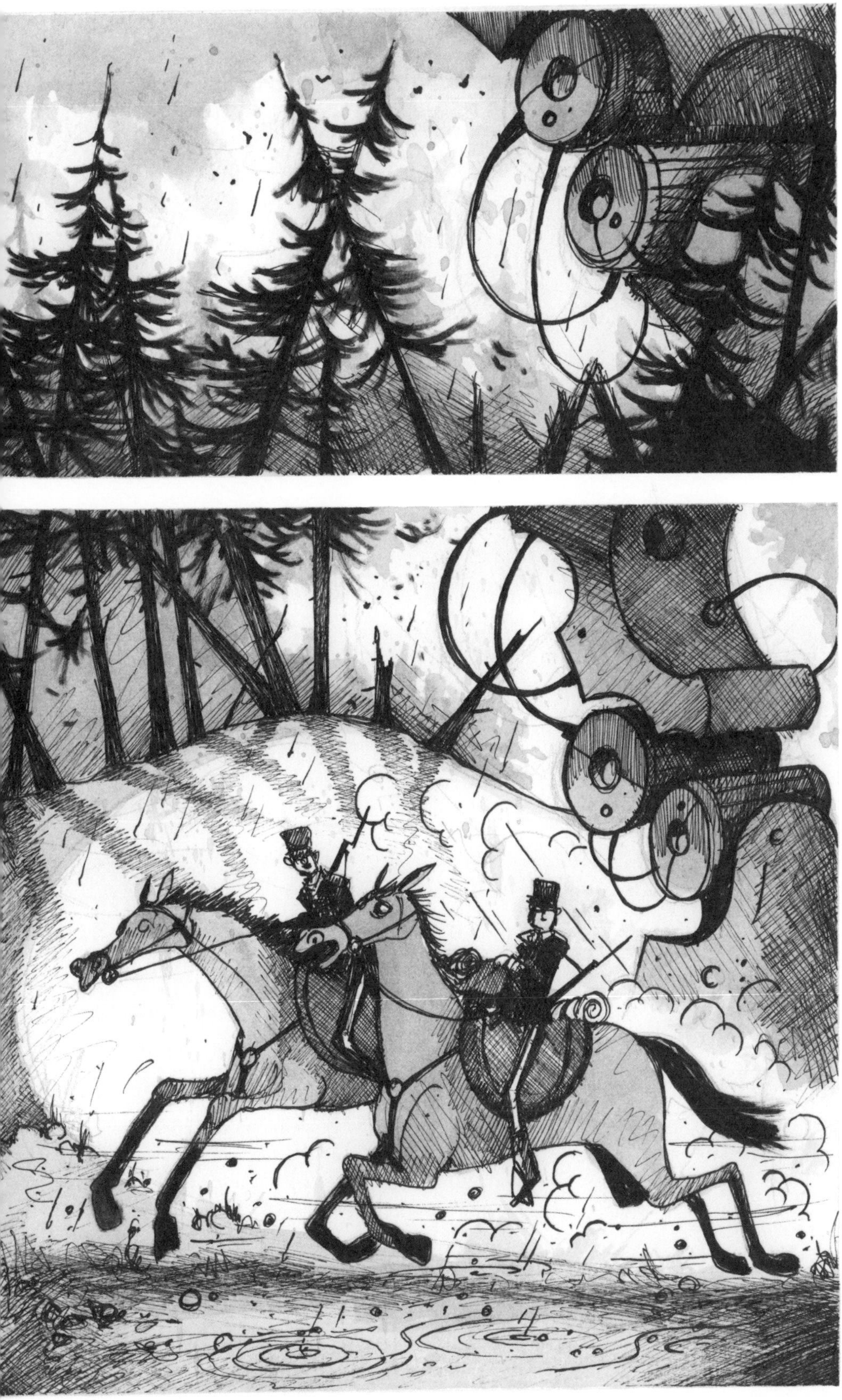

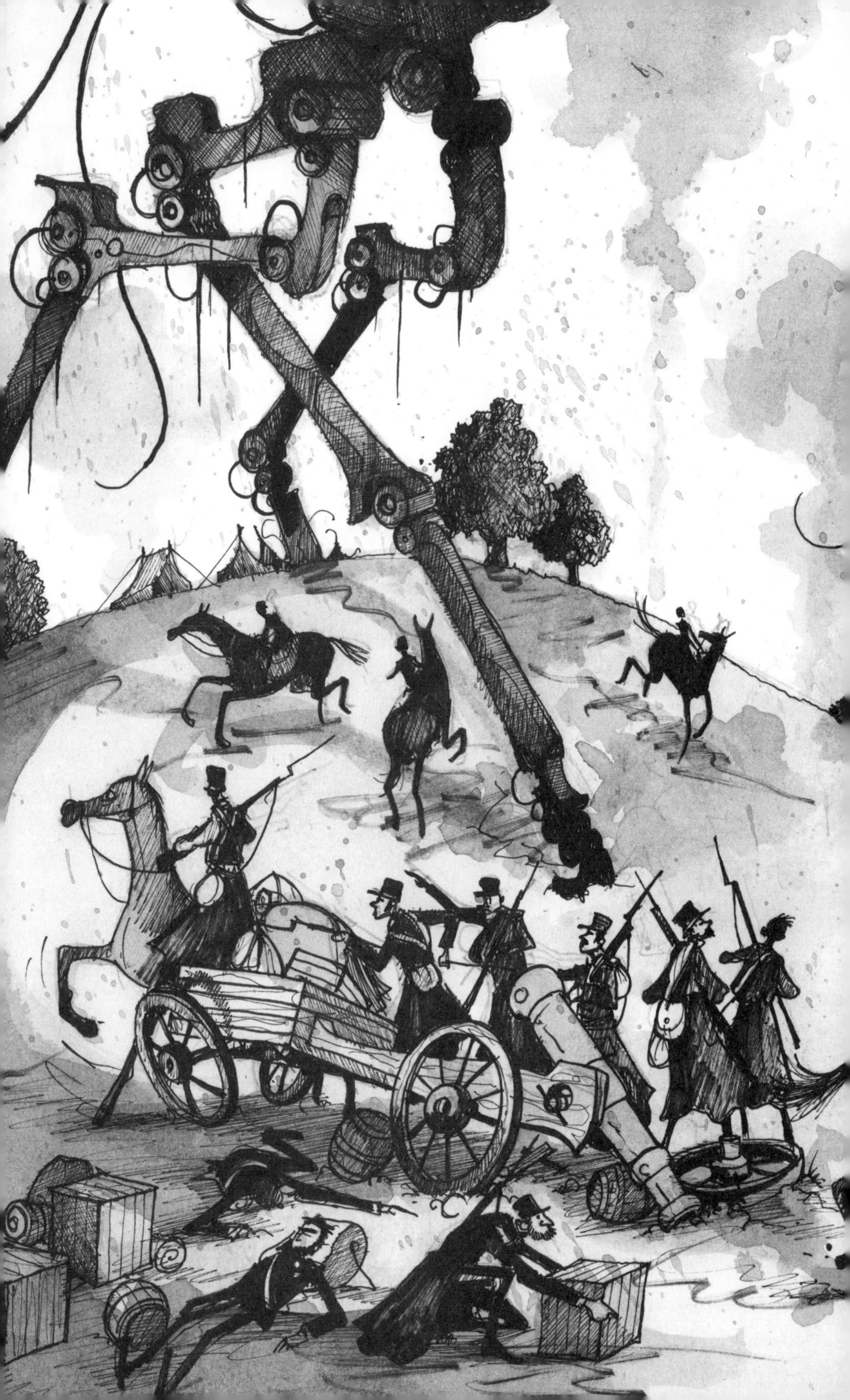

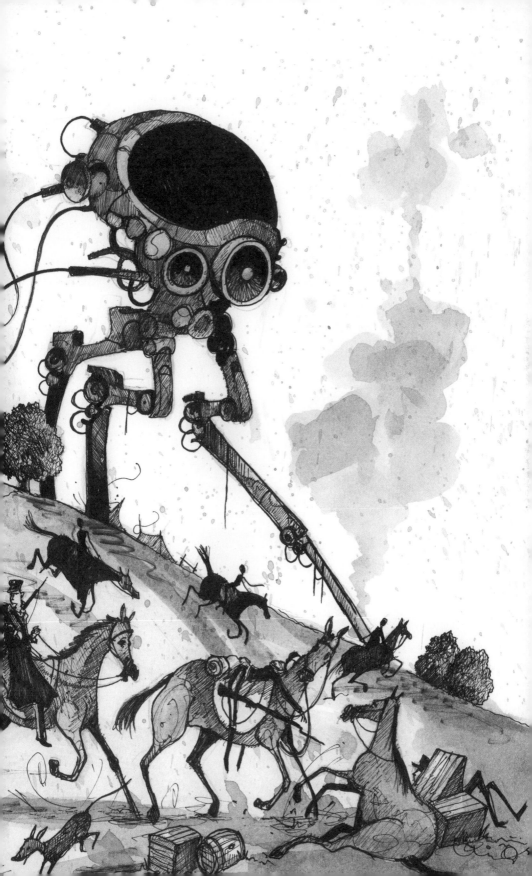

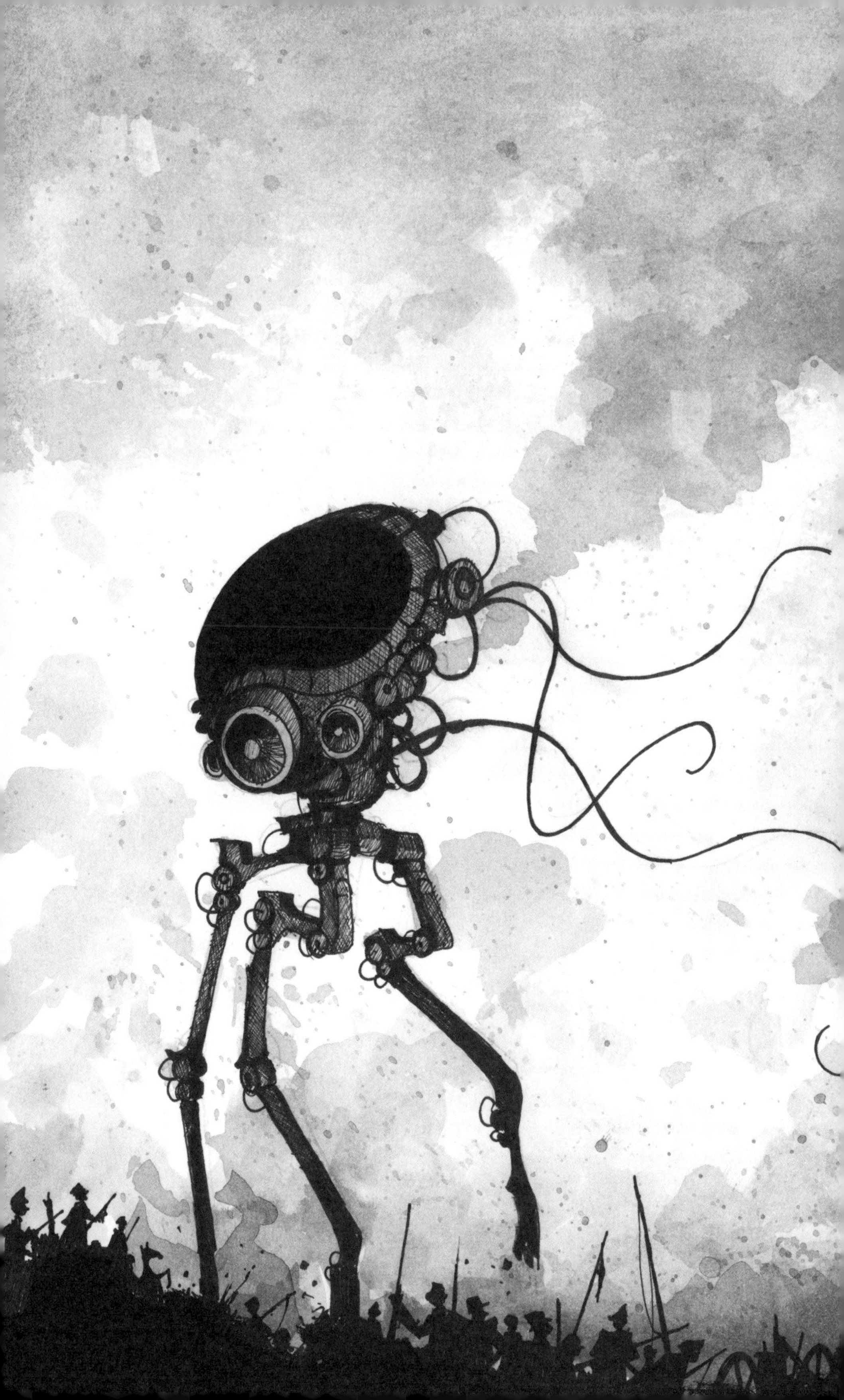

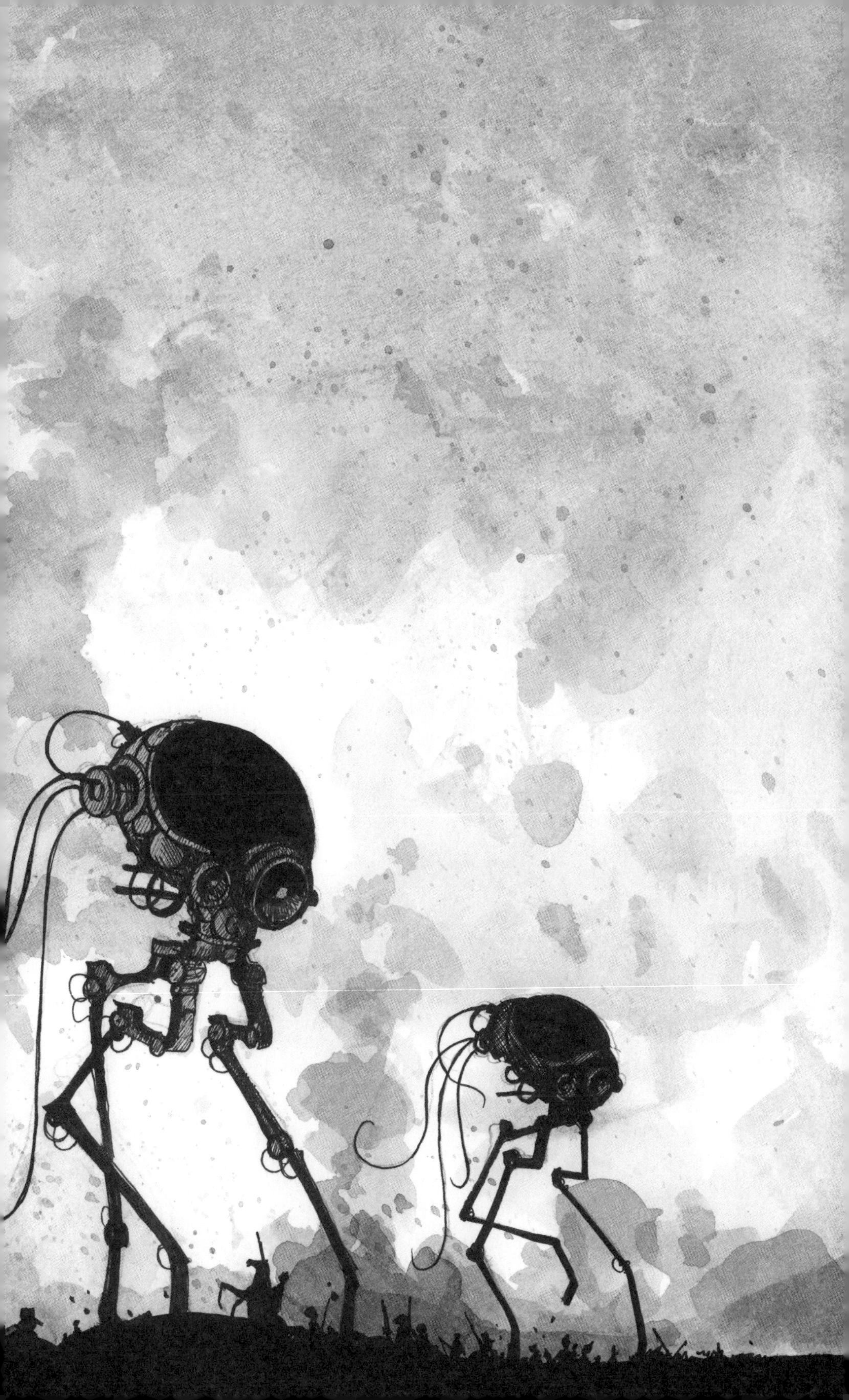

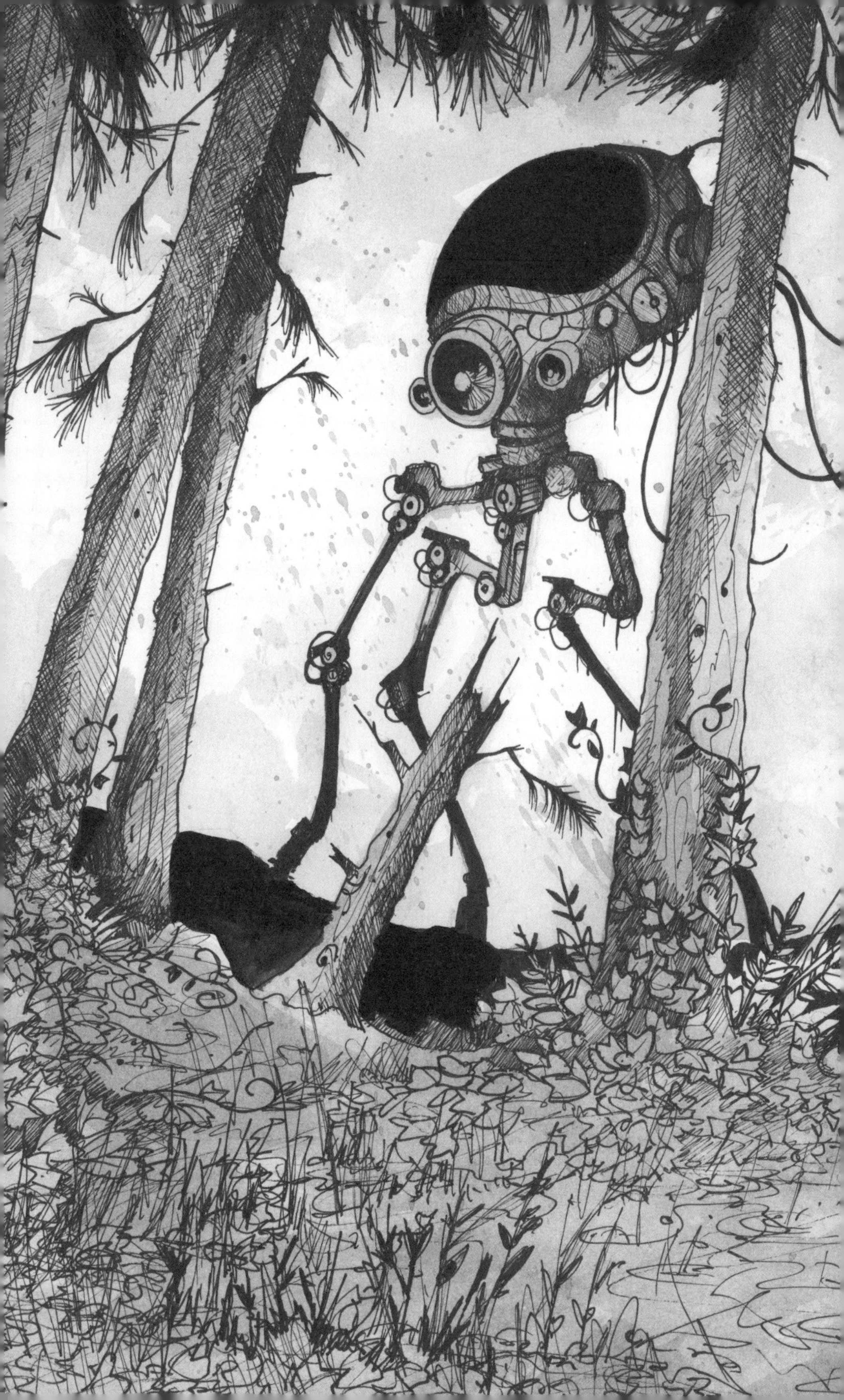

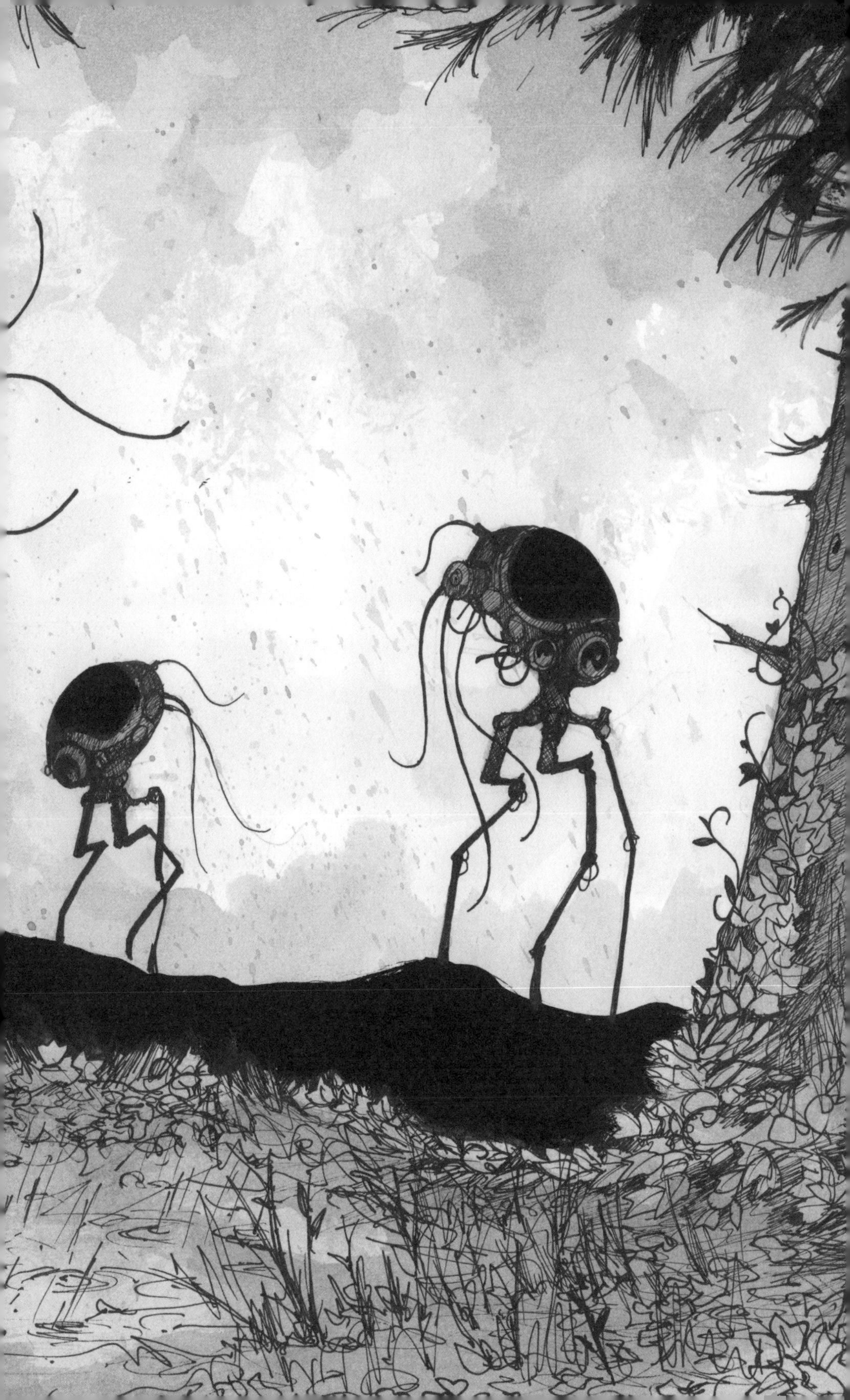

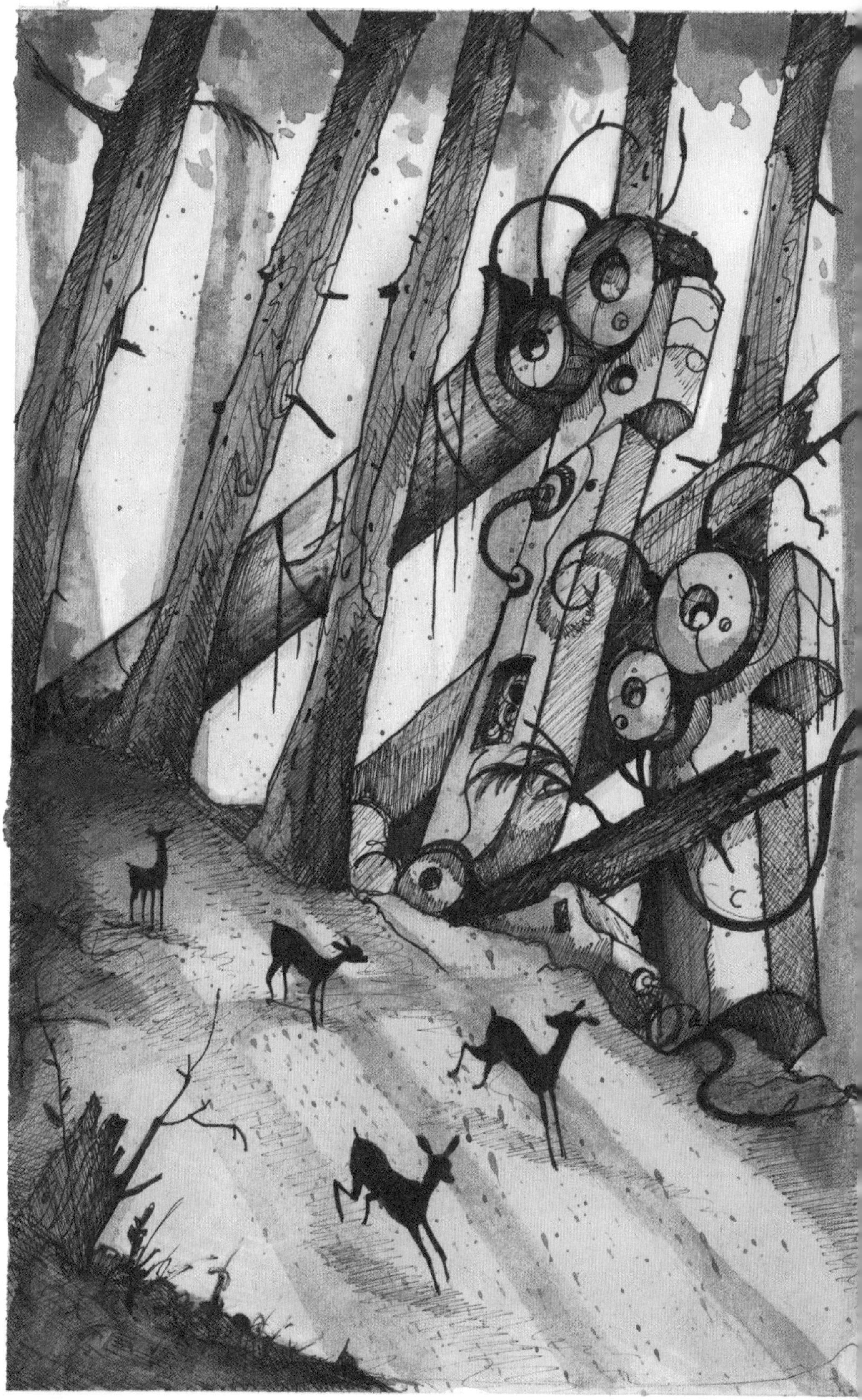

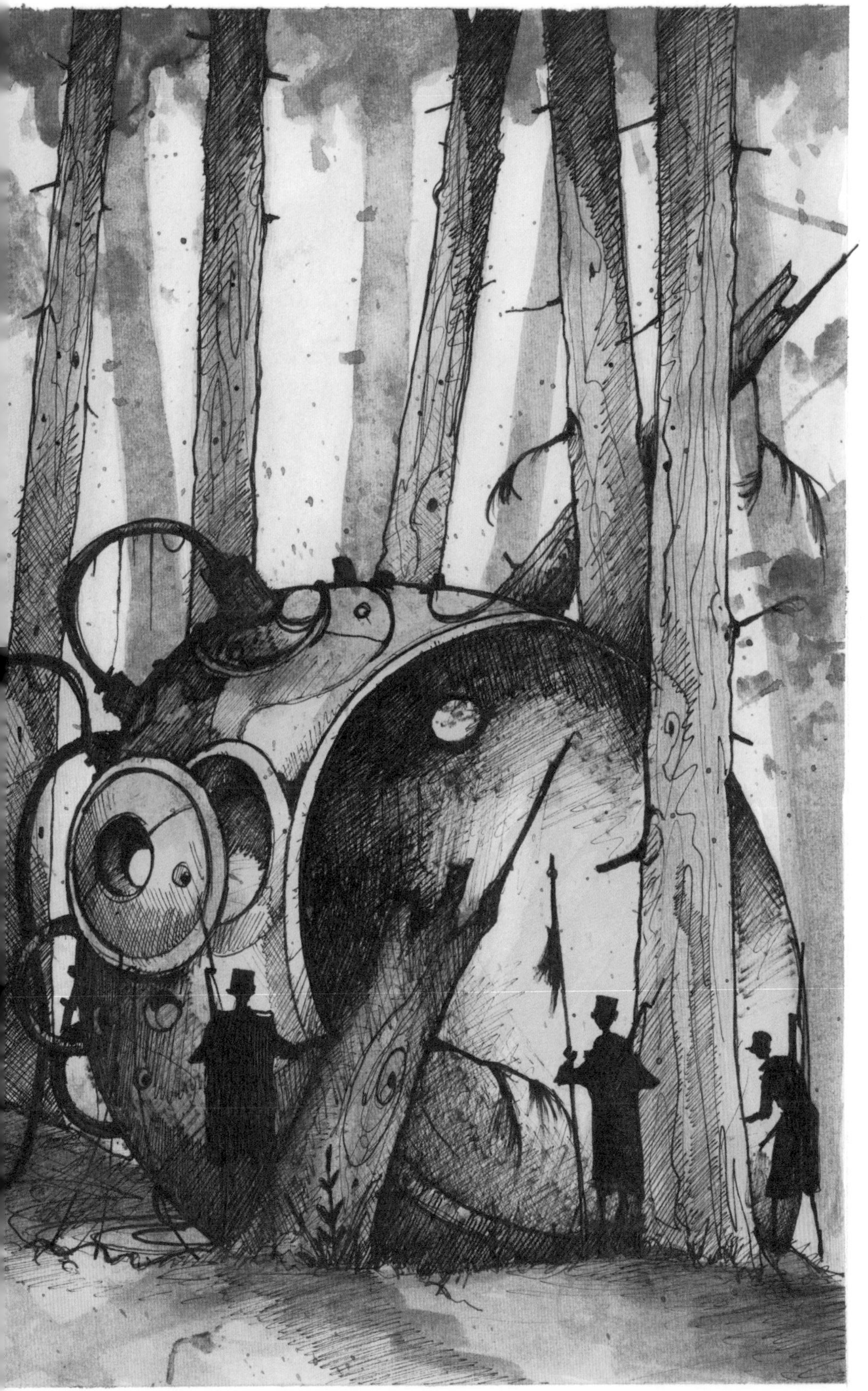

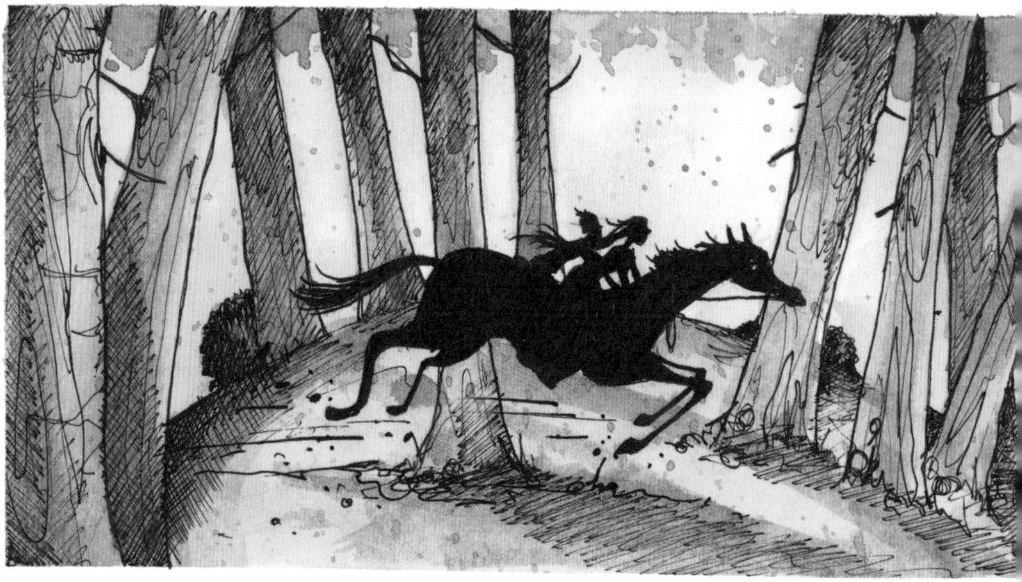

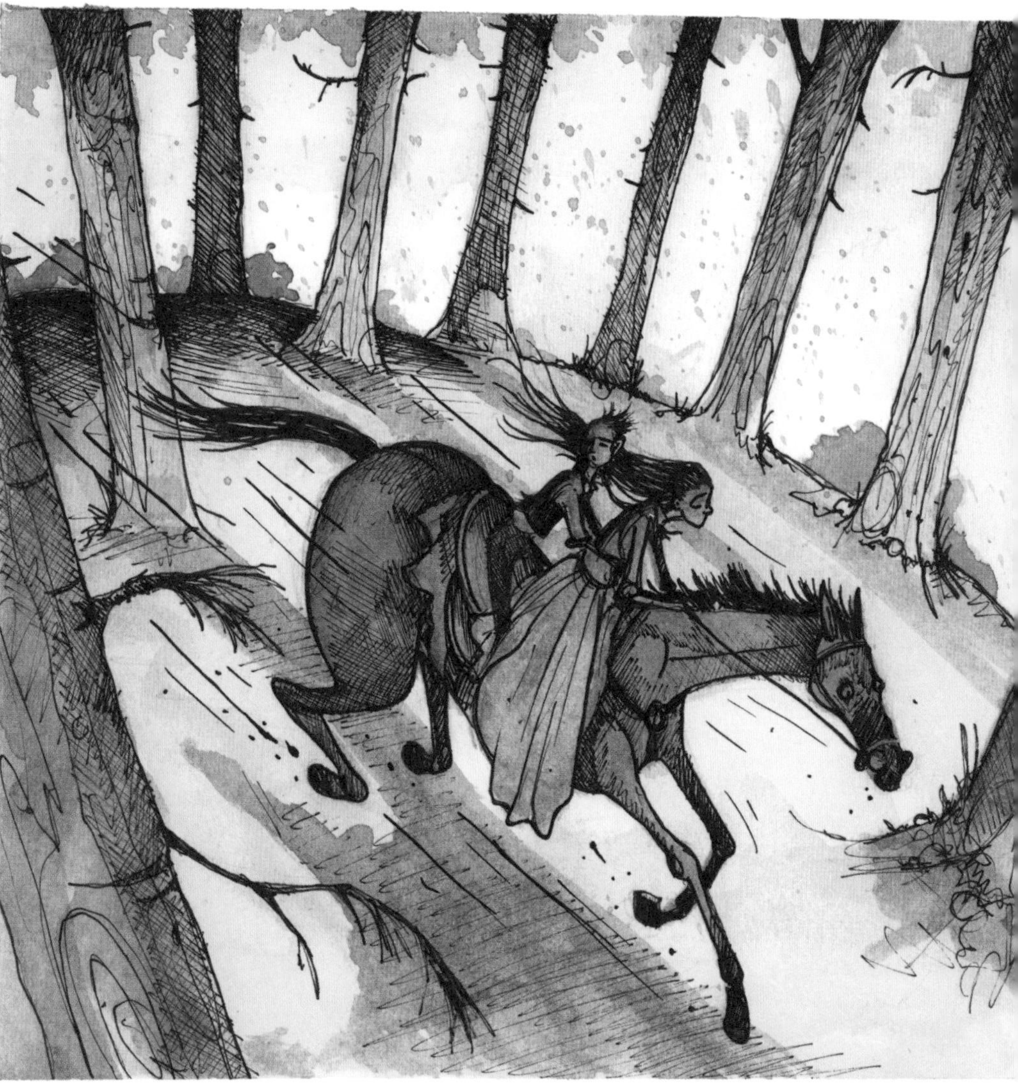

The onslaught continued, the two sides seemingly undeterred by the force of nature around them. The skies unleashed their own power, harder and faster until pools filled in the divots where the earth had been churned up and rivers formed and ran. Fire and smoke billowed endlessly, choking the forest. The noise from the storm grew louder, fighting to drown out the song of war.

Something thundered behind me under cover of the trees. I almost didn't dare to look. Through the pouring rain, a horse cantered between the uprights. It was Anya, soaked through, her hair lank across her shoulders.

'Climb up!' she shouted.

I scrambled onto the horse's back, and we were off before I had even climbed comfortably astride. I managed to drag myself upright, and we pounded through the forest, narrowly avoiding the dangers.

I glanced back. A creaking, groaning echo sounded through the trees as another colossus collapsed into the earth. And another, smashing its way into the soaking ground. Incredibly, despite our lack of impact and inferior firepower, our army made progress. But I couldn't see how. Everything was against us. As we fled the scene, the machines were either fallen or had ground to a halt.

I shouted over Anya's shoulder, 'I think they're struggling.'

'Yes, I know,' she said without looking back. As if she somehow expected it.

The sky grew darker and then, ever so slowly, the battle grew quieter, and the only sound that could be heard was the lashing drum of persistent rain. In the distance, as night turned in, silhouettes of the machines made themselves known to the sky. Motionless.

In the next moment, we were tucked under cover, away from the downpour. We laughed at each other, soaked to the skin.

'I had to come and find you,' explained Anya. 'We've made good progress at the lab with your sample.'

'You have?'

'We placed it under water. The metal reacted strongly and appeared to move without agitation. What's more, it seemed to ignite on its surface while immersed. A purple flame. Barely visible but under the microscope it caused sparks and what appear to be minuscule explosions.'

'So that means what?' I asked. 'They're dangerous underwater. Harmful?'

'No, quite the opposite.' She raised her head and pointed back at the scene. 'Where there is moisture, they're under attack – infected by organisms in the water. Eating away at the surface. Bringing their alien forms to a grinding halt.'

Men had stopped in their tracks and stood in disbelief, ceasing their fire. Up above, those tripod walkers that had not crashed to the ground had been hypnotised into a stillness. Static towers loomed, while flocks of birds circled their hoods. Their oily surfaces began fizzing and bubbling and rusting instantly in front of us. Steam and smoke rose from them as their lives ebbed out.

The night brought a velvet-black sky that erased the silhouettes of the machines and peppered bright white stars into the world above us. I heard shouts from the soldiers amid wheels rolling, hooves marching and calls from one man to another. Gradually it faded.

'This all makes perfect sense,' I said as the horse slowed to a trot.

'It does?' asked Anya.

'Yes, I read of a tripod collapsing into the Thames. It must have been the water.'

'Of course,' she agreed. 'And the prolonged journeys of the machines as they walked their routes around the towns and cities!'

'Yes, but what did that mean?'

'They avoided the rivers wherever they could,' Anya explained. 'And where they couldn't, they got into trouble and crashed headlong into the water.'

As we neared home, we came to a stop and I got down from the horse.

'I'm so proud of you, Anya. Your work will be remembered for a long time.'

'And yours too. I didn't do this alone.'

'Shall we bring the children home?'

Anya nodded. 'Yes, but in the morning. They're settled now.'

'Let me prepare the house then. I want to be sure that you don't return to any surprises. It should look as it did when you left.'

She smiled. 'Till morning then.'

With that, she turned and galloped into the distance as I took the short walk towards home.

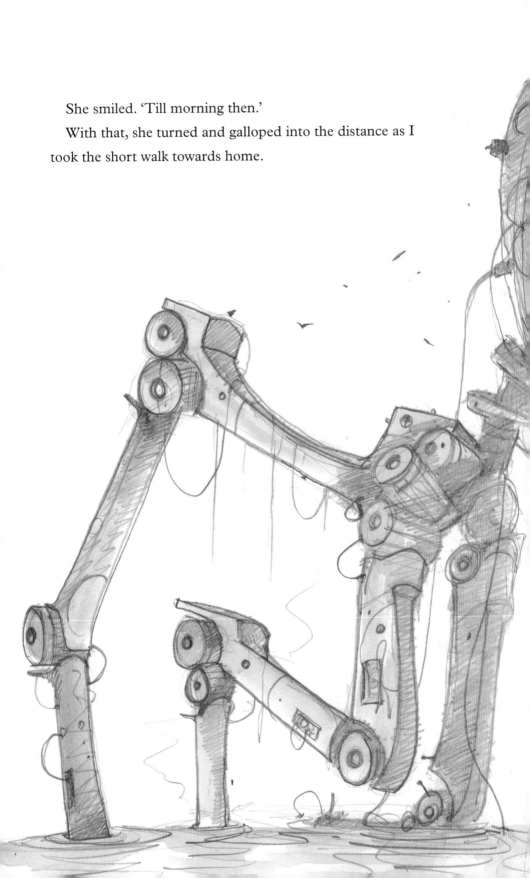

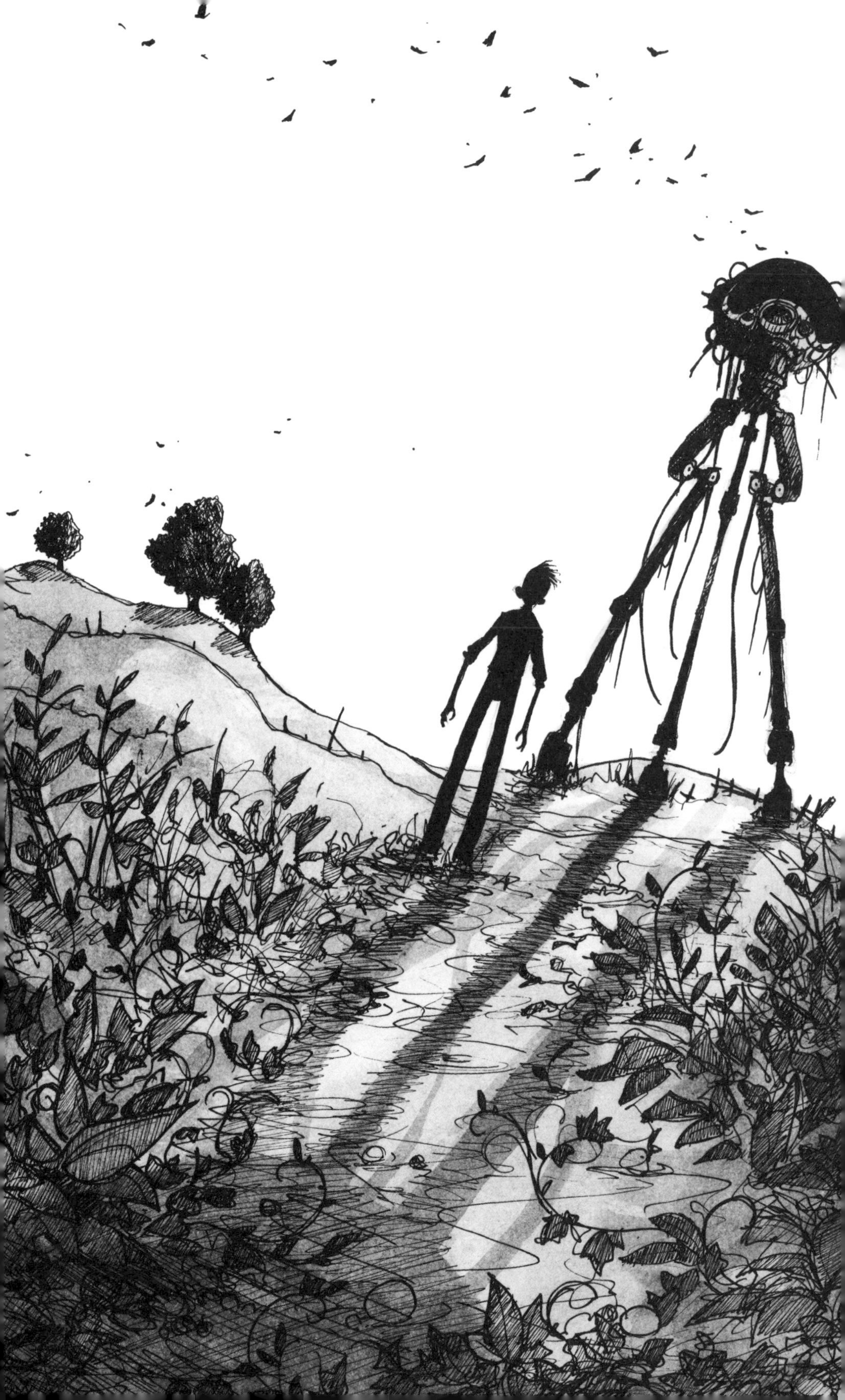

Chapter Twelve

What We Dreamed Of

A STILLNESS LIKE THIS I had never
known. The return of birdsong broke
the morning silence and I stood in
the warm air and dared to feel a small sense of
relief. I clung to the hope that the alien storm
had cleared. I walked freely over the common, the
grass still wet beneath my feet.

And then I detected a new sound. A low rolling
and rumbling. Wheels upon the ground. And, if I
wasn't mistaken, a chatter, almost like bird noise
but somehow bigger. Voices maybe. I looked up
and in the distance a horse led a cart along the
brow of the hill towards me. I stood perfectly still
and watched and waited.

It stopped some distance from me. I watched Anya alight from the seat. Her every movement was unmistakable. It could not have been anyone else. One by one, she lifted the children down and they ran towards me. Anya followed at the back, selflessly allowing them their moment before we were together again. They laughed and shouted and all at once we embraced in a huddle, climbing and screaming and bringing me the wonderful chaos I had longed for. And then Anya. I always remembered every tiny detail of her face in the times that I did not see her. I can't explain how the sight of her overwhelmed me in that moment of knowing that we were free again.

I held her so tightly that I was almost unable to let go. Tears flooded my face and ran streaming into her long dark hair. We had no words. Only a tight embrace and a long gaze that reminded us both that in that moment nothing else mattered.

And then something else, following on behind. Two figures, holding each other as they walked. I stood and watched them come closer and then it made sense. Orla and Ivan. Alive and well.

Esme tugged at my coat. 'I told you the nightingale would look after you.'

'Of course he did,' I said.

We hugged tightly.

'I've learned to read,' she told me urgently. 'I won't need to ask so many questions any more.'

'That's good,' I said. 'But you can always ask me anything you want.'

'Anya says I've learned to fly.' Then she ran to join the others across the meadow, skipping together and laughing out loud with their arms waving.

Anya told me of their adventures and I spoke as little as I could of the things I had seen.

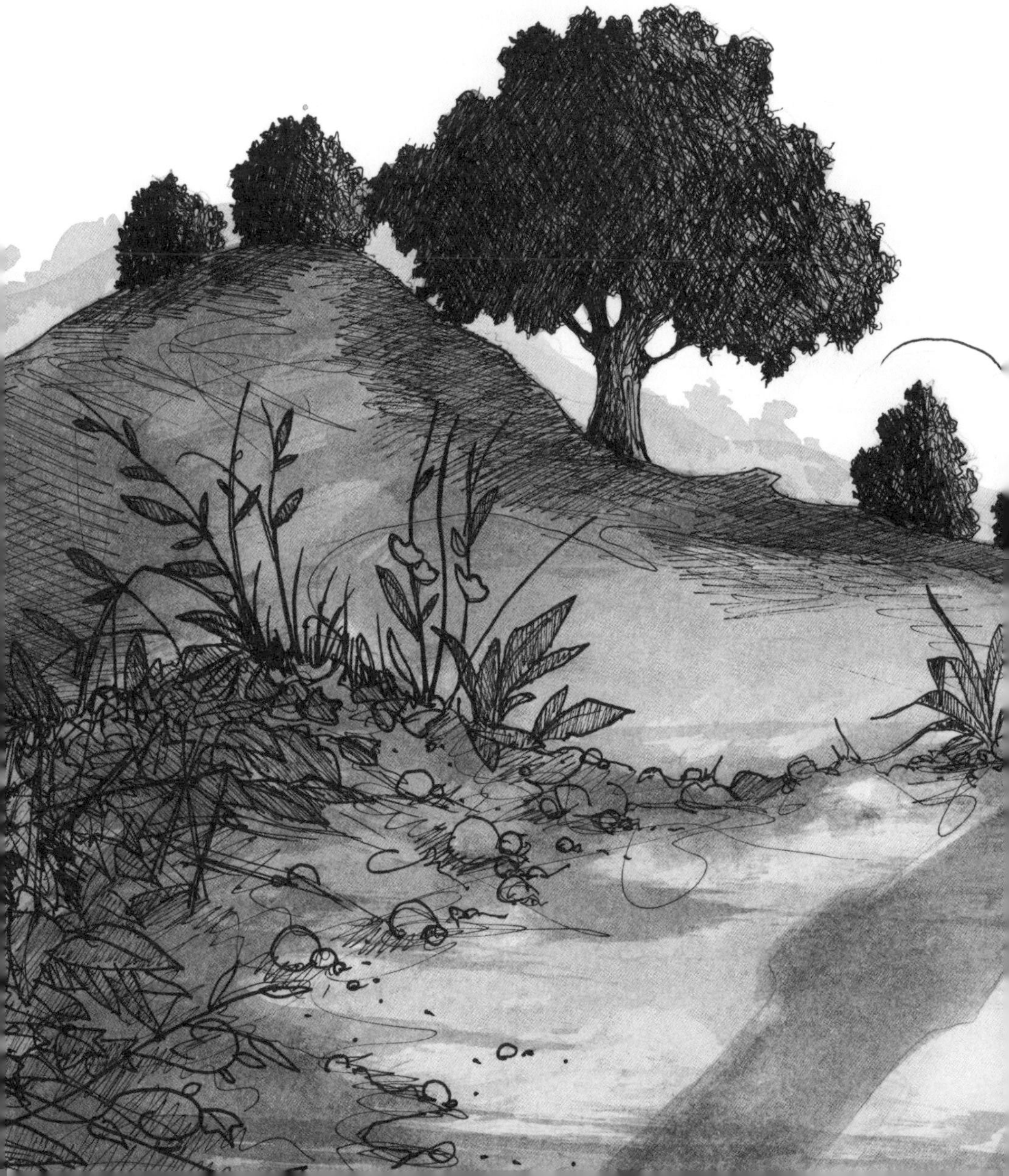

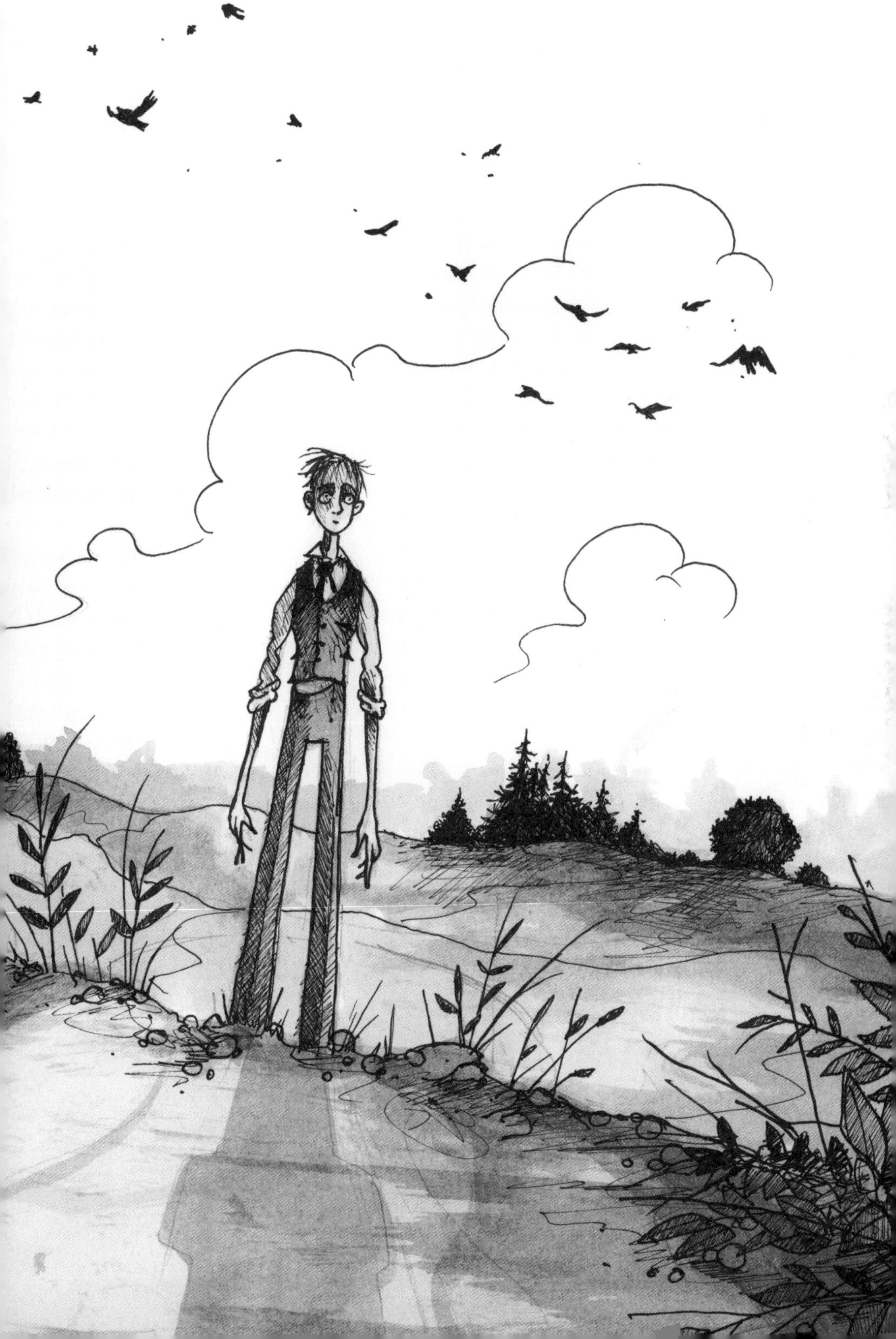

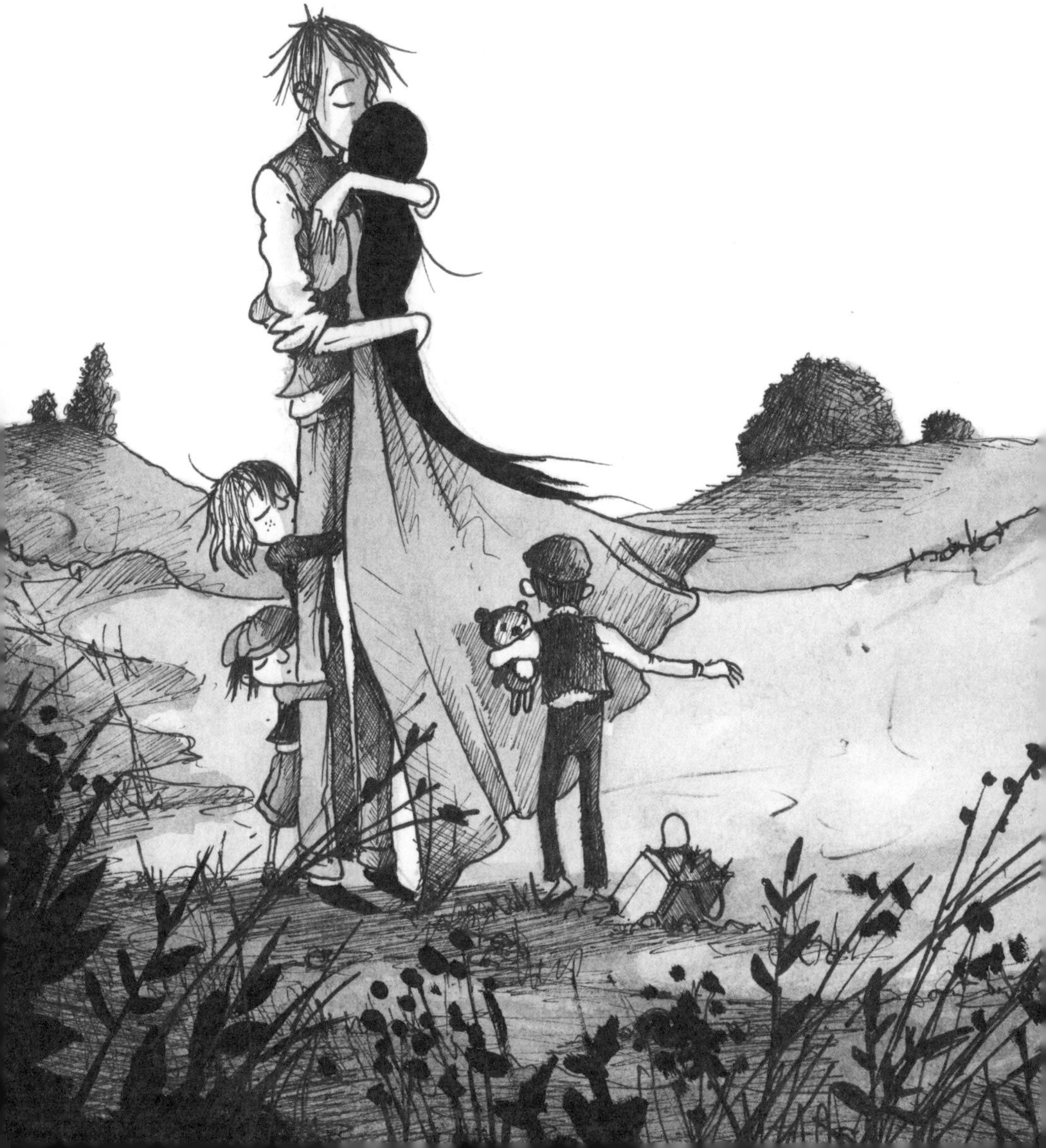

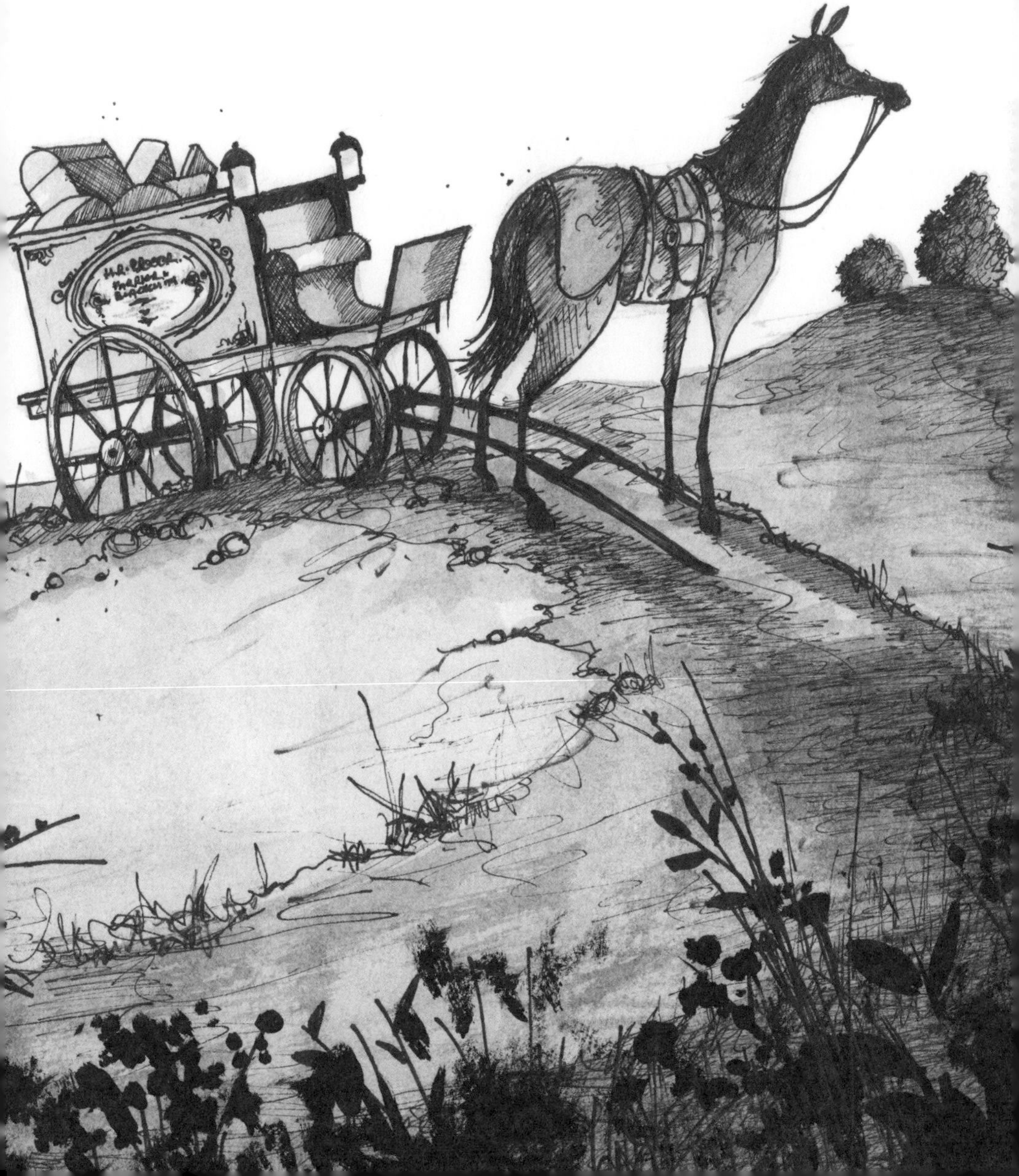

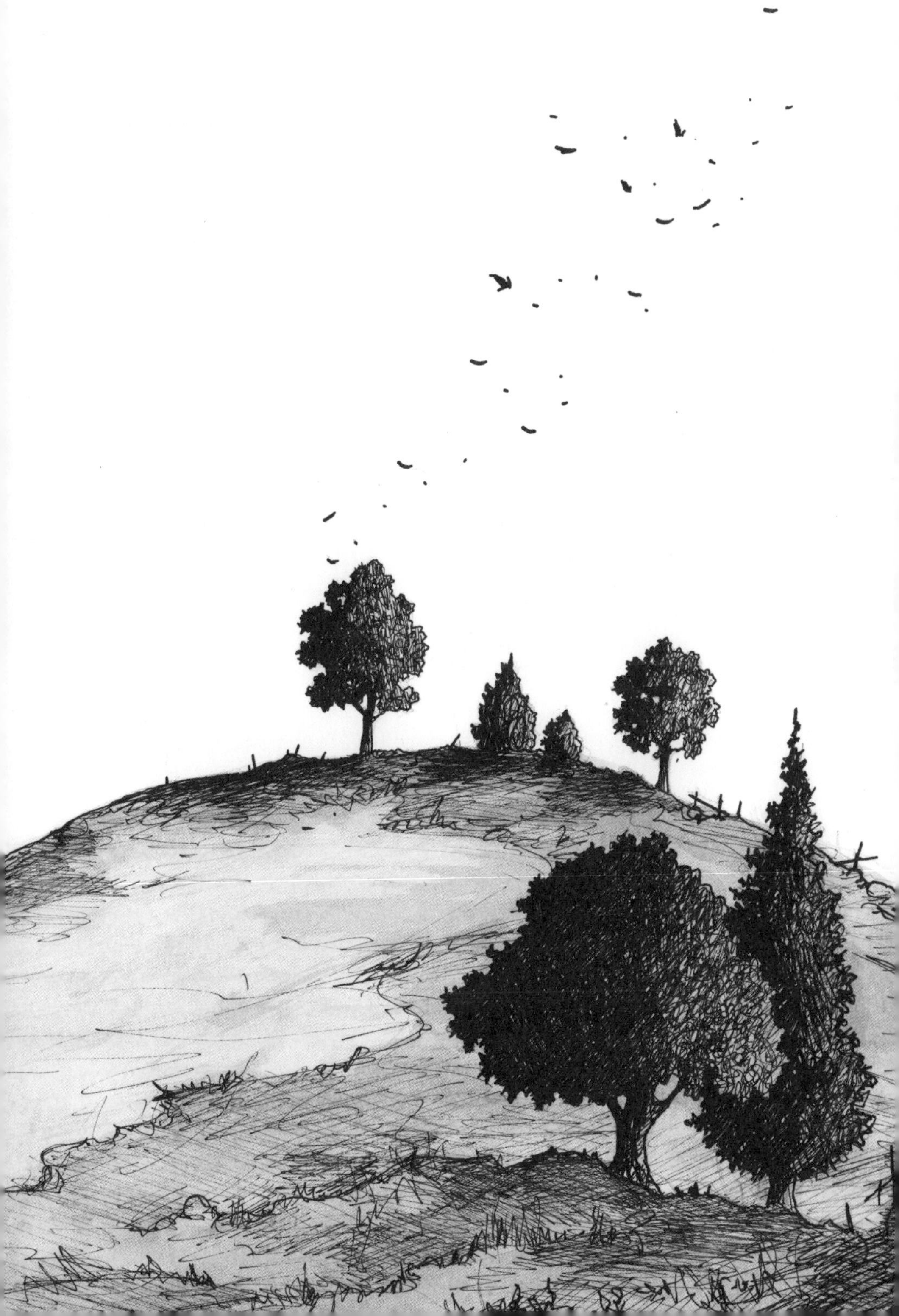

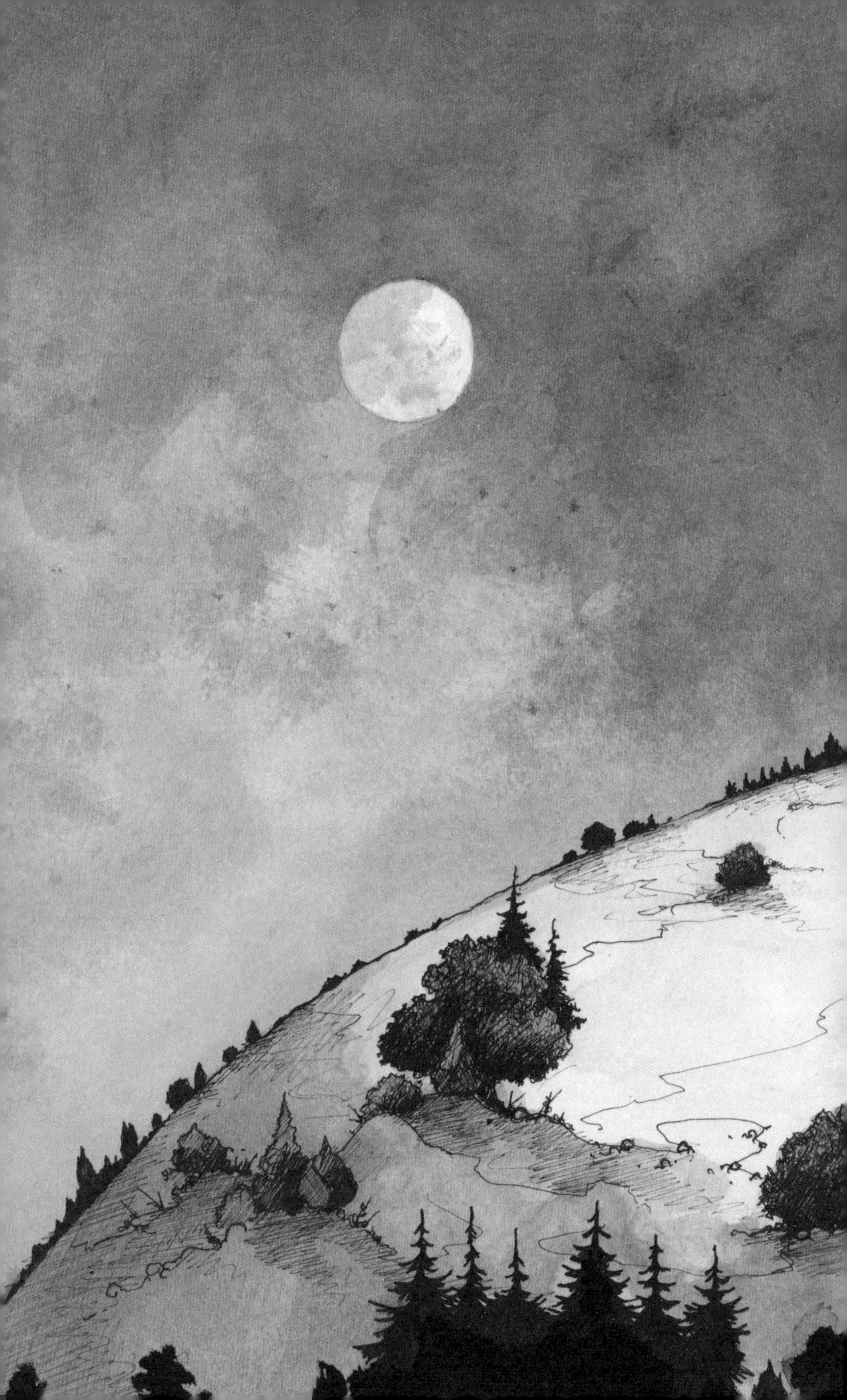

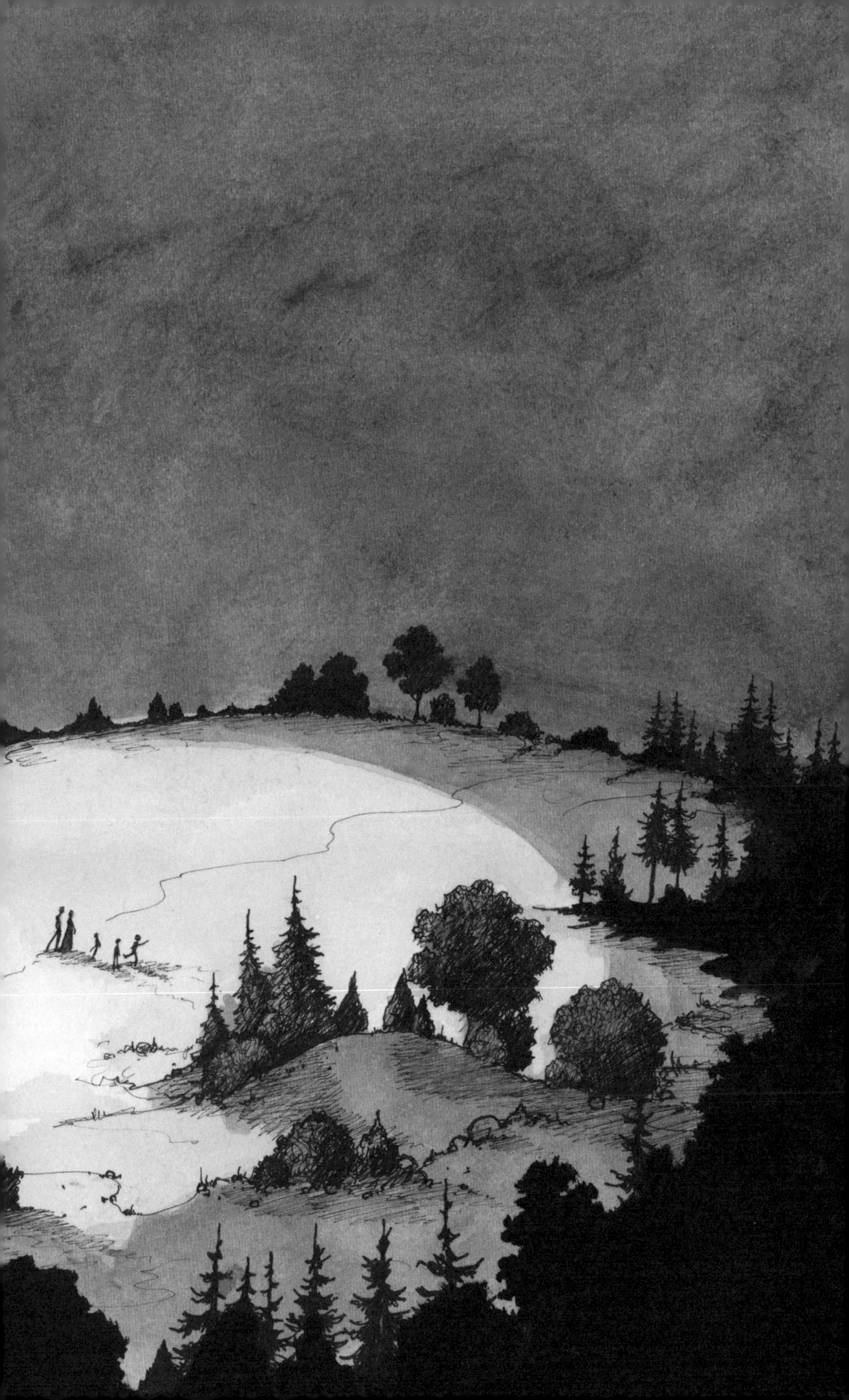

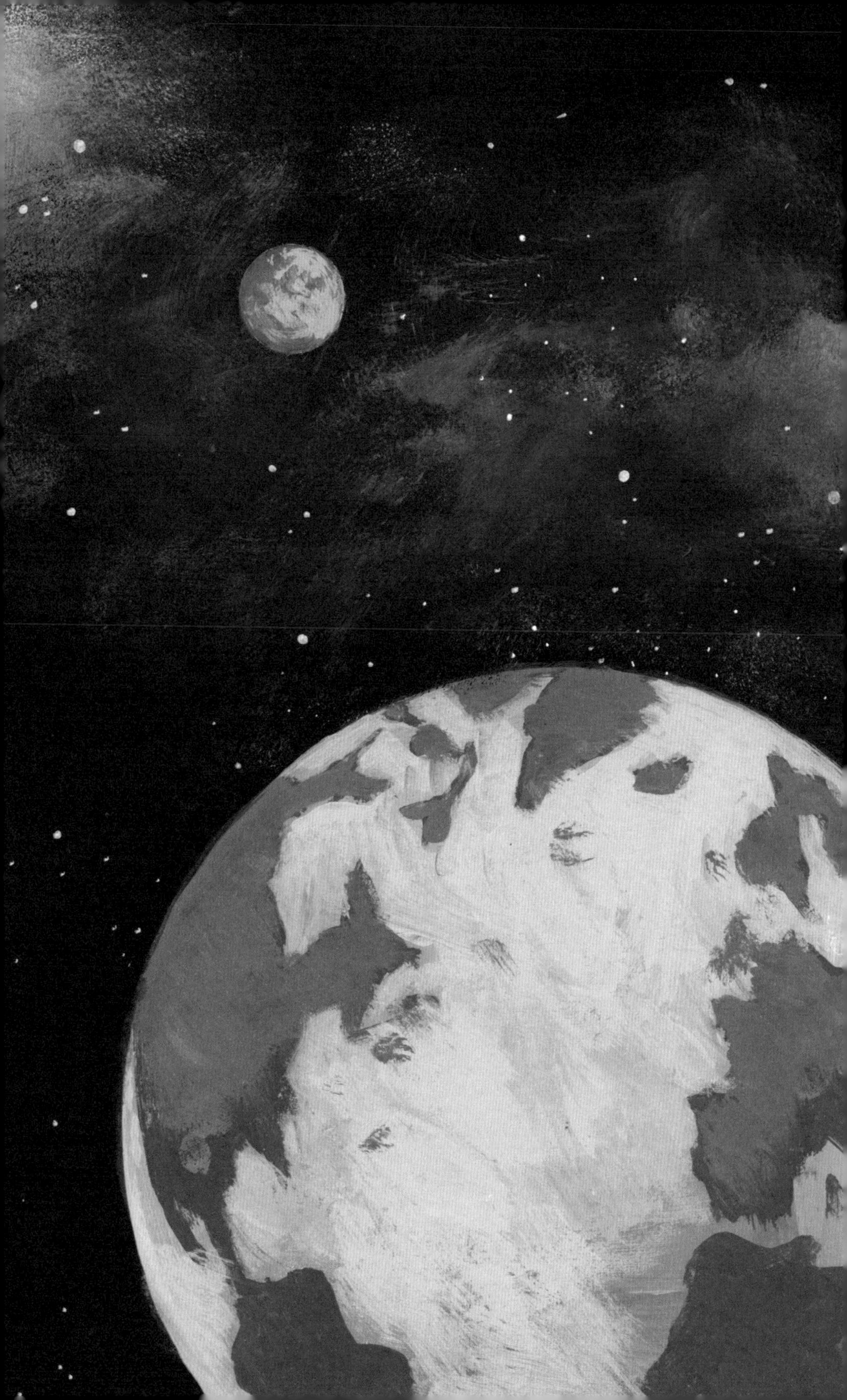

Chapter Thirteen

How It Ended

THERE ARE NO BACTERIA on the
planet Mars. It is not possible for them
to exist. It seemed that the moment
our invaders arrived, and drank and fed from our
world, our microscopic allies began to work their
overthrow. From the very moment I watched the
Martians walk down Maybury Hill they were
doomed, dying and rotting even as they marched
onwards. It had been inevitable all along. Every
drop of moisture, every molecule, had worked
against them. From the smallest drop on the
tiniest leaf on the smallest tree to the might of
the flow through the Thames. The living, moving,
constantly evolving state of the glimmering metal I
had seen was in fact a sure sign of its decay. These
things could not exist within our realm. This
world they envied could not accommodate their
kind.

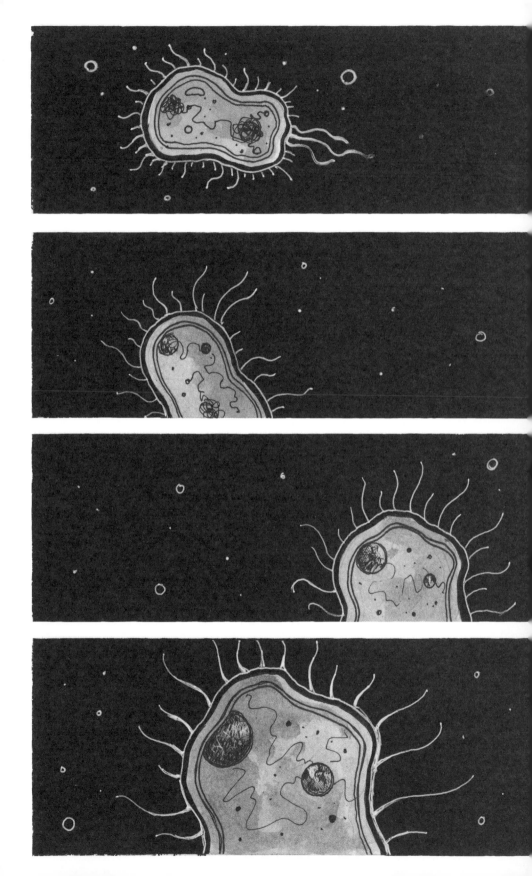

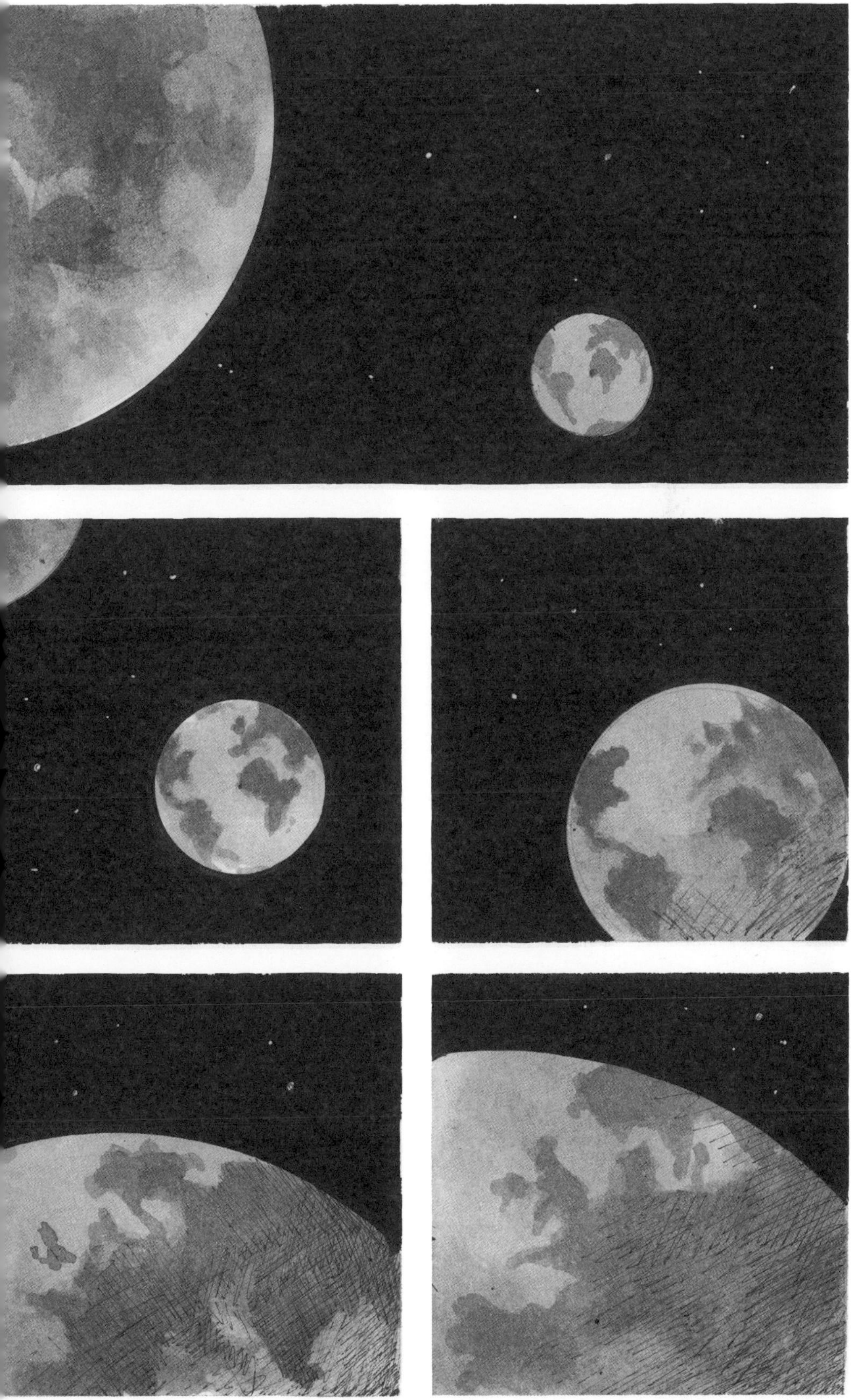

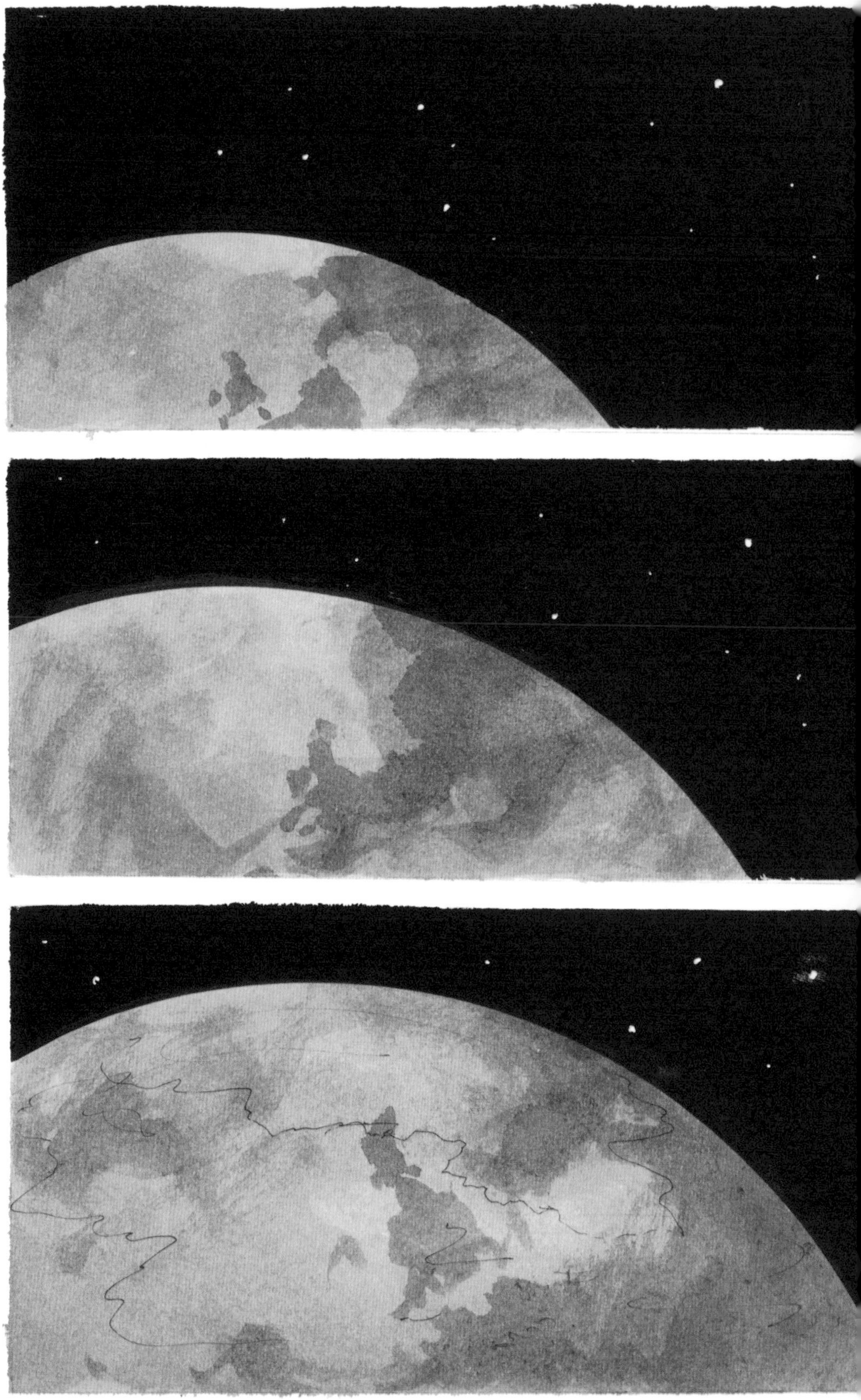

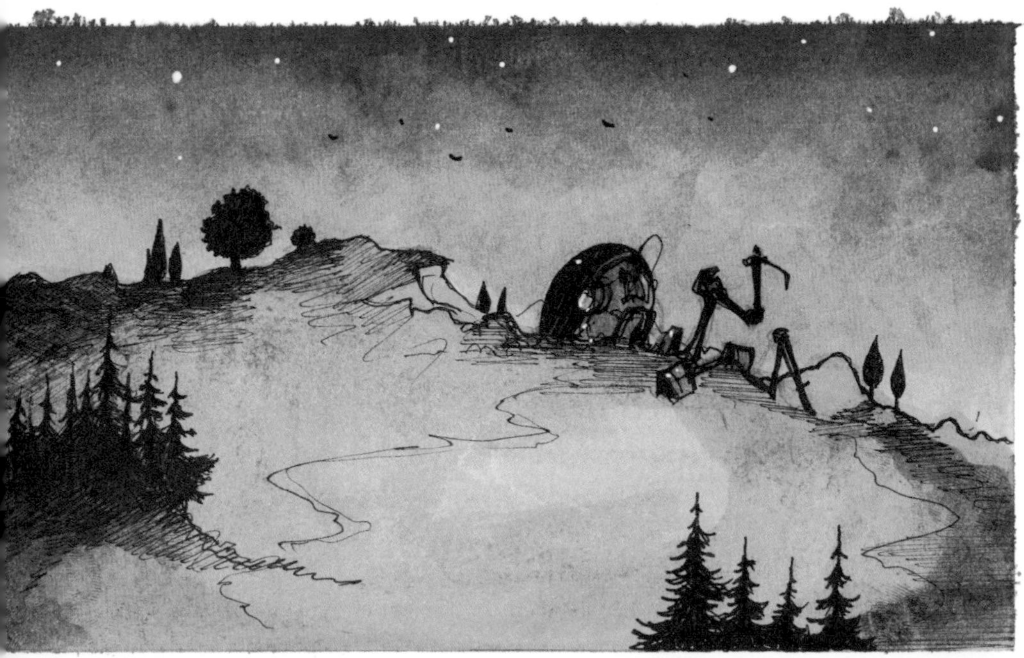

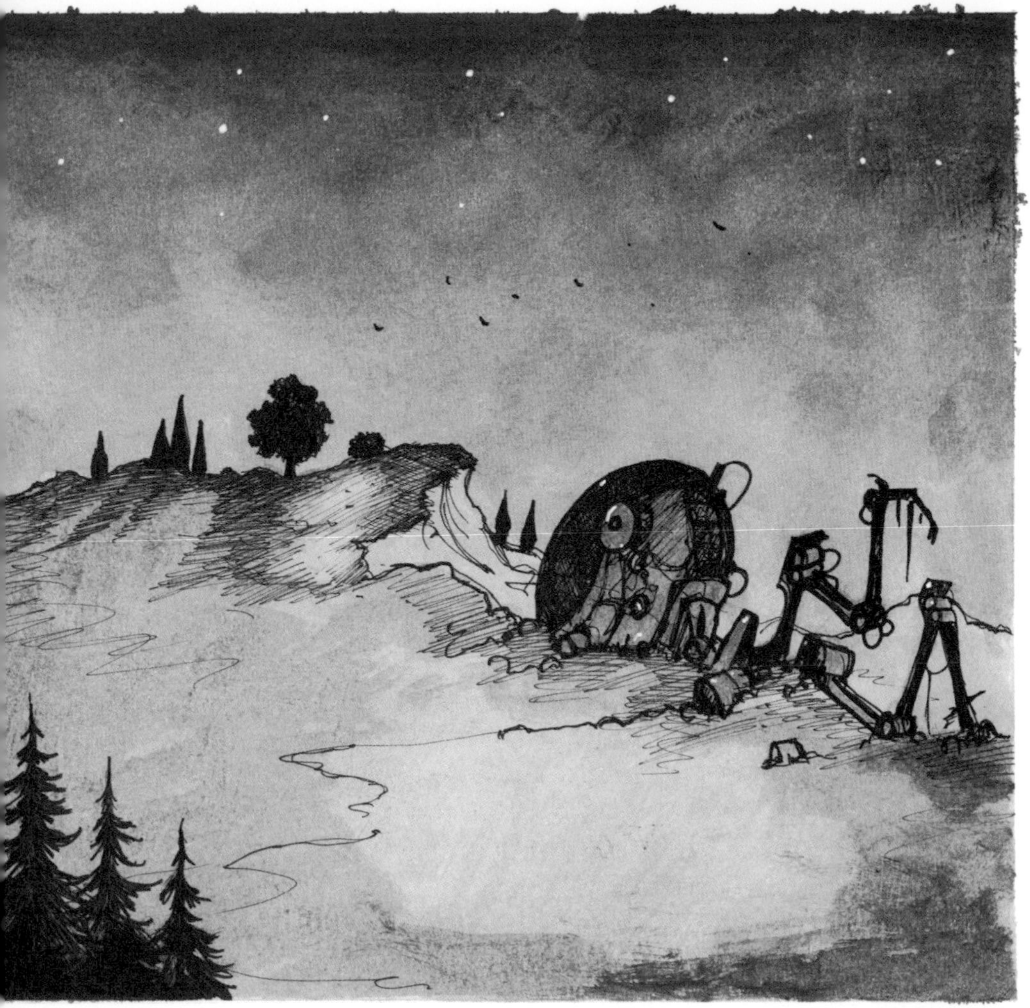

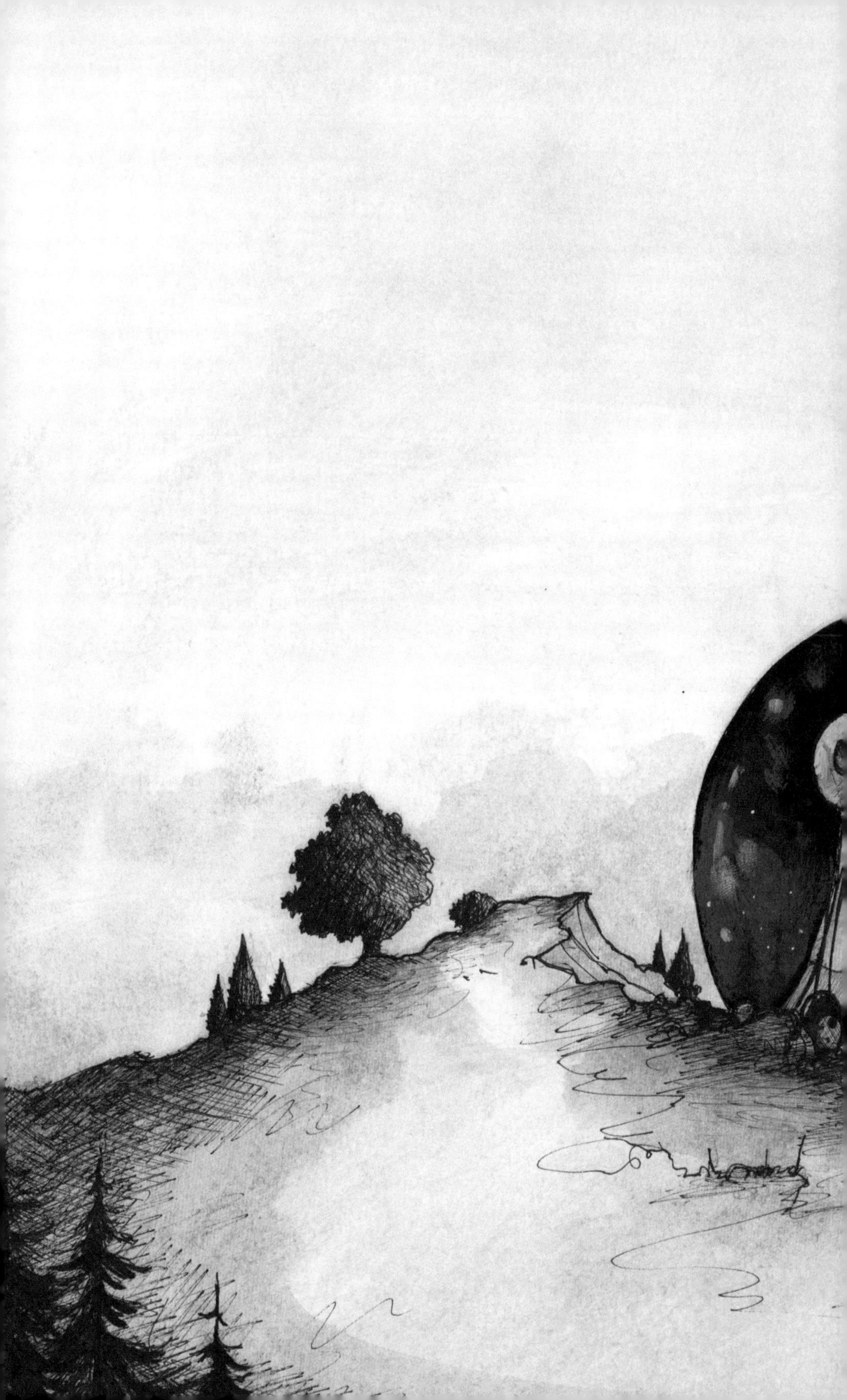

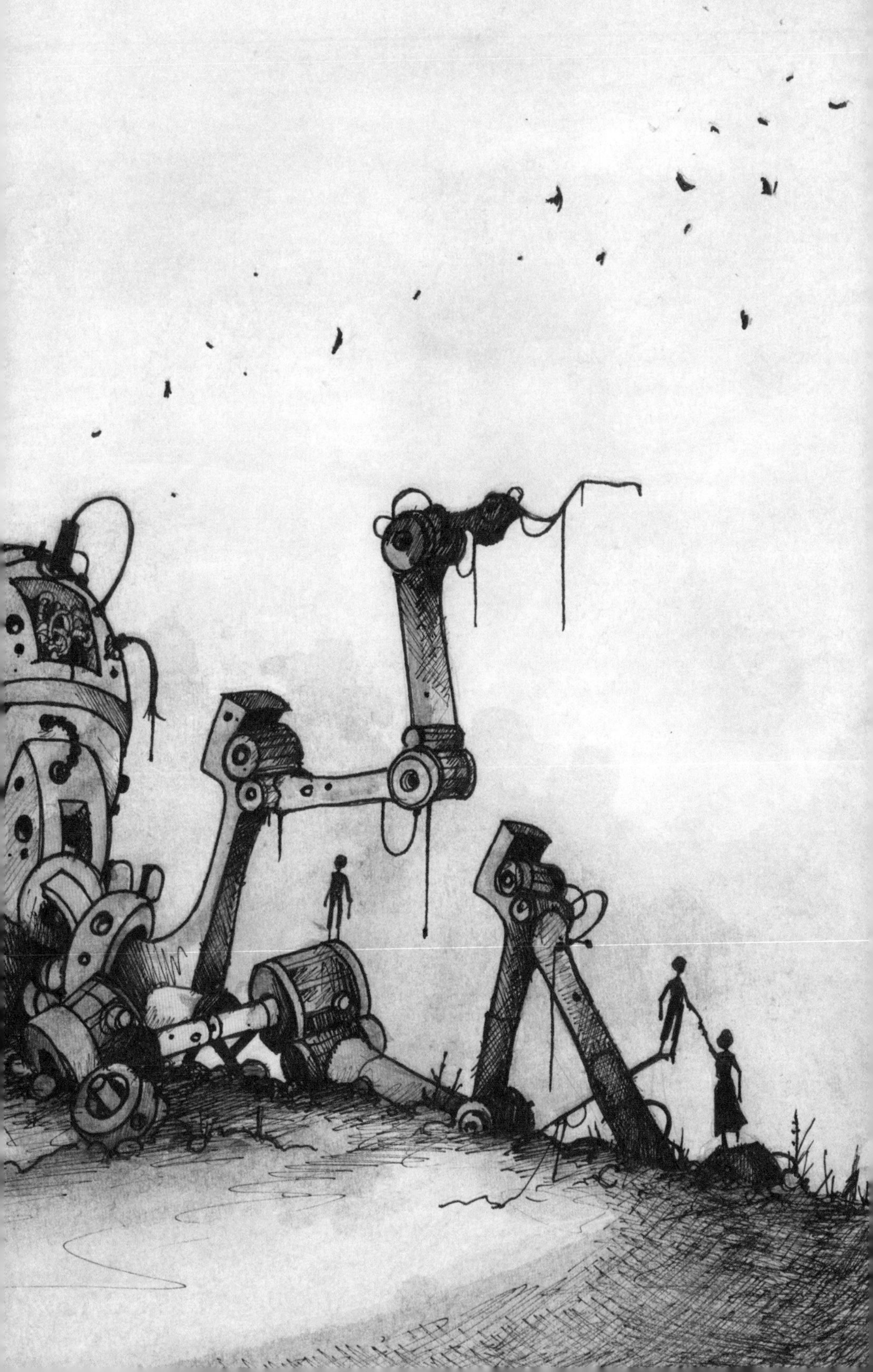

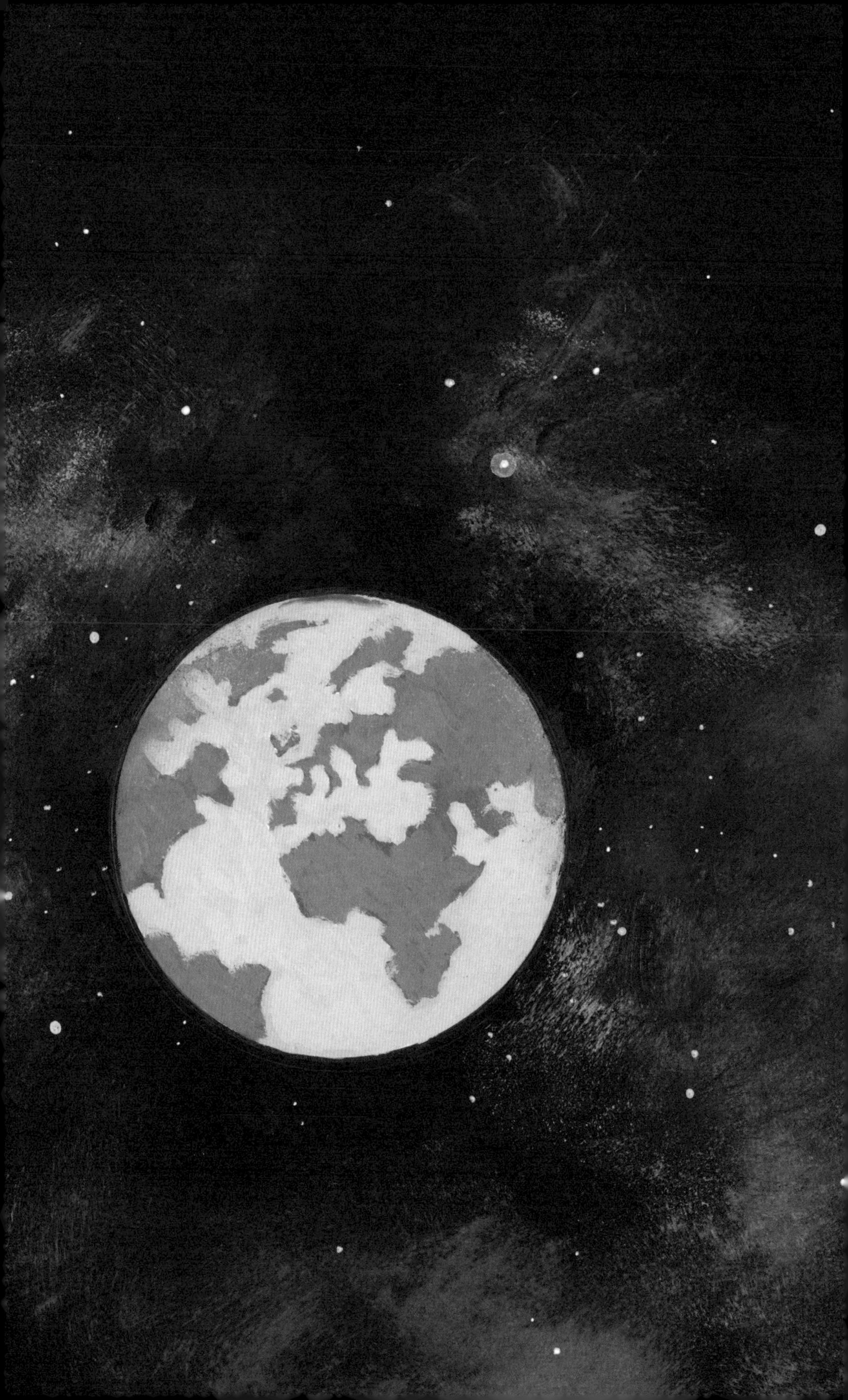

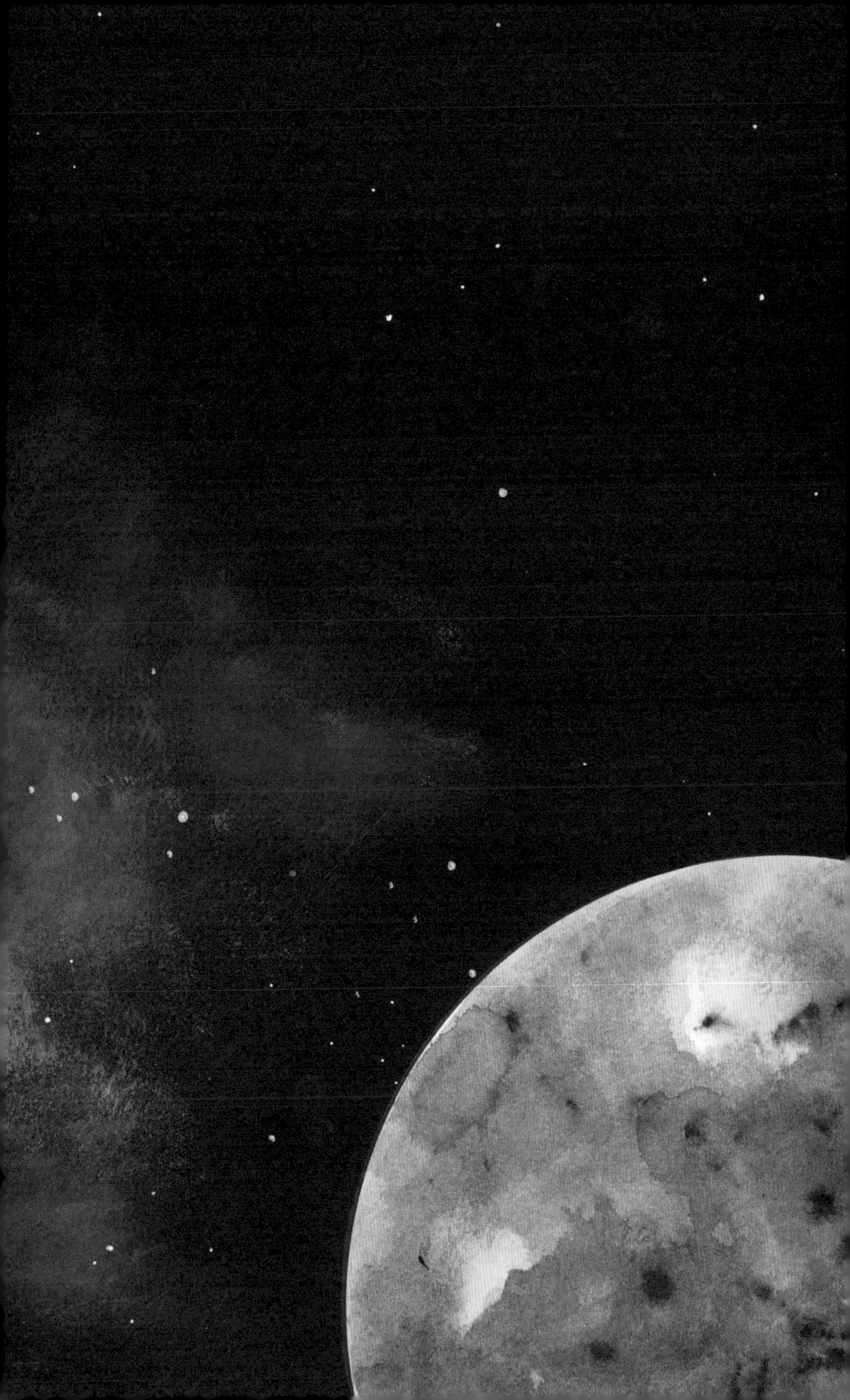

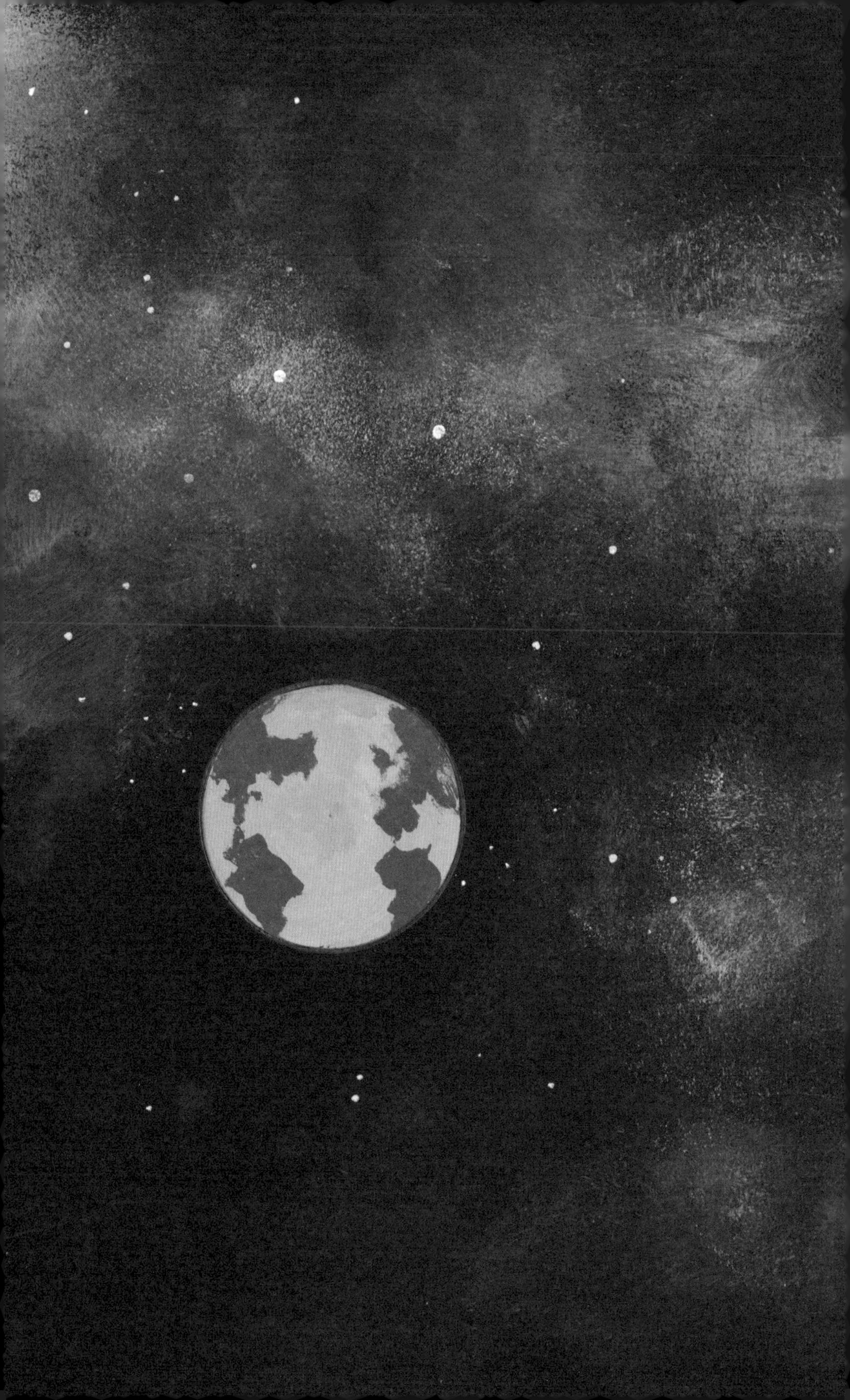

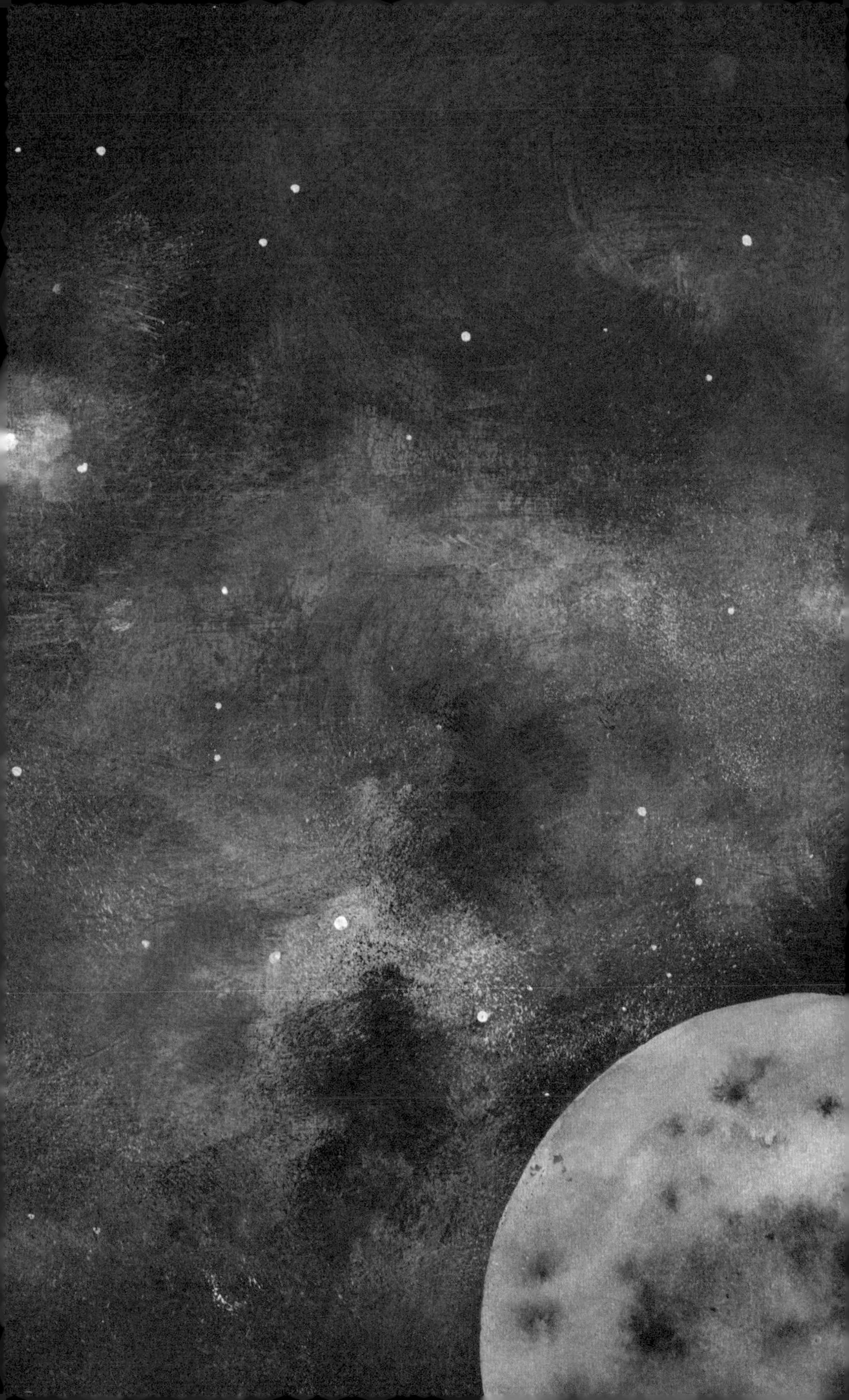

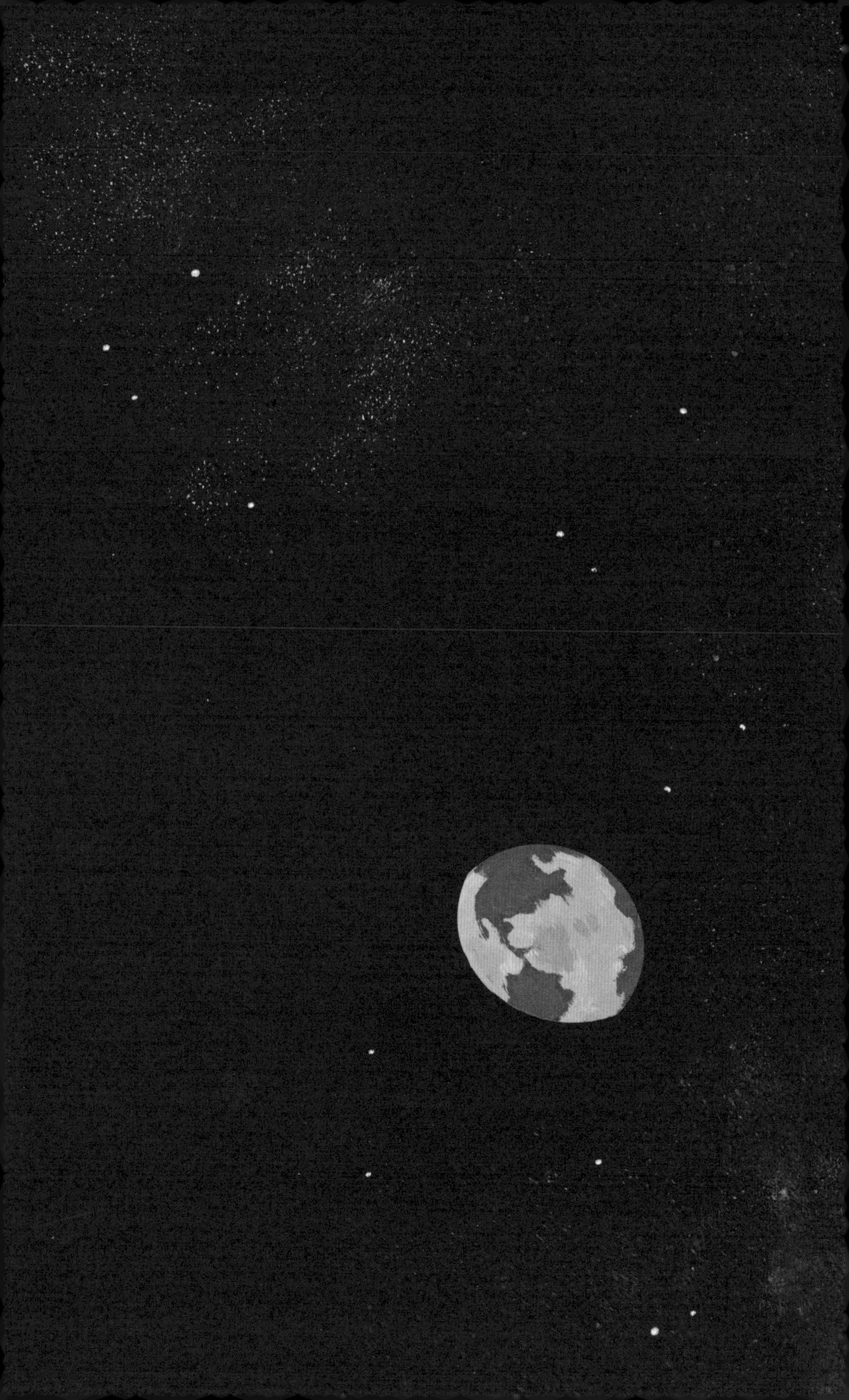

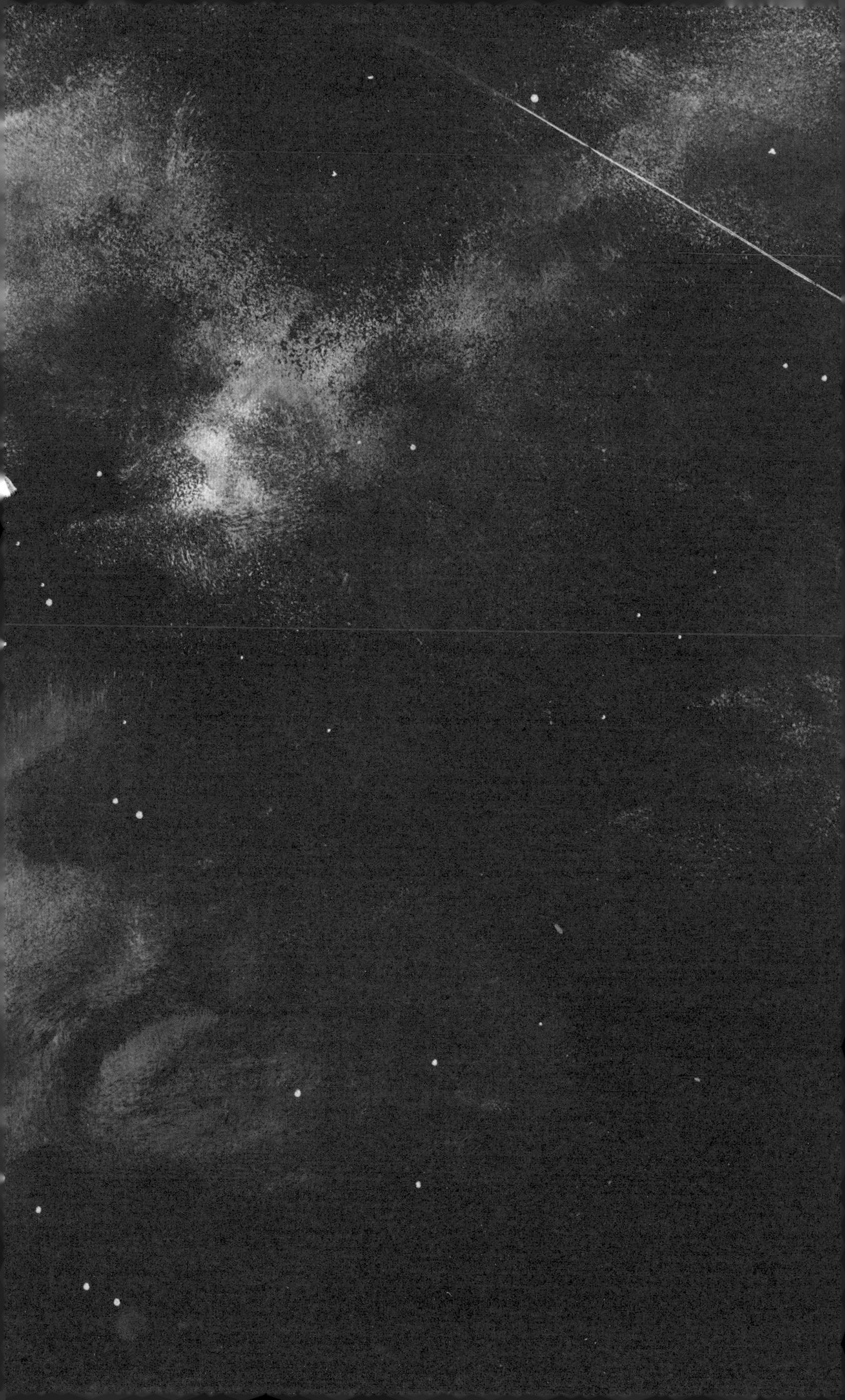